SCRAMBLING BACKWARD across dry ground that was becoming increasingly more rocky and treacherous, Lark tried to force her mind to comprehend what she was seeing. That creature, clearly large enough to eat a syphod whole, was where Lark drew the line on bravado. How long had that thing been sleeping under the surface of this planet? How many of them were there?

How quickly could she get the *fuck* off this world? And how long would she see this thing in her nightmares?

Surprising exactly no one, the raiders had abandoned their pursuit. Though, with all the rising dust their absence was hardly noticeable. The wind was whipping around her, tearing at her hair and nearly blinding her. "Mags!" she screamed at his back, raising a hand to shield her eyes from the stinging wind.

What in all bloody hell was he doing? Lark was all for pushing the envelope when it came to dangerous decisions, but this was straight up stupid. She had just gotten him back—as tenuous as that return had been—she was not prepared to watch him die for no reason. "If you're tryin' to impress me, this ain't the way to do it!"

DARKSPAWN

M.A. Short

For David.

PROLOGUE

JIKTAR AVROK—six hundred and forty-fifth d'javu-khan of Kyro, first of his name and of his dynasty—could not say he found himself surprised to be neck deep in bloodshed.

Swinging his great darksteel sword, Jiktar fought with all the might inside him. He took down a gray uniform, slamming his dark blade into its wearer and cutting clean through him. Hot blood splashed across his face. Swiftly, Jiktar wiped the gore from glowing orange eyes to survey the rest of the battle.

Bathed in the red light of Kyro's sun, hundreds of his fellow d'javu had gathered here at Katarak Keep for a last stand against the Protectors. Jiktar felt a proud smile rise on his lips. Men and women in shades of darkened reds, blues, and greens—heads topped with horns and darksteel weapons in their hands—fought wildly, hissing and growling like animals against the crisply uniformed humans.

An explosion of hot energy seared through the flesh of his comrades. The Protector catalyst weapons spat fire, the edge of every blade burned with it. The d'javu had their ancient, handcrafted darksteel blades, but the hands to wield them had dwindled swiftly. Unbridled brutality and ruthlessness had failed miserably against the tactics and strategy of the organized Protector military.

Jiktar gathered his free hand into a fist and held it out before him. Calling upon the mystical power of his blood, he slammed an invisible battering ram into the Protector line and pushed them all back. Humans shouted and fell over one another. The darkspawn cheered, but Jiktar knew this was only a momentary victory. Dread roiled in his throat as he watched the Protectors rise as quickly as they had fallen.

If only there had been more d'javu left like him; more of the pure blood, powerful darkspawn who could command that dark magic. But the Protectors had murdered them all. Somehow, before Jiktar had even known what was happening, their greatest weapon against this invasion had been destroyed.

"D'javu-khan!" someone called over the din. Jiktar, recovering from the use of his dwindling power, scanned his allies quickly before he realized it had come from inside his head. The call of the Kabalak. "It is time."

"Hold them as long as you can!" Jiktar shouted to anyone who could hear him. "We may die this day, but we will rise again!"

Jiktar had never before left a battlefield while the fighting continued. He found himself running now, the sounds of the clashing weapons and dying warriors fading at his back, and he had no remorse. Inside Katarak Keep something much more important called for his attention.

The sound of his pounding boots on the polished black floor echoed against the high walls. Unimpeded by any passersby, Jiktar thundered up the stairs. When he entered the corridor that led to his living quarters he heard a cry, swiftly silenced, and hastened his pace.

Throwing the door open, he found the air in the room was heavy, dank with the smell of blood and sweat. It was not unlike the battle he had just left.

Fosta sat up in the broad bed. Her father's sword lay next to her on sheets stained red and, wrapped in her dark purple arms, was a tiny child still slick with blood. Jiktar moved hastily toward her, sheathing his darksteel sword over his shoulder. He tore his left gauntlet from his arm and threw it to the side. Yanking his knife from his belt, he cut his arm and approached the bed.

The Kabalak, an orange male with horns ground flat, dipped his fingers in the blood on Jiktar's arm then spread it over the child's smooth head. Jiktar stared at Fosta, who smiled at him. It was an old custom, offering up his own blood to claim the child as his own. If he'd doubted the bloodline, now would have been the time. But Jiktar had never doubted Fosta, not once.

"Brought to life by the blood of the mother," the priest murmured. "Anointed in the blood of the father. Proud d'javu, glorious warrior."

Jiktar could not pull his eyes from his wife. She had never been more beautiful than she was in this moment. Her dark hair plastered against her face, and her aubergine skin aglow despite her recent ordeal. A warrior, a wife, and now a mother. Was there anything Fosta could not accomplish?

She allowed one of the baby's dark gray hands to coil around her finger, "A son, Jiktar, and a lucky one." She referred to the child's rare skin pigment; like the darkest clouds heralding a hellish storm. Jiktar would have given up anything for that prophecy to be true, but his dread only compounded. Luck appeared to have abandoned the d'javu.

"D'javu-khan, they are coming," someone spoke from the corner. Jiktar hadn't even noticed there were others here. Several of the Kabalak stood, chanting quietly, along with Crotis, the human governor. It was Crotis who had spoken with his face blanched and morose. "Things are far worse than I had foreseen."

"Worse?" Jiktar frowned.

"The Protectors did not stop at killing your warriors. As I understand it, they have a test to identify the blood powers even in children as young as your son here." Crotis swallowed hard, his ice blue eyes held Jiktar's. "And they have been murdered in their mother's arms."

Jiktar's eyes turned unbidden to his son. Fosta was smiling down at the tiny warrior, running her purple finger over a chubby, slate-colored cheek.

Crotis went on. "A scientist by the name of Nyhman— a man I thought was my friend... He is the one who took the d'javu to the Alliance the first time. He is the one who devised this test..."

Jiktar had stopped listening. His attention was on the bed, with his wife and infant son—his family. "Let them come," Fosta said without looking at them. Her baritone voice was somehow warm and ominous at the same time. "They can kill every one of us. Magnimus will be the glory of the d'javu, and he will avenge us all."

Jiktar's mouth formed a silent question. Who? A silent moment passed before he realized this was the name she had given their son. Fosta turned her head and met her husband's eyes; resolve made her features hard. "Hold your son, Jiktar, and give him to Crotis."

Fosta did not flinch when she offered up the child to his father. She shed no tears, but her fingers sought the darksteel blade at her side.

Jiktar looked down at Magnimus. The child's unseeing eyes glowed dimly, like tiny embers before they had taken a full breath. "Our pride," Jiktar whispered to him. "Will be your armor."

Moving across the room, he looked up at the governor. The human man's face had become pale. He stared at the child, then he straightened his spine and Jiktar saw that there was no other who could do this. "Teach him," he said to Crotis. "So that he may be a warrior but a better ruler than I. So that he may defeat his enemies and lead our people."

Crotis took the child gingerly, giving a tense nod, "Of course, d'javu-khan."

The Kabalak who had aided Fosta in giving birth

spoke, "We will go into hiding, to protect our heritage from those that would destroy it. When the time comes, we will restore the pride of Kyro."

Jiktar gave him a nod and pulled his sword from his back. The priests ushered Crotis from the room and fled with the child, leaving the d'javu-khan alone with his wife. Fosta, belly still swollen, gripped the sword against her chest. "Jiktar," she said fiercely, without evidence of the pain he knew was in her heart.

He glanced at her, but before he could respond the door flew open.

"Back!" Jiktar screamed at the humans that entered brandishing catalyst weapons. They pointed the weapons at Fosta, and Jiktar felt rage surge through him. A roar escaped him fueled by the agony of this day—the loss of his home, his people, and now his son. With two hands on the hilt of his darksteel sword, he charged forward, bloodlust flooding his mouth.

The pulse of energy that tore through his leg left the stink of charred flesh in his nostrils as he fell, another in his chest stole his breath.

Fosta screamed and Jiktar saw her bloody feet on the floor as she leapt from the bed to attack. She took two steps before she fell beside him, a steaming hole in her shoulder. The Protectors spoke, but Jiktar could not understand their language. One of them bent over Fosta, examining her swollen belly. She slapped his hand away protectively, and her body jerked when he shot her again.

Fosta's eyes met Jiktar's. He saw no sadness in their glowing depths, only pride and hope. Fosta had never given up, not even now. He reached for her, though her fingers remained outside of his grasp.

Together, they left the fate of the d'javu in the hands of their newborn son.

1
TWENTY YEARS LATER

"SORRY, FRIEND," Lark purred without remorse, digging the toe of her boot under the man's shoulder to flip his body over onto the metal sidewalk.

She pulled her goggles down around her neck and crouched over him in the neon-lit alley, tugging twisted fabric from his neck and pressing her thumb into his skin. She watched the readout on the gauntlet that sheathed her left forearm. The information fed from a subdermal implant in the pad of her thumb, through the plug at the base of her hand, and into the gauntlet. It flashed when the information was confirmed; she had killed the right guy.

Not that there was a chance she had been mistaken. "Nothin' personal."

Once she logged the completion, a crew would seek out and remove the body. If he had a family, it would be returned to them. If he didn't, which was likely for scum bags like Barr Osko, it would be destroyed. Either way, it was better than he deserved. Lark left him in the reeking alley she had cornered him in and headed toward the closest lift that would get her out of this skanky part of the city.

Niks Serlec's face was slashed in half, thanks to a deep crack that ran from corner to corner across the digital screen at the transaction console, evidence that a previous conversation here had not gone as planned. When the young man grinned, spots of neon light glittered in the cracks across his teeth as if he'd had them replaced with ludonite diamonds. Someone like Niks, she wouldn't put it past him.

"Barr Osko was a rapist and a slaver," he said to her, still smiling that glittering smile. She looked up from the keypad and cocked her head at him, the Fringer equivalent of a raised brow. "Killing him was charity."

A grin spread across Lark's pink lips, "No big loss to the galaxy. But didn't kill him for charity. And you ain't payin' because he was a rapist."

"True," Niks smile faded slightly. "Did rip me off a few times. Guess I should pay you then, after all."

"Bet you should," Lark's grin didn't fade in the least; in fact, it spread to her turquoise eyes and gained a hint of sadism in the process. "Killin' you'd be the real charity."

He laughed. It was not the anxious laugh of a man who had been subtly threatened by the killer he had failed to pay as of this moment, but the confident laugh of a man that knew paying her was a drop in his bucket. "What would the Fringe be without pluggers like you, Lark?"

The digits in her bank account began to tick upward. She dropped the grin and gave him a knowing look. He knew the answer, everyone did. Without a government, without laws or enforcement, Lark and her fellow headhunters were the only things standing between the Fringe and, "Chaos." She shrugged, "Or maybe a damn good party. Probably never find out since I don't plan on goin' anywhere."

When they had disconnected the call, Lark stepped away from the console and onto the mid-level streets of

Cuttah City. Metal pedestrian platforms carved through the open area between buildings piled one on top of the other. People were rushing in every direction against the biting wind, crowding around lifts and hovering outside food stalls. Above towered offices, penthouse apartments, and docking garages were built one on top of the other as far up as the eye could see.

At night all of the buildings and docking bays sparkled with lights. Now, on the cusp of evening, their smooth glass and metal surfaces mirrored the expansive sky. It was a flat white sky, just barely touched with gray. A perfect winter's sky.

Lark breathed in the chill air which carried, among various malodorous city smells, the aroma of snow. Nostalgia pricked her skin and called her to find her way onto a rooftop and watch the snow fall all night as she would have done years before. Instead, she pulled the hood of her jacket up over her head, shoved her hands into her pockets, and joined the flow of traffic just as the first flakes began to float down through the buildings.

She had only made it a few blocks before the tone of her communicator alerted her to an incoming call. "Boy, am I popular today," she muttered to herself, activating the speaker system in her hood and answering. "Yeh?"

The man's voice filled her hood but remained mostly inaudible to those around her. It was an emphatically jovial voice, which one would be careful not to mistake for friendliness, "If it ain't my favorite plucky blonde plugger. I knew you were on Cuttah."

"Not for much longer," Lark answered, already disinterested in whatever it was he was calling her about. Something was in her right pocket. She pulled it out and squinted at a fortune ticket from her favorite golgi house on the other side of the city. It promised that with patience came good fortune then encouraged her to visit the Viox

8

Casino. With a scoff, she shoved it back in her pocket, "Got appointments to keep."

"More important than old friends?"

Friends. To Jaris, the word was a convenience. Lark had gotten caught up with him in a short-lived spot of desperation a few years back, and he'd tried to stiff her. Come to think of it, that was more or less the definition of friendship in the Fringe.

"For you?" Lark paused but gave it very little thought. "Definitely more important things to do."

"Pay you in full this time."

Unlikely. "Up front?"

He laughed, "Who do you think I am?"

"Who do *you* think I am"" Lark moved to the side of the walkway and looked down through the expanse between the platforms to see the snow swirling about in the wake of aircars. Further down, the lights of the rust streets glowed meekly through the haze of winter weather. "Ain't some start-up begging for scraps, I'm the best fucking plugger the Fringe's got." Passersby glanced her way. Lark waved, an acrid smile telling them to move on unless they wanted to challenge the proclamation. No one did. "Find someone else to fuck over, Jaris. I'm busy."

"Lark, c'mon," he pleaded. "Have a drink with me."

Her voice dropped angrily, "Lost your teeth, Jar?"

He paused and must have considered that he may have lost his mind. "Meant coffee, s'all."

With a snort, Lark disconnected the call even as he continued to protest. She took a few steps before he called again. This time, she yanked the plug from her wrist before turning the call away. If that didn't get the point across that he was playing with fire, nothing would. He did not call a third time; there were plenty of other pluggers for him to harass.

The Quilsek Street market, shielded from the elements by the giant silver-glass office building that had grown over it, was packed full of people rushing to collect frivolous supplies before the storm picked up. Wine and beer were hopping off carts as fast as, if not even faster than, fuel cells and dry food. People were pushing and shoving, heedless of others doing the same, as if the incoming weather somehow negated the need for certain common civilities.

As the snowfall outside the alcove began to gain weight, the crowd thinned and carts began to close. Wandering through the emptying market and procrastinating, Lark browsed the unpurchased wares. The last cart was at the end of the alcove, flakes of snow blowing in and sprinkling across the table. A small hand-sewn brado cub perched at the edge of the table caught her eye.

The shopkeeper was involved in hurriedly packing his cart. Lark waited for him to notice her, but he failed to do so. "Hey!" she called out and offered him her credit chip. He seemed less than happy about having to pull out his tablet for such a small purchase, but she was unmoved.

With the transaction complete, Lark tucked the cub into her bag and headed out of the market. At the edge of the platform, a group of children sat huddled against the railing and whimpered at passersby. They were wrapped in crimson fabric that matched the ruddy dirt on the bare toes that stuck out from beneath their wrappings. They had come all the way up here from the rust streets; it was a miracle they hadn't been chased away already.

Digging into the inside pocket of her jacket Lark pulled out a stack of coins. She doled them out to each, then set her bag down and knelt beside them. She spread her hands before them; fingerless gloves revealed fingertips and nail beds tattooed dark red before she pressed palms to frigid cheeks. "Snow's gonna get worse," she said to them. "Should get home. Warmer down on the rust streets."

Their smiles were missing a few teeth, but they nodded agreeably. Hopping to their feet, the children ran full tilt toward the closest lift, ignored by those rushing through the cold to a warm apartment or other shelter.

Lark watched them until they disappeared into the crowd. She found herself strangely envying their freedom. It felt like another lifetime. So much had changed for her since she had been just a little girl from the rust streets—a lot of it for the better.

Breaking from her reverie, Lark nodded at a passing familiar face then dipped her head and started walking against the snow-strewn breeze.

Was it the snow or the rust street children that had made her suddenly so reflective? The only thing she was sure of was that spending so much time in the past wasn't helping her one bit. It was an invitation for darker things to come out to play—regrets, lost opportunities, memories she wished to forget—and they never missed a party.

Lark marched forward, that was what she did. Returning to where her ship, the *Starsigh*, waited patiently, she left the introspection on Cuttah. The snow slipped to the sides of the starshield until she rose above the clouds.

2

"A DEMON GOD."

That's what Crotis had told him before he sent Magnimus on what he referred to as his final task. The people of the planet Sulok worshiped a demon god whose coming had been foretold by a priest with a devil's visage.

Too coincidental, Crotis had decided. This was the call of the Kabalak.

Diminutive, moon-faced humans with small, kind eyes, the Suloki had scrambled out of their homes and thrown themselves to their knees before him when Magnimus had exited his craft. Now, they were singing low into the dry yellow dirt. They still had not answered his initial request, and he was beginning to wonder if their innate stupidity was what had stranded them in this isolated part of the lawless Fringe.

This was what he had been reduced to? Magnimus already found his frustration rising, his fists gathering at his sides and glowing eyes narrowed in anger. Crotis had ordered him to convince the Suloki to bring him to their demonic priest. If it turned out to be the Kabalak, then it would be time for his training to end and their rebellion to begin.

"All your training, all your missions and practice have led you to this moment," Crotis had told him. *"The diplomacy I have taught you will be the key to moving forward from here. I know you will not disappoint me this time."*

This time.

The words echoed in the rhythmic chanting of the Suloki, mocking him.

This time... This time...

Magnimus did not have many failures to dwell upon. It was not difficult to determine which 'time' Crotis was referring to with that last backhanded comment. He glowered at the groveling Suloki, letting their disregard for his question stoke his frustration needlessly. He found it difficult to believe they did not speak universal. They *had* to be intentionally ignoring him. Had the old man finally discovered a task that would force him to truly flex his tolerance?

"Who is your leader?!" he demanded a second time, his voice deepening to a threat. He felt as if wiping out half the population might stir up some of the diplomacy Crotis was always trying to force down his throat.

The elderly woman who accepted the package of supplies Lark had brought back from Cuttah was small and round, with little deep-set eyes like buttons sewn too tightly onto an overstuffed pillow. She smiled gratefully and pressed a piece of round, golden fruit into Lark's gloved hand. The little woman muttered something and gestured toward Lark's shoulder.

Craning her neck, Lark found a splash of congealed blood staining the left side of her gray jacket. "Oh..." lodging the fruit between her teeth, Lark rubbed at the stain and the dark brown blood smeared. She nodded her thanks to Sherra and started to follow the path around the metal shacks that comprised the Suloki settlement.

The fruit was tart and fresh, at a severe juxtaposition to the scenery around her. Dry and dusty, Sulok was a backwater world even by Fringe standards. It was populated almost entirely by the native people who had yet to seek a way off-world. Anyone else who came to this place was hiding from something or someone.

Speaking of, Lark again lodged the fruit between her teeth and dug the fingers of her right hand into her glove to ensure the wiring that fed from the gauntlet on her left forearm to the plug at the base of her thumb was still disconnected. It was the only way to ensure she was officially off the clock.

Sufficiently unplugged, Lark began moseying toward where she had left her bike days ago, chewing on the fruit until she found the stone buried within.

An excited cry made her half-turn, and Sherra pushed passed her, running full tilt toward the square at the center of town. Lark squinted her turquoise eyes, toying with a piece of fruit stuck between her teeth as she watched the woman run. "Demon god?" she said aloud, translating the Suloki language for herself.

The fruit stone disappeared into the dirt when she threw it, turning to follow behind Sherra toward the square. At the edge of a particularly rusty building, she slowed as the gathered Suloki came into view. The entire population of the town had thrown themselves to the ground in front of—

Lark felt the last bit of fruit juice catch in her throat as she recognized the broad, demon-faced creature standing shirtless over the crowd. Gunmetal skin gleamed in the sun like brushed velvet, ridges on his shoulders reflected the light in a prism of gray purples, greens, and blues. The horns on his head, the bright glow of his eyes despite the afternoon sunlight—there was no mistaking him.

Flinging herself backward against warped aluminum siding, Lark hid in the shadow of a building and forced herself to breathe. Of all the planets in the Fringe and civspace, he had to show up on this one?

Over the humming of the Suloki, she could hear him shouting in universal to be brought to their leader. He must have been on another mission for Crotis. Could the old man know that he had, once again, sent Magnimus right into her path?

As many times as Lark had wished for him to show back up in her life, as many coins as she had cast into the dream pools on Fisk, she knew there was no such luck in this universe. He was not here to see her.

Far be it for Lark to leave well enough alone. Potential heartbreak be damned, Lark tugged her goggles over her eyes and then strapped her respirator over her nose and mouth. Twisting her long blond hair into a ball at the base of her neck, she pulled her hood up and started out into the square.

3

"PROBLEM?"" a digitized voice cut over the humming, and Magnimus whipped around, his hand instinctively shifting to the knife he kept tucked in his belt.

A few paces away from the gathering of Suloki, a figure stood. Human, though the face was hidden behind a set of large round goggles and a respirator half clogged with dust, head covered by a gray hood. A splash of blood, hastily wiped away, stained the left shoulder of a cropped hide jacket. The verbalizer in the respirator disguised her voice, so he was unable to determine an accent or age.

Magnimus stood still, studying her for signs of threat as she started forward, carefully picking her way around the genuflecting populous until she stood a few feet from him, cocking a hip and looping her thumbs into her utility belt. The sun glinted off the polished chrome of two holstered catalyst pistols, their white enamel inlays gleaming with hot neon blue detailing. He could see several packs of nefarious weapons and traps studding the gauntlet on her left wrist.

Mercenaries and pirates may have been similarly accoutered, but they didn't travel alone. This was an independent contractor, a bounty hunter if he had to guess. Unscrupulous, void of loyalty or honor.

"What're you tryin' to get at here, friend?" the digitized voice inquired.

"Their leader," Magnimus answered testily, flexing his fists. "They refuse to answer my questions." He added with disdain, gesturing angrily around them, "What are they doing?"

The goggles scanned the mass of people on their knees, whirring and clicking as their innards focused and reported upon her surroundings. When her face moved back up in his direction he could see his own reflection in the glass, dark against the overcast sky. He didn't often see his reflection and he had forgotten how terrifying he appeared.

"Looks like they're worshippin' ya," replied the disguised hunter.

Magnimus frowned and turned away. Succinct, if unhelpful. The hunter did not seem to notice his antipathy and spoke again, "Lookin' for that darkling priest supposed to live here, ain't ya?"

He passed her a sidelong glance, annoyed by her presence and her prying. "What business is it of yours?" he asked without fully looking at her.

She laughed; the sound came out choppy through the voice digitizer. "Hurshek the Wise is a friend of mine," she told him casually, shrugging when he looked at her with intense scrutiny. "These people've been waiting for the coming of their demon god for years. Hurshek's been tellin' 'em to expect you soon. Don't speak universal, but they understand d'javu well enough." He sensed she was mocking him even though he could not see her face. "Well, what're ya waitin' for? Go on, demon god, give 'em the business."

Narrowing his eyes in her direction, Magnimus set his jaw. He did not appreciate her smug demeanor nor the fact that she appeared to know more about this than he did. So, he turned away from her and spoke to the mass on their knees before him in clear, loud d'javu, *"People of Sulok, I am Magnimus Avrok. I have come to you—"*

A digital snort of laughter interrupted him, and he turned to see the covered head shaking. She waved her hand for him to go on and crossed her arms. Magnimus rolled his eyes, but that only seemed to amuse her more.

Glaring at her, he found himself curious as to where a bounty hunter from the Fringe had learned to speak d'javu when her body suddenly went stiff. Her head twitched to his left, and Magnimus saw in the reflection in those goggles the looming mass in the sky over his shoulder. He whipped around and peered upward at the roiling cloud of sand that was barreling toward them from the distance.

"Raiders," the digitized voice said. Then repeated, in d'javu, to the scattering Suloki. *"Kaeata! Yat! Yat!"* Then she looked up at Magnimus, who had not moved. "You a demon god or not?"

Smirking, Magnimus turned back toward the rising cloud. The Suloki were retreating into dwellings and hidden burrows when the bounty hunter came to stand beside him. Magnimus breathed deep and tasted the malice heading toward them. His long knife was in his hand, the grip fitting perfectly into every crevice of his palm.

The hunter had settled gloved hands onto her catalyst pistols beside him. Loosened in their holsters, the chunky weapons' indicator lights glowed green and blue. With a soft whine, they were powered up and ready, the chemicals contained within prepared to flood the reaction chamber and burst forth in white hot energy pulses.

The cloud was moving closer. A few straggler Suloki passed before them, panicking as the sound of the raiders' motorbikes rolled over the small settlement like thunder. The deafening sound preceded the raiders into the square where Magnimus stood tall, gripping his knife.

A scraggly group of dirty young men on primitive motorcycles, they all wore matching armored vests along with goggles and respirators similar to those worn by the bounty hunter at his side. Magnimus felt the dust coating the inside of his mouth and nose, and he understood the need for such paraphernalia.

The gang circled Magnimus and the hunter, whooping and randomly firing their rudimentary weapons into the air until they finally came to a stop and began to dismount.

The hunter's digital voice rose above the clarion, "What have I told you, Laredo? Leave these people the hell alone or one of these days their demon god'll show up and make you."

One of the raiders stepped forward, removing the goggles and the respirator to reveal a youthful face obscured by a thick layer of dirt. He was tall and lanky with jeering blue eyes and a mop of grimy blond hair. He radiated the arrogance of a man who'd confused himself with a king on a world too remote and underdeveloped to challenge him. Laredo laughed at the bounty hunter, "This him then? Don't look so god-like to me."

"Be my guest," she waved a hand toward Magnimus. "Don't say I didn't warn you."

As if he had been waiting for his cue, Magnimus started forward. A grin spread across his face as the raiders scrambled to offensive positions before moving to engage him. Two of them hefted clunky energy weapons, taking aim at Magnimus from his periphery. Before they could discharge their weapons, catalyst pulses splashed and sizzled against their armor. The barrage went on until they fell back, and his hunter companion laughed in delight as she bounced into the fray. After a high kick to one raider's head, she conjured a knife and started in on another without missing a beat.

With several of the combatants otherwise occupied, Magnimus focused on the four that stood between him and Laredo. The first came at him with arms outstretched, intent upon securing him so the others could wail on him freely.

Magnimus slipped around behind him and leaped, driving the handle of his dagger into the young man's skull. Another swung a baton at him and he barely ducked. He dropped to the ground and swept the raider's feet from under him, picking up the baton and slamming it down into his chest. That made quick work of the first two, but the others had given up the ghost by the time Magnimus pulled himself to his feet.

Their large guns made an appearance and Magnimus growled. Bad form. Lunging toward them, he shoved one muzzle toward the sky and the other straight back, into its owner's face. Blood cascaded from a broken nose while he tore the first gun from the raider's hand.

It was an unwieldy thing, heavier than necessary and grossly inaccurate if he was to believe the digitized laughter coming from behind him. It made a better battering ram than a gun, and he put that into practice by bashing the last raider's head with its ungainly muzzle before dropping it on top of its prone owner.

Laredo was no longer smiling. More raiders had dismounted and were moving to intercept Magnimus. He pushed them aside with a wave of the hand, pointing to Laredo and beckoning him forward. Much to the raider's chagrin, he complied.

When they were face to face, Magnimus pressed his hand over Laredo's heart. The man's body went rigid, and he felt the heart as if it were in his hand, pounding wildly against the unnatural grip around it. Magnimus smiled darkly, revealing his sharp teeth, as he willed the heart to beat faster. Laredo grunted, his mouth opening soundlessly as he wrapped trembling hands around Magnimus' wrist and tried weakly to push the hand away.

The bounty hunter wandered over. Her goggles reflected the chaos they'd inflicted upon the raiders. Laredo could hardly move, he stared at his captor, blood beginning to fill the sclera of his eyes. With effort, the young man forced his hands up into a gesture of surrender, and the other raiders ceased what would have been a supplementary attack.

"Move out," Laredo said to his men, his voice strained and hands falling to his side. "We are done here," he choked out to Magnimus, hoping to be released.

This deluded raider meant nothing to him, so he released the man's heart and stepped away. The young man may never know how many heartbeats this darkling had stolen from him. Magnimus watched with amusement as the leader clung to his dignity, trying not to falter as he returned to his motorbike. They gathered their dead and injured and slunk off into the dry plain around the settlement.

The hunter fired after them before sliding her CCPs back into their holsters and turning to face Magnimus. For a moment, he imagined a grin on that unseen face and a shudder borne of nostalgia ran through him.

4

"WAIT HERE and I'll get my bike," she told him. "We'll go see Hurshek in the morning, yeh?"

Magnimus sneered after her and tucked his knife away. Wiping the dust from his hands on his black pants, he considered her offer—if that was what that had been. His knee-jerk reaction was to spurn her charity and send her on her way. Despite her obvious skills in battle, he had no use for an unreliable brigand.

Had she said she was friends with Hurshek the Wise? Clearly an outstanding boast, but even if it wasn't true she at least knew where the Kabalak was hiding. Staying with her was the smartest course. It was also the opposite of what Crotis would want him to do which made his decision that much easier.

The woman returned with a dusty red and blue motorbike. She threw a leg over the bike and nodded for him to do the same. He hesitated a moment before he swung on behind her awkwardly.

"Don't be shy now," she muttered a split second before slamming on the accelerator. Magnimus pitched backward and was forced to grip around her waist lest he tumble backward off the bike. Over the whipping of the wind and the roaring of the engine he couldn't be sure, but he thought he heard her laughing at him.

They blasted away from the settlement, heading out into what appeared to be an endless craggy mesa. He closed his eyes to prevent being blinded by the rush of dust.

The hypnotic whine of the engine made it feel like hours. Eventually, the motorbike seemed to be slowing. He chanced opening his eyes and saw that they were approaching a small mudbrick house below a dead tree.

She drove the bike around and a small roll-up door opened for them, allowing access to a minuscule garage meant to hold little more than the bike. The two of them together made an uncomfortably tight fit. As the garage door sealed shut behind them, she turned her head to glance over her shoulder at him.

"You make it?" the digitized voice asked, an impertinent tone somehow finding its way through the speakers of her respirator.

He smirked at her and slid off the bike, shimmying around to the only egress other than the way they'd come in. She followed, pulling her jacket tight to keep it from catching on the bike. When she reached under his arm and punched a security code into the panel, the door slid open and Magnimus stepped through swiftly—eager to get out of close quarters with her.

"Whew!" she breathed as she sealed the door behind her. "Make yourself at home, friend. Grab some water and I'll be right back." The hunter disappeared through a doorway at the opposite side of the room.

It was a small house, primitive in its lack of the technology that was ubiquitous in the rest of the Fringe and the galaxy at large. A kitchen occupied the corner to his left. He rinsed his mouth and face of dust in the sink. The rest of the main room was dedicated to living space; weapons and gear stored in corners.

Magnimus watched the sunset through the dust tinted window, blood staining the blue expanse as darkness threatened the opposite horizon. Until he heard her re-enter the room behind him. Without turning, he inhaled through his nose to dispel some of the gathered tension.

He flinched as the smell of her sweat stung his nostrils, sending him plunging into a deep rush of memory. A world and a time he'd put far behind him; the smell of sunshine, peaches, and captivity. And *her*.

Magnimus whipped around and found the hunter facing away from him. She had removed the hood, goggles, and respirator. Her honey-blond hair, plaited across the right side of her head, sat knotted and twisted in a pile at the base of her neck where she had tucked it into the hood. She was pulling her jacket off, revealing a sleeveless armored tank.

Breaking the smooth skin, thick lines of scars carved across her shoulder blades and onto the backs of her arms. His memory, determined to take him back to that place now, saw them when they were brand new, raw and bleeding. Even though they were now healed but destined never to fade, he'd know those scars anywhere. He had been an integral part of how they'd whipped their way onto the back of that young girl.

Magnimus was moving before he even knew what he was doing. His fist wrapped around her left arm and spun her around, shoving her against the wall.

It *was* her. That same girlish face, though her pinks lips were normally set into a smile. He had never forgotten her eyes—not for lack of trying—that brilliant turquoise had been burned into his mind along with the abyss she had left in his life.

"What the hell is going on?!" he demanded, his arm trembling with the effort not to shake her. "What are you doing here? And why did you hide from me?"

24

Lark stared at him, seemingly surprised by his reaction. "I live here, Mags," she answered flatly, as if explaining something that was obvious. That was the first time in years he had heard that stupid nickname she had given him and, for a moment, it distracted him from how angry he should have been. "Sorry I didn't tell you right off, didn't want to surprise you in front of your adoring fans."

The Suloki. Now the entire exchange with them was that much more mortifying. She had been laughing at him, mocking him, while the entire time knowing he had no idea who she was.

Anger forced his voice into a growl, pressing her into the wall, "When I saved you from slavery on Izlatana and took you back to my home, you didn't want to get *involved*." She opened her mouth to defend herself, but Mags' voice rose over hers. "Now, here you are. Of all the planets in the Fringe, you are here—in my way yet again. And making friends with a darkling priest."

Lark sucked in a breath between her teeth. "Yeh, ain't so sure Hurshek sees it that way…"

Mags released her and stabbed a finger in her face, "More of your lies."

Lark's brow drew together, her eyes studying Mags' face for a moment. "What the hell are you so mad at me for?" she asked him, her jaw tight.

Was she pretending not to know or was she just that ignorant? Either way, the question enraged him. "You used me to get out of that place, provoked me into staging a riot so you could escape. But the moment I asked for anything in return you ran way."

Her face took on an expression as if he had struck her. He took no pride in the pleasure her reaction gave him.

"*Used* you?" she repeated, her voice rising. She pulled her arm out of his grasp and gestured broadly. "Mags, I was in love with you! I didn't provoke you. I didn't ask you to do anything about what happened. I would just as soon have forgotten the whole fucking thing!"

Then her eyes narrowed, her head shaking slightly from side to side. Disbelief or denial? "I did *not* run away," she insisted punctuating the statement by pointing at the floor. "Crotis told you I wasn't reliable, that I wasn't worth risking your damn rebellion for."

Mags paused, for the first time doubting his memory of what had happened on Kar'ju two years before when he had returned from that ruined mission on Izlatana accompanied by a human girl. Crotis had said those things about Lark, and he had repeated them often enough since then that Mags now found it difficult to remember his own feelings from that day.

He remembered one thing very clearly. "You didn't argue or speak up for yourself when Crotis accused you," he growled at her, crossing his arms over his chest. "You turned and left without so much as a word."

"You didn't exactly jump to my defense, you know!" she spat at him. "I saw it in your face that you believed that old cock. You lost faith in me that easy. Figured if you weren't even going to try to stop me from going, I'd already lost you."

"It isn't that simple, woman!" Mags' frustration bloomed. He unfolded his arms and thrusts his fists to his sides, closing his eyes to block her out. He had come here to complete this final task in order to free his people from oppression, not to throw down with his ex.

When he opened his eyes again, he tried not to see her. "Your involvement in this ended two years ago. So why are you here? Who are you working for?"

Lark threw her head back and laughed. "Don't be stupid," she said to him, her voice frigid. "Needed a place to hide and, lucky for me, I knew enough d'javu to convince Hurshek that you and I were friends. I was alone, and I had to survive." Lark's eyes became sad as she stared up at him, her tone softening into submission. "Ain't your enemy; I would've stayed with you and fought with you." She shook her head, more to herself than to him. "But as long as Crotis has that leash around your neck, there'll be no room in your life for anyone else."

Her shoulder struck his when she shoved past him and, again, Mags felt powerless to stop her. "Get some sleep," she muttered as she disappeared into the corridor. "I'll take you out to Hurshek tomorrow. Then you'll be rid of me for good."

Trapped between his past and his future, Mags could do little more than stare at where she had stood in front of him. Lark, as she had been on Izlatana, was the wrench in his plans.

Why was he so happy to see she hadn't changed?

5

L<small>ARK'S EYES</small> opened to the stillness of a house that had never been home. She scowled and grumbled, irritated by the reminder that nowhere had ever really been home. Although to outward appearance nothing had changed, she felt as if she had been ravaged inside. All her pieces lay out in the new sunlight, strewn about by a storm. She had grown practiced at pushing feelings like that away and plowing forward. How else did a girl survive in a galaxy like this?

She opened the door to her bedroom as quietly as possible. The hall and the rest of the house were just as silent and peaceful as the bedroom. Mags was standing in the middle of the living area, shirtless as he always was when not armored. Facing away from her toward the windows, he was silhouetted by the morning sun that shown white and hot even this early.

Whereas Lark had been cut with a dull knife from the rough stone of survival, Mags had been built from the ground up for the sole purpose of fighting his impending battle for the freedom of his people. She tried not to stare at him, even if he was as beautiful as the first day she had set eyes on him.

Mags turned his head to glance over his shoulder at her when she entered the room and her cheeks grew hot, hoping the blush didn't show. His face, she noticed, had adopted a loftiness that it hadn't had before.

It was not his anger that had surprised her—Lark had always been apt at bringing out the worst in people, and he was no exception to that—it was the high and mighty routine. He was falling into the role of king of the darkspawn, and it just did not fit him at all. Not the young man she had known anyway. It had only been two years, was Crotis really able to work that fast?

"Mornin'," she muttered as she stepped into the kitchen. He nodded in response and turned back to the window.

"Figured you'd be awake already," she went on, unable to stop herself. "Never were a late sleeper…" She trailed off as she realized the familiarity that statement implied.

His head nodded slowly, considering her words with far more focus than she had. She hadn't expected a reply, but one came anyway. "I didn't think you'd be up for a while."

Lark offered him a quick glance and a thin smile, "Feel like I could sleep for two days, but that ain't gonna happen." She shrugged and pulled some plates down, feeling the distance between them stretch as she sought to say as little as possible. Involving him in her life was the last thing he wanted. "Bound to catch up to me at some point."

"I could have waited."

Lark turned to look at him. His eyes lingered on hers. At one time, she would have known exactly what that look meant. Mags could have told her anything with a glance.

"And hold you up?" she smiled at him, then shook her head, returning her attention to the task at hand. "Hungry?" She asked a few minutes later, setting a plate of eggs and bacon on the bar and nodding for him to take a seat. "Won't get fresher eggs anywhere, the Suloki give 'em to me. And that's Sarlo sweet bacon from Cuttah."

The stool squeaked on the stone floor when he moved it to sit and for a long moment that was the only sound that had broken the tenuous silence other than the sizzle and pop of the griddle. Lark poked pointlessly at the bacon.

Then he spoke suddenly. "No peaches?"

At first, all she heard was him critiquing her cooking and a caustic retort was on her tongue even before she had turned fully toward him. When her eyes met his, she froze. He was grinning, in that soft, lopsided way she had been sure she would never see again. She stared at him for a moment, surprised into silence, and then a light chortle escaped her. Mags was still in there after all.

"Never again," she answered with a cautious smile. Peaches were the calling card of the resort on Izlatana where Lark had been a servant when they met. After picking and serving enough of them she was unsure if she would ever be able to enjoy one again. She filled her own plate and leaned on the bar opposite him.

They ate in a comfortable silence for a moment and for that moment Lark settled into a contentment she had not felt in a long, long time.

When he spoke again, she looked across the bar at him. "How is it you came to know Hurshek?" It was a lead-in for more information, but the request was conversational, not demanding.

She gave a sigh and answered him directly, "When I came here and spoke d'javu, the people brought me to him. He wanted me gone at first. Thought I was just another raider. Told him you and me were...friends. Wasn't exactly happy with me that it turned out I stretched the truth, but he can't get rid of me now, I guess..." Mags' face became contemplative and they sat in silence for a little while longer.

Lark found she wasn't entirely hungry. When this meal was over, everything would go back to the way it had been last night. He would go back to Crotis, and she would be alone again. For right now, it was like it had been once upon a time. She was going to cling to that.

Scraping the side of her plate mindlessly as the pregnant pause droned on, she resigned herself to the fact that their friendly banter was over. Mags had all the information she could give him, and he would have no interest in small talk—

"Are you still a plugger?"

"Uh," came Lark's profound reply. She stared at him, completely taken off guard by a question that had no answer that could benefit his cause in any way. "Yeh—yes," she answered dumbly. She was able to right her conversational skills a moment later and she added with a grin, "Best in the Fringe, say so myself."

His lips quirked into a smile that told her nothing other than he hadn't smiled in a long while. "So, why aren't you on Cuttah? All you ever talked about was getting back there, you loved that place."

Her mouth dry, Lark found the words gathering in her throat even as she battled to hold them back. He was not staying and there was nothing she could do about that. What she could do, after all these years of being in his way, was not make it any harder for him than it had to be. "I loved a lot of things I had to let go of..."

Mags fell silent and, for an extended moment, Lark couldn't bring herself to look at him. She just stared at the place on the plate she had been scratching at with the fork. When she finally did raise her eyes to his, he was just looking away. Her words had the intended effect; Mags had clearly slammed back into the reality that was this a failed exchange. He had more important things to focus on.

He pushed his mostly empty plate away and stood up, moving away from her toward the opposite side of the room. Lark lifted both their plates and spoke softly, "Ready when you are." He paused, peering at her over his shoulder. "Better head to Hurshek's place soon," she explained. "Ain't gettin' cooler out there."

The air was tense and tangible between them as she pushed her bike out of the garage. Lark gave Mags a long look before climbing onto the motorbike and then shook her head, pulling her goggles back on.

Beneath her respirator, Lark was biting her lip hard as she propelled the bike across the bleak plain. It mirrored her mood all too well.

This was for the best, honestly, because she told herself that she liked being a working plugger, that she wasn't lonely. Her life was damn good enough, and she wasn't about to give it up for anybody.

Reaching beneath the steering column, she switched on some music and cranked the volume until it could be heard above the roar of the engine. It was an old song, from a band that had long ago succumbed to the lure of drugs and fame, but it was about justifiable good riddance.

Lying to herself and listening to music written by seventeen-year-olds did nothing to assuage the hard, cold feeling in her stomach—though the feel of his arms around her, even just to hold on while they flew across the plain, went a long way toward changing her perspective. What wouldn't she give up for him?

There was one thing, but it hardly mattered now because he *wasn't fucking staying*. She slammed the throttle and turned up the music again.

Hurshek lived in a cave carved out of a rocky rise far to the North. At top speed, it took almost two hours to get there. Icy regret turned to heavy anxiety as the rise appeared on the horizon. How was Hurshek going to react when he saw her? She hadn't laid eyes on the shut-in darkspawn for over a year and then he hadn't left in the best mood. From what she had heard, he appeared to the locals a few times when she was away, and nothing had seemed amiss. That did not give her any confidence he had forgotten that day.

Lark pulled up and stopped the bike, allowing Mags to dismount before she unclipped her dusty respirator and climbed off. She didn't look at him right away as she was trying to determine if this would be where she would say her goodbye. He was watching her thoughtfully while she pushed her goggles down around her throat. Then his hand moved toward her face, and she flinched.

For a split second, she saw something resembling despair in his eyes before he got his emotions under control. Lark didn't really think he was going to hit her, but she had been wrong about people before.

"You need to stop biting your lip," he told her, and he ran his thumb over her bottom lip. The gunmetal skin came away with a streak of red. Lark's heart lurched at the touch, the softness and care in his voice as he repeated that suggestion for what had to be the hundredth time.

Lark licked her lips and tasted the blood. She was not as good as he was at hiding her emotions. Considering the situation, she envied his ability to swallow his feelings. Unable to come up with an appropriate response, she forced a thin smile onto her lips and started into the cave.

The first several yards of the tunnel were pitch black, but Lark pulled a flash torch from her utility belt and held it up. It was for her benefit only, Mags could see perfectly in the dark.

Lark had navigated this cavern several times, and it never got more comfortable. It was as if Hurshek made this cave as dank and uninviting as possible as to discourage friendly visits. When the dim light of the living space appeared before them, Lark put the torch away and hesitantly strolled inside.

Lit by smokeless flames, the air was heavy with spiced incense and cut with sharp decorations and stone figures of darkling gods.

"Hurshek?" Lark called as she cautiously walked forward. She did not wish to catch the man off guard. He was already likely to be upset with her just for breathing his air. "It's Lark. Where you at, friend?"

"Friend?" his cool, flat voice preceded him from the shadowed doorway at the end of the room, the door directly to the right of his altar. He stepped out from the darkness and through the plume of incense smoke, regarding her coolly.

Hurshek was taller than Mags, with skin the dark blue of the sky just before midnight that had even slashes of ridges amid decorative and symbolic scarring. His horns were thick, but they had been ground down flat and level with the crown of his head. He had told her this was the symbol of his order, a pledge to the old ways. It set him apart from warriors and kings.

Speaking of, she realized belatedly Mags was not behind her. Lark glanced over her shoulder and then back at Hurshek. He was wearing a long sleeveless coat of dark blue seamed in silver. His hands were on his hips, pushing the coat open at the front to show the intricate carvings on his chest. He had not moved from the doorway. "When exactly did you begin assuming we were friends?"

Lark smirked. "S'a metaphor, don't worry about it. Look—"

"I told you I have no time for liars," he interrupted her and turned toward his altar dismissively.

Her eyes narrowed, and she crossed her arms over her chest, "Yeh, looks like your schedule's real packed. And I didn't lie, I was... Wrong, that's all."

Hurshek did not turn to look at her, but his voice was uncharacteristically sharp. "I have no reason to trust the words of a whore. My time would be better spent idle than—"

"Continue to speak to her like that, and your time will be much shorter than you realize," wherever Mags had gone, he was back now. He stepped around Lark and stood slightly in front of her, shoulders squared. He lifted his chin slightly, favoring Hurshek with that lofty very un-Mags-like look.

Hurshek about gave himself whiplash snapping his head around. His mouth dropped open briefly, the only reaction of surprise he allowed himself. It was enough for Lark; she memorized the expression and filed it away for later. Brightly, she gestured toward Mags and smiled widely, "Look what I found!"

Turning fully to face the newcomer and choosing not to acknowledge Lark's outburst, Hurshek smoothed his robes. "Magnimus."

"You know me."

"Of course," said Hurshek, clasping his hands in front of him. "You are Magnimus Avrok, son of Fosta and Jiktar. I was there on the day the mantle of your destiny was passed on." He studied Mags silently for a moment. "And you have come here to find me. Sooner than expected."

"Crotis sent me."

Hurshek nodded. "The natives gave you no trouble?"

Mags paused before answering, glancing at Lark whose attention was focused on something just out of his line of sight. He turned back to Hurshek. "If it had not been for Lark, I may never have made it here."

Hurshek glanced at Lark and growled in d'javu, "*I told you last time not to touch that!*"

Lark dropped a black dagger down onto the side table and stepped back, hands raised. Mags grinned and went on, "Crotis wishes for me to exercise patience. Luckily, Lark saved me from that. Yet again."

Lark gave a wide smile to Hurshek and crossed her arms, "And you said I'd never amount to anything."

"I did not say that," countered Hurshek. "I said you would never realize your true potential. Now come."

Hurshek walked between them and back out through the tunnel. Lark looked at Mags. "Told you he's my friend."

6

LARK YAWNED, stretching backward in her saddle and making a loud squealing noise. Mags raised a brow, but Hurshek ignored her completely.

"Where're we going anyway?" she asked, propping her boots on one thick horn of the large reptilian syphod she was riding. The animal gave a mewling groan of protest. It had a wide back with heavy shoulders, allowing the locals to ride with a saddle across its shoulders and strap their bulky goods to its back. Lark had wadded up her hide jacket and wedged it up under the back of her neck, so she could lounge during their long journey.

"To the gathering place," answered Hurshek evenly. "Where we will meet the other Kabalak."

"Sounds like fun," Lark quipped sleepily, settling into her saddle. It was midday, and the sun was at its zenith, pounding down across the dry, rocky landscape. Lark baked in the sun; her body was not as well built as her traveling companions' for extremes of heat. Pack animals included.

She had dozed off when her syphod came to a stop, waking up when Mags started to pull her from the saddle. They were in the shadow of a rock plateau. At their back rose a small settlement not dissimilar from the one Mags had landed in the day before. The sky shot upward in cloudless blue high above their heads.

"Damn," Lark dragged the back of her hand over her forehead to wipe away the sweat. "We all the way out by Inlan?" She peered around the ridge where their syphods stood soaking in the sun.

In the middle of a haphazard circle of upright stones stood seven d'javu of varying colors. All were wearing sleeveless robes similar to what Hurshek wore, and all had their horns ground flat and smooth. They were speaking in low tones that could not be heard from this distance.

At least Lark couldn't hear them, Mags was silent and clearly listening. If he was picking anything up, he didn't indicate as such.

Finally, Hurshek turned back toward Mags and waved for him to join them. The Kabalak were shuffling back to form a wider circle. Mags stood and began to climb the short ridge up to the circle. He stopped at the apex and turned, reaching down.

Lark stared at him stupidly. She hadn't expected to be included in what was clearly some sort of darkling conference. Least of all by Mags, who she knew had been working hard for this moment. When she didn't move, he hooked his other hand around a rock and stretched to grab her by the elbow and haul her bodily up onto the ridge.

Feet scrambling for purchase among the loose rocks, Lark tried to get her brain and body to catch up to what was happening. Maybe it was being in the sun too long, but she just couldn't fathom why he was pulling her up to him. He then took her by the wrist and, keeping her just behind his left shoulder, began to walk over to that circle. Lark had no choice but to follow, her brow furrowed with concentration while she tried her best not to trip and embarrass him in front of his elders. The priests didn't object to her presence, so they must not have been outright offended by it.

Hurshek spread his hands as he addressed Mags in a gesture that, for him, qualified as theatrical, "Magnimus, you were born in a time of hopelessness and turmoil for the d'javu. Your mother and father were the last of our greatest warriors. They, among many other of our kind, were slaughtered because of the power they possessed. The ancient jak'tu that were the pride of our race."

Another stepped forward, he was taller like Hurshek and a dark red color. Hurshek called him Ladek. He had a calm face, and he spoke in a dusty tone that Lark had to strain to hear. "Our people are too savage, too brutal to be ruled by a human like Crotis, regardless of his intentions..."

Lark gave a quiet snort. Mags shot her an angry look. She peered back innocently and patted her throat, pretending to clear it. He rolled his eyes and turned back to the priests. When he looked away Lark suppressed a smile.

The Kabalak went on, hardly skipping a beat. "But our people are still too proud. No one left on Kyro would survive an attempt to rule them. The d'javu are not known for..." A pause to choose his words, "Temperance."

Hurshek moved toward Magnimus, "Crotis agreed to raise you as the leader of the d'javu, to teach you all he knew as a military leader and to train you for the task ahead." Hurshek assessed the younger d'javu before him.

"But your time has not come yet, boy." A shorter and squatter darkling with an ugly face and mangled, claw hands that Hurshek identified at Qatlo spoke up, "Crotis still has much to teach you."

'Twenty years is a long time for our people to remain repressed by the Salvans," Ladek mused. "But given current circumstances, we have decided it is not yet time for that exile to end."

Lark peered at the side of Mags' face that she could see. He was stunned, she could tell by the subtle shift in his expression and the way his hands tightened at his sides.

"Current circumstances..." Mags murmured, his voice like boulders grinding together.

"You are too young," the one that answered was a burnt orange color. Lark couldn't wrap her mind around his actual name, so she decided to refer to him as Tangy. "The task before you is monumental," Tangy went on to say, as gentle as any d'javu male could be. "We cannot embark on this until we are certain you will not fail."

"Too young," Mags repeated.

"Untested," Qatlo chimed in.

A gross underestimation or patent ignorance. He was wrong. Even in Lark's limited experience, she knew Mags was far from untested and several years passed being too young for what they expected of him. She decided it was not the time to point this out, so she pressed her teeth together and continued to listen, with great effort, silently. "You will have to be as even-tempered as you are vicious. Crotis promised us he could instill that in you."

Mags squared his shoulders and lifted his chin, "He has."

Tangy turned his head to look at Qatlo, who cast his gaze over to Ladek. "That decision will be left to us."

The Kabalak all looked at each other, and Lark sensed there was something unsaid, something they knew shouldn't be said. Lark had discovered that most people found it impossible to keep things like this to themselves. The Kabalak, it seemed, were not exempt from that observation.

Qatlo's harsh visage turned back to Mags, and he spoke slowly, as if careful to ensure Mags understood every word. "After what happened on Izlatana, we are not sure you are prepared for the task ahead of you."

Lark found it suddenly very difficult to swallow. Her throat had tightened painfully, and she felt her eyes go round as she stared at Mags' back. It took every ounce of her pride to stop herself from shrinking behind him and hiding from the judgmental gaze of his elders.

Deathly still to the point where Lark had to resist the urge to push him to see if he'd fall and shatter like a statue made of glass, Mags did not speak for a stretch. "What happened on Izlatana," he said finally. Lark noticed that he'd hardly been able to form a statement that wasn't a reiteration of what the Kabalak had said. She was beginning to worry these withered d'javu had broken his brain.

Tangy answered him, spreading his hands. "You were meant to show the captive d'javu on Izlatana that you were beside them, that you shared in their burden."

Ladek interjected, "Instead you staged a riot; the news of which became very public very quickly. You nearly revealed yourself and destroyed twenty years of waiting and planning."

Mags eyes settled on Ladek, studying him for a long moment. When he finally spoke, his hands were in shaking fists at his sides. "I allowed an innocent girl to suffer as a result of my actions."

My actions. That was the first time Lark had been absolved of the blame. Not as a result of a *distraction* but as a result of *my actions*. Lark realized that Hurshek was looking at her, though he remained silent. It was obvious he'd inferred she was the girl. There a hint of conspiracy in the man's eyes that made her think, along with the fact that the other Kabalak had not even spared her a glance, that he was the only one who was aware of her involvement in the apparently notorious Izlatana incident.

"When I instead focused my efforts on the task at hand, that suffering continued," Mags went on, gaining steam now. His stillness had left him, and his tension was suddenly and frighteningly dynamic. Lark wasn't sure what she would do if he ruined this for himself now, but she wasn't going to try and stop him. "I will be damned if I was going to allow the same thing to happen to my people as a result of my *in*action."

Qatlo seemed undeterred by Mags' speech. "You are reckless," he claimed. "Impulsive. We have not waited twenty years—"

A rumble in the ground cut off the elderly d'javu. Good thing, too. Lark was unsure how much longer she could keep from assaulting them.

All heads swiveled to determine the direction of the disturbance. Lark broke away from Mags and took a few steps toward the edge of the circle, squinting into the bright sun in the direction of the Inlan settlement.

She spat a sudden curse, whipping around and heading back toward the syphods at a sprint. "About had it with these fuckin' raiders." At the edge of the flat rock, she slid down onto the earth below, eyes flitting to the horizon.

7

MAGS BROKE into a run, following Lark and watching her scramble up the side of the syphod. Hurshek was shouting at him. Lark was already spurring her syphod into a run when Mags turned to look back at the Kabalak.

Hurshek called across the open ground, "These raiders do not concern you." Mags replied only with a smirk and pulled himself into the saddle. Lark was already distant. Her battle whooping could be heard clearly over the rumbling of the approaching raid. "*Magnimus!*"

Ignoring the priest's haranguing, Mags kicked his syphod and leaned forward, determined to catch up to Lark. When she caught movement out of the corner of her eye, Lark turned to cock her head at him. "Show off," she yelled over the sound of the syphod's pounding feet.

Her lips curled into a smile, mirroring his own. He held out his hand, and Lark pulled one of her catalyst pistols from its holster, tossing it across the distance between their mounts. Mags caught the pistol and held it down by his leg as he leaned forward again to focus on their attack. Lark held her other pistol aloft and whooped loudly, firing into the air.

A dozen or so raiders were galloping across the landscape toward Inlan on syphod-back. Behind them, the wind was whipping the dirt into a cyclonic storm of dust, making them appear to be dragging a captive cloud behind them.

"Oh, bring it you sons of bitches," Mags heard Lark muttering as she leaned forward in her saddle and tugged her goggles up over her eyes.

Lark evened her firearm and took the first raider down just as the dust cloud enveloped them all. Mags followed suit, leaving her side. He fired a series of shots and took down two more before circling back to flank them again. The raiders commenced firing back, a barrage of inaccurate catalyst fire.

Lark's syphod caught a pulse and crumpled mid-step. She bounded off the animal and tumbled clumsily, springing up to one foot covered in yellow dirt, brandishing her pistol and cursing into the dust cloud. On both feet, she fired at the next raider who challenged her; barely dodging when his syphod collapsed as well.

The beast went skidding to a stop atop its rider a handful of yards away. The man screamed in agony, and Lark gave no second thoughts to shooting him.

Amidst the chaos, a greater rumble shook the ground—deeper, hollow, and growing louder. Lark stood still for a moment and pulled her goggles down around her neck. She looked down at her feet as her balance left her, and she fell backward onto her rear.

Gazing forward, she watched as the ground pitched upward and birthed a great red claw. It reached out to grab one of the dead syphods, dragging it down into the pit it had created.

Scrambling backward across dry ground that was becoming increasingly more rocky and treacherous, Lark tried to force her mind to comprehend what she was seeing.

That creature, clearly large enough to eat a syphod whole, was where Lark drew the line on bravado. How long had that thing been sleeping under the surface of this planet? How many of them were there?

How quickly could she get the *fuck* off this world? And how long would she see this thing in her nightmares?

Something appeared through her daze and wrapped around her arm, pulling her from the ground. Lark shrieked and turned, thrusting her knife at the offending appendage. Mags caught her wrist before she could stab him. He released her once recognition flashed in her eyes then focused beyond her at the churning soil. Without a word, he pushed her gently aside and began to walk toward it. As soon as Lark got her feet back under her, she started after him.

Surprising exactly no one, the raiders had abandoned their pursuit. Though, with all the rising dust their absence was hardly noticeable. The wind was whipping around her, tearing at her hair and nearly blinding her. "Mags!" she screamed at his back, raising a hand to shield her eyes from the stinging wind.

What in all bloody hell was he doing? Lark was all for pushing the envelope when it came to dangerous decisions, but this was straight up stupid. She had just gotten him back and, as dubious as that return had been, she was not prepared to watch him die for no reason. "If you're tryin' to impress me, this ain't the way to do it!"

He glanced over his shoulder at her, but his pace only quickened. The churning of earth had stopped, leaving a gaping hole from which clouds of sand belched into the gale.

Out of the blinding dust, another hand appeared to forestall her from following him. "Hurshek?" Lark turned, for the first time glad to see the priest. Maybe Mags would listen to him. "You gotta stop him."

"No."

She blinked at the simple response, "Then I will." She turned back in Mags' direction.

"You will stay right here," he told her firmly, holding on to her arm. "Magnimus!" he called out over the slowly dying howl of the wind, and Mags turned at the mouth of the pit.

Hurshek pulled a long black sword from his back. It had a wicked sharp, curved blade on one side, notched and angry on the other. Lark had never seen a sword like it. Even against a controlled catalyst weapon, she would put her money on that thing. It shown in the sun like black blood, and she could only imagine what kind of damage could be done with something so heavy-handed and vicious.

Swinging it back, Hurshek tossed the thing across the expanse between them. It stabbed into the ground a few paces from the younger darkling. Mags hooked Lark's catalyst pistol into his belt and pulled the black blade from the dirt with one hand. Without ceremony, he leapt into the pit.

"Mags!" Lark cried, pulling forward against Hurshek's grip, which only tightened as he fought to keep her with him.

"This is not your battle, girl."

"Not my...?" she stared up at him, incredulous. Then angry as hell. "Get bent, priest!" lifting her boot and shifting her weight away from him, she jammed her heel into his hip. Hurshek grunted and had no choice but to let her go. Lark tumbled to the ground with the sudden release, rolled and hopped to her feet.

She ran full tilt, without any idea what she was going to do when she got there, and slid to a stop at the edge of the pit. Below the gaping wound in the earth, several meters of emptiness sprawled out before her. Walls of dank earth retreated out of sight, belying a humongous cave system underneath the planet's surface. Most of the dead syphods lie at the entrance to one of those caves. Lark didn't want to consider where the missing parts had gone to.

Where the sun shone in she could see the pair of them. Mags was dark and small compared to the creature which was at least five times his size, its back covered in a great shell shining in the sun in a prism of black and green. It snapped great red pincers at Mags, looking like a giant beetle-crab. It also looked pissed, and Lark was wondering if Mags had lost his mind down there.

Hurshek joined her, wrapping a hand around her elbow. "He can handle this," he said low, staring down as the two monsters circled each other.

"He doesn't have to do it alone," answered Lark, almost introspectively, without pulling her eyes from Mags. She may as well have been talking to herself for all that Hurshek listened to her.

Even from here, she could see Mags' grin as he lifted the sword in one hand and swung, hacking through a pincer that had shot out at him. Thick, green blood flooded the ground, and Mags hopped back to avoid any incoming counterattack.

The creature roared, skittering backward and slamming into the wall of the pit. The ground shook and Hurshek yanked Lark back.

By the time Lark was able to wrestle away from the Kabalak, Mags was in hot pursuit of the big bug. He took a great leap and slammed the sword through the shiny shell, breaking through the glazed surface and going straight to the hilt. Mags swung his body, and the sword cut its curving way across the back of the shell leaving spider webs of cracks across its surface until the blade released. Mags dropped to the ground gracefully.

With a high-pitched screech, the creature swung his remaining pincer and caught Mags in the center of his chest. His back slammed into the stone floor with a sickening sound that even from a distance made Lark's stomach drop. The shelled creature recoiled while its enemy was down, screaming and screeching as it tried to reach back to where Mags had stabbed it.

Mags was barely moving, Lark couldn't help but notice. He was lying there on the ground not far from where the bug was throwing its tantrum and not making any attempt to get up. His arm was shiny with fresh blood.

Lark's chest was open and raw, her breath stolen by a paralyzing fear that he'd never get up. That creature would overtake him and... She couldn't.

Ripping her pistol from its holster, she screamed as she fired several times at the advancing creature. Hurshek was pulling her back away from the edge, but she didn't fight him this time. She just kept firing until the reaction chamber of her pistol began to strain. If it weren't for him, she may very well have fallen to her death. The frustrated howls of the giant beetle were lost among the crack of Lark's heavy fire.

Finally, Hurshek gave her one hard yank and the edge of the pit fell away. She had lost her shot.

It didn't matter. She had distracted the creature long enough, and Mags had pulled himself to his feet.

"You must have faith in him," Hurshek's voice was in her ear. "He is capable."

"I have faith in him," Lark shoved him away. "Don't need him to die to prove himself to me. And I certainly ain't gonna let him fucking die to impress you withering pricks." Dodging the darkling as he attempted to grab her again, she slid on her knees to the edge of the pit.

Mags was cornered now, his right hand void of the sword. He had her pistol in his left, but even Lark knew it was useless against that thing. His face turned up to hers, and she squinted across the expanse to assess his wellbeing. She saw pain there, that was to be expected, but nothing even resembling resignation.

Something swelled in Lark that she found hard to squelch, even with the fear and adrenaline still running high; overwhelming, and nerve-wracking at the same moment. Her throat tightened uncomfortably, and tears stung behind her eyes. He was grinning at her and she found herself smiling back without asking her lips to do so.

Mags held up his empty, bloody right palm then pointed at his belt. Lark's hand instinctively fell to that same place on her own belt, where her charges were stowed. He pointed at the creature that was still advancing on him then trailed his indication up along the edge. Lark followed his line of sight, studying the curve of the wall where it met with the ground at her feet. Looking back at Mags, she cocked her head. He smiled smugly and began to move.

Good thing she knew him so well, otherwise, this would have been anticlimactic.

Lark snapped a handful of charges off her belt, as many as she could gather and hook together in the time it took Mags to leap and run across the rise of the wall. The creature was following him, skittering on the rocky wall and trying to catch up to its prey. Lark was tracking the thing with one eye while she gathered the charges.

"What are you doing?!" Hurshek demanded from behind her. She had already almost forgotten he was there. Lark ignored him and pulled back her arm to chuck the charges to Mags. He caught them and in a smooth motion, activated and dropped them, springing himself off the wall and to the opening of the pit.

His body impacted Lark's just as the explosion battered into his back and the air ripped from her chest as it erupted around her. Mags' bloodied arm broke their landing as they fell to the ground together. He wrapped his arms around her, shielding her from the blast of rock and sand and bug guts. Hurshek had been blown clear, his nagging out of earshot for the moment. The only sound above the shattering explosion was the screeching howl of the creature at its epicenter.

"You're hurt," Lark told Mags when she could get a full breath of air into her lungs. Her hand slid up his slick arm toward the wound on his shoulder. He was smiling when he looked down at her, and he shook his head. Lark chuckled lightly, "Must've been how you felt when you found me with that pack of duncats on Narber."

"Do you regret that?"

Did he mean getting cornered by a pack of the wild cats while tracking a mark through the woods or the month they'd spent together out in the Fringe dodging responsibility? Either way, Lark shook her head, and Mags laughed. For a moment, it had felt like being back there— that brief blink of time that they'd been free and together after their escape from Izlatana. Before it had all gone to shit.

"Do you think this is funny?" Hurshek asked them. He wrapped two hands around Mags' bulky arm, pulling him to his feet. He reached next for Lark, but she waved him away, getting herself up and regarding him as if he were a parent that had crashed her party. "That was a baracs," he said as he watched them wipe sand from their eyes. "Omens of death—"

"If I were that fuckin' huge, pretty sure people'd see me as bringin' death, too," Lark was pushing her unruly hair away from her face and pretended not to catch the caustic look Hurshek cast her.

"Something isn't right..." the priest went on, almost to himself.

Lark released her hair and turned her ire directly onto the priest. "Yeh, that something is you lettin' Mags stand in that pit by himself and tryin' to keep me from helping him."

Mags put a steadying hand on her shoulder, "Lark..."

"No," she shrugged him off and stabbed a finger into Hurshek's chest. "What isn't right is whatever you're trying to pull here. You said he's not ready, but you were willing to bet he'd survive against that fucking monster. You're just like Crotis. You want to be in charge, but it's Mags who has to do the fighting." She let her hand drop and shook her head in disappointment. ""Nobody's doin' anything in this fucking galaxy alone."

Hurshek clenched his jaw and studied Lark. "The time isn't right," he forced through his teeth. He turned his gaze to Magnimus. "Return to Crotis, continue on your current path. When it is time, we will join you."

"Until then," Lark interjected before Mags could think of anything to say. "Why don't you keep your damn tests and your black daggers and your omens to your damn self. C'mon, Mags."

She looped an arm gingerly around his midsection and pulled some of his weight onto her shoulders. He must have been grateful for her interference because he allowed her to steer him away from Hurshek.

The syphods had gathered near the edge of the pit like the stupid animals they were. Lark grabbed her jacket from the back of her dead syphod then hoisted Mags up behind her on another.

He was still putting up a good front for Hurshek's sake, but she could feel the way he leaned into her, the weight that he was having trouble keeping up with. Lark decided not to say anything. Mags had his pride but he was alive and in one piece, so she let him keep it for now.

The trip back to Hurshek's house was slower than she would have liked. Midway through the silent ride, Lark glanced back to see Mags holding up his injured hand, sticky with drying blood. He flexed his fingers into and out of a fist then glanced at Lark when he realized she was looking. His grip tightened on her for a moment, pulling her closer to him.

"Hang in there, tough guy," she said to him, reaching back and patting his knee. "Once we get my bike, we'll be home—I mean, back to my place, and I'll get you fixed up." He didn't answer. Lark shifted slightly against him, finding that her cheeks were growing hot, and her heart was pounding despite the fact that the adrenaline had all but drained away.

The sun stroked the horizon by the time they made it back to Hurshek's place, and Lark glared at the priest when he came to join them at the mouth of the cave. "How did you get back here so fucking fast?" she asked accusingly as she slid off the syphod.

Without acknowledging her, Hurshek approached Mags as the younger darkling dropped unsteadily to the ground. "You are welcome in my home, Magnimus. I would be honored." He paused to shoot a hard look at Lark when she snorted at that. "I am a healer."

Mags waved his bloodied hand. "Thank you, but I'll go with Lark."

Lark was much smugger about that than Hurshek was disappointed. The priest gave no indication that Mags' decision bothered him in the least.

"Very well," he reached into his sleeveless robe and produced the black dagger that Lark had been fondling earlier. "The d'javu have few weapons left, most were taken by the Protectors when they invaded our planet and oppressed our people. Those that remember the craft are growing old, and soon it will be dead." Holding the dagger by the sharp blade, he held it out to Mags. "Take this. It is a weapon of our history, one of the very last we have. It is yours."

Mags took the blade's hilt in his left hand, felt the weight and examined the blade. The blade was the length of his forearm and light but sturdy and sharp as hell. Lark guessed he should have been a little more careful with that big sword he'd left in that monster in the pit.

Mags handed the dagger to Lark. She smiled, forgetting that Hurshek had denied this blade to her on many an occasion and this was an opportunity to rub it in his face. What was more important was that it meant something to Mags, and he was giving it to her. Carefully, she tucked it into her belt and tried to hide the flush in her cheeks.

"When the time is right, we will come to you," Hurshek's sigh was one of resignation. Mags nodded and began to move toward Lark's bike, but the Kabalak blocked his path. Hurshek's voice dropped in an urgent and conspiratorial way. "Crotis has an inflated sense of his role in this. He was allowed to raise you in order to impart upon you the patience and wisdom necessary to rule an angry and vicious people."

Hurshek's glowing eyes seemed to grow brighter as the light of day began to fade. Mags listened intently, the weight of the Kabalak's words almost tangible. "He thinks he controls the destiny of the one who will usurp dominance in this galaxy. He thinks he is the only one to whom you owe your allegiance." Hurshek watched Magnimus carefully. "Crotis' work is not done, but you must understand his role in this."

"What does it matter what he thinks?" Mags asked lowly, his brow furrowing.

"Because he will try to steer you on this path as if it were his own to walk."

Lark crossed her arms and spat sarcastically, "Crotis? No, never..." She harumphed and gave Hurshek a sour look. "Sounds to me like you don't trust him. How could that be?"

Hurshek looked at her, his expression unreadable. "The rumors that swirl about in this galaxy should answer that question for you."

Lark gave a chuckle and had another retort on her tongue when Mags growled. "That is *enough*," he took hold of Lark's arm with his good hand to silence her and spoke harshly to Hurshek. "Crotis has been nothing if not a father to me. You will not speak of those rumors again. And you," he glanced at Lark and released her. "You don't know what you're talking about. Let's go."

He moved toward the bike, and Lark turned a questioning gaze on Hurshek, who gave her a meaningful look that had her shaking her head furiously in response.

Everyone in the Fringe and in civspace took great pleasure in the gossip and rumors—how Crotis had fallen from the Alliance elite because he had shown an obscene interest in the darkling boys the Protectors had brought back after their first excursion to Kyro.

It wasn't like that, Lark insisted to herself. Mags would never let Crotis touch him. He was so much stronger than the old man and far too proud. Lark stepped away from Hurshek, not appreciating what she saw in the Kabalak's eyes. As if he had accepted those rumors as truth. She wanted to ask him if he had known about them before they let Crotis take Mags when he was a child. If they had, then why would they put him in danger like that? She wasn't entirely sure she would like the answer.

The ride back to Lark's place was uneventful. Mags seemed to be regaining some of his strength; he didn't slump against her as heavily. When they reached her garage, he got off the bike and ambulated inside under his own power.

Once they were in her home and she had locked down the place, Lark pushed him into a chair. Show's over.

"Just let me wash up," she told him, throwing her jacket onto the sofa and heading into the lav to wash her hands. She grabbed a med kit on her way back out.

Mags hadn't moved, he must have been exhausted. "You alright?" she asked gently.

"I was waiting for you," he answered. "You were just screaming at a darkling that could kill you with one hand." Mags gave the breath of a chuckle. "I am not going to argue with you."

After dropping the med kit on the table beside them, she bent over him to take a look at his wounds. The rock had dug deep into his shoulder and while the wound was deep and painful it was not life threatening. His wrist was swollen, this knuckles nearly crushed. Nothing was broken, but the skin had cracked and bled from the creature's unforgiving exoskeleton.

Lark pretended not to notice that he was watching her. She rested a hand on his good shoulder and leaned over him to check his back. Gripping his jaw gently, she examined his face and neck. Mild contusions, a few lacerations, nothing else that would leave even a scar on his thick, gray hide.

Finally, she allowed herself to realize he was staring at her. "What" she said with a laugh, reaching over to grab a medical pad and tearing open the packet with her teeth. She pressed it gingerly to the wound in his shoulder, and he winced.

"Seems like years ago that I was doing the same to you..." he answered reluctantly.

"It *was* years ago," she reminded him, dabbing at the blood so she could get a clear look at the cut. She pressed her lips together. "This ain't so bad..." she muttered and reached for the wrappings.

Words gathered from the pit of his stomach, but his teeth clamped shut around them. She deserved to know. After everything he'd put her through... He'd made everything harder on her than it would have been if he'd just stayed out of her life. And she had never missed a stride. "Lark..." he murmured finally.

When her eyes darted to his, oblivious to his inner turmoil, his stomach flipped. Even still covered in dirt, her face streaked with blood, and her hair framing her face in wild knots, she was beautiful to him. Too beautiful for the life she had been stuck with. The life he had left her in.

Mags braced himself, stubbornly forced his jaw to open and the words to come, "I feel... I haven't been alive since you left."

"What?" Lark froze, staring at him in disbelief. A shaking hand, sticky with his blood, pushed her unruly hair behind her ear, leaving crimson streaks in the honey strands. She swallowed with difficulty, shaking her head and turning back to the job at hand. "What are you talking about?" she muttered under her breath, trying to sound dismissive.

Mags caught her hand in his left, pulling her fingers away from his injured flesh. "I couldn't allow myself to think about you, so I didn't... and I stopped breathing." He pulled her closer.

Despite the way she stared at him, she gave no resistance. "Mags, you did fine without me," she said in a near whisper.

"Being alive is not the same thing as living," he told her. "I didn't see that until you were back in my life. I don't want to live that way..."

Lark's bright eyes studied his, her tongue caught between her teeth. He could see the protests forming behind her eyes. It would be easier to allow her to continue to believe that she was in his way. Holding him back. Nothing more than a distraction from his true purpose. All things Crotis wanted both of them to believe so they would remain apart.

"Mags..." she breathed, stalling for time to form an argument she didn't have.

He seized her then, dark fingers tearing through tangled hair to grasp her and pull her lips to his. He kissed her deeply and savagely, full of all the passion he had felt when their love was secret and all the time he had missed being away from her.

Wounds forgotten, arguments thrown aside, he stood from the chair with his hands still clasped around her face. Lark's fingers looped between his armor and she pulled him backward, leading him without uncertainty toward her bed.

8

Lark awoke in a different world, in sheets that didn't smell like her own. The feel of the man pressed against her was at the same time reassuring and terrifying. If she moved or if she woke him, would it be over?

He shifted and pulled her closer. He was awake, had been from what she could tell, and he seemed startled to find that she was as well. "Mornin'," she whispered with a sheepish smile, too nervous to break this fragile moment with full volume.

"I didn't mean to wake you," he replied, just as lowly.

"You didn't. How long have you been awake?"

Mags shrugged, "I didn't sleep..." Lark's brow furrowed in concern. He ran a finger across her forehead, willing those lines of worry away.

"Why not?"

A moment ticked by, and his ethereal glowing eyes studied her face, his fingers traced the line of her jaw, down her neck and across her shoulder. Pinpricks of chills rose along her skin at the tenderness of the touch. "Because I've missed watching you sleep."

Lark's stomach twisted with agony. She almost wished he wouldn't say things like that, wouldn't fill her with these feelings only to burst her bubble when he had to leave.

Without answering she rolled into him, pressing her face into his shoulder and going still. Maybe if she pretended to sleep, this moment could go on...

"And I was thinking," Mags continued, running his fingers over her hair. "About what Hurshek said. About Crotis."

He paused at the painful sound that escaped Lark's throat. That name was the last one she wanted to hear in this fragile, fleeting moment. Mags rested his cheek against her head to reassure her. He spoke into her hair, his voice a gravelly whisper. "I'm not going back there if I can't take you with me."

She rolled back to look into his face, incredulity in her eyes. "What?" she asked flatly, the whispering gone. She must have misheard him. What he'd said was insanity.

"I will not continue on this path if it means losing you again." His hand rose and pressed against the side of her face. "Hurshek said it himself. Crotis thinks he has more authority than he does, that he will try to steer me. I am going to be the leader of the d'javu, not him." He pulled her hair just a little, the strength of his conviction tightened his fingers faster than he knew. "And he cannot make me leave you behind."

His stare was unwavering, and Lark found herself a prisoner to it. Of all the times she had dreamed of him coming to her, she had never imagined these being words he'd say. Swallowing the lump in her throat, she licked dry lips and spoke again in a whisper. "What about the darkspawn? They'll never accept me."

"They will accept you if I tell them to," Mags said with certainty. "If I am to be their ruler, they will have to do as I say. The d'javu have a deep respect for marriage."

"*Marriage*?" Lark heard her own voice squeak.

"Yes," he confirmed, smiling at her and holding her chin between his thumb and forefinger. "It is the only thing they will understand. I will claim you as mine and no one will challenge me. They will accept you, or *they* will be cast out." He chuckled at the disbelief on her face. "Hurshek will do it if I tell him to." His smile faded slowly. A serious expression that seemed more at home on his features overtook it. "Will you come with me? Will you be my wife?"

Lark stared at him, her breath held in her lungs. She seemed to be waiting to be woken from a dream, and Mags allowed her time to come to the conclusion on her own that this was not the case.

"Mags," Lark seemed to accept reality. She sat up, tucking her hair behind her ear. She paused, smiled at him and slid her hands into his. "You know I will. But..."

She watched his face, the slight cock of his head when she seemed to have conditions. Her smile lost its strength and she took a deep breath, "There's something I gotta tell you—"

A chime interrupted her. A voice called from inside the house. Lark turned her head toward the door, caught her lip between her teeth, and climbed out of the bed. She dressed quickly and glanced back at him. Without explanation, she fled the room.

Was she denying him? Mags hadn't considered she would, he realized now that was probably arrogant of him. But she had said yes, hadn't she?

With apprehension, Mags pulled on his discarded clothing and followed her into the main room.

Lark was standing before a Suloki woman, her weight distributed oddly while she engaged in conversation. When the woman saw Mags, she gasped. Lark was able to catch her before she threw herself to the floor at his feet. "*Thank you*, Sherra," she said to the woman in d'javu. *"You should probably head back now, be careful."*

After a few half-started replies, the woman finally settled on a deep bow in Mags' direction and hurried out of the house. Lark pushed her tousled hair back away from her face and timidly turned back toward Mags. He realized, in that motion, the reason for her awkward stance.

Swinging from her leg with all his weight was a human boy. A little over a year old, he had pretty features with green-brown eyes and a mop of dark hair. Lark followed the line of Mags' sight and reached down to press a hand to the boy's head, "Mags... This is Gunner. He's... he's my son."

When Mags didn't say anything, Lark grew uneasy. The child pulled on her, oblivious to her distress, and she bent to lift him. Her arms ached to pull him closer, to protect him from some terrible thing she couldn't readily identify. Curling him close, she chewed her lip and glanced at Mags.

The silence was torture, so she opened her mouth and the words tumbled out, "I didn't know I was pregnant when we left Izlatana. When I figured it out, I... thought he was yours. I was too much of a coward to go back to darkling space, so I started looking for a place to hide—"

Mags grimaced, closing his eyes and pressing a hand to his forehead. "Izlatana... that night... the man that—"

"It's not Gun's fault," she blurted, her voice trembling over words she had said so many times in her own head. Lark squeezed her son against her and closed her eyes as well, sucking in a heavy breath to calm herself.

Even in dreams she had dreaded this moment, torn between two things that meant so much to her, convinced there was no reality where she might keep them both. Her son was everything she had; Mags was everything she had lost.

When Lark opened her eyes, she looked at Gunner instead of at Mags. She could not bear to see him lose faith in her again, but she would not hold him accountable to the things he had said this morning, the things he had said before he knew the whole truth. She said, "I know this changes everything..."

Silence reigned. Gun gently tangled his fingers in her hair, and Lark watched him. Her throat choked with tears that she had repressed over countless nights without Mags at her side. Now that he had returned, she was unsure if she would be able to hold them off until he left.

"This..." Mags began, not without reluctance. His voice was low, rumbling just over a whisper. "This changes nothing."

"Less than a week, Magnimus," Crotis muttered into the writing film on his desk without raising his eyes to see who had entered his office. "This is early, even for you. Tell me, did the Suloki people respond so positively to your terrorizing..."

He finally looked up, and his last few words died on his tongue. The writing utensil dropped from his hand. He pressed his palm to the top of his desk. "Lark," he spat her name, the features of his face—which resembled a skull even more now than it had years ago—twisted into an expression much more disappointed than surprised.

"Did'ja miss me?" Lark replied buoyantly. She offered a wide grin in response to his non-greeting.

"Hardly," Crotis retorted without skipping a beat, his thin upper lip curled away from his teeth momentarily. His graying blue eyes flashed to the darkling standing next to her. "Am I to understand that this...girl is, in some capacity, responsible for the swiftness of your return?"

"Yes," Magnimus answered him with meticulous restraint. Crotis would not be convivial toward their decision, and how Mags chose to present the scenario to him would greatly color Crotis' argument. "By chance or by fate, she was on Sulok when I landed. She knew the location of Hurshek, and she brought me to him."

Crotis nodded agreeably but falsely so, then folded his hands on the desk before him. His voice, like everything else about him, was a dagger seeking blood. "And you decided to bring her here in front of me. To what end?" He leaned forward and regarded them both. The light in his eyes was hungry. "I rarely have to repeat myself, so I will allow it this once." He held up one crooked finger. "If you wish for the d'javu to accept you, this human girl will only—"

"They *will* accept me," Magnimus interrupted. From the look on Crotis' face, this may well have been the first time he'd ever done so. "And they will accept my wife. They will have no choice."

"Of course, they will—" Crotis closed his eyes and waved his hand dismissively before he registered all that Mags had said. Then he froze, and his eyes fluttered open, his hand hovering in the middle of the gesture. Crotis stared at Magnimus, his face slowly paling and his mouth falling open slightly.

A peal of laughter broke the heavy silence before Lark was able to contain herself. Mags glanced at her, and she chortled, "What? He looks like he just bit into a rotten tormirander."

Crotis went on as if she wasn't even in the room, his eyes falling to the new straight-line scar on his protégé's forearm, "Magnimus, what did you do?"

Mags lifted his chin and answered simply, doing his best at hiding the unease he had displayed the last time they'd had this conversation. That time, it had ended with Lark backing out of the room and fleeing from heartbreak. This time, she wasn't going anywhere.

Fists at his sides, Mags' chest rose, and he steeled himself, "I ordered Hurshek to make Lark my wife."

A slight misrepresentation, Lark realized but chose not to point out. It had gone quite a bit more like this:

"Hurshek, I'd like you to make Lark my wife."

"Of course, Magnimus. Whatever you wish."

What had followed were a series of d'javu prayers or chants, only a fraction of which Lark could understand. Then he had Lark and Mags clasp each other's forearms as he drew that darksteel blade across their skin, matching scars as evidence of their eternal bond. How romantic...

In any case, Crotis didn't seem like he was bursting with well-wishes for the newlyweds. His face was turning a murky shade of puce, his jaw working like he was gnawing on something especially foul.

Without warning, so suddenly that Lark flinched, he slapped his palms flat against the desk and stood. "You disobeyed a direct order!" he shouted, drops of spittle showering the writing film on his desk. "I told you to let the girl go. I *told* you to focus on our plans, to let nothing deter you from your destiny. You stupid, selfish child! Everything your people have been through, everything I have risked for them, and you will destroy it all for a fleeting fancy!"

Now, it was Mags' turn to yell *Surprise!*—or at least something in d'javu that Lark hadn't heard before but sent Crotis whipping backward away from him.

Mags brought his fists into the desk hard enough to buckle the metal top, his dark gray shoulders heaving as he stared glowing orange daggers across the desk at the man who had raised him.

"Listen to me, old man," Mags growled, danger in his throat. "Rebellion for my people, victory for you. I want nothing of *your* plans, *your* destiny, if I cannot have *her*," for emphasis he jabbed a finger behind him at Lark, who was thinking about how good it would be if she were anywhere else at this moment.

Crotis stared at him, one hand on the back of the chair that he had run into when he backed up so quickly, the other still flat on the desk. "Magnimus," he began, his voice having lost all the fervor it had when he thought he was the only one in control. Now he sounded humbled, speaking as if trying to calm the overreaction he had elicited out of the young darkling. "I cannot—"

Mags stood to his full height, suddenly and coldly calm. He stared Crotis down, "I am not asking for your permission." He held his arm out to Lark, and she took it, averting her eyes from Crotis. "Or your blessing." He tugged on Lark's arm, pulling her around.

"And what of the darkspawn, Magnimus?" Crotis asked, some of the former hubris returning to his words. "What happens when they will not bless this union between you and a human?"

Mags turned to the side and looked at his mentor, his eyes still leveled coolly. "You have always told me that when I reveal to them that you are on their side, they will accept you because of your connection with me. Lark will have that same privilege."

"And if she doesn't? Working with a human is one thing, Magnimus. It is quite another to lie with one."

Mags turned away from him, wrapping his arm around Lark's shoulders and leading her from the room, "I am sure you expect them to feel the same way about you."

9

THE FOREST trees were black as night, slick with steaming rain that smelled like sulfur. Kar'ju, Kyro's moon, hung low and heavy in the sky, brushing the tops of the trees. The red-tinted moonlight that filtered through the heavy canopy revealed almost nothing of the creatures that moved amongst the trees.

Mags was ahead of her now, though all she could see of him was his glowing orange eyes between the black trees when he glanced back toward her. She lifted her right hand from where it rested on her utility belt and saluted him. His sharp teeth glinted in the ruddy moonlight when he grinned back. His eyes blinked out again a moment later as he headed into the trees. Lark started to step forward to follow, but another shadow stepped in front of her, blocking her path.

Galkun. A tall d'javu with skin the color of blood and a lot of bottled up rage that was reflected on his viciously grimacing face. Galkun kept his horns shorter than most, coming to sharp points just above the top of his skull, and one of his pointed ears was scarred and crumpled where it had been half torn off.

He stepped around her and sent a look of malicious

provocation over his shoulder as he passed, daring her to respond. When he turned away, he muttered a nasty intonation in the d'javu tongue. Something to which she took great offense. Something he wouldn't have uttered if Mags had been in earshot.

Lark's hands tightened on her holstered CCPs, wanting more than anything to shoot the tall darkspawn in the back. After seven months, their scorn was starting wear on her pride. It would do nothing to win her friends among the darkspawn if she attacked Galkun, it would only make Mags' task of winning them over that much more difficult.

Then again, risking her ass for their freedom hadn't warmed them to her either. Lark figured they would cancel each other out.

Her earpiece came to life, bringing her back from her dark fantasies. [Patrol ahead,] Mags' gravelly voice spoke to her. [They are becoming desperate; this is the third patrol since we returned from Nak'jin.]

"Gettin' wise a little late in the fucking game, ain't they?" Lark replied. She had a pair of goggles dangling around her neck, and she tugged them up over her eyes, depressing the button that engaged their sensors and showed her the heat signatures of the patrol. "It took 'em this long to figure out we're here. I say bring 'em on. It'll be fun to have a real fight on our hands, don't ya think?"

[We will have to discuss the differences in our definitions of the word 'fun'.]

Lark chuckled and pulled her hood up. "You can show me whenever you want, my love, but I got some pricks to kill first."

Kettlewood was a massive forest, named by the Protectors for the thick black bark on the trees. It was one of the only places on Kyro the humans had yet to infiltrate, and it had been the natural place for the rebellion's base of operations throughout the dry Kyro winter. The season had not been exceptionally cold, but food and supplies had been scarce and the forest wildlife especially aggressive.

For months, they had been embroiled in guerrilla warfare, ambushing Salvan patrols for supplies and ousting Protector control from the smaller cities. Any other enemy may have given in when they saw the slaughter the darkspawn were capable of. The Protectors, unfortunately, were boosted by generators of self-righteous rhetoric and the belief that they were shielding the rest of the galaxy from the demonic creatures of Kyro. Not to mention the population of the planet Salva and its well-supplied fleet. They could outlast the darkling rebellion by years upon years.

Pulling a mask up over the bottom half of her face to hide her fair skin, Lark moved quietly through the trees. Her goggles told her the patrol was about thirty yards ahead and moving slowly westward. Lark remained hidden as she planted her charges and prepared to put a stop to their progress.

When the charges were secured to several trees in the patrol's path and Lark was well out of shrapnel range, she pressed the detonator.

The boom shattered the serenity of the dark forest, followed in short order by the war cries of the d'javu as they poured out of the trees like an army of demons. Lark left her hiding place and hurried to join them, pulling a CCP from each holster and wielding them in both hands.

She broke through the trees; the air was so thick with black smoke even her goggles were struggling to sort out the action. The transports had stopped and dumped more Salvan soldiers into the forest to engage the rebel darkspawn. All around her, people and darkspawn were screaming and fires were spreading. Somewhere not far off, a heavy repeating rifle was spitting into the trees relentlessly, filling the forest with its deafening report.

A loud bang split through the din, the sound of lightning cracking open the sky followed by the smell of burnt atmosphere. Lark whipped around at the familiar report of a catalyst pistol, but the white-hot pulse hadn't been meant for her. To her left, Galkun had taken the catalyst pulse to the face.

His already ugly, ghoulish visage was melting before her eyes. Sizzling and popping, the chemical concoction ate away at his crimson flesh until he collapsed before her. His clawed hand reached out and briefly wrapped around her ankle. His hold went limp almost immediately. Lark understood the gesture, or at least interpreted as she needed it to. They were allies, after all, and she wasn't here to dance naked in the forest.

Lark raised her own pistols and unloaded into the fray, aiming for the human woman who had taken out Galkun but assassinating any others within her sight with extreme prejudice.

In the darkness and the smoke, they couldn't tell she was human beneath her goggles and hood. They were, however, clearly tipped off by her use of catalyst weapons, because they responded to the report like birds to seed.

Lark whooped. She'd been waiting for some action all week!

The onslaught of pistol fire drove her back, but the darkspawn fell upon the distracted Protectors and ended it before they could corner Lark any further.

All in all, the skirmish lasted only a few minutes. The d'javu attack had taken the Protectors completely by surprise. Their native camouflage in the familiar territory was decimating even against the Protectors' numbers.

Out of necessity as much as innate cruelty, they left no survivors. They could not risk anybody running back to headquarters to confirm their whereabouts. Not now when they were so close to the final phase.

◻   ◻   ◻

Their tent was dark, and the canvas walls buffeted the midnight wind that shuddered through the trees outside. A small green light blinked slowly from the makeshift desk— a comm station Lark had cannibalized from her ship. Her gear lay thrown over the back of a flimsy chair, another held Mags' sword and his leather duster.

A light gray and sky-blue uniform, freshly cleaned and holes mended, hung from a far support to dry for its final use in the morning. Lark stared at it across Mags' chest as she lay curled against him. He was sleeping, probably for the first time in days, and she was determined to make sure he did so for as long as he could.

Tomorrow was going to be a big day. If all went as planned, it would be the culmination of over seven months of rebellion and the end of the Protector occupation of the planet Kyro. Twenty years of oppression would turn to blood and fire and the d'javu would be free.

For her part, Lark was looking forward to the victory for more than just the d'javu's freedom. She didn't mind roughing it out here in the woods, but she did look forward to building a real home with her husband for the first time.

"*It isn't the Fringe.*" That's what Mags had said when they first arrived on Kyro. He had pointed out the far-off valley city of d'jaku and the dark stabbing spires of Katarak Keep. "*But I will make it your home.*"

The sound of footfalls passing outside the tent along with the smell of rekindled fires and cooking food woke her before she realized she had dozed off. The camp was coming alive, and when Lark opened her eyes, slivers of sunlight had broken through the openings in their tent.

A ray of the warm, red light sliced across the tent and onto the gray fabric of their enemy's uniform. Anticipation stirred inside her like coffee in a percolator.

When Mags finally awoke, Lark had donned the uniform and finished braiding her hair tightly against her scalp. She glanced over at him as she tucked in the ends of the strands, her pink lips curling into a smile. "Mornin'."

"I hate it when you wear that," he said in a growl.

Lark chortled darkly, "Everything goes as planned, this'll be the last time I'll have to."

He rose from the bed and dressed while she put on makeup in a dirty, warped mirror she had scavenged. He cut her a disgusted look, the decorative ridges of his brow that gave him an omnipresent scowl pulling together as he secured his woven leather jerkin across his chest. Lark caught the look in the mirror, and her bright eyes cast him one right back. "Keep lookin' at me like that and I'll get into character early."

Mags fell silent for a moment, "I still don't agree with this scheme of yours."

"Scheme?" Lark turned to look up at him, her face pinching into something between a glower and a pout. "Ya know, I was a damn good plugger before you walked into my life."

"When I walked into your life you were a captive servant on a resort planet," he retorted, his eyes teasing even if his voice was indignant. "And you weren't plugging anyone from Izlatana."

"Could've gotten outta there without your help."

"Yes, you were certainly flying under Izla's radar," he said sarcastically, leaning down to kiss the top of her head and pinching her side as he did so.

She narrowed her eyes at him. "Little bit more time, and I'd have been out of there. But you had to bring that gorgeous gray body into it and distract me."

Mags smiled at her, and her heart skipped a beat. She remembered the first time she had seen that smile, in the peach orchard back on Izlatana. She had stolen his knife to cut a peach and hadn't been able to tell if she had impressed or irritated him. Then he had smiled, an uncommonly beautiful expression on his intense face, and she had been hooked on him for good.

"You would know all there is to know about distractions," he tugged gently on her ear before bending to gather the rest of his gear.

When she rose, Mags pulled his hooded duster jacket across his shoulders. He held the tent flap to the side so she could exit and followed her out. In this getup, she received even more dirty looks than normal from the darkspawn in the camp.

They ate breakfast in a tense silence, and then Lark prepared to head out. Mags walked her to the stolen transport bike she had fixed up in anticipation of this farce. "I hate this," Lark commented, tugging on the light gun belt of the commandeered uniform. "I miss my CCPs."

"I'll have them with me when I reach the platform," he assured her.

After putting the uniform jacket on and buttoning it up to the sky-blue lapel, she could easily be mistaken for a Protector. Lark kissed Mags swiftly, not wanting the other darkspawn to see. Even if they hadn't exactly gathered to see her off, they always seemed to be watching and judging.

"Sundown," she said, tucking a strap of his armor away. "Don't get yourself killed."

Mags stared at her, the depth in his eyes threatened to swallow her. "Be careful," he said, his voice was not cautionary but imploring. Careful was not particularly her jive, but she would try anything once.

"I will," she lied, patting his cheek. She turned away, but he pulled her right back to kiss her again, lingeringly this time. "Alright," she said with a light laugh when he released her. "I promise."

Then she climbed up on top of the transport bike, saluted him, and headed off through the trees.

10

DEVIN MENT brought her pike up over her head, letting out a shout as she brought the weapon down on her enemy. Her voice echoed in the training room. The dummy shook with the impact of the attack.

"Killing blow!" the panel on the wall told her. "Keep it up!" She had no intention of stopping.

It was early, even for the military lifestyle of the Salvan people, and the only company she had in the training room of the barracks outside of d'jaku city was three rows of training dummies. They all stared at her emotionlessly, as if her outrage was perplexing to them. Fitting, since the darkspawn here on Kyro seemed oblivious to the Protector's reaction to their deadly rebellion.

Wiping sweat from her forehead and pushing a dirty blond curl back into its binding, she reset and swung again. She imagined the demon-faced rebels she had killed in the past months. She imagined the faces of the many more to come. They had declared that they would not stop until every Protector was either dead or had fled from Kyro.

At first, that had been laughable. After over seven months of non-stop skirmishes in Protector controlled cities, the Salvans had been forced to face the reality that the darkspawn were going to wipe themselves out trying to accomplish their goals, and they might just take a generation of Salvans with them.

"Devi."

Her fingers tightened on the pike, and she turned to glance over her shoulder. Rykstar Os had entered the training room. His tall frame moved tentatively toward her, dark eyes forlorn under heavy brows.

Devi turned back to the dummy, "I don't want your pity."

The pike cracked against the dummy's midsection, the jarring vibration travelling down the staff into her fingertips. She gripped it that much tighter and swung again. She could sense Ryk's presence as he stopped out of range. "Devi, we lost another patrol in Kettlewood last night."

She paused mid-swing, then brought it back and slammed the pike into her adversary with brutal force. The dummy shook back and forth, and the panel on the wall congratulated her on another imaginary takedown.

Devi spun around to look at Ryk, her milky green eyes on fire, "I *knew* it!"

To Ryk's credit, he didn't flinch at her outburst. Perhaps he was expecting it. She had known him almost her entire life; it made send he wasn't surprised by her ire. Especially today, of all days.

"You knew what?" he asked carefully, remaining outside of her swing radius.

"I *knew* they were hiding in there!" she pointed in a random direction, far too distracted to determine which one would be correct. "Let's get a battalion together and wipe them out."

"Devi, we don't even know how many there are. They have the advantage in that forest." He held up a hand to forestall further fiery ideas. "I'm already setting up a system of watches to try to contain them in the forest. But

Kettlewood is large and we are short on available people. And…"

"And, what?" Devi could only imagine more bad news could be coming. He certainly wasn't going to follow that up with a surprise party.

"A transport coming in from Salva was destroyed on its way through the Devil's Tongue this morning," Ryk sighed as flames licked the sides of Devi's face. "Somehow, they've placed proximity mines in the nebula. I sent a drone out this morning to tell them not to send anyone else in until we can find them all. I won't know if it made it to the other side." He paused, and his brows drew together. "Dev—"

She turned and threw her pike into the dummy, hard enough that the thing bounced around on its bearings and the panel gave an unreadable spurt of code before shutting down entirely. The pike clattered as it fell to the floor.

"*Someone* is helping them!" Devi shouted, rounding on Ryk again.

"Who?" he asked her calmly.

"Crotis!" she blurted without really thinking about it.

Ryk paused before picking up her pike and following her to the entrance of the training room. "Governor Crotis has nothing to gain from this rebellion except putting his own life and power in danger."

"I don't trust him," Devi snapped, yanking a folded towel from a shelf and causing several others to fall. "And neither does the Consul."

Ryk watched her in silence as she wiped her face and interacted with a computer console, angrily swiping away alerts about the damaged practice dummy. "He was sent out here because no one in civspace likes him," she growled. "You don't think Crotis wants revenge for that?"

Ryk gave a sigh and took over the console to bring up what little information they had on the previous night's attack. Devi crossed her arms, studying him as he spoke in that same calm tone. "Governor Crotis will be on the main platform at sundown. He'll want to see us. If he was responsible for this rebellion, why isn't he in hiding?"

Devi dropped her hands in exasperation. "I don't know, Ryk. I also don't know why we don't just blow this place up. And all the darkspawn with it…"

Ryk put a hand on her shoulder. "We are Protectors, Devi. Not murderers."

On the northern side of the landing platform, in front of the barracks, Devi recognized the governor's shuttle craft beside a line of bound darkspawn. She breathed an embittered sigh. "Nyhman's here, too…""

At the end of the column of d'javu, the *Cartographer* stood waiting. An old, ugly ship, with a name that made little enough sense considering it was basically a prison transport.

Somehow, the man who owned it had managed to make even less sense. The enigmatic scientist, tall and thin with hair that was black and wild, stood speaking with Crotis beside the mouth of the transport. D'javu were being forced into heavy collars by large, armed men. The pair were old Alliance socialites from what Devi had been told. From back before the d'javu had been discovered, when the Alliance of Civilized Planets had been all parties and pleasures. Then, as now, the Protectors carried all the serious burden.

"Governor," Ryk said as they approached, bowing his head slightly to Crotis. Devi followed suit.

Crotis acknowledged them with a friendly nod, "High Commanders. We were just talking about your efforts to put down this piteous darkling rebellion. Nyhman, you remember High Commanders Devin Ment and Rykstar Os, don't you?"

"Protectors," Nyhman purred in his strangely melodic voice. Devi suppressed a chill as the man swept into a bow. "It is my privilege to work beside you."

His mismatched, oily eyes lingered on Devi before spending approximately the same amount of time on Ryk and then burned through the closest d'javu. "I am not a warrior like yourselves," he said. "But I hope that by taking a few more of these creatures off your hands. I am contributing to your efforts to get the darkspawn under control." He smiled thinly, his odd face taking on a skeletal cast in the weak light of Kyro's muted sun. It wasn't yet dusk, but it always felt like the sunlight was dying here.

"Certainly," Crotis answered for them. The two men then shared a smile that made Devi look away. The rumors about Crotis' infatuation with young darkling boys and the experiments that Nyhman ostensibly performed in his laboratories made that conspiratorial exchange almost sickening. The pair of them just had too much interest in the darkspawn. "I had heard, Commander Ment, that you are engaged to be married. To Baelfor Ritgar, if I remember correctly. Is that right?"

Ryk's head swiveled to Devi. Her jaw tight, she swallowed and forced herself to sound as cordial as she could manage when she answered. "That's right, Governor."

"Splendid!" Crotis' smile was full of delight that he simply could not be feeling; his hands made a papery sound when he clapped them. "We could use a little light in these dark times. Tell me, when is the special day?"

"Today," Devi answered between her teeth, feeling her hands ache with fists she did not know she had gathered. She took a breath, pushing at the pang in her chest. "It was supposed to be today."

Crotis blanched, his smile turning into an expression

that reminded Devi a little of a frog. "Well then," the old man's voice honked slightly as he tried to offer sympathy and optimism, neither of which he was accustomed to conjuring. "Where is our good friend Bae? We have a ship's captain, don't we? I see no reason we can't make this happen..."

Ryk interjected, trying to deter the conversation from travelling any further into such territory. "Bae is on Salva." He sent a tentative glance at Devi who simply turned her eyes to the ground.

"I see," Crotis cleared his throat. "When this rebellion is put down, we will have that much more to celebrate then." He forced another smile onto his ancient face. "In any case, I am sure you all have more important things to do than to listen to the dithering of an old man." Crotis bowed to each of them again, "Good evening, all."

Nyhman turned to the Protectors after Crotis had shuffled away. "Indeed. Here is to a quick end to this rebellion, my friends." He dropped his head to them. When he rose, the light caught the skin of his gaunt cheek and highlighted the three parallel scars he'd acquired a few years ago, most likely from an unfortunate encounter with one of his 'collection'. "Do not allow me to hold you up. I will be out of your hair—along with several of these creatures—in no time." He tapped one of the passing d'javu with the prod he had in his hand. The darkling sneered at him, bucking his shoulders.

The scientist didn't move when the darkling snarled at him, but Hithlis did. Devi hadn't even seen Nyhman's oversized lackey who she now imagined had been lurking over the scientist's shoulder the entire time, smirking his ugly smirk. The other d'javu were forced to watch helplessly as the large man laid into the offending prisoner with such savagery even Devi flinched away.

Nyhman made a strange noise in his throat, somewhere

between amusement and disappointment. "Come, come, my friend," he spoke to Hithlis. "We have a schedule to keep."

Hithlis rose and roughly set the darkling on his feet. Bleeding and swollen, the d'javu staggered but stubbornly stayed vertical.

The darkspawn were tougher than humans, but Hithlis was no normal threat. The man was impossibly huge, if not especially clever. He had olive skin stretched neatly over bulging, round muscles. Hithlis stood to his full height, at least a head over Nyhman, and his ice-chip eyes gleamed with sick satisfaction.

"Well," Nyhman said evenly, moved by neither the disrespect of the darkling nor the violence of his counterpart. His eyes took in Hithlis' bloodied knuckles without reaction, then he bowed to Devi and Ryk again.

"Safe travels," Ryk said to him, returning the bow hesitantly. They stepped back as Nyhman disappeared into the *Cartographer* and the line of boarding d'javu dwindled then ended.

"I do not know which one of them is creepier," Devi commented, suppressing a shudder as the craft took off.

"We live among demons," Ryk agreed with her somberly. "And sometimes, it is the humans here on Kyro that concern me."

Devi shook her head. "I don't know about that..."

Ryk's communicator flared to life at his hip; a garbled, indiscernible noise roaring from it. He lifted it and spoke, "Repeat." The response came back, nothing but more static.

Devi frowned, and her eyes rose to scan the platform. One of the transport pilots was climbing on top of his craft, seeking the broadcast panel at the top. On the opposite side of the platform, a young blond girl was pushing off the advances of one of Ryk's boys. Devi's brow gathered as the girl began to run. Ryk was shaking his comm as if that would make it work.

"Our signals are being scrambled," Devi told him before starting toward the blond girl. "HEY!" she yelled. Her target didn't look back, but her pace quickened so Devi began to run.

And then the world exploded.

11

THE *STARSIGH* was miraculously untouched. Months ago, Lark had left her beloved ship under a tarp among the shipment piles on a neglected end of the Protector platform, and there it waited.

The blurry red orb of the sun was now heading toward the horizon, casting a deep shadow underneath the ship that had facilitated Lark's entry onto the well-guarded platform. Mags would be here just after dusk to catch Nyhman before he left Kyro with his shipment. For now, Lark crouched under the wing of her ship and anticipated her next move.

Luckily, though the Protector uniform was tailored and slim fitting, Lark had been able to hide her wrist gauntlet beneath the long sleeves. This gave her direct communication with the *Starsigh* and any devices therein, along with all the little tricks and gadgets she had hidden within the gauntlets themselves.

Nyhman was on the platform, as was Crotis. Lark seriously considered calling on the *Starsigh*'s catalyst missiles and blowing both men up. It would solve two of her biggest problems in life.

Mags would never forgive her for taking the satisfaction of Nyhman's murder away from him, unfortunately. Nor would he be thrilled that she had killed the man who was, for all intents and purposes, his father. Even if she claimed it was an accident. Even if it would save her a metric shit ton of frustration down the line, it wasn't worth it.

Checking her chrono, she pulled the sleeve of the jacket up over her forearm and keyed in the access code that logged her into the *Starsigh*'s command console remotely. She activated the ship's scrambler and immediately, her own readouts and comm signals went dead. Shifting her weight onto her right leg, she leaned out from under the ship and listened. It didn't sound like the sudden radio silence had alerted anyone enough to sound any alarms.

That meant she still had time.

Shifting back, she pulled her sleeve back over the gauntlet and scurried between the shadows to the first transport parked along the eastern end of the platform. A handful of charges placed just over the fuel cell, and the first transport was a ticking time bomb. The next had several Protectors on board, playing cards and shooting the breeze. The terrorists and the rebellion seemed far from their minds, at least for the moment.

Their laughter only feet away, Lark slipped silently behind the ship and planted the charges. Then she turned and did so to the ship parked behind her. As she passed from under the transport to move on to the next, she noticed that the *Cartographer* was gone. The High Commanders were engaged in low conversation as they walked away from where the ship had been loading. Searching the skies, Lark caught sight of the clunky ship just as it ignited and punched through the atmosphere.

Crotis had told them he planned to meet the scientist at dusk, and Mags would not be here for another ten minutes! How could Crotis have miscalculated something he knew was so important to Mags? Hands in fists, Lark began crossing the platform in search of the old man, intent on asking him just that.

"Are you lost?" someone asked her and Lark pulled her eyes from her pursuit to engage him. A stupid-looking young man with a stupid smile. Lark was unable to stop her lip from curling. Boys like this would not have survived childhood in the Fringe let alone until manhood, and she wasn't in the mood to be polite.

"No," she answered shortly, moving away from him. "I'm looking for the Governor."

"Governor Crotis?" the kid was still following her, and Lark growled audibly.

"Who else?"

"The Governor and his entourage just left for Kar'ju a few minutes ago. I might be able to reach them on the comm if you have something you need to tell him."

Lark caught movement out of the corner of her eye, his arm rising from his belt. She whipped around and hardly kept herself from screaming 'no' as she wrapped her hands around his comm to pull it away from his lips. He stared at her in bemusement, and Lark gave a nervous laugh. "Don't bother the Governor now. It can wait." Releasing his hands quickly, she turned to go. He caught her arm.

Her hidden knife triggered; the steel was cold in her hand. It was all she could do not to slice his throat right there, but she'd had the presence of mind to keep the knife well hidden behind her. He didn't seem to notice her murderous instinct because he smiled and waved his other hand back toward the transport she had just rigged. "I'm Jak. Do you want to come have something to eat? We've got Gudbars and Crackle, straight from home."

Lark smirked. Last thing she needed, starry-eyed lover-boy over here. "No, thanks," she pulled her arm from his grasp. "I'm busy."

She scurried off before he could protest and turned back to ensure he wasn't following before sliding behind the next transport and attaching the last group of charges to the hull. Then she got the hell away from that end of the platform. She had enough scars stitched across her body; she felt no need to add burns to that canvas.

They were yelling at her, but she was done with the pretense. Time was ticking down, and panic was spreading across the platform. Someone had realized their communications were being scrambled.

Lark checked her chrono again and broke into a run. More demands for her to stop, more inquiries about her name and her assignment. All of them ignored.

Out of time. She couldn't very well go through with her plan from Protector custody, so this ruse was over. The sleeve of the tailored Protector jacket tore as she wrenched it back away from her wrist, coming to a sliding stop and diving under one of the safe transports.

Keying in the code for the detonator, she covered her ears with her hands and curled away from the incoming blast.

12

DEVI FOUND herself staring at the crimson sky. Her hearing slowly crept back, and with it came pain. Her skin was burned and her back ached, but Devi got up.

"Ryk!" she cried out as she forced herself to stand. Her voice was muffled and weak in her own ears. She yelled it again, louder this time.

"I'm here, Devi," his voice came from far away, but she found him only steps from where she had landed. "Are you alright?"

"I'm alive," Devi bent to help him to his feet, grunting painfully with the effort. "What the hell happened?"

Ryk shook his head to clear it, peering around him at the wreckage. Several ships had been destroyed or thrown aside; smoke and fire filled the air. All around them bodies lay sprawled—some unmoving, some no longer whole. "Another bombing. They must be going for d'jaku city next."

"How are they doing this?" Devi asked with desperation softening the edge in her voice. She could not pull her eyes from her dead comrades.

As if in answer to her question, the d'javu appeared. Hardly visible through the smoke, the dusky skinned crowd of darkspawn was dripping in blood, wide mouths split with jagged smiles. These were the terrorists who'd murdered and looted their way from Tak'ar to Filsek. They had appeared so suddenly, but over the last few months, their numbers had swollen to what stood before them now. An army.

Their leader, the one responsible for all this carnage, stepped out of the crowd of d'javu and stood before the battered Protectors, surveying the damage with eyes that glowed brightly even in the dingy light. He leered at them, his teeth sharp but perfect and even.

"A jak'tu..." Ryk muttered in disbelief, pulling his weight from Devi and drawing his catalyst sword from its sheath across his back. It had been so long since Devi had heard the term, she almost didn't recognize it. It dawned on her as she stared at the terrorist leader who looked so different from his brethren.

A pure blood d'javu, the ancient black blood Devi and Ryk's parents had attempted to expunge from the galaxy. Devi shook her head in disbelief, "That's not possible, they're all dead..."

The darkling's thick arms spread wide. He held a black sword in one hand, shining red with blood. "High Commanders!" he called to them in unaccented universal over the din of blazing fires and dying soldiers. Devi's brows pulled together in confusion. How could he have survived?

"Protectors!" the leader went on, his voice booming across the platform. "I am Magnimus Avrok, leader of this rebellion. You!" He pointed at them all. "You came here twenty years ago, and you brought nothing but pain and blood to Kyro. You repressed my people, you destroyed our history, you murdered all the jak'tu because you were afraid." His lips curled into a snarl and his voice dropped, "You should have been more thorough."

Ryk activated the controlled reaction in his sword. The edge of the blade ignited in bright chemical alloy. Devi had her pike in her hands as she stared at this Magnimus. "You can't do this!"

Another voice responded from behind them, "He can, and he'll have a little bit of help."

Devi turned to see the smirking human dressed in a dirty, torn Salvan uniform. "*You!*"

The girl clucked her tongue in contempt and waved a compact CCP around carelessly. "Name's Lark," she gave a sweeping bow, a flourish of mockery. "Best plugger in the Fringe."

"An assassin," Ryk muttered under his breath.

Lark spoke loudly across the expanse between herself and the army. Devi could only gawk; the girl was speaking d'javu, a language the Protectors hadn't even attempted to learn. It was an ugly, guttural and devilish tongue, and it sounded no prettier coming from the pink lips of the young Fringer who spoke it.

Whatever she had said to Magnimus seemed to anger him deeply and whipped the horde of d'javu into a frenzy behind him. He pointed at what was left of the Protectors and gave an order. Then he waved at the plugger to follow him.

The d'javu swarmed over the already dwindling Protectors—a whirlwind of teeth and claws and retribution. Devi raised her pike to defend herself as the two Salvans to her right were taken down, blood splashing to mingle with the crimson light from the sun.

She drove her pike into her attacker's chest and scanned the chaos around her. Human screams were lost amidst the vicious roaring of the darkling horde.

Magnimus had been lost in the wave, but Devi could still see his hired assassin, her fair hair and the light-colored uniform made her a beacon in the dark tide. Devi's temper flared. She left Ryk's side just as he met two d'javu in combat.

"Traitor!" Devi screamed, charging passed the attacking darkspawn and slicing at Lark with the blade of her pike. The assassin turned back just in time and caught the weapon on her wrist—an armored gauntlet absorbed the energy and deflected the blow. Pushing the blade to the side, the assassin moved swiftly within Devi's guard.

Lark coiled her arm around Devi's and yanked, threatening to dislocate her shoulder until the catalyst pike clattered to the smooth stone ground. With her free hand, she attempted to get Devi into a headlock. Not so easily overpowered, Devi took advantage of the movement and speared her shoulder into Lark's gut.

Grunting, the plugger swept Devi off her feet and they both tumbled to the ground. Lark laughed brightly as she rolled to her feet and cast a shock dart in Devi's direction.

Ryk batted the thing down and swung his sword at the Fringer, who bounded backward, pouting, "No fun at all."

"Devi, we have to go," Ryk said to her, still brandishing his sword at Lark in case she got any ideas about coming closer. Devi stood up, looking around her and realizing that they were the only ones left alive and that the darkspawn were still coming.

"Runnin' away?" Lark taunted. She didn't come closer, but she pulled her pistols and smiled. "Can't get far. This is their planet now, and you got no place to hide."

Devi recovered her pike and spun it, standing beside Ryk. They rushed together, dodging Lark's fevered blasts as she backpedaled and was finally forced to jump to the side. Devi dove into an empty transport with Ryk at her side and slammed her palm against the board to get the doors to close. Ryk jumped into the pilot's seat. His hands scrambled over the controls.

As they were lifting off, Devi peered out the window. The landing platform was enrobed in dark forms, still fighting or killing or dancing in victory. Magnimus ducked inside a ship that had been covered by a tarp, and Lark was sprinting to follow him.

"How did this happen?" Devi asked Ryk as she dropped into the copilot's seat and studied the horizon. Smoke billowed from Katarak Valley to the north. The last of the Protector control on Kyro was burning.

Ryk shook his head as he brought up the comm display. "We were careless," he said to her. "And we failed."

Garbling, panicked voices filled the cabin and Devi breathed. Other Protectors were still alive. Once Ryk had their coordinates, that was the direction in which they headed.

13

LARK WINCED as a proximity mine activated only yards from them, and shrapnel scraped its way across the hull of her ship. She winced again when something slammed below her. She had her jacket half on, the ruined Protector uniform lay in a heap on the floor.

"For fuck's sake, Mags! Stop it! The *Starsigh* didn't do a damn thing to you, don't take this out on her!"

"He was *supposed* to be there!" His breath on the back of her neck startled her. He'd climbed the ladder without making a sound.

Mags moved around her slowly as she pulled the collar of the jacket up around her neck, his movements smooth and quick like a slithering shadow. "Crotis said that Nyhman would be on that platform at the exact time we arrived. He promised I would have my opportunity to strangle the life out of him."

Lark cast a sidelong glance at her husband. "Crotis ain't exactly the most punctual himself," she pointed out, shifting her eyes back to the starshield and flight controls, narrowly missing another mine that would have pulverized the *Starsigh* and the both of them. The last half of her statement, she muttered under her breath. "Ain't the most honest, either."

Mags curled his fist and stared at it. "Nyhman," he breathed the name to himself darkly. "Crotis knows how badly I want him dead. Nyhman discovered the gene of the jak'tu and sold us to the Protectors. He alone is responsible for their systematic genocide of that ancient bloodline. The murder of my mother and the destruction of my culture." He tightened his fist and ground his teeth. "Every moment he is allowed to live, more d'javu become victims to his vile experiments."

Lark swallowed, choosing her words carefully but keeping her eyes steadily on the ruddy atmosphere through which they flew. "Mags, you'll get your chance."

As if he hadn't heard her, he continued speaking in that same low tone, tightening his fist. "I will tear him apart as he tore apart each one of my people, seeking that secret to our power, finding ways to break us... to *use* us. A thousand years of torture is not enough for him."

Without warning, he bashed his fist against the control panel. Lark jumped and glared at him, but he simply returned to his pacing.

Rubbing the panel as if to soothe the ship, Lark scowled to herself. Nyhman deserved everything Mags wanted to do to him, and Mags had every right to be angry about missing out on his chance. Lark wondered how Crotis, knowing how much it meant to Mags, could get something like that wrong.

Lark wanted to tell her husband that this was evidence that Crotis wasn't on the same page as they were, but another crash from behind her made her think he wouldn't want to hear it. Right now, it hardly mattered. They were so close to finishing this. Nyhman would just have to wait.

Mags was not aware that the *Starsigh* lacked an air lock. And he found the way Lark said 'in a pinch' when she assured him the cargo bay could be used as one less than comforting.

"Have you done this before?" he asked, watching her with narrowing eyes as she flitted from one side of the bay to the other completing various tasks that seemed in no way related to each other or their ultimate goal.

"Yeh," she answered immediately, then paused with a fist full of rags. "Well, no. Knew a pirate once and he showed me how."

His gaze withered as she began packing the rags into the cracks of the door that led back into the ship proper. She stood back and propped her hands on her hips, admiring her handiwork.

"What?" she frowned when she noted he was unimpressed.

"A pirate."

"Yeh."

Then she was moving again, raising the hood of her jacket and activating the short-range field within that would protect her from the vacuum of space. "Hey, how long can you hold your breath?"

He hadn't realized he'd been pinching the bridge of his nose until he dropped his hand. "What—Why?"

Lark chewed her lip, slowly raising her hand toward the panel to open the bay door, and looked at him with round, bright eyes. "Left the breathing tanks in the cockpit."

The door sealed shut and gravity slammed into them. Mags bent his knees to absorb the impact, but Lark crumpled from her graceful floating to her normal rough and tumble self.

"Don't look at me like that," she caught her breath and chuckled at his smirk, brushing the dust from her pant legs. "S'what you get for doubting me. I know what I'm doing."

"I don't doubt you," Mags retorted, pushing back his hood and adjusting the strap that held his sword to his back.

Around them, the airlock had finished cycling and fresh, recycled oxygen passed through vents above their head. The door to the lock opened, revealing a long hallway in shades of white and gray. "I doubt your methods. You still haven't told me how you plan to do this."

"Easy," she said casually, pulling out a stubby knife and using it to pry open an access panel on the wall directly to her right. The airlock door closed behind them. "Put the ship into emergency lockdown, seal everybody up in all their little compartments."

She grunted, and the panel door finally peeled away, revealing a flush mounted computer panel surrounded by a mess of wires. Lark dug her fingers into the wires and began twisting and pulling them out in handfuls like a noodle chef at work. She hissed when one of the wires sparked in protest and then yanked the offending wire completely out of the panel. "There we go," she shifted to interface with the computer panel.

Slamming began at the far end of the hallway, moving ominously toward them as compression doors sealed and overhead lights popped off. The hallway fell into darkness, the glow of the computer panel and Mags' eyes the only light for several seconds before the orange emergency lights glowed on.

An overtly calm woman's voice came from overhead, *"Emergency lockdown activated. Please remain in place until further notice."*

"Too easy," Lark grinned at Mags, the orange light gave her an impish air. "Now we go to the bridge."

She started skipping down the hall, Mags following at a normal pace. Every few minutes the woman's voice reminded them to remain where they were.

"How do you even know where you're going?" he called to Lark as she came to a ladder that disappeared into a tube in the ceiling. Pausing, she pointed upward at a sign that said 'Bridge' with an arrow pointing up the ladder. He should have figured.

They were moving toward the bow of the ship, Lark still skipping ahead and pausing at corners to wait for him to catch up. She skipped past one turn and then whipped backward at the report of a CCP. Her armored jacket sizzled at the shoulder and she was cursing in several different languages as she activated her catalyst pistols.

"How many?" he asked her rapidly, watching her activate a pulse from her gauntlet that would disable their comms temporarily.

"Didn't have time to count, more than five less than a hundred." She looked up at him, but he was gone. "I hate it when you do that."

Lark could blend in, as she had done with the Protectors, or avoid being seen, but Mags had been blessed with the preternatural power to dissolve into the shadows and appear almost invisible so long as he moved in an economy of light.

"Save some for me!" she called as she came around the corner, dual wielding her catalyst pistols and taking out two before Mags appeared out of the reddish darkness.

Moving like a deadly specter, he grabbed the first man's arm and broke it before slamming him face first into the wall. The next was still firing at Lark until he found a darksteel blade protruding from his chest. By now the other handful of men were distracted and terrified, staring in horror as Lark's catalyst pulses ripped through them. Mags chased down the smart ones that tried to flee, snapping a neck and slashing another through the belly.

The discarded canisters of Lark's pistols made hollow noises when they hit the floor. She reached inside her jacket and pulled out new, sliding them into their compartments with a click. The catalyst pistols whined low as they warmed up; she holstered one of them.

Lark stole an access pass from one of the dead men, wiping the blood off on her pant leg before skipping to join Mags at the end of the hall. A large set of double sealed doors stood before them and Lark swiped the pass over a card reader.

The doors opened, bright lights flooding the hall. "Jeesh!" Lark raised her left CCP to shield her eyes, "Ain't you guys get the memo?" she drawled into the bridge, a dozen heads snapping toward them in surprise. "Emergency lockdown! Somebody's commandeering your ship!" Then she lifted her right pistol and, squinting one eye against the lights from the bridge, began to fire.

The crew responded in admirable fashion, dropping into defensive poses and sending a volley back her way. Mags grabbed Lark and shoved her to the side, swiping the chemical pulses away with a wave of his hand. Extending his arms at his sides and closing his eyes, he dipped into the well of power within him.

"You'll feel afraid," Mags said low. Lark glanced at him, unsure if he was talking to her or the crew. Then her expression changed, fear creeping over her skin like a sudden, rising tide of freezing water. She shook it off a moment later and turned her attention back to the bridge crew.

Panic. As if they had just realized there was a monster in their midst, the orderly defense crumbled, and the crew flew into hysteria. Lark moved closer to Mags, noting the smell of brimstone and the intensity of the fear that peeled off him. Out in the hall, warning bells sounded and the woman's voice, once calm and cautionary, had become assertive as she demanded the crew stay put. Completely ignored, those captive in the compartments could be heard breaking free and trampling each other to get to the escape pods.

Turning back, she raised her CCP and resumed her assault.

14

LARK HEAVED the overweight and bloody captain onto the security console. She pulled his right eye open then pressed his face onto the scanner. The lights glowed blue. She let the body drop. After muttering a sarcastic thanks to Mags, who had helped not at all, she headed toward the ship's maneuvering controls.

Magnimus stared out the starshield that took up the entirety of the bridge's concave wall. To the port side of the *Salvation*, the great red smear of the Devil's Tongue swirled angrily. Lark rotated the ship, and the shining, bright home world of the Protectors came into view; all blue oceans and lush, green land.

Beyond lay the rest of civpsace. No obstacle, natural or otherwise, kept Salva from the galaxy, foreign commerce, or military protection. In short, it was the polar opposite of exiled Kyro.

Mags moved toward the starboard side of the bridge, the only area directly in front of the starshield not taken up by panels and navigation equipment. His dark hand reached out and pressed against the thick glass. "The missiles are ready?"

Lark pushed off from the piloting controls to roll across the bridge, but her seat didn't budge. She realized belatedly that the chair was riveted to the deck instead of rolling on casters. After a quick, embarrassed glance at Mags to see that he had been staring out the starshield and hadn't seen her awkward slip-up, she hopped out of the chair and moved to the weapons station, shoving the dead gunman out of his seat. The *Salvation's* armaments were listed in a touch screen format; missiles, torpedoes, and other outboard guns.

"Wow," she murmured. "Got warheads on this thing..." Lark's face twisted. "What do they need warheads for? Protectors my ass—"

"How long before we can launch them?" Mags snapped impatiently. Lark glanced at him. Though he was looking away from her, she could see his reflection in the starshield glass. His eyes were bright as he stared out at Salva. "I cannot have Nyhman," he growled to himself. "But I will have the Protectors, and then Nyhman will have no one left to hide behind."

Lark hummed an old pub tune to herself as she ran a finger down the touch screen, activating a dozen warheads all at once. "Thirty seconds to launch," she answered him, using the captain's access card to bypass launch codes.

"Twenty," Lark updated and a targeting screen lit up to her left, displaying a digital view of what they could see through the starshield. Swiveling in the weapons tech chair she listened for the tell-tale whirring of warhead chambers moving into place. Metal slammed and locked far below the deck. A brilliant amber light illuminated at the top of the weapons station. Lark pressed all her fingers to the panel, targeting reticles appeared beneath her fingers tips. "Ten. Mags, you ready?"

"I am ready."

"Targeting..." Lark swept all her fingertips together and the reticles amassed at a single point on the planet's southern hemisphere, just above its southern pole. "Launching."

The *Salvation* shuddered, and twelve deafening booms shook the craft. For a moment their view went into white out, the propulsion engines on the warheads filling the starshield with blinding white fire. When it cleared, the fires had decreased and the quickly dissipating exhaust left trails across the stars, each falling in line behind the last.

Mags grit his teeth, his outstretched arm and back showing the tension of his effort. His palm strained against the glass. A grunt escaped his throat as he concentrated his power on the warheads.

Lark glanced down at the targeting panel and noticed that the bombs had sped up, their course taking on an orderly but curved path toward the planet.

The starshield cracked. A single thread of danger sliced outward from Mags' palm as he continued to strain. Lark jumped up and stared. If that glass shattered, if the vacuum of space reached into the bridge, she would have no time to save herself let alone Mags. He didn't seem to notice but his shoulders heaved, his eyes closed, and his mouth opened in a grimace, hooked teeth glinting against starlight.

The atmosphere pockmarked when they struck, piercing through with unanticipated speed and accuracy, before the starshield exploded with light again. The impact shook the *Salvation*. Mags stumbled backward and Lark slammed into the weapons console as she tried to jump over it to get to him. On her unsteady feet again, she found Mags staring out at the planet of Salva, watching the colors change as the planet was swallowed by fire.

15

"*SALVATION*, COME IN," Ryk demanded for what had to be the eighth time since they had passed through the communications darkness of the Tongue. "This is the *Contribution*. Please respond."

The large warship hadn't responded, not even once. As they approached the vessel, nerves in the Protector transport ship began to run high. Devi stared out the window, finding nothing remarkable about its behavior. Until the white fire blinded her, and the *Contribution* was thrown so suddenly off course that every last soldier crashed to the floor. The pilot himself struggled to stay in his seat and regain control of the transport.

"What was that?" Devi asked, pulling herself and a younger woman named Eiley to their feet. There was a general murmuring of confusion, and Devi moved back to the viewport out of which she had been peering before they had somersaulted through space. Trails of exhaust were bleeding out of the warship's firing tubes. "Did the *Salvation* just fire?"

The pilot was still trying to right the craft; he rotated it so that they could see the planet of Salva. Ryk grimaced as Eiley stepped forward. "What could they be firing at? That assassin's ship… maybe it's cloaked, but they can still see her on their scopes…"

Devi's brow drew together, and she glanced at Ryk. If that Lark character was any good type of assassin, her cloaking device would scramble any scanners as well. She was about to give voice to that thought when she spied something clinging to the side of the *Salvation* like a parasitic insect.

A ship. The very ship they were, in fact, discussing at this moment. Ryk read her facial expression and turned to see it as well. The *Contribution* shook again, and Devi steadied herself, turning to peer through the viewport at Salva once more.

The atmosphere was changing. From the southernmost pole, an explosion of blinding light consumed the planet's surface. At its edge, the wave ignited the atmosphere and created a squall line of fire and death. Eiley gasped and the Protectors behind her moaned in realization and anguish.

Devi watched, her face unmoved as the planet was swallowed by the toxic cloud of fire. Then, all at once, it dissipated outward with no atmosphere to contain it. What was left behind was the gray, charred husk of Salva. In mere minutes, everything on the planet was gone.

Ryk was speaking over the ringing in Devi's ears. "Get us out of here, now!" he ordered the pilot. "We need to get to Lystor. Get the Consul on the comm! Someone stop her panicking!"

A loud crack as someone slapped Eiley to break her. Devi realized she hadn't even heard the girl's uncontrolled weeping.

Slowly, Devi turned to Ryk. He was in the midst of damage control, but he paused when their eyes met. He said her name and she blinked as if she didn't even recognize it. She could not stop staring at him. What had happened? Why was Ryk's voice so far away? "Devi!"

His hands were on her arms, shaking her gently, but Devi just continued to stare. "I guess we'll have the wedding on Lystor," she said to him.

Ryk shook his head. The last thing Devi remembered was the jelly feeling in her knees and the impact of Ryk's shoulder on her forehead.

16

THE *STARSIGH'S* antigrav landing boosters stabilized and the craft landed softly on Katarak Keep's private landing pad. Any Protectors that had survived were fleeing through the Devil's Tongue, pursued by Salvan ships flown by darkspawn pilots.

Lark stepped out of her ship behind Mags to look out over the valley city of d'jaku. For twenty years the Keep had sat nearly empty, though Crotis had kept it up in anticipation that he would one day live inside it.

The walls were cut from satinite stone, polished to an inky black. They appeared almost liquid, absorbing the light instead of reflecting it. The corridors themselves fell off into unfathomable lightlessness, making the Keep as a whole feel endless and labyrinthine.

Lark wondered as they walked if Mags knew where he was going, or if they were just wandering aimlessly through the dark halls. She got the distinct, unsettling feeling that they were not alone. As if the shadows hid silent onlookers that were eager to do them harm.

A quick look over her shoulder confirmed that she was not wrong. They were, indeed, being followed. Slowly, as they had passed from the landing platform and moved within the Keep, a gathering of d'javu had joined them.

They trailed behind, a silent procession, and Mags paid them no mind. In fact, he reached behind him and gripped Lark's hand, leading her through an especially dark passage.

For a large portion of the journey, Lark's eyes refused to adjust, and Mags' hand was the only thing keeping her from being swallowed up. When he slowed, she squinted through the shadows and found that they had approached a set of large double doors, outside which stood Crotis surrounded by several large d'javu. She recognized a few of them from Kar'ju, Crotis' bodyguards during the rebellion.

"Magnimus," the old man purred. The darkness magnified the cadaverous angles of his face, and he spread his arms wide beneath a dark robe. "The clans have assembled to celebrate your victory. Kyro is yours."

Mags grinned at him. Nyhman was forgotten for the moment now that he had the taste of victory on his tongue. He turned to the gathered darkspawn around him. "The Governor and the assassin are here under my protection from this moment forward. Without either of them, we could not have defeated the Protectors and won back our planet."

Lark glanced at Crotis briefly, simply because she was still trying to adjust her eyes to the darkness and he was easier to see than anything else. To her surprise and discomfort, she found he was casting her the most hideous, deadly look she had ever seen. In that expression was all the ire he held for her, unmasked for a moment while he thought she couldn't see him. Her heart skipped a beat and her skin prickled, the unfamiliar feeling of fear for her own safety ran through her.

Mags tugged her closer suddenly, and Crotis was out of view. "If any harm comes to them, swift and lethal retribution will come from me." His glowing eyes turned to her, and she saw a flash of affection before he turned toward the door.

The deadly visage had disappeared from Crotis' face when he joined Magnimus at the door. One of the old man's large bodyguards pushed it open and before them was the war room.

Vaulted ceilings made the room breathtakingly huge, tiered platforms full of d'javu of all shapes and sizes made it feel cramped. Mags held tightly to Lark's hand and she stayed at his elbow, crushed among the press of ebullient darkspawn. He started down the stairs, and all around them, the darklings were losing their minds. Roaring and screaming in their native tongue, cursing the Protectors and damning Salva.

Mags and his entourage pushed through the throng of darkspawn whose joy was unintelligible from their anger down to the bottommost tier of the room upon which stood a large satinite table. It would have taken ten of the strongest d'javu to move this thing it was so thick and heavy. Carved in relief on its dark surface, Lark recognized a map of the known galaxy, each planet and every system.

Lark noted the Fringe, its far-flung reaches clinging to the furthest edges of the table. In the center area were the main planets of civspace, gathered together like a clique of teenage girls as far from the rim planets as it could be. At the farthest corner, Kyro was separated from the rest of the planets by a swath of blood red crystals set into the satinite. There, standing sentinel on the civspace side of the glittering Devil's Tongue was the planet Salva.

The satinite table and its map of the galaxy was a relic from another time, Mags had told her. When the Kabalak had been more than just priests and mystics, they had also been star travelers. Their wisdom came in all forms, including knowledge of the galaxy at large. That was before the ancient people of Kyro had been forced into hiding and forgotten by the universe.

Mags released Lark's hand as he approached the table. He stared down at the carved planets as the room slowly quieted.

A door opened between the stairs to their right. Several large d'javu led in a group of humans. Chained and beaten bloody, the light cloth of their Protector uniforms was hardly recognizable under the stains of blood and dirt. Lark couldn't count them all, but they filled the doorway and out into the hallway.

"Hostages, Magnimus," said one of the big creatures, tugging on the chain. The Protectors stumbled forward, much to the delight of the gathered darkspawn. "We caught them trying to escape the Protector juggernaut."

"Good," Mags answered, the boy-like vivacity had dissipated to reveal that all-business exterior he'd developed for his moments as a leader. "Let them witness this." His eyes rose to address the room at large, and all the d'javu went silent to hear him. Lark's chest swelled with pride.

"Clansmen!" he called out, arms raised, his gruff voice un-echoing in the high ceilings. "Today we reclaimed our world and destroyed our greatest enemy. The Protectors are gone and Salva is no more. But we are not done here!" he assured them, his lips curling into a bloodthirsty smile. "We will rebuild, we will be strong once again! And…"

Reaching out, Magnimus grabbed a great ax from one of the closest darklings. In one smooth movement, he lifted it up high above his head and brought it down on the black carving of Salva. The rock clove, breaking the planet into jagged, ruined shards.

The darkspawn went wild. They roared and leaped around, clamoring as Magnimus somehow yelled over them. "We will show them the meaning of chaos!"

17

FOUR YEARS LATER

GLOWING ORANGE eyes peered from beneath a heavy black hood. A mask covered the face below from nose to chin so that even in the light only his eyes were visible. A black duster hung from broad shoulders to the knees, beneath which could be seen a jerkin made from strips of woven darklite—leather made from the boiled skins of d'javu who had died in battle. A large, crooked dagger was tucked into the front of his belt. No pistols or other technology were apparent on his person. He could be mistaken for any brigand tooling around the Fringe; one to be avoided for sure.

And the galaxy knew that now. He was everything they had feared. But Magnimus Avrok was not finished yet.

Ghery Long should have known better. Crotis had been given detailed information on the pudgy man's work with Nyhman—namely, moving darkspawn throughout the Fringe. After the rebellion on Kyro, those that worked with the infamous scientist should have known that it was only a matter of time. The information dealer must have anticipated his number was up and that his organization and his life were in danger, though he was certainly trying not to show it.

Mags stood in the foyer of Ghery's townhouse. In stark contrast to the sharply cut world of concrete and metal that made up the Fringe city outside, Ghery's home was pleasant and welcoming. The large entryway was paneled in imported wood and warmly lit, lined with lush red carpet. Ghery walked with controlled steps toward where his large, armor-chested bodyguard waited outside the office at the end of the corridor beneath a staircase that curved onto a dark second-floor landing.

"Please, Magnimus," said Ghery, his voice flat in its effort to remain calm, gesturing passed his bodyguard toward the office door. "Join me."

Passing his glowing eyes over the guard, Mags stepped forward over the deep carpet and followed Ghery into the office. Within, another bodyguard was posted at the end of a broad wooden desk. Magnimus found himself stifling a laugh beneath his mask at the superfluous security. Ghery was indeed under the impression—not wrongfully—that he was in real danger. It was a useless gesture. Mags could deal with this half-assed security detail with ease. But if it made Ghery feel better, he would allow it for the moment.

Ghery slid around to the opposite side of the desk and waved a hand toward one of the large, low-set chairs that sat facing him. Mags ignored the request to sit and the following offer of liquor from a cabinet beneath a window that overlooked a docking bay and the city-scape of Cuttah. Ghery poured himself a drink and sat in the high-backed desk chair, leaning into the empty desktop. "You're lucky I was available to meet you."

"Trading secrets for barely legal favors has been keeping you busy?" Mags asked facetiously, his eyes tracking the pudgy man.

"Legality is a matter of little consequence here in the Fringe," Ghery answered, dropping three ice cubes into his drink. "And secrets are called information when they are paid for." He looked up at Mags and then sat back in his chair. "Judge me all you like. That is how things are done here. Fringers don't need honor codes or juries to keep us straight. If I get on someone's bad side, they'll send a plugger after me. Cautious men don't end up at the wrong end of that transaction."

"Men who know not to piss off those that can afford a plugger."

Ghery spread his hands and gave an ugly version of a smile. "A Fringer's motto if I ever heard one."

Mags scoffed behind his mask, "Every man for himself seems more appropriate."

With a shrug, Ghery leaned forward. "Tell that to the Alliance pioneers that tried to bring their civspace garbage past the Brink. We can be surprisingly united in defense of our anarchy." Mags shifted and passed a glance at the bodyguard. The man had hardly moved. "But you know the ways of the Fringe, don't you?" Ghery said into his drink. "Little lady grew up on the rust streets, I hear? You know what they say about girls from Cuttah City—"

Ghery must have realized he had said too much because he looked up at his guest suddenly and his eyes grew as wide as the great disk of the moon behind him. "Come now, Magnimus," he stuttered just slightly before regaining his composure. "You may have the rest of the galaxy fooled, but I know that plugger isn't hanging around on Kyro, far from her money, just because she likes the view." He set his drink down and jingled the ice inside it. "Nyhman spoke briefly about her. Fiery thing, I hear, and quite attached to you."

"You will not speak of her," Mags snapped before he could stop himself. Jumping to her defense only validated the rumor, but Mags couldn't stand to hear Lark and Nyhman referred to in the same breath. Gritting his teeth, he sought a way to change the subject. Ghery seemed to sense his tension and raised his hands in a placating gesture.

"Understood, Magnimus, please sit down." When the darkling still did not move, Ghery cleared his throat, all that congeniality replaced with impatience. "To what do I owe this pleasure?"

"I want you to tell me where Nyhman is."

Ghery's knuckles went white as he clutched the glass in his fist. His eyes flashed fractionally, a near slip for a man so accustomed to hiding his fear. "Magnimus," he said with a nervous laugh. "I haven't spoken to Nyhman since before the rebellion. I—"

Mags moved faster than the guard could react. He was on the desk and in Ghery's chubby face, their noses centimeters apart. Close enough that Mags could see the skin beneath a day's worth of stubble was flushed and irritated. "You're lying," he growled through the mask as he pulled the glove from his right hand.

"No!" Ghery cried out, but Mags grabbed him and all he had to do was touch the man's forehead with his dark hand.

The guard finally clamored into action. With a wave of Mags' left hand, the big man shot backward into the wood paneled wall. His catalyst pistol discharged, showering the incapacitated guard in splinters of overpriced wall covering. Mags returned his hand to Ghery's shoulder, holding him in place while he focused his abilities into the man's mind and forced it to release its secrets.

"Tell me," Mags demanded. His claw-like fingers dug into Ghery's skin and the man whimpered. "Now!"

"Aah... he has a base on Vargo... In Hartun City," Ghery blurted mechanically. "The darkspawn he gave me come from there—Ah! I don't know what he's doing, I swear!"

No, he didn't know any more than that. Nyhman wasn't foolish enough to allow that much information into the hands of a weak minded, greedy man like Ghery. Mags poked at his mind just to make sure there was nothing else feasible hidden there. A lot of information, but nothing useful to him.

"You will release the rest of my people you are hiding," he ordered, shoving the man backward into the desk chair. "You will provide them with transports to Kyro. And if they don't make it there unharmed, you will see me again." A smile spread across his lips, one that would have frozen Ghery's already straining heart if he could have seen it, "And not just in your nightmares."

The *Starsigh* was an unobtrusive craft; one Lark had taken better care of than was immediately obvious. It was a small ship, originally built as a personal transport vehicle, with a double bunk and an open room for lounging and eating. The cargo space—a subdeck that bulged out of the back of the ship, complete with its own dedicated hatch—was limited, but it wasn't an amenity Lark was terribly interested in.

The cockpit was perched at the bow just above the rounded nose that flared out to thrusters and batteries at her side. Within, every bit of technology had been retrofitted or modified to make the *Starsigh* fast, accurate, and advanced. As for the hull, carbon scoring marred a gray and red paint job that couldn't even remember if it had seen better days.

Mags found Lark with her feet propped up on the control board, swiveling back and forth in the co-pilot's seat. In her lap, she was cradling a tablet on which she was scrolling through available bounties while she popped sugar encrusted crancherries into her mouth, the juice staining her tongue and lips a brilliant pink-red. He kissed the top of her head before reaching over her to flip a switch which would lock the ship down for take-off.

"You got your mark?" he inquired as he pulled off his duster. Her eyes still trained on the tablet, she didn't answer him but made an intrigued sound and cracked another crancherry with her teeth. Mags spoke louder, "Something interesting?"

She dropped her feet to the floor and swiveled to face him, chewing on the fruit as she spoke. "One of the Coin Brothers got a bounty on his head. Big'n, too..." Mags raised a corrugated brow and Lark went on without looking at him, "Strange to see a bounty hunter with a hit out on him... Somebody'd have to be real pissed to go after Jaimy Lecorza." She scratched her head, talking more to the tablet than to her husband. "Funny, always thought Liem would be the one who'd get himself into trouble..."

Mags was standing over her suddenly, and he plucked the tablet from her hands, "Friends of yours?"

Lark gave a shrug, "Not really... Met 'em back in the old days. Big boys with reputations." Finally, she looked up at him and fluttered her eyelashes. "Why? You jealous?"

Rolling his eyes to the ceiling, he dropped the tablet back into her lap. "Your bounty has gotten higher," he added as he turned to leave the cockpit, unbuckling his jerkin as he went.

"Oh..." Lark hadn't noticed, but there it was listed above the Coin Brother bounty. She whistled when she saw the amount they were offering. "Don't worry about it, Mags," she told him, standing and moving toward the ladder to regard him. "Nobody comin' after me. Had that bounty on my head for years and nobody even fucking tried. Protectors can throw as much change at me as they want, ain't gonna scare me."

He turned at the top of the ladder and looked at her. "What have I told you?' he asked with a grin, tugging off the leather jerkin and pinching her chin. "If you had any idea what was good for you, you would be afraid of me."

"Never did figure out what was good for me..." Lark watched him descend, then looped one leg over the railing and slid down. The sound of her utility belt scraping on the metal followed her down, deepening a gouge that ran the length of the railing before her boots hit the metal deck with a clang. "You didn't ask me about my mark."

With a chuckle, Mags threw his jerkin over the back of a chair and moved toward the box of food left on the counter. Perhaps one day they could eat together in public, but for now, he would have to settle for take-out. "Tell me about your mark."

She slid up to sit on the counter next to him, "Thought it was gonna be a cake walk until he turned out to be a fucking lightbender..." She ran her hand through her hair. Tricksters who could manipulate light were a pain in the can when you were trying to kill them. "Had to chase him through parts of the city I ain't been in years. But I got him—What are you *doing*?!"

Mags froze, a bottle of kachi sauce poised over the meal she had brought him. She snatched the bottle from him his hand. "That's the best damn ploi-ploi in the Fringe! You do *not* put kachi on that!"

Mags blinked at her a few times as she placed the bottle of sauce protectively against her leg and stared at him, daring him to try for it. He considered it, but Mags knew that taking a dare from Lark was dangerous even if he knew he could get it from her. Shaking his head, he turned his attention back to his sauceless meal. "You've enjoyed your time on Cuttah?"

Lark shrugged. "It's as much home as anywhere else." She splayed her fingers, displaying her rust-red nails. Those from the ground levels—the rust streets as they were affectionately called—were known to carry an accumulation of the planet's red dirt beneath their nails. Tattooed fingertips and nail beds, a common custom among women from Cuttah, had been adopted as a symbol of pride. "How about you? How'd your meeting go?"

"Well, he wasn't a lightbender," Mags grinned when she slapped his arm. "He had the information I required," Mags answered after tasting the food and finding it palatable even without the kachi sauce. "And he said something interesting…"

"Ah yeh?"

Mags regarded her, and Lark gave him a perplexed look, waiting for him to go on. He did, smiling at her, "Do you know what they say about girls from Cuttah?"

Lark laughed throatily and hopped down off the counter, "Oh, honey, I can show you what they say about girls from Cuttah, but it ain't nothing compared to what they say about me."

18

THE WAR was over. Not won, and most certainly not forgotten, but over.

Even now, years later, to the citizens and governors of civilized space it felt like mere months had passed. The rebellion of the darkspawn had traumatized the galaxy proper like a child who had seen their worst nightmare come to life. Although the battle itself—if it could even be called a battle—had been limited to the space around Salva and Kyro, the Alliance had been shaken all the way to the Serian Run on the opposite end of its reaches.

Rykstar Os, Consul of the Alliance of Civilized Planets, was standing among those traumatized children. His dark eyes took in a room full of governors and counselors from every corner of the Alliance, and they were all looking to him.

His hand shaking, he pressed it to the side of his dreadlocked hair, smoothing it back. All his life he had known honor and responsibility, duty and sacrifice. He had learned how to lead his people to death if that's what it took to save the galaxy from what had once been a forgotten evil. He did not know how to lead an unsafe galaxy with that evil unrestrained on the periphery.

"It is not in the nature of the darkspawn to be satisfied," he said to the gathering, forcing strength into his voice. "They will want revenge. We can no longer hide under our bed and wait for this monster to find us. We must prepare." He took a breath, meeting eyes that betrayed fear and indifference. "The Alliance of Civilized Planets granted me the position of Consul because I know this enemy. I know what they are capable of. Protecting this galaxy is all I know. And with Salvan culture all but disappearing, I see no other way but to turn to you. To ask the people of this galaxy to pick up arms against a foregone conclusion."

They all stared, shifted in their seats. No response came. Ryk sighed. Finding no more to say, he dismissed the Consul's meeting and asked everyone to hold on a few more months until Devi was on her feet again. He knew it was a lot to ask, for an entire galaxy to put their fears on hold so that a new mother could rest, but Ryk assured them that nothing could be done without the help of his co-Consul.

"How is your wife doing?" the governor of Qelnash had gold eyes and dark skin, a small woman known for having an even head and deep pockets. The question was nearly lost in a wave of conversation from the other governors as they overtook him before he could escape the chamber, but it was the only one he heard.

"She is not my wife," he answered quickly, his head buzzing. The Consul's meeting had been longer than ever—or maybe it had felt that way without Devi's combative presence keeping segues to a minimum. Ryk was too kind and too gentle. Leading soldiers was one thing; dignitaries had always been the ones he had knelt before. He could not find it in him to be callous to them. Devi had never had that problem.

In his haste to correct the Qelnashi governor, he felt he may have sounded impatient or unkind, so he held up his hand and added gently, "Devi and our daughter are doing fine, thank you."

Another governor piped up then, and Ryk could not get his tired mind to stretch far enough for the man's name. "Will the Consuls be getting married? Will you take on new titles?"

"No, no," Ryk gave the man a pleading glance. It seemed cruel considering what she had just accomplished in bringing a new life into this world, but right now he would gladly change places with Devi. The quiet sanctuary of her hospital room and the soft coos of the baby would have been great improvements over this horde starving for information about their new addition.

"It isn't like that. As much as I admire and respect Consul Ment—" speaking her name formally made him sound more removed from her emotionally, or at least that was what he hoped. "She has been my friend since we were children, and we remain so."

It was so hard to explain this without making it sound like they had made a mistake in the heat of guilt and pain that had brought unexpected consequences. That made it sound as if he regretted it, which he didn't.

"I could not think of another who would make a better leader or a better mother, but we are not lovers." This seemed to throw the assembled governors and representatives into squawks of confusion—or scandalous chittering, Ryk could never tell. He knew it was his duty to work with these people, and he did not wish to make them feel as if he were keeping secrets from them.

This is where Devi would tell them all it was none of their business and ask them simply to leave it alone. "If you'll excuse me..." he slipped quickly out of a gap in the crowd, finally understanding why they'd wanted him to take on personal guards. He'd thought it had been a silly concept at first, considering his training, but he had not anticipated how terrifying the Alliance governors could be when seeking information about a child.

The crowd did not follow him, thankfully, though the guilt that he had done something inappropriate did. Duty had been at the heart of everything to the Salvan people. Here, he wasn't sure what ran deeper; fear or greed. Both were equally as malicious to what they were trying to accomplish.

The capital palace on Lystor served many purposes. It was large enough to hold the Grand Consul Chamber where the leadership of the galaxy could meet en masse to discuss policy, as well as the many offices of the administrative staff and the home to the Consul and his family.

The Consuls and *their* family, he amended.

It was a long but uneventful walk from the Chamber Tunnels to the living quarters, and here in the halls of their new home things were quiet. He turned a corner to the medical wing and opened the door to the room where Devi and their daughter would be.

He paused in the doorway, his eyes trained on the single bed where Devi lay curled under the blankets. She appeared to be sleeping, and he did not wish to wake her. A moment passed in which Ryk could not make the decision whether to stay or go and then she sat up. Her dark blond hair curled just to her ears and was bedraggled as she blinked at him, eyes rimmed in pink, sunken and tired. "You look awful," she commented, shifting to sit up.

Ryk let out a soft laugh. "You look better," he answered, palming the door closed behind him as he entered the room and approached the bed. "I didn't mean to wake you."

"You didn't," Devi pushed a curl from her eyes and leaned over to peer into the bassinet by her bedside. "You didn't wake either of us."

Right, the baby. Ryk had almost forgotten, somehow. He really must have been tired. But Nadia had only been in his life a day or so, and for weeks his mind had been torn between worry for Devi's health and the insurmountable obstacles that lay before him as Consul. Singular, for the moment.

He sat on the edge of the bed and looked in at the sleeping baby. "You're both alright?" he asked Devi, his hand floating mindlessly up to touch the top of his head, again pushing at the mass of knotted hair that gathered just to his shoulders.

Devi looked at him, eyebrows raised. "We are. Are you?"

"Just tired," he told her, his hand falling back down into his lap. "It isn't easy without you."

"You need to be tougher with them," she commented, turning back to the baby before lounging back onto the pillows. "I know you've got it in you. I've seen you order a hundred men to fight against the darkspawn, and you can't get through a consul meeting on your own?"

"Those people are not Salvan soldiers. They need something from us. But they aren't willing to take any of the responsibility on themselves or ask anything of their people."

Devi gave a noncommittal shrug. "They wanted you to do this; they need you to do it. If they can't stand beside us... they're going to have to learn how to fight the d'javu." She laughed. "Can you imagine Mantel fighting a demon? His chins would have to hold their own."

Mantel. That was the man's name that he'd forgotten earlier.

"Come here," Devi said suddenly, and he stared at her dumbly as she shifted in the bed and pulled the covers down for him to lie next to her.

"Devi..." he began in protest.

"What are you afraid of?" she asked him, a rebellious look on her face. "They might think we've been sleeping together? I think our secret's out..." she nodded toward the sleeping bundle.

Ryk didn't have the strength to argue with her. He pulled his boots off and crawled into the bed beside her. It would be a lie to say he felt nothing for her. They had grown up together, had worked and fought side by side their entire lives. He did love her, but not romantically.

She was not wrong, though. They shared a child, what difference did it make if they shared a bed? They both needed rest and at least no one dared to bother them here.

An arm draped around her and they both watched their daughter sleep for a time before Devi would realize Ryk was snoring softly in her ear.

19

THE FACTION leaders of the d'javu, along with their clansmen, had gathered in the war room of Katarak Keep. They were quickly becoming restless, and Crotis' efforts to calm them were beginning to fall on deaf ears. The longer they were forced to wait, the less they wanted to listen to the platitudes of a human.

Crotis eventually gave up on gently requesting their patience and stood quietly beside the satinite table, staring at the doors at the top of the room with his hands folded in front of him. His agitation was as well-hidden as the darkspawn's was tangible.

When the doors thundered open and Magnimus stalked in, the room fell into tense silence.

His pace was intentionally measured as he walked down the tiered steps between the gathered darkspawn. They stared at him in silence and watched him pass. It had been over twenty years since the last true darkspawn ruler had stood before these people. It was easier to forget how to be ruled than it was to accept a new ruler.

To this day, they were still not entirely sure about Magnimus, regardless of his bloodline or his abilities. The patience, strategy, and even-headedness Crotis had drilled into him made him different from nearly every d'javu in this room. He was more capable than any of them, but he still had to prove that he was darkspawn to his bones. They would test him until they knew his human upbringing had not denied him the savagery required to rule them.

Magnimus moved to stand beside Crotis, who murmured, "You're late."

"Forgive me," Magnimus replied rapidly, shooting the old man a silencing look. Crotis was only angry out of principle. If Mags hadn't been out with Lark, there would be no comment from the old man.

Magnimus turned his attention back to the gathering. There was wariness, even disdain in their eyes. They wondered who was truly in charge. They may have been a short tempered and crude bunch, but they were not stupid.

Magnimus lifted his voice and called into the buzzing silence. "For four years we have reclaimed our homes, our cities, our lives. But the time for repairing has passed. Now, we build further than we ever have before. We build for revenge, we build for war. They stole twenty years and thousands of lives from us—brothers, wives, children. They tried to steal our power because they feared us." He put a fist to his chest. "They know now they were right to be afraid. But I promised you they would soon learn the true chaos they had awoken. And now is the time for that lesson."

"Why now?" Sylis, a red-skinned d'javu from the Shank clan stepped forward. Standing tall and gangly above his brothers, he leaned on the table toward the leaders on the other side. He spoke with a slight lisp, given that his fangs were over-sized for his mouth. Mags tried not to sneer at the interruption. "We have waited for four years, for what reason? We could have invaded civspace and be living like kings on the graves of the Protectors by now!"

"Like kings?" Laus raised a great brown claw and pointed at Sylis, stepping out of the press of darkspawn and standing beside Magnimus and Crotis. The d'javu were moving closer, their eyes bright with the rising tension in the room. Laus came from a warrior clan out in the west, a group of fighters, guards, and laborers. He was at least twice Magnimus' size, and his voice boomed with accusation as he stared at Sylis across the table. "You mean you'd be living like kings while the Stridjar continue to fight your war for you!"

An unidentifiable voice called out from the crowd, "Take all the glory for yourselves!"

This bickering was as commonplace as it was pointless. The d'javu simply could not make decisions without ripping each other apart. Spreading his arms, Magnimus raised his voice calmly to quell the intensifying anger that was brewing amongst them. "We all have a part to play, and we all—"

Another broke in. Though thin framed, the female's arms were cut with muscles. Her black hair had been shaved on the sides. Lantine, Sylis' wife. "Why are we still even listening to this one?" She pondered loudly, gesturing toward Magnimus. "He's not one of us, he takes orders from Crotis."

It figured they'd rally behind dissent rather than face the bigger issue. A cry rose up from the crowded hall in response to Lantine's yammering. Magnimus ran his eyes over them. They just seemed to enjoy the noise of it, the anger and bloodlust in the air. They preferred this to getting things done. Having grown up under Crotis' draconian rules, Magnimus detested this type of time-wasting. His teeth ground against each other as he watched them rabble around dissidence.

Sylis went on, "How can we follow someone who shares his bed with a human?" Over the sound of the gathering, Sylis could not hear the warning growl that was in Magnimus' throat. His eyes narrowed. Every notion of calming this and speaking of progress was forgotten now as he tracked Sylis like newly discovered prey.

"Yeah!" Laus chimed in, banging a fist on the table. Mags' sharp gaze turned to him. "And he drags around the half-breed and the human bastard. Does he expect them to succeed him?" Magnimus crossed his arms, withholding the impulse to remind Laus that he stood right before the man he was badmouthing. "I will not be led by that child—that half-breed son of a whore!"

Crotis' eyes rose to the ceiling in exasperation a moment before Magnimus snapped.

In a dark gray flash, he was on the other darkling. He grabbed Laus around the throat and, with the help of the blood powers that the larger darkling did not have, lifted the giant off his feet, slamming him down upon the heavy satinite table.

A sickening crunch and Laus screamed in agony, the shattered form of Salva cutting into his spine. Magnimus held him there, shoulders heaving in anger. Laus struggled but seemed to be having trouble moving his legs and arms, blood trickled from his mouth as it opened wide, gasping for air. The room had gone silent save for Laus' wailing.

Without releasing the big d'javu, Magnimus' glowing eyes locked onto Sylis. "If there is anything else to be said of my wife," he snarled, loud enough for all to hear. The tall darkling stepped in front of Lantine as he eyed Magnimus. "Or of my son. Know that every one of you can be replaced by one of your clansmen." Finally, he let go of Laus, but the darkling didn't move. His eyes grew distant and glossy, his hands limp at his side.

Now, Magnimus addressed the rest of the gathering. "Your enemies say they take no joy in killing you," he said loudly. "I can assure you I will have no such difficulty."

¤   ¤   ¤

Crotis had Laus removed from their presence. The big warrior would live, but he would be crippled. Any darkspawn would have prayed for death rather than a life of uselessness. Mags saw this as an appropriate punishment. If he was going to lead them, he needed to be as cruel and vicious as they were. There was very little that made him act more like a darkling than insults strewn at Lark.

After he appointed one of Laus' nephews to take his place—a young warrior who seemed more than eager to prove his loyalty—Mags moved on. He assigned each clan their role in the coming months. It should have been enough to have them follow him but despite the fear he'd put into them today, there would still be doubt.

Doubt, Mags was prepared to deal with. He was not, however, prepared for the scolding he knew was coming from his mentor when the clans filed out and left them alone. Crotis stared at him for a long moment and Mags directly avoided eye contact, studying the satinite galaxy before him.

The old man sighed in resignation and spoke quietly. "Magnimus, accompany me to my home."

This had his head snapping up, blurting incredulously, "To Kar'ju?!" No more than a handful of minutes had passed since the other darkspawn had left and Crotis had already managed to make him feel powerless.

"Yes," Crotis responded simply, folded his arms within his robes, and started up the stairs.

Mags watched the man climb for a moment, considering his course of action. It was not a short trip back to Kar'ju, and it put several hours between Mags and his bed. Arguing wasn't his best option, especially considering he already had a lecture coming. Disobedience had always been something Crotis had an extremely low tolerance for. Something Mags had never quite been able to avoid.

Tonight, though, he chose not to create a battle when they already had so many others to fight. They walked in silence through the dark halls of the Keep, taking a long elevator to the highest tower in the valley city where Crotis' private shuttle waited.

When they were alone, surrounded by the muted colors and plush fabrics of the sky shuttle, the old man spoke. "Stirring words," he said with mock adulation. "I was especially moved by the part where you crippled one of your most powerful faction leaders over a girl."

Mags felt his eyes begin to roll but stopped them. It was difficult not to feel like an indignant teenager when Crotis spoke to him like this. His mentor seemed to miss the would-be gesture, or he simply let it go without retaliation. That would have been unlike him. The darkling said nothing but cast Crotis a sidelong glance as he went on.

"Magnimus, do you see now why I advised against this marriage? Keeping her here, flaunting your relationship with a human in front of those you hope to lead?" He let out a sigh, heavy with unwarranted disappointment. "I hold nothing against the girl." A lie. Mags had to withhold a snort of disdain. "Your people are more powerful than any other in this galaxy of ours, and that is why they are feared from here to the Fringe. If they are going to harness all that power, they require leadership.

"That is why I saved you, Magnimus. I made every effort to give you the tools you need to rule your people and bring them to victory, and beyond."

Mags shifted to look away from Crotis. He'd heard this speech a thousand times and it irked him that he was going all the way to Kar'ju just to hear it again.

"You will conquer this galaxy, Magnimus. You will bring the Protectors to their knees and rule all of it. But your people will never…"

Finally, Mags rounded on Crotis, slicing the air with his hand to cut the speech short. Crotis stopped and stared into those glowing eyes, bright now with aggravation. "I have already told you. Unless I have her, I want none of that."

Crotis smirked as if hearing this argument for the first time. Then, he held up his hands in a placating gesture. "I know. I will not ask you to get rid of your family, Magnimus. Believe it or not, I do know how much they mean to you. I am simply..." he waved a hand slowly, searching for the right word. "Suggesting that you perhaps think about relocating them temporarily, somewhere safer while you work to gain a deeper foothold with your brethren without her..." He paused again, and Mags saw his lip curl in just the slightest expression of disgust. "Distracting you."

An old, crooked hand lay gently on Mags' shoulder, and Crotis smiled at him kindly. Another lie, but one Mags was used to seeing. "Surely, she could see the wisdom in this and she would go without argument?"

With a mirthless laugh, Mags shook his head. The shuttle came to stop, and the doors slid open. Mags gestured for Crotis to lead the way, commenting under his breath as he followed. "You don't know Lark very well..."

Hours had passed by the time Magnimus walked through the silent corridors of his own apartment within Katarak Keep. Exhausted and irritable from his discussion with Crotis, he opened the door to his bedroom and found Lark asleep in typical gracelessness. Her hair splayed across the pillow, arms and legs similarly stretched across the bed. Without speaking, simply by existing, she calmed him.

She had come into his life unexpectedly, and since that day she insisted on continuing to find ways to surprise him. As a rule, Magnimus Avrok did not like surprises. He preferred control, to make every calculated decision as he saw fit. Resourceful, clever, and adaptable to nearly every situation, Lark's unpredictability at times frustrated him, but it had done nothing to diminish the respect he had for her.

Mags pulled the blankets away, fully prepared to drop bone-heavy into the bed. Luckily, he looked before doing so, because he discovered that she was not alone.

Gunner, nearly seven now, lay sleeping there with his arm wrapped protectively around a darkling boy of only three. The d'javu child had skin the color of ash and his arm stretched out, fingers holding tightly to Lark's hand. Mags gave a sigh that was not wholly in admiration of the familial affection before him.

Before he bent to lift the boys, he noted that Lark's other hand was underneath her pillow. More than likely, she had a weapon hidden there.

Slowly, watching Lark closely, he bent and slid a hand over the human boy's back. "Gunner," he whispered. "Come, you have to go back to your bed."

The child's eyes opened, a muddling of brown and green, and he sat up slowly. Gunner's dark hair was rough and often unmanageable, and now it stood straight up on half his head as he moved to wrap his arms around Mags' neck and allow himself to be lifted from the bed. The other child was more likely to give him trouble, but Mags was able to scoop him up without waking him.

Not lucky enough to keep from waking their mother. Magnimus had not even stood to his full height before she was up, her hold-out CCP.42 aimed squarely at his forehead, and her bright eyes open without a hint of grogginess. She had always been quick to pull a gun, but in the last few years, motherhood had sharpened what she had once considered paranoia into an alertness that, to Mags, often smacked of premonition.

"You're late," Lark said. Mags felt his jaw tense. If it wasn't Crotis, it was her. She lowered the pistol and folded back down into the bed. Mags brought the boys to their rooms, and when he returned she was waiting, arms crossed. "What took you so fucking long?" she watched him lay down and then scooted closer.

Mags could hear the exhaustion in his own voice when he answered her, "Crotis wished for me to accompany him home."

"To Kar'ju?" she asked, her brow drawing together in anger. "Why does he do that to you?"

"Because he knows I won't argue."

Lark snorted, drawing the blanket up over them, she rested her head on his shoulder. "Argue with me all the damn time, ya know."

Mags gave the breath of a chuckle, and his shoulders relaxed against the pillows. He pulled Lark close and let his eyelids fall. It had been a lot more work to get here than it should have been, and he had a feeling things weren't going to get easier.

20

RYK AWOKE to the sound of a baby crying. Immediately awake, he sat up and gazed through the darkness at Devi who stood in the doorway with Nadia in her arms.

"Are you alright?" he asked her, rolling out of the bed and approaching them. He was surprised and concerned by her presence. Though she had access to his room at all hours, she had not chosen to visit him until tonight.

"I haven't slept all night..." Devi said over the baby's squalling. "I don't know what else to do..."

"It's alright," Ryk reassured her, taking Dia from her and folding the squirming mass into his arms. He nodded to his bed. "You need sleep. I will take care of her."

Devi's voice betrayed as much relief as it did desperation as she pushed a wild curl of hair back away from her face, "Thank you, Ryk..."

"Please don't thank me," he gave her a soft smile. "The least I can do is to hold my daughter occasionally. Get some rest. We will be right out here."

He closed the bedroom door behind him and rocked the baby gently. At first, her cries subsided, but they picked right back up again. "You have your mother's temperament," he told her in a whisper, not wanting Devi to hear.

Dia's lip trembled as dark brown eyes examined her father. "I know," he murmured, sliding onto the couch and tightening her swaddles. "There is a great weight on your tiny shoulders, my love. You are the first generation of Protectors without Salva to call home. But I promise you, we will never put down our guard, and one day you will lead them in peace." The child's crying quieted slowly, and she cooed as Ryk ran his finger over her soft cheek.

"All of that is a long time from now, Dia," he told her and laid a kiss on her forehead. "Today you focus on growing and thriving and letting your mother sleep. Tomorrow is for worrying about tomorrow's things."

Tomorrow's worries came too soon. Devi had insisted she was ready to join him in the smaller Consuls' meeting that involved only the leaders of the major planets in the ACP. Twelve delegates sat in an inverted V before the double podium that had been constructed for Devi and Ryk to address the gathering.

Immediately upon her entry, Devi had been overwhelmed with a wave of well wishes and questions about the baby's health. She answered with a tense smile, and Ryk could tell she was annoyed by all of it. If she hadn't had a baby a few months ago, they wouldn't have cared about her health. They would only be asking for things from her.

Ryk had warned her that they were starved for information on her and Dia, so he grinned as she gave them all her thanks and then asked them politely to take their seats. The moment her face turned from them, she sent him a bruising look that did nothing to deaden his amusement.

"Thank you all for coming," Ryk said as he settled himself behind the podium. "I—We brought you here to discuss fortifications against continuing threat from Kyro."

Sheba, a thin and dark woman from Riton with a crest of black hair, raised a hand. "Civspace has gone unprotected for over four years," she told him amid nods of agreement from the other eleven that flanked her. Her large golden jewelry clattered when she waved that hand across the room, "If there have been efforts to build these fortifications against the darkspawn, our people have not seen it. The people look to us to protect them, and we look to you. Tell us what it is you are doing to make sure the darklings will stay on their planet."

Beside her, a man with large balloon cheeks and a pig-like nose added, "Streibo has given many men to the new draft. Mothers, wives, and daughters protest openly. Am I to ask them to sacrifice more or will the Protectors do as we have asked them?"

Grumbles rose then faded when there was no response from the podium. Ryk had gone very still. Devi looked at him when he said nothing, and he waved for her to go on before briefly pressing his fingers into his eyes. She smirked and looked back to the assembly. "We have all sacrificed much, some of us more than others."

"No one here denies the sacrifice Salva made for us," Sheba responded with little of the sympathy they all seemed to hope to get from the Consuls.

"You don't?" Devi shot back angrily.

Sheba was unconcerned with the threatening glance the other woman was sending her way. "We remain eternally grateful. But if our people continue to suffer, what will that sacrifice have been for?"

Ryk's fingers wrapped around Devi's wrist as she drew breath to form her no doubt caustic retort. "I assure you all that the suffering of your people has not gone unnoticed," he said before she could speak. "You have asked us to defend you, and we are doing all we can with what is left.

"But it will take a lifetime to rebuild what was lost on Salva. Our child represents the first of the new generation of Protectors, and she is only months old. Would you ask her to change the universe in just those few months?" He released Devi's wrist and regarded the gathering sternly. "We are starting from the ground up, but time is our greatest enemy. Every planet in this system will need to fortify, raise up armies, put your people to work. We need ships, we need weapons, and we need hands to wield them."

There was a general shifting and harumphing in the room. Devi leaned forward, her words as hard as always. "For generations, the Protectors have lived between you and the greatest evil in this universe. If we all stand together, what happened on Salva won't happen to another planet. When the darklings come again—because they *will* come again—all we can do is be ready. And pray to every god in the universe they give us enough time to prepare."

It took some more convincing and a lot of hard words from Devi, but the Alliance delegates eventually resolved that they needed to do more and that it was their responsibility to break that news to their people. When they were leaving, they had clearly run themselves dry on well-wishes, because they said nothing to Devi. Her smile was genuine at their backs, and she turned to Ryk with joviality he was not used to seeing in her. "I think that went well."

"Better than I thought it would," he allowed. "Considering we're basically asking them to prepare for war."

Devi gave a bitter laugh as they started out into the hall. "We lost everything for them and they act like it's too much to pick up a damn gun and defend themselves."

With a sigh, Ryk nodded. "They don't know any better. Our people were the only ones that remembered the darklings and what they were capable of."

"They sure got a reminder, didn't they?"

They walked in silence for a long time, acknowledging bows or salutes from staff passing in the halls. Rubbing her belly, a habit from being pregnant she hadn't lost yet, Devi looked up at Ryk finally. "Are you alright?"

"Of course, I'm alright. How are you feeling?"

"Stop that," Devi came to a halt, and he took a few steps before turning to look at her.

"Stop what?"

"I had a baby, I didn't lose a limb. I saw your face in the chamber when they mentioned wives and daughters. I know that look. I've seen it a million times since that day." Ryk's dark eyebrows knit together, pain rippled across his features. He leaned against the wall and shook his head, unable to find words. Devi pushed on, "Those people forget what we gave up so they could sit in a room and berate us."

"The magnitude of our tragedy is the only thing that makes it any different from theirs."

"And what about the little tragedies that are still ours?" she crossed her arms and gave him a hard look. "What about Selmi?" Ryk flinched at the name, his eyes closing. He shrank away as if she were physically assailing him.

"What about Ryka?" Devi closed the gap between them, and her hands cupped his cheeks. "Look at me." His eyes opened, and tears sat upon his lashes. "You had a wife and a daughter," his breath trembled. "And you lost them."

"And you were getting married," he pulled her hands from his face and pushed them back toward her chest. "That life is gone now. We must push forward. For the galaxy, and for Dia."

"And for us," Devi added darkly. "Call me selfish but we deserve a resolution to all of this."

"Consuls," a deep voice announced itself, and Ryk turned, wiping his eyes to find one of the Consul guard bowing.

"Yes, soldier?" he acknowledged the man with fortitude he had become accustomed to faking.

"A transport just entered the atmosphere."

"And?" Devi smirked impatiently, she had not stepped down from her soapbox just yet.

"Consul," the soldier bowed his head and paused, apparently having trouble forming words.

Ryk approached him gently and settled a hand on his shoulder. "Go on."

When the soldier looked up, he seemed overcome with emotion and Ryk's heart went out to him even if he was unsure what had caused this. "The transport," the soldier forced out. "It's Salvan."

Medical staff had already responded. They had swarmed over the hostages and were actively scanning, testing, and checking vitals. For once, the ever-present drizzling rain had subsided, and the setting sun dyed the round white buildings of Lystor pink.

Below the platform, the thriving plant life bathed in the last few hours of sunlight. The captives were spread out at the end of the landing platform next to a battered old Salvan shuttle with the *Salvation's* faded insignia painted on the side.

Ryk walked among them, Devi uncharacteristically silent at his side. He stared at the people—faces he should have known but were unrecognizable, tattered rags far from the crisp gray uniforms they'd all once worn. All of them were emaciated and dirty; several of them were injured.

One by one, as Ryk and Devi passed, those that were able pulled themselves up to stand tall and placed a fist over the middle of their chests. A Salvan salute. Ryk numbly returned it, feeling as if he were outside his body.

"Would you look at that," one of them spoke. He was tall but thin, his face disappearing beneath an unkempt beard. "Isn't that just the prettiest girl you've ever seen?"

Devi stepped up next to Ryk, her hand on his shoulder. She squinted her eyes at the man but said nothing. Then it struck Ryk like an open hand slap. "Bae?"

The beard split, his smile appeared and a great laugh filled the platform, somehow the same even if he didn't look anything like himself. Bae had been a big man, with big muscled shoulders and a big laugh. That laughed seemed to be the only thing that survived imprisonment on Kyro, though it sounded a bit rusty.

He laughed until Devi moved toward him, wooden as her eyes pierced suspiciously into the figure before her. Bae's smile softened, and he reached out to her. Something dropped heavily in Ryk's stomach.

"You..." she began, allowing his skeletal fingers to touch her face but failing to respond to the affection. "You're dead..."

"No, Dev," he smiled again, and his blue eyes twinkled. "I'm here, it's me."

Devi paled and pulled away abruptly. "You are *dead*!" she screamed and backed up so quickly she nearly fell into the lap of a Salvan who'd just sat down in a hoverchair. Ryk grabbed her shoulder to pull her away from the injured man and from Bae. Once she had regained her balance, she broke free from is grasp violently and fled inside.

Silence fell like the weight on Ryk's shoulders. Devi was not known for emotional outbursts though he wouldn't ever have called her level headed. On a normal day, he would not mind smoothing things over in her wake. Today though, it took more than his usual perseverance to find the strength to face this on her behalf.

He half turned and glanced at the med team who had frozen during the hysterics. "Get these people inside," Ryk ordered, less gently than he had meant to. "I want them in fully stocked rooms with anything they need. Food, drink, medicine, anything at all."

The med team jumped into action and began helping the Salvans inside. "Bae," Ryk approached his old friend and settled a hand on a shoulder that lacked the girth it once had. "Devi..."

"I get it," Bae forced a smile but it didn't make it to his eyes. The distance in those eyes made Ryk afraid they may lose him again. "As far as she's concerned she's seen a ghost."

"Let's get you something to eat," Ryk led him toward the entrance. "We can analyze Devi all day, but that is not something that should be done on an empty stomach."

"Consul, huh?" Bae asked as he surveyed the veritable feast spread out before him. Ryk had asked them to bring something from every category on the menu to his quarters. It had arrived in his room about the time they did and since then, Bae had eaten as much with his eyes as his mouth.

"Yes," Ryk smiled ruefully. "Consul Frer stepped down after the rebellion. He felt incapable of dealing with the d'javu threat. I think he retired to the beaches on Lepthys."

Bae had filled up his second plate and was taking less time to study his food before eating it. He sopped up some gravy with a roll and took a bite, crumbs collecting in his beard. "You were the obvious choice to replace him."

"I suppose," Ryk shifted uncomfortably. "They would have offered me anything to take his place even though I had no experience in politics. In the interest of the Alliance, I took the position, only after they agreed to allow me to share the duties with Devi."

Bae grinned, revealing a missing tooth. Ryk struggled to recognize him in that moment. "I'm real proud of both of you."

Ryk sighed, his chest heavy with a profound sadness. "It hasn't been a simple task. We know the d'javu will strike again, but we have no idea how or when. And with Salva gone..." His eyes snapped to Bae, unsure if the captive Protectors knew about the loss of their home planet.

"They told us," Bae replied grimly. He put down the roll and brushed off his hands, sitting back in the chair. "Once they had us all trussed up, they paraded us into the war room of the Keep. Crotis was there. He was with Magnimus. That's where they told us they destroyed Salva. They said we were all that was left of the Protectors. I didn't believe them. Somehow I knew you and Devi got away."

Bae had gone back to eating. Ryk was willing to let him, he wished for Bae to be his over-sized, over-enthusiastic self once more. For Devi's sake as much as for his own.

"She never truly stopped mourning you," he found himself saying without thinking. Bae paused and looked at him. "Devi. I know you probably imagined she'd be happier to see you. I don't think she knew what to do, she has been fighting grief for so long."

"I don't blame her," Bae gave a slight shake of the head and pushed his food around on his plate. "Seeing her again... it was the only thing that kept me going. Sounds like you were short on hope around here."

"We didn't know they had hostages, Bae."

"It's for the best you didn't." The rapid words were spoken harshly. His blue eyes snapped up from the plate and adopted a seriousness he'd never quite been able to accomplish before. It sent a chill over Ryk's skin. "It would've done the Alliance no good to have you rush back in there to free us."

Ryk grew silent, his eyes falling to the half-eaten kila pie before him. For the first time, he felt as if the d'javu had failed to take everything from them. So long as the Protectors, however few they may be, held to their beliefs the darkspawn could not truly win.

"I wish I had some inside information to give to you," Bae said with a sigh, wiping his mouth on a cloth napkin. "They kept us locked up and we hardly saw anyone but the wardens. It's only in the last few weeks Magnimus and Crotis came." Ryk watched him, hesitant to prompt Bae to relive anything but wanting to know all the same. "Even then, all they said was they were going to send us to the Alliance. They thought we couldn't understand them, but I guess they were still cautious about speaking in front of us."

"You can speak d'javu now?"

"Tiska was with us," Bae reminded him. "She's a linguist, and she had a lot of time to piece it together and then to teach us all. Don't know how conversational I could be, but I can get the gist of a conversation.

"Crotis, he's been on the darkling's side since we took down Jiktar. He raised Magnimus up, taught him everything he knows." Bae smothered a belch and surveyed the food in front of him, decidedly reaching across the table to drag a plate full of meat closer. "Strangest thing I've ever seen—a darkling who talks like a man. Calculating type of guy but, man, what a temper!" He took another oversized bite of roasted meat and spoke while he chewed. "They never said anything useful in front of us. But what I can tell you is the rumors are true, all the darkspawn talk about it."

"Which rumors?"

"The ones about Crotis and the darkling boys. We all took bets, just to pass the time, and we'd listen in when they complained to each other about Crotis. I think Oll won in the end. Guess I owe him a lot of money..." Bae pressed a hand to his lips and thought for a moment, then looked back at Ryk. "You can see it when Crotis looks at Magnimus, but it isn't the other way around." He let out an unkind laugh. "I tell you, when you haven't seen the sun in years and you're starting to lose it a little, you live to see the old man disappointed."

"What about Lark?" Devi's voice startled them both, and they turned to see her standing in the doorway with the door sliding closed behind her. Ryk had been so distracted by Bae's story he hadn't even heard it open.

Her eyes were pink, her hair curled in disorderly tangles around her face. Devi was carrying Dia in her arms, the child wrapped in soft ivory blankets. Ryk furrowed his brow as he watched her approach the table. He'd always thought Devi's infatuation with the Fringe assassin who'd teamed with the d'javu was unhealthy. Now, looking as she did, it bordered on obsession.

Bae cocked his head at her, his eyes running over her quickly. What he determined from the bundle in her arms remained unclear. "Who?" he asked.

"The assassin that helped them, her name was Lark," Devi sat at the table, seemingly unaware of what Dia's presence was doing to either of the men at the table.

Ryk sat very still, his eyes going from the child to Bae while the big man seemed to be trying not to notice. Devi leaned forward in an almost conspiratorial way. "I've researched her as much as I can. She comes from the Fringe, but you know what their record keeping is like. All

I could find was a laundry list of people she had killed—what the Fringe considers a resume—and an asking price you wouldn't believe. The only thing we have on file for her here was an arrest on an Alliance world when she was very young." Devi pulled her tablet out of her pocket and set it on the table among the food, pushing it toward Bae.

"You kept a copy of that file?" Ryk asked her incredulously. She cast him a knowling look then turned excitedly back to Bae.

"Ah," he nodded his recognition at the picture. "She was in the war room that first day with Crotis and Magnimus. Only other human there." He looked up at her and realized Devi was staring at him hungrily. His eyes went wide, and he added tentatively, "Haven't seen her since then." Bae set his elbows on the table, watching Devi's disappointed reaction. His eyes studied her, thinking deeply. "Who's baby is that, Dev?"

As if she hadn't expected the question or she had forgotten the child was there, Devi immediately looked down at Dia. She went suddenly still, her mouth opened but only a pinched sound came out.

Ryk, eager to get the damn thing over with, leaned forward. "Bae," he noted the suspicion in Bae's eyes when they turned on an old friend. It frightened him to see how much the d'javu could change someone. "Nadia is my daughter. Devi is her mother." It sounded stupid on his lips, but it was the only way he could think to say it without leading him to the obvious conclusion.

Bae immediately looked to Devi who slowly raised her eyes to meet his. Ryk wondered what had happened to the fire-child that very nearly ran the Alliance on her own for the past four years. He hoped Bae realized the type of power he was playing with here. Bae's hands knitted together, and he pressed them to his forehead, closing his eyes. "So, are you two...?"

"No!" Devi and Ryk both exclaimed at once.

A pregnant pause followed, one in which Ryk tried to form a million excuses for his behavior. Even if Devi was the one who'd shown up in his room... climbed into his bed...

"I only have one more question then," Bae began quietly. Devi trembled and bowed her head. "When do I get to marry you?"

Bae opened his eyes. Devi stared at him for a long moment before she burst into tears. Dia followed suit shortly thereafter.

21

"Can I go with you, ma?" Gunner asked in what was little over a whisper. Lark was buckling her utility belt at her waist when she looked up at him. He was sitting at the foot of her bed, peering dejectedly into the steaming bowl of slathered noodles in his hands. Behind him, Sever was jumping on the bed tirelessly.

The tumultuousness of the beginning of Gun's life and the fact that he was growing up a human on the d'javu world made Gun quiet and paranoid for a child so young. Despite all her efforts, Lark was certain that she would be unable to undo what her decisions had already done to him.

She leaned down and pushed the flop of brown hair out of his eyes. "Who's gonna stay here with Sev?" she asked with a smile.

His answer was spoken without much strength, already resigned to the fact that he had no argument. "Daddy..." he said, looking away from her. "Sal..."

Lark pressed her lips together into a thin line. It wasn't fair, but she saw no other choice. She couldn't very well take him with her to hunt and kill. At least he was safe here...

Mostly safe, anyway.

"Things are gonna change, Gun, just a couple years. I promise."

He nodded slowly, and she rose, kissing his forehead. He was a tough little thing, for that she gave him credit, but she feared he would never know the freedom she'd had in her own life.

"Crotis got the message to you, then?" Mags entered the bedroom and regarded her. He glanced at Sever who was still jumping and squealing at his father. "Stop."

The little boy stopped jumping. He could not contain himself for long, though. A giggle burst out of him, and he threw himself face down on the bed where he remained, thoroughly amused by himself.

Lark's response came with mostly ignored sarcasm. "Yeh. Ain't got a problem callin' when he needs me. Couldn't give two shits if I lived or died rest of the time." Mags hooked a thumb into Gun's bowl, peering inside to see what he had. The pair exchanged twin looks of revulsion, and Mags sat down on the end of the bed next to him.

Lark crossed her arms and gave him a cold look.

"What do you want me to say?" he asked her bluntly, pitching forward when Sever jumped on his back.

"That you see what the rest of the damn galaxy sees in that crotchety old fart," she answered, and Gun tried to cover a giggle. Mags shot him an angry glance, and the boy silenced immediately.

When Mags stood up, he didn't seem to notice that Sever was clinging to him like a Taknu monkey to his tree. "Is he paying you?" he inquired neutrally.

Lark did not seem to like the taste of her own answer, "Yeh, he's payin' me..."

Before she was even through responding, he was already heading out the door. "Then what are you complaining about?"

Lark narrowed her eyes as she watched him go. "Ass," she muttered under her breath, then looked at Gun. "Stay here while I'm gone. With Sever and Sal." He nodded slowly, and she grabbed her rifle from where it was stashed in the corner.

If the Fringe had been organized enough to have a capital, Cuttah would have been it. The most populated and diverse planet in the Fringe, it had the most thriving economy.

Cuttah City had grown upward as quickly as it had grown out. Wide avenues of foot traffic on the rust streets, the notorious ground level streets where only true Cuttah natives, Lark among them, walked without some degree of paranoia. Docking bays lined the roofs of buildings while traders and sellers of all things—some more sinister than others—covered the lower level streets.

At any point, one may have felt they were strolling through a bazaar from hundreds of years before, only to take a step and wander into some of the most modern casinos in the entirety of the galaxy.

Lark had lived here on Cuttah, sometimes on the streets and at other times in the higher apartments, for longer stretches of time than she had ever lived anywhere else. Here she had learned her craft, honed her survival skills, and gained her reputation. Though those old times had not been the best, and a Fringer city was far from the ideal place for a child to raise herself up, Lark loved her home.

She pushed open the gilded doors of the Chronicle Casino. It was one of the newest to open in the casino district—referred to by the locals as the fortune borough. The ceilings soared, and globes of light floated unrestricted over the vast gambling hall. It was lined with machines, rimmed with tables, and all-over populated by crowds of well-dressed patrons. Most of them would be worth a lot less by the time they left here.

Casinos, as a rule, were not welcoming to pluggers and hunters. Their profit came from people staying and dropping money into machines for as long as possible. Anyone who would abbreviate a customer's betting run was likely to be hindered from the moment they entered. For that reason, Lark had abandoned her armor and her CCPs for something more appropriate.

A royal blue dress with slits up to her hips—as much fashion as utility, she had determined that between the high slits and the stretch of the fabric she had almost as much freedom of movement in this dress as she did in her gear. The gathered bodice offered several places to hide knives and other small weapons.

The dress had been custom-made for her, with all her nefarious intentions in mind, by a good friend who specialized in this sort of thing. He'd done her makeup and her hair as well, curled over one shoulder and scattered with sparkling pins that could disable a man if deposited in his body in the right away. Thredare was an artist in so many ways.

The beautiful nightmare of a frock fit her like a glove and she received many a compliment and lingering stare as she strolled into the luxurious casino. Mags would have hated it. He greatly preferred her in her warrior state. Lark, herself, would never tell him that she enjoyed playing dress up from time to time. Especially when it made her that much more deceptive and deadly.

The only thing she wished she could have kept was her wrist gauntlet. It made her feel naked and disconnected to have left it behind. So much of her sensory and communications equipment was wrapped up in the technology that constantly occupied her left wrist, not to mention the weapons that she kept within. A set of silken gloves covered the area where it normally sat, hiding the telltale plug at the base of her left thumb. Although she was certain she would be recognized, she needed to at least retain the appearance of being off duty.

She scanned the room and touched her hair, making a show of checking the chrono before heading for the bar. A well-dressed man was tending bar and he set a napkin on the bar before her. "What can I get you, miss?"

"Water," she answered, still running her eyes over the vast room.

"Water?" he repeated, puzzled. Lark studied him. He was a big man with a meticulously shaved head and just a touch of eyeliner. His muscles bulged beneath this starched shirt, just about a size too small. He most likely doubled as a bouncer and probably moonlighted as entertainment in the gentleman's club she had passed on her way here. A flavor for every wallet on Cuttah.

She blinked slowly, knowing that trying to charm him would be fruitless. "Ya heard me," she answered, her frustration belying her less than polished nature beneath the disguise.

The bartender raised a pretty plucked brow and wiped the inside of a glass with a towel. "Who drinks water?"

Lark bit her tongue between her teeth. "A girl who knows better," she snapped after a moment, tugging on her gloves.

"You know you can't turn tricks in here unless you work for the casino," he dropped his voice and leaned forward, speaking to her privately. "You'll have to take your business elsewhere."

Her eyes cut like turquoise glass as they fastened onto the bartender's. His smile disappeared, and he backed up quickly. Lark watched him until he walked away, then she did her best to re-focus. That conversation had been a waste of time and energy. Meanwhile, she hadn't been looking out for her mark.

A few moments later a glass of water appeared in front of her along with a blush orange piece of candy wrapped tightly in clear paper.

The flavor burst on Lark's tongue. The sickly-sweet sugar and peaches filled her mouth, and she hadn't even touched the damn thing. It took her right back to Izlatana. Her pink lips twisted in repugnance that had nothing to do with the ugly taste. This was an unexpected reminder of a private part of her past and she needed to know where it came from.

Her eyes rose to the bartender who gave her a nasty smile and tipped his head toward the farthest corner of the bar where a man sat. He had *not* been there when she sat down.

Her pride and her paranoia throbbed in tandem. She considered herself an observant gal, and her general mistrust of, well, everyone gave her several habits of the over-observant type. Had she been so distracted by the bartender that she allowed this character to enter the casino and sit down without checking in first?

The only other option was that he was just that good. 'That good' would be very bad for Lark. She watched as his dark face turned up toward her, a sinister grin sliding across his lips. This was her mark.

And if he knew about Izlatana, then he knew too much.

Mersulo Garrehr. Crotis hadn't elaborated much on why he wanted the man dead. Then again, Lark didn't really like listening when the old man spoke.

Lark produced a small shiny coin, setting it on the bar top next to the glass while she slid from the stool. "No charge," the bartender called to her.

"Ain't for the water," Lark responded without looking at him.

Her right hand slid one of the small knives from within the folds of royal blue fabric, the other rose to fist the peach candy. Her knee jerk reaction was to stalk across the room, shove the damn candy down the man's throat and then stab him in the eye. But she wanted—no, *needed* to know how much he knew about Izlatana and how he'd gotten to know it.

She was on her way over to him, reviewing each of the ways she knew to get information out of people, when he jerked around to smile at her. "Hello, Lark." He had large eyes and a voice that was deep and smooth.

"Garrehr," Lark acknowledged him, stopping just within arm's reach and keeping the knife hidden at her side.

"You've decided to come have a chat with me, I see."

Lark gave a derisive snort and held up the candy between her gloved thumb and forefinger. Even at arm's length, she could smell it. "Where the fuck did you get this?"

His smile revealed a line of white teeth, "Where do you think I got it?"

Her temper flared, and she lost track of her own motions for a split second. When she regained them, he was choking. Lark's fist stung where she had punched him in the throat. Not entirely regretful but aware she should have known better, Lark tightened her fingers around the sweet and glared at him, ignoring the attention she had garnered with that ill-timed punch, "Tell me."

"Nyhman," he wheezed. Lark's eyes grew large. She stared at him, suddenly unable to move, as if the man's name alone had restrained her. Garrehr chuckled, rubbing his throat and watching her. "Yes, Nyhman. He sent me to look for you, to deliver a message."

Lark scowled, speaking through tightly clenched teeth. "What message could that asshole have for me?"

With a grin, Garrehr leaned toward her. He reached out to touch her fist and she jerked back at first then allowed him to open her hand. "Nyhman said to give that to you. He said you'd get the point."

Lark tore her hand away, dropped the candy and stomped on it. "Got a message for him," she sneered. "But you ain't gonna be around to deliver it."

"Ah," Garrehr held up a finger. "I think you've forgotten where you are, my pretty friend. Chronicle security is already alerted to your presence," he waved his hand toward the line of uniformed officers heading their way. They wore shaded glasses and hoisted catalyst prods.

"Five," she said, slowly fluttering her eyelashes at him. "For little old me?" Her hands shot out, grabbed Garrehr by the back of the head and slammed his head into her knee. Blood burst from his nose and splattered across the shining blue fabric. Thredare was going to kill her.

The security detail picked up the pace, but they were nowhere near close enough to stop her now. Lark slammed the small knife into Garrehr's right lung then tore the thumb of her right glove with her teeth. Pressing the reader in the pad of her thumb to Garrehr's neck, she counted.

Four… three… two…

Maybe it was a second too short, but without the confirmation beep of her gauntlet, she just had to hope the scanner had taken its vitals and it would be enough to prove to Crotis the man was dead. She didn't have the choice to wait, security was on her.

Normally, there wouldn't be much they could do to her. They would have preferred to interrupt her business before she could get blood on their polished floor. They could detain her for a few days, demand payment for their damages, bar her from entering the casino again.

If she were any other plugger these would be mild inconveniences. For Lark, a few days in a casino where

Nyhman knew exactly where to find her shortly after killing one of his men was just too risky. Considering she had succeeded in causing a deadly scene in the middle of the gambling floor, the Chronicle would not be above turning her into the Alliance for her bounty. There, she would stand trial for war crimes against civspace.

Probably be executed, too, if Mags didn't lay waste to half the galaxy first.

Foregone conclusions notwithstanding, Lark's choices were limited. Being detained was not one of them, so all she could do was run. She dropped Garrehr and bolted, slamming straight into the solid form of a Chronicle security heavy that had joined them from out of her line of sight.

Lark finally admitted to herself that this was not her day.

Shoving backward from him, she kicked and knocked him in his crotch. The painful crack against her shin told her he'd come prepared for that. It still racked him, but he wouldn't be out of the fight for long. When he doubled over, she slid around him and tossed the knife she'd been holding behind her without really aiming. She was at full speed before she could find out if it hit anyone.

The impact of the full body tackle stole her breath and her feet left the floor. They fell for what seemed like ages before the unforgiving marble floor slammed into her chest, the guard's weight on top of her made her feel like a balloon about to pop. Her face collided with the shiny surface and white exploded before her left eye.

She was still dazed when a flood of pain overtook her; the epicenter appeared to be at the junction between her right shoulder and her neck. Every muscle in her body panicked, writhing and seizing as an electric current rushed through them. She tried to scream, felt it rising in her throat, but her teeth clamped closed and all she managed was a frustrated growl.

When the hot electric agony ebbed, she felt her body go limp. Sucking in a harsh breath and tasting blood, she clawed against the darkness seeping in from the edges of her vision. Lark repeated to herself that she could not be detained. Even as the guards dragged her puddle of a body from the floor and she felt her grip on consciousness slip away.

Lark found herself in a small cell when she awoke. The three walls, floor, and ceiling were all that same marble that she remembered so clearly coming up to meet her left cheekbone an indeterminate amount of time earlier. Without thinking, she lifted her hand to touch the area around her eye and winced as pain shot through the swollen flesh.

The fourth wall of her room was occupied only by polished steel bars. Through them she saw a desk with a monitor; behind which sat one of the burly Chronicle security officers with his feet propped up and crossed at the ankles.

"There she is," he dropped his feet to the floor and stood.

She hadn't gotten a good look at them when her only concern was getting away, which she had failed to do anyway. He wore a black armored vest, the sleeves of a heather navy sweater over his arms. The insignia of the casino, something that looked like an analog compass, had been embroidered over his left breast pocket. The name Halys cut into a gleaming silver name tag on his right.

As he approached she discovered he had a handsome face but a mocking smile. He leaned on the bars and grinned in at her, "You came to sooner than expected."

She could tell by the way he spoke that he wasn't Fringe-born. He started all his sentences properly, instead of cutting out the subject outright, without even a hint of the frontier drawl that most Fringers tended toward. Lark knew her own accent, thicker than most, had evened out over the years but the rust streets still came out when she was angry.

Civspace emigrants were not wholly uncommon, especially on Cuttah and especially in security positions; bastards who couldn't make it in ACP employment, so they went where their character flaws were a commodity and not a liability.

"Take more than a shock stick to put me down," she put a hand in her hair and found it knotted but void of the sparkling, deadly pins. A quick pat to her midsection revealed the hidden knives were gone too. "Get your rocks off while you frisked me?"

"You'll never know." The quickness of his reply made her think he'd been in the Fringe awhile, but she found it hard to judge his age. He slid a card over a reader and rolled open the bars. "C'mon," he said, not unkindly. "You get to make a call. Think you got a friend who'll bail you out?"

A long time, she decided. He'd been in the Fringe long enough to consider her an equal. Lark stood on bare feet and followed him out of the cell. There was a comm station at the other side of the office. He handed her an ice pack, and she cocked her head at him, knowing he'd understand the gesture, "Totally makes up for smashing my face into the floor."

"I'll call us even." He winked at her and returned to his desk.

Lark turned to the comm station, hissing as she pressed the ice pack to her raging cheekbone. She stared at the monitor and at her bruised reflection in the glass, dark blue and purple already creeping across a solid half of her face. There were few enough people she knew who would respond to a call such as this, fewer still she would want to involve in the side of her life that involved darkspawn and men like Nyhman.

She sucked in a deep breath and pressed her fingers to the comm screen to initiate a call, hoping he still had a soft spot for her.

It had to have been about an hour. She entertained herself while she waited by chewing on a half-broken fingernail (after swearing she would leave it be until she could trim it) and endlessly berating herself for how badly she'd screwed up this job. Letting Garrehr bait her into attacking him in the middle of the gambling floor had shown great weakness, and it had not only opened an opportunity for Nyhman but had forced her to involve an old friend. If she had been smart or level headed at all, she would have gotten him outside and then beaten him senseless.

For a millisecond when she first heard the voice, she thought it was Mags and her heart skipped a beat. The low, grumbling tone brought her back from her thoughts and she yanked her finger from her mouth, annoyed but unsurprised that the nail was no less uneven.

It wasn't Mags. The voice belonged to a tall human who hailed the guard with false amity. She was too ashamed to look him in the eye but too proud to show it, so she settled on glancing in his general direction when he came into view on the other side of the bars. "Liem."

"Yeh," he nodded to her, his expression serious from what she could see. The rest of him was about the same as she remembered; brawny shoulders beneath a heavily worn jacket with the sleeves pushed up over tattooed forearms. "What's the damage?" he asked Halys.

She didn't hear the answer, but Liem didn't flinch when he offered up his tablet to make the payment. Lark stood up and smoothed her tangled hair, suddenly and inexplicably self-conscious.

Halys slid his card again and waved her out of the cell. Lark did her best to appear dignified while her bare feet slapped the marble floor, and she held her dress closed where it had torn up to her midsection. "My effects?'

He turned over her comm and a single earring. Lark touched both her ears to find one missing and begrudgingly removed the other one. Halys chuckled at her, holding up a handful of knives before dropping them back into a desk drawer. "We'll keep these if you don't mind."

"Cost of doin' business," Liem agreed, not that he'd been asked. He wrapped a hand, rough and over-warm, around her bicep and squeezed to discourage her from arguing. "Look good all dappered up," he commented as he turned her toward the exit and pushed her into a walk.

Lark glanced up at him, saw that he was making fun of her, and scowled then sucked in a breath when pain shot into her skull via her left eye socket. She yanked her arm away and Liem let out a rumbling chuckle, "Your eye almost matches your dress, know it?"

"Thanks for noticing," Lark grumbled, shoving at her hair to keep it behind her ears. "Where's Jaimy?"

"Where d'you think he is?" Liem's retort came just as they stepped out of the corridor and onto the gambling floor. Straight ahead of them was the exit to the fortune borough. Across the sea of clanging pachinko machines and crowded card tables, Lark recognized the bar where she'd lost her temper and nearly everything else. The bartender was still there. He smirked at her when their eyes met then turned his attention back to the closest bar patron.

Liem whistled so loud that heads across the floor pivoted in their direction. Lark turned her face away from the unwanted attention and gave Liem a jab in the side which he ignored. One of the heads that had turned belonged to a body that unfolded from the bar and strode toward them.

Jaimy Lecorza. If Lark hadn't wanted to look Liem in the eye, all she had to do was look at his brother. They had the same face, angular jaw, and hazel eyes, but Jaimy's brown hair flowed sinfully over his shoulders where Liem kept his cropped short.

"You look nice," Jaimy commented as he approached. He slid his hands into his pockets casually and offered her the smile that had opened dozens of legs.

"Ah yeh," Lark scoffed and rubbed at her neck, the skin still tender where they'd hit her with the shock stick. "Look a hell of a lot better than I feel."

"More reason to keep moving," Liem growled, nodding toward the gathering security force watching them from the other side of the room.

"Let's go," Jaimy put a hand on the small of her back and Lark felt her cheeks flush without her permission. She concentrated on clinging to her pride while she scurried out of the Chronicle in what was left of her pitiful disguise.

The metal grates of the walkway outside were grimy under her feet and hot from cooking in the summer sun. She had gone barefoot for years at a time as a child in worse parts of this city, but doing it now made her cringe. She hurried forward, propelled by an itching instinct in the back of her mind directly related to her escorts.

Jaimy and Liem were aloof at her back and she didn't like it. The pressure of Jaimy's hand was still on her back even if his hand wasn't. Dozens of women had fallen into the trap that was Jaimy Lecorza. Lark was far from being one of them, but that didn't mean she was immune to the effects of his charm.

"This is my stop," she turned abruptly outside a lift that went somewhere she didn't need to be. She caught them sharing a silent, conspiratorial expression. "What do I owe you?" she asked after a moment in which they tried unsuccessfully to appear guilty of nothing.

"I'll call us even," Liem waved the comment away.

That was the second time today she had heard that, and it was still untrue. It may have been a long time since she had come face to face with the Coin Brothers, but they certainly didn't owe her anything.

Her current state, torn frock and bruised face, had to make her less than intimidating, but she was beyond caring. She let go of the dress and let it fall open, peeled off her remaining fancy glove and tossed it over the railing. Then she stepped inside Liem's personal space, a tactic that made most people back up.

Liem didn't move. Lark was suddenly reminded of why she had put space between herself and the Coin Brothers all those years ago. His guard should have gone up, she should have tried to keep her distance. Instead, she felt the same spark of chemistry she always had and, again, she tried to ignore it. "Lost your teeth if you think I'll owe you a fucking favor, Lecorza," she poked a red fingertip into his chest. "How much?"

Liem grabbed her hand and held it, staring down at her like she had just tried to pick his pocket. When his face darkened, she noted he had collected a few more scars since the last time she had seen him. She also realized he hadn't ever looked at her like that before, like she was something less than human. Lark felt the need to pull her hand away, to turn and run, but she didn't. She couldn't decide if she felt afraid of Liem Lecorza or saddened that she seemed to have lost him as a friend.

Jaimy sprang into action after their stare down lasted a moment too long. He wrapped an arm around Liem's chest and forced him back a step, tearing his hand away from Lark's and placing himself between them. "This is just what friends do, Lark." His voice took on a soothing tone as if he was weaving some type of spell. "Why don't you go get changed and we'll go have a drink—"

Rubbing her hand where Liem's grip had pinched her skin, Lark narrowed her eyes at the Coin Brothers as if she could squint and see through this fake sweet-and-sour candy shell they were wearing. They were playing the same roles they had always played. Jaimy was the diplomat who could charm just about anybody into anything and Liem was the threat of violence if Jaimy's charms didn't work. Behind that façade, though, something wasn't working quite like it used to.

Unfortunately for them, Lark wasn't impressed by charm and violence was more tempting than threatening to her. Liem cocked his head when her visceral response to the offer quieted Jaimy, his eyes searching her as much as his own memory. "Don't drink, do you?"

"No."

Jaimy pulled a face, genuinely puzzled. His alluring mask dropped, and judgment filled his tone, "Why the hell not?"

It wasn't worth the time to explain to a boozer like Jaimy. Rolling her eyes, she tugged at a torn part of the dress before answering. "More trouble than it's worth. Listen, got appointments to keep. Thanks for springing me; I'll make us even my own way."

Liem smiled in an entirely insincere and disturbing way that froze Lark momentarily to the steel walkway. "Sure, you will," he said. "See you 'round, then."

A pause while Lark studied them both before Jaimy regained his composure and gave her a smile meant to be comforting, the type that begged forgiveness for his twin's behavior. "Hang in there."

Lark waved and waited for them to melt into the crowd on the other side of the platform. She scratched a place at the back of her neck that wasn't really itching before taking the next alley toward the finance borough and the lifts that would take her down to the rust streets.

22

STILL FUMING about the encounter in the Chronicle, Lark left her dress with Thredare to be mended. He had been less than happy but not entirely surprosed to see the condition it was in. Lark hadn't been in the mood to trade snark, so she'd forced some extra change on him. She wanted to get home, where she could be with her sons and then fall into Mags' arms with Izlatana far from her mind.

She had forgotten to trim that nail. She discovered this when she found herself nibbling at it again while lost in dark thoughts. Her communicator toned, and she tugged her hood up to accept the call, "Yeh."

The response came hurriedly, the words slurring together in their haste to make it out of the speaker's mouth, "Thank the stars, Lark, where the hell are you?"

"Ma... li?" Lark responded slowly, unsure if that was the voice she was hearing. It had been years since they'd spoken—a trait intrinsic to the survival of Lark's friendships.

"Yeh!" Mali sounded relieved, but impatient. "Where are you?"

"On Cuttah, running a job. Why?"

"You need to get off Cuttah. Now!"

Lark stopped walking, cocking her head at the image of Mali in her mind. Her old friend was tall and strong, with waves of dark red hair and hard violet eyes. The woman she knew had a cold, military calm to her that Lark had never seen shaken. This person, with her voice shrill with panic, did not fit the memory. "Look, Mali, you got a job here, I get it. Think this planet's big enough for the two of us…"

"This isn't a joke, Lark!"

"Ain't laughing…" A strange feeling had suddenly overtaken her. Her right hand rose ponderously to the side of her face and found that the skin of her cheek had been replaced by something rubbery and soft.

There was something in her mouth, too, thick and heavy that was keeping her from speaking. After a long moment in which she idly moved the thing around between her teeth, she realized it was her tongue. Numbness spread across her face, subtle tingling as if she had walked into a spider's web. She cursed, but it just came out as wet gibberish.

"Lark!" Mali was screaming at her, but her voice was quickly fading from Lark's ear. Belatedly, she realized she had allowed her hood to fall back.

"Caln bluvvers," Lark slurred, sliding to her knees.

"What?" she heard Mali's voice from a great distance but was unable to reach back to pull her hood back up. "The Coin Brothers are after you!"

If Lark had an answer, it never found breath as she crumpled to the ground in a heap.

The smell of campfire, dirt, and wilderness assaulted her senses as consciousness hit her like a bucket of ice water. Her eyes shot open to find uncovered ground and foliage before her. Beyond the ring of light thrown by the fire at her back, everything dissolved into darkness.

Just below the sound of the crackling fire, she could hear two male voices speaking in hushed tones. Her hands were bound in front of her and, as sensation trickled into her limbs, the chill night air stroked the skin of her arms. They'd taken her jacket, which left her arms exposed— scarred and naked. Her utility belt and pistols, along with the rest of her weapons, seemed to be gone as well.

Slowly, she regained motor control and pulled herself to a sitting position, turning her head to see the source of the light. On the other side of the fire sat two large human males. Twin faces, broad shoulders. The Coin Brothers.

"Welcome back," Liem Lecorza quipped. He was picking at something that may have been a bird but was now heavily charred and mostly eaten. "Didn't think you were ever gonna wake up."

Jaimy added with a chuckle, taking a sip from a flask, "Kind of hoped you wouldn't."

Lark feigned hurt and rotated her body to face them, crossing her legs in front of her and cocking her head at them, "Aw, and here I thought we were all friends." She tested the bindings on her wrist. After finding them sound, she dropped them back into her lap and blew a puff of breath at a piece of hair that had fallen into her face, sending them a narrow-eyed glance. "What's with the rope work, fellas?"

"Don't want to get knifed," Jaimy answered matter-of-factly.

"Good call," Lark admitted with a shrug, then her face took on a mischievous smile. "Partyin' or what?"

Liem laughed in exasperation, but Jaimy was in disbelief. "Aren't you at all concerned about what we could do to you in this situation?"

Lark gave a low chuckle, shaking her head at him. "First of all, ain't afraid of much, least of all two hunks with a set of tranqs." Liem gave her an indignant look. Jaimy seemed genuinely flattered. "Second, you two ain't gonna hurt me. No money in it. 'Sides," she grinned widely. "Only murderer here's me."

Liem scowled at her and muttered under his breath, turning his attention back to his meal.

"Where are we anyway?" Lark asked after a moment of listening to Liem grumble and chew.

Jaimy ignored his brother and answered her question, tucking the flask away with a sigh, "Can't take you through the spaceports, so we're going the long way. I think this is officially the middle of nowhere."

"Ah," Lark nodded dramatically as if she had just been clued in on a galactic truth, "Don't wanna be caught turnin' in a fellow Fringer on an Alliance bounty, eh?"

"Do the same thing if you were in our position," Liem snapped.

"Maybe," Lark replied in kind.

Lark and Liem glared at each other before falling into silence. Liem chewed noisily on the rest of his food, and Jaimy zoned out on the fire, focused internally.

Lark assessed them as they seemed to forget her presence entirely. Now that they had given up the act they had been trying to pull in Cuttah City, they were more themselves. The predictability of their more natural state put Lark at ease, relative to the situation.

Lark had seen the bounty out on Jaimy, second only to hers in payout. The only difference was that her bounty was put out by the Alliance which meant no one in the Fringe was going to take it. Not unless they were desperate enough. Even with the number of zeros hovering over Jaimy's head, Lark was surprised by this turn.

"That's a funny name, *Lark*," Liem said suddenly, throwing the bones of the bird into the fire and wiping his hands on his pants. His disingenuous smile made the words sound more mocking than curious. "Where'd you get a name like that?"

She shrugged. "Just what everyone's always called me. Guess it's 'cause I got one tattooed on me." At least they weren't asking about her scars. Few people ever did. It was rare, if not impossible, to find a Fringer without the scars of a sordid history. Lark just wasn't interested in sharing hers.

"You got a bird tattooed on you?" Jaimy asked incredulously, his flask had somehow appeared back in his hand without motion.

"Nope, just always had one. Ever since I can remember." She moved her bound hands up to the neckline of her armored tank and pulled it to the side, revealing her left shoulder and the tattoo of the dark silhouette of a small, delicate bird with its wings spread in flight. "Don't know who tattoos a kid, but..."

"Lemme see that," Liem's urgency was startling as he jumped up and rushed around the fire to squat in front of her. One of his large hands wrapped around her arm while the other gripped her shoulder. He leaned in and took a good hard look at the tattoo.

Lark, who was as surprised by his sudden proximity as she was by his interest, shifted back against the pull of his hand to put some space between their faces.

Having not taken a close look at Liem since this encounter had started, she had failed to notice that his eyes were vaguely the color of a lake—a blueish green brown—and that his face had grown harder than his twin's, more suited to scowling than it was joviality. His nose had a crooked cast to it, a tell-tale sign that it had been broken to one side at least once and broken back the other way at least twice. Frown lines and scars roughened his skin, showing age Lark didn't remember from the last time she had seen him. Whereas Jaimy's face was still smooth, clinging to youthfulness, Liem's belied the effects of stress, unending work, and a quick temper.

His seriousness notwithstanding, Lark still could not deny that innate connection to Liem. Maybe her own temper and recklessness would show on her face one day as the lines and scars did on Liem's. She felt a sudden need to look in a mirror in search of wrinkles before she remembered the bruised swelling and decided she'd rather not just the same.

"It's not a lark," he told her, releasing her swiftly and standing up.

"What?" Lark looked up at him and then to Jaimy, who was still staring at the tattoo with a strange, unreadable expression.

"*It's not a lark,*" Liem repeated impatiently, moving back across the fire. He dropped himself back into his seat with something that resembled resignation. "It's a moonshadow." He pressed his thumb to his lips and looked away as if contemplating this deeply.

Lark stared at him, mouth slightly agape, "A... moonshadow?"

"It's a kind of bird," he answered without looking at her. "A type of owl, actually."

Suddenly embarrassed by her body art, she pulled the strap of her shirt back over her tattoo. Eager to change the tone of the conversation, her face took on a malicious grin as she chaffed him, "Didn't know you were a bird guy."

"There's a lot you don't know about me," he replied tersely. The two brothers looked at each other so intently Lark wondered if they had some sort of psychic connection.

Finally, Liem broke the silence, "Let's get some shut eye." He lay down on a sleep mat with his back to the fire.

Jaimy glanced at Lark briefly. "You can get some sleep."

"I just woke up," she reminded him. "Could offer me something to eat, ya know."

He glanced into the fire then offered her a sympathetic look, "I think Liem ate it all..."

"Figures," Lark shook her head and leaned back. "You know there are better ways to make money. Ain't about to beg for my life, but this will end your career real fast. Only say this cause we've known each other so fucking long— but you guys are damn good hunters."

"We don't want to do this, Lark," he looked away from her, holding the flask in both hands and staring at the fire.

"Don't think you do, Jaimy," she smirked at him.

He let out a breath that was heavy with regret, "Don't have a choice."

She pressed her lips together and rocked her head back and forth. "Don't you?" Shrugging, she slid to the ground. "Probably do the same fucking thing, it were me."

He didn't respond to that, so she turned her eyes up to a starless, moonless sky. Off in the distance, she could see the muted glow of light pollution that she could only assume was Cuttah City. They were still on-planet then. Dimly, she wondered where they'd left their ship before her eyes closed without her knowing, and sleep reclaimed her.

The sound of shuffling awoke her to the thin light of early morning. She could hear Liem and Jaimy muttering to each other and smelled coffee brewing as she opened her eyes to survey the world in daylight. All that the darkness had cloaked the night before was now shrouded in a milky fog. A ring of dark trees was just barely visible through the fog about twenty yards to the either side of their campsite. Their figures were shrouded in white gossamer, the trees looked like a ghostly forest army standing sentinel over the land.

A chill ran through her that was not entirely related to the cold, wet morning air.

Lark sat up and pivoted to the face the campsite. She brushed ruddy dirt from her face, ignoring the dull pain. "Coffee..." she murmured, her eyes closing to slits. Jaimy and Liem had been breaking camp, but when she spoke their whispering stopped. "Feed me..." she added.

Liem turned on his haunches and grimaced at her. "What are you, some kind of undead thing in the morning?"

"Dun like morning," Lark replied. She yawned and tried to stretch her bound wrists above her head, "D'you like morning, Liem Lecorza?"

"Can't say I'm too fond of it myself," he admitted, rising and pouring some coffee from a carafe that sat at the base of the fire.

After he shoved the paper cup it into her hands, she sniffed it and looked up at him petulantly. "No sugar?"

"Are you fucking kidding? This ain't a vacation—"

"*Liem*," Jaimy rebuked him sharply. The Coin Brothers looked at each other. What followed was a conversation that occurred almost entirely with frustrated facial expressions and culminated in a rude hand gesture from Liem, who then stalked off into the mist. Jaimy laughed nervously and sprinkled some sugar from a tin canister into Lark's coffee. "Not really a morning person either, Liem."

"Ain't really an anytime person, is he?"

"That either."

Lark chuckled and leaned back against a log, crossing her ankles and looking decidedly like she was on vacation. "So, where we off too, brother?"

"Brother?" Jaimy paused in bending down to put the sugar canister away, his eyebrows raised.

"That's what you are, ain't it?" He stared at her silently. "A brother. A *Coin* Brother? Do you want me to call you sister or sweetheart or princess?"

"Oh..." he gave that nervous laugh again and returned to his work of gathering their equipment.

Lark drank heavily of the coffee. It was watered down and gritty, even for frontier coffee, but it was coffee and she could feel it working its magic from her forehead to the tips of her toes. "Somebody once told me you don't like to be called Jaimy by anybody but your friends."

His large shoulders lifted and fell uneasily as he faced away from her, bent over their sleeping mats. "That's not really true."

It was too early for Lark to think of a good response to that. So, she turned her attention back to her glorious drink of the gods and went quiet for a while.

As she came to the bottom of the cup, she stared down at the dregs of grounds left from the primitive method they'd used to make it. The black globs reminded her of an old gypsy woman on Cuttah who would throw stones and read tea leaves. Lark rotated the cup, trying to make heads or tails of the images and wondering what that old fortune teller would have read in her cards.

It occurred to her to ask Jaimy what he thought, seeing as she knew the Coin Brothers were gypsies. As she opened her mouth to ask, she had the supplemental recollection that they had both been pretty drunk when they had admitted that to her outside that pub on Thrantos. It was unlikely they remembered and, if they did, they probably regretted it. Lark wasn't sure if it would offend him to bring it up. Even the Fringe had its outcasts.

She was just debating whether or not she cared about offending him when a groan came from Jaimy's direction. "Need help?" she asked, receiving another groan in response. Lark pulled herself awkwardly to her feet, dropping the empty paper cup in the fire as she stepped around it and approached him. "Seriously, big man can't pick up a fucking sleeping mat?"

"What?" Jaimy looked up at her from where he was crouched.

"Over here grunting like you're pulling a damn Bufari steamship out of the fucking atmosphere." He blinked at her and she heard it again.

Well, it wasn't coming from Jaimy. And it wasn't exactly a groan either. More like a... growl.

"Run!" Jaimy shouted. He jumped up and pushed his hand in between her shoulder blades, forcing her into a run just as several large creatures crashed out of the trees and into the campsite. A howl echoed against the trees, and Lark chanced a peek over her shoulder in between Jaimy's shoving.

Silver fur, black spines bristling on their hackles. Lips curled, hungry drool slid through their bared teeth as their black eyes tracked what they had to be considering was a sure bet for breakfast. Three more materialized from the trees.

When the pack of briar wolves let out a bark and moved forward as a unit, Lark stopped looking. She could hear their great paws in the undergrowth as they spread out into the trees, navigating the tight spaces with ease, and that was enough information for her.

Lark discovered it was difficult to run effectively with her hands bound, her balance was all off and she couldn't get a proper arm-leg rhythm going. She had no idea she used her arms this much when she was running.

Jaimy's hand was still on her back as the briar wolves gained ground. Around them, the fog was beginning to dissipate. Over the tops of the trees, Lark could just see the shadow of distant Cuttah City floating in the rapidly depleting mist.

Another howl and Jaimy shoved her suddenly. Lark gasped, struggling to keep her footing as she clumsily circumnavigated an especially tight grouping of trees. Chancing another cautious glance behind her, she realized the reason for Jaimy's sudden rush forward. The pack was almost on top of them.

Off the trail, it was their only option. If Jaimy could climb a tree, maybe he could hoist her up... Maybe he *would*...

Lark never got the chance to turn off their path. The closest creature lunged, a loud snap as the jaws slammed closed mere centimeters from Jaimy's ankles. The big man jumped forward, facilitating the near miss but knocking Lark off balance for a final time.

Lark fell, hitting the ground hard on her shoulder without being able to break her fall with her hands tied. Jaimy called out her name as he fell on top of her. She thought it was just because they'd been running so close, but he stretched his arms out. She realized he was shielding her body with his own.

Over Jaimy's large shoulder, Lark could see the pack beginning to encircle them. Victory and hunger shone in the black hollowness of their eyes; the largest one pulled back to leap onto Jaimy's back.

Lark saw those long canine teeth shredding through her throat and there was not a damn thing she could do about it except watch as the world went silent and slow and her death inched toward her. She closed her eyes, swearing she never thought it would end like this.

But that strike never landed.

A barrage of catalyst pulses shattered the silence and, over the din, a voice could be heard whooping and hollering as the blasts went on and on. Lark opened her eyes to find the pack of wolves gone, and Jaimy rolled off her to reveal Liem unloading his catalyst pistol into the dead carcass of the pack leader. The rest of them had fled into the trees. He reached the end of the reaction chamber and the blasts changed from hot white to cool blue as one or the other chemical emptied.

Jaimy took a deep breath and ran his hands over his face as his brother's steam ran out shortly after his ammo. Lark propped herself up on an elbow, face pinked with adrenaline, and she gave Jaimy a cold look. "You guys really must be fucking desperate..."

"What?" he seemed surprised by her tone, dropping his hand to look at her. "Why?"

"Just risked your damn life to save me," she shook her head at him and pulled herself into a sitting position. "Stupid or something? Can't spend the money when you're fucking dead, Jaimy."

Liem gave a last, half-hearted howl and kicked the dead beast, oblivious to the conversation beside him. He holstered the gun, tromped over to them and helped his brother up, then reached down to pull Lark to her feet. "Are you alright?"

Lark slapped his hands away and growled at him. "Fucking fine, thanks to my hero over here." The boys glanced at each other, another one of those silent communications she was quickly growing tired of. "What the fuck is with you two?"

"C'mon," Liem said, turning away from the carcass and heading back toward the campsite. "We're taking her to dad." Jaimy followed without tugging Lark along like the prisoner she was.

"Wait," Lark hurried to keep up with them, again reminded of how awkward running was with her hands tied. "Why are we taking her to dad? Why ain't we taking her to cash in the bounty?" They kept walking, ignoring her because there was no way they hadn't heard. "Boys? Boys!"

Jaimy finally turned to look at her, putting a placating hand on her shoulder. "Just calm down," he said softly. Too softly. "We just... need some guidance."

Scowling, Lark spat, "I'll give you some fucking guidance." Jaimy sighed and turned away.

Liem spoke up without turning. "Something tells me we don't want your kind of guidance." Lark stomped her feet and stopped walking. When they both turned around, she was glaring at them like a petulant child.

Liem's mouth twisted with frustration. His boots pounded over the undergrowth as he crossed the distance between them to stare her down. "Ain't got time for this, now get fucking moving," he ordered her, the gruffness in his voice revealing the edge of his temper.

"*I gotta pee!*" Lark yelled shrilly into his face.

Bravado seemed to be doing nothing for these two, and she was finally losing her patience. She felt as childish as she was acting but she didn't rightly care. "Know you two can just whip out your fucking space worms and go wherever you want, but I don't got that luxury."

Jaimy suddenly turned an odd shade of puce. "Please... don't... talk about stuff like that."

"What?" she peered over Liem's shoulder at him. Any other day, the thought of the infamous womanizer Jaimy Lecorza being at all prudish would have her in stitches. Not today. She was hungry, severely lacking in caffeine, and believe it or not she really did have to pee. "Can't talk about your fucking boy parts?" While Jaimy looked like he was going to faint, Liem's anger had disappeared and he closed his eyes, pinching the bridge of his crooked nose.

True to form, Lark kept pushing. "Like I never fucking seen one before?" Lark went on, only half teasing at this point. She pressed her knees together and tried not to hop up and down. "Like you two don't know the difference between—"

"Alright, just fucking stop!" Liem's gruff voice rose over her own, and he held his hand out to shush her.

"Jeesh," Lark said, letting out a laugh. She hadn't expected to get under their skin so easily. She wondered what kind of women they spent their time with. "How do you two ever get fucking laid?"

"Just go!" Liem pointed into the trees. "And don't run off."

"Ain't exactly my idea of fun, Liem, but I ain't stupid. Got a better chance with you two clowns than I got against another pack of wolves while I'm half naked and squatting in the woods."

"Please?" Jaimy pleaded, and Liem waved her toward the tree line.

"Alright, alright..." she laughed lightly as she tromped into the cover of the trees.

23

THE *STALKER* was a slightly larger vessel than the *Starsigh*. Boxy but meticulously well cared for, it was an older style, re-purposed small cargo freighter equipped with several armament upgrades and stealth capabilities. Staring up at the shiny black paint job made Lark want to go back and give her own ship some well-deserved attention.

The inside was as beautiful as the out, having been renovated to allow for two people to occupy the ship for long periods of time without killing each other. At the end of the corridor from which the bunks split off, Lark could see a passage to the cargo hold.

Much to her surprise, the hold was not her destination. Instead, they showed her to a bunk room. Liem unbound her hands, nodded to the lav and left her alone. Lark tried the door and found that it was not locked.

What the what? These two were freaking her right the hell out. She would have been a lot less disturbed if they were treating her like a bounty and not a damn princess. Could they at least have locked the door?

Lark knew that despite the freedoms they'd allowed her, no opportunity to escape was going to present itself while they were traveling through space. Regardless of her own abilities, it was not likely she could overpower both Coin

Brothers on their own ship. Lark had enough respect for them remaining not to make trouble fruitlessly trying to escape just to prove a point.

For a community built upon the shaky foundations of an every-man-for-himself attitude, there was a great amount of mutual regard among Fringers. One of the great uniting factors of life in the Fringe was not being in civspace; the Alliance was the enemy of all the disorder the Fringe had striven to maintain. Turning a Fringer—any Fringer—over to Alliance authorities was the only true crime in the Fringe.

That bounty on Jaimy's head was a heavy one, and she couldn't blame him for wanting to pay it off quick. However, the backlash from this would end their careers and make them pariahs in the Fringe. Whoever held that bounty must have been one scary mother.

The bunk itself was unremarkable. Lark found a bed that folded out from the wall beneath a viewport. The desk was littered and stacked with computer printouts of news clippings and prison ledgers.

Lark shuffled through the papers quietly, aware they could be listening, and found several slave ship manifests and purchase receipts. Whatever they were looking for here, it must have been a long-running bounty. Some of the dates went back to long before she'd even gone to Izlatana. Out of boredom, she tried several drawers and found nothing of interest though one was locked.

While she was trying to pry it open, the door slid to the side and Liem walked in. His gaze shifted from the drawer to Lark's not-so-innocent smile, and he gave her a cool look. "Find anything interesting?" he asked, setting down a tray of food on top of the printouts.

"Only that you been looking for someone since the dawn of time," she touched the edges of the printouts.

"Bounty's gotta be as old as I am, can't imagine anybody gonna pay out now."

Liem gave the breath of a chuckle. "Probably wouldn't understand. Plugger's about instant gratification, ain't you?" His eyes lingered on hers for a moment, and Lark found herself shifting uncomfortably. "Some bounty's don't pay off right away, but they're worth it in the long haul." The eye contact broke abruptly, and Liem Lecorza turned away from her. "Get yourself a shower and settle in, it'll be a few days before we get where we're going."

Once he was gone, Lark didn't even hesitate. The prepack meal he'd left her could have been poisoned and she wouldn't care. It wasn't as good as handmade food, but when you were in space for weeks it was the closest thing. Right now, she was so hungry it was as gourmet as she'd ever had.

After she gorged herself, Lark went into the lav. There was a small laundry refresh unit and a set of Liem's clothes sat freshly ionized inside. Lark folded the clothes and set them on an empty shelf then deposited her own in the laundry refresher before hopping into the shower.

By the time she had finished washing, her clothes were quite a few ticks down from filthy. Uncomfortable walking around naked, she dragged her clothes on over damp skin and then stepped out into Liem's bunk. Again, she tried the door and found it unlocked.

For two days it went on like that. She'd had less comfortable captivity and worse wardens. They didn't even bother her except to bring her food. Most of the time it was just left for her.

A rash had developed on her left arm, more than likely from some poisonous plant she had run into in the Cuttah wilderness. A small medkit she found in the lav had a tube of cream for just this occasion as well as a set of small scissors she used to trim down the fingernail that had been bothering her. Afterward, she found it felt just as annoying to have one nail shorter than the others, so she trimmed them all.

While she considered the fact that, if the time came for her to defend herself, she had just cut off what could have been her only weapon, there was a polite knock on the door. Lark turned to look at it, holding the dull trimmers in her fist. When it didn't open immediately, she rolled her eyes and called for her visitor to come in.

Liem opened the door and said, "C'mere." He gave a grin like none she had seen on his face before, glowing with pride. "Something I wanna show you."

Even if she didn't have a choice, it wasn't an order. It was an invitation.

Neither of them spoke, but Lark watched Liem's back as she followed him through the cramped corridor and through the lounge. His broad shoulders were more relaxed than was customary for him. She remembered them as being tense the way Mags' always were.

Considering she hadn't thought about him in years, Lark was struck by how much Liem reminded her of her husband. He was taller than Mags and slimmer at the waist, but the bulkiness of their shoulders was the same. As well as their attitudes. Liem was always so serious and gruff, especially in stark comparison to his brother. Then there were those moments of morbid, often inappropriate humor. Lark thought that was where the two of them were most alike. It made her smile to herself to think of Mags' dark grin.

In the cockpit, Jaimy was sitting at the controls. Liem gestured toward the starshield, and Lark stepped up next to him to peer through. She gaped at what lay before them.

Floating out in the black sea of space, against the pinprick of stars, was a crippled starship. Broken, floating dead in space, but painted in bright slashes of purple, green, and blue. It was a huge transport vessel, built to accommodate a small city. Smoke belched from the fuselage; a cloud of shrapnel surrounded one end of the craft.

"Ship's been hit," she said to Jaimy's back. "Better get the fuck outta here. It's pirates, we don't wanna be fucking next."

With a chuckle, Liem crossed his arms. "Girl after my own heart," he nodded to his brother. Jaimy opened up the comm and began speaking in a language Lark had never heard.

"That..." Lark began, bewildered. She looked at Liem, pointing at his twin. "That your gypsy language?"

"It's called Zingari but yeh, that's our language," Liem gave her a patronizing smile.

A voice filled the cockpit, squawking out what sounded like an affirmative. Then Jaimy began to bring the ship in for landing. They were aiming for what Lark had originally thought to be a gaping hole in the hull, but she could see now it was a docking bay.

Lark's brow knit above her eyes as she watched that multicolored behemoth draw closer. "I thought you were taking me in for the bounty..." She was talking to Jaimy, but he didn't turn to look at her. She watched his face tighten as he stared determinedly through the starshield.

Liem answered for him, "Change of plans."

They didn't cuff her. They didn't stick a pistol in her back and push her forward. Liem helped her into her now empty jacket, and then the two of them just sidled out of the ship and expected her to follow.

She did, of course, but more out of a dearth of anything better to do. She welcomed the familiar sensation of her old jacket on her shoulders, the pleasant feeling of knowing her scars were covered even if the weight was wrong and they hadn't returned her gauntlet. They'd removed all her hidden knives and poisons, but she pulled the jacket tight, zipping it up as far as it would go.

Lark had been on nearly every planet in the Fringe, and she had never seen a more disorganized docking bay in her life. Ships were parked—some with inch thick layers of dust across them—willy-nilly across the dirty metal floor. Many of these ships probably hadn't seen flight in ages, and it was doubtful they'd be space-worthy even if they would start up.

They passed through the dim bay and through a set of doors that opened about three-quarters of the way before stopping unexpectedly with a jarring clang. Lark jumped, but the Coin Brothers didn't seem to notice. "Where are we?" she demanded, flinching when the doors slammed closed behind her.

Ahead the corridor was warmly lit and wide; music and voices could be heard echoing from within. "This is the *Udancea*," Jaimy answered, turning to glance at her over his shoulder. It was the first time he'd spoken since they left Cuttah. She stared at him stupidly when their eyes met. "This is home."

His face was forlorn, and Lark was unable to fathom why. Maybe it was just regret for what they had been planning to do. Jaimy had always been the more compassionate of the pair, it made sense he'd be the one to crack.

No, if he'd changed their plans Liem would be much grouchier. And why wouldn't they have just let her go?

"The *Udancea* is a piece of junk," she grumped before she had fully run the thought through her logic filter. She regretted it immediately. Jaimy turned away, burned by the comment and Liem bristled.

"Better than nothing," he growled over his shoulder. Then added, with emphasis and a poor Cuttah accent, "*Ain't it?*"

Lark's eyes narrowed. Was that supposed to mean something to her? Sure, she hadn't ever had a home, per se. Not until Mags had given it to her, but they didn't know that. And maybe she had a bad habit of speaking like a pirate, but it wasn't her damn fault she'd grown up on the rust streets.

"Whatever," she muttered, fiddling idly with the zipper of her jacket. She knew she'd deserved that for wagging her tongue, but their unpredictable behavior had her in a foul mood.

They continued on in a tense silence for a few yards. The music and voices became louder and the smell of rich, spiced food and fire drifted toward her.

Wait, fire? What in the hell?

They turned and stepped through a large arched doorway into a dimly lit common room bigger than even the docking bay had been. Within, something that more closely resembled a gypsy camp than any cruiser bay confronted them. At the center, proving Lark's olfactory correct was a large, low brazier on which several hunks of spiced meat and sweet-smelling vegetables roasted, filling the huge room with choking smoke and mouth-watering scents. A crowd of people sat around the fire singing and chattering in a mix of Zingari and universal as they poked the cooking food.

Other clumps and groups of people were scattered about the rest of the room dyeing fabrics and fixing machines while children ran amongst them. When the Coin Brothers entered, a cry went up from various places across the hall. Lark stopped, taken aback by the sudden noise that she was just barely able to translate as Jaimy and Liem's names shouted at the same time.

Lark hung close to the boys as they walked through the camp. Gypsies kept to themselves even more so than most Fringers. Tight knit groups that were dangerously suspicious of outsiders, found sporadically in large cities doing their troupe thing—entertaining, selling wares, and pickpocketing for the most part.

The Coin Brothers had been more or less the extent of Lark's interaction with gypsy culture, aside from being screamed at by a gypsy woman during the Cuttah festival when she was a child. (In the woman's defense, Lark had been attempting to con her out of some sweet cakes without paying.)

As a rule, Liem and Jaimy did not make their cultural affiliation public knowledge and, as far as Lark was aware, she was the only one that knew. She had kept their secret, and they had never brought it up again until now.

An old woman surrounded by a gaggle of children accosted them, babbling in Zingari as she slapped each boy gently on the face and shoved wrapped cakes into their hands. The children swarmed around them, babbling questions in both languages. Jaimy handed the wrapped cake to Lark, and she stared at it. Was this the same kind she had been trying to steal all those years ago?

As the boys waded out of the crowd of children, Lark peered at the older woman. She couldn't tell if it was the same one from Cuttah, but she tucked the cake into her jacket and hurried after the Coin Brothers. It felt prejudiced to her, but Lark was keenly aware that she was unsafe among these travelers.

A tall man with dark hair caught their eyes from across the cook fire. He rose slowly and spread his arms, leaving the group gathered around the food to stand before them. "Well, the infamous Coin Brothers return to us," the acrimony in his voice was not terribly welcoming. He crossed his arms over his chest, his lips twisted in irritation. "Early for once..."

He was as tall as the boys, with eyes that may have been kind but had been masked steely as he surveyed the twins. Lark noted sprinkles of gray at his temples and in the days' worth of patchy beard growth on his chin. "Which one of you is in trouble this time?" Lark was still taking note of his facial features, trying to determine his age when she was surprised by the ice in his voice. Was this their—

"Dad," Jaimy spoke up, not really in response to what the man had said. Reaching back, he pressed a hand to Lark's shoulder and pulled her forward. "We need to talk."

The man took one look at Lark and then his eyes changed, disappointment morphing into austere judgment as they sternly passed to each of his sons before rolling toward the ceiling. He stepped around them toward the hallway through which they'd come.

Lark cocked her head and both Coin Brothers glanced at her before Liem clamped a hand around her arm and forced her to follow their father. Lark tried to root her feet to the floor simply out of a deep-seated need to be stubborn, but Liem tugged her hard and gave her a look that sliced right through her. She gave in and allowed herself to be pulled out into the hall.

Their father stayed a few paces ahead of them as he strode through the tangle of airy corridors. The main hallway that sprouted off the common room was lined with doors, most of which were standing open. Within, parents could be heard yelling at their children to get in bed and children could be heard whining for more time.

Lark's heart ached for her boys. She was used to the pain, but considering the bizarre trip she'd been on so far so, she had no earthly clue when she would be seeing them again.

After a brief ride in a loud lift, Liem and Jaimy's father turned into an apartment of his own, and the twins hustled Lark in before closing the door behind them. She tore her arm from Liem's grasp; greatly wanting to bang their damn heads together. Her patience was beginning to grow thin with this charade.

Crossing her arms, she stood between the Coin Brothers and regarded their father as he made his way to the other side of the round table that took up most of the space in the apartment's small main room.

Everything in here was old and used as if the whole place had been done in sepia tones. Even the draperies that softened the walls had dust settled in the folds of the cloth.

Three doors led off into a hallway, a canteen, and a smaller room that appeared to be meant as a study—if one could get in there passed several large storage cabinets. A weathered coat hung on the wall, the leather having gone stiff from neglect, and a shelf above it catered to a stack of dirty drinking glasses and a half-drunk bottle of liquor Lark didn't recognize. She felt very solid in her observation that a woman had not set foot in this place in eons.

"My name is Rem Lecorza, I apologize for being rude," he began, turning to look at Lark as he pulled a chair out with his foot. His voice was deep and soft but tired. "These two don't normally bring home pretty girls. So..." He tugged a small box of cigarillos from his pocket, removed one then threw the box across the room toward Liem. "What kind of trouble have these two idiots gotten you involved in?"

Lark plucked the cigarillo box from the air. In the following silence, she pulled one from the box before throwing it over her shoulder at Liem. She stuck the small brown cylinder between her lips and spoke around it, hands on her hips. "Name's Lark, by the way. Think you got it backward, pretty good at findin' my own trouble."

◻   ◻   ◻

He stared at her for a moment. When a smile cracked his weather-worn face she thought she saw something that made him look terribly familiar. Lark turned to Liem, holding a hand out. With an eye roll, he produced a lighter and held the flame against the tip of her cigarillo.

"Where did you two find a woman with such good taste?" their father asked with a chuckle as a thin line of smoke dribbled out of the end of the cigar. "And what did you bring her here for?"

Jaimy chose to answer, taking the box from his brother but holding onto it for the moment. He nudged Lark with his elbow and nodded to her. "Why don't you tell him where got your name?" his eyes flashed to her shoulder where he knew that tattoo was.

Lark cocked her head. Then shrugged off her confusion. "They called me Lark because of this tattoo..." She had told Liem and Jaimy that out of boredom and a need to make conversation, it felt odd to be repeating it on command now.

"Ah yeh?" Rem dragged on his cigar and let a mouthful of smoke float toward the ceiling. His disinterested eyes wandered to the neglected items that littered the table top. That was probably the most attention any of it had gotten in years.

Lark nodded and unzipped her jacket. Clearly, the Coin Brothers were trying to make a point, and she wasn't going to do anything but delay the inevitable by playing dumb. She pulled her jacket and shirt aside to reveal the bird tattoo on her shoulder. She looked back at the old man, expecting to see that they were still sharing in that state of bemusemen.

The moment he laid eyes on her shoulder, the cigarillo dropped from his mouth, falling to the metal table top and scattering a small fountain of hot ash across its surface. By sheer chance, nothing caught on fire. Lark's brow gathered, and she resettled her jacket over her shoulder, feeling suddenly sheepish now that she had shown it off so much. "Something wrong?" she asked him, tugging on the zipper.

"That's no lark," muttered the increasingly sullen man, picking up the discarded cigar and tossing it into an overflowing ashtray.

"Liem mentioned that," Lark crossed her arms. "Had no idea you gypsies were so into birds..."

"It's not that..." Rem answered her and then he sent a glance over her shoulders to his sons. Lark heard them shift behind her, but she couldn't pull her eyes away from their father. There was something in his eyes she had seen somewhere before and a sensation she couldn't place blossomed under his gaze.

Tearing her eyes from the older man, she turned slowly to look at Jaimy and Liem. Both of them had pulled the collars of their shirts over their shoulders to reveal twin tattoos of a bird flying in silhouette against a full moon. The same one Lark saw every day in the mirror.

Lark stared, having lost the ability to speak or move. Her mind raced. How had they gotten that same tattoo? And why didn't they say something before?

Seeking explanation, she looked at each of their faces. Jaimy looked like a lost puppy dog having finally found its way home. His eyes were large and poignant, his smile full of a long, deep sadness. Liem looked as determinedly sour as she had ever seen him. As if whatever it was that was making Jaimy so emotional was poisoning him slowly.

Neither of them offered her any answers, so she turned to their father who pulled his shirt aside as well.

◻   ◻   ◻

It wasn't a lark. It was a moonshadow. A night owl from the Zingari homeworld. The Lecorza family tattooed the image of the bird on their children at birth—an old gypsy tradition.

The locket Rem had given her sat open on the table before her next to a glass of untouched Zingari hephywine, the two digital images glowing softly in the smoky room. The top picture was a youthful Rem and a pretty blond woman. The picture on the bottom was of three young children; two boys about Gun's age and a young girl of maybe four years old. The boys were identical, and both the blond woman and the little girl had bright turquoise eyes.

Lark hadn't had a drop of alcohol since before Izlatana, but she needed the spicy, fruity liquor to loosen up the tight feeling in her chest and to lubricate her brain, which seemed to have gone into a hard shut down.

Liem and Jaimy flanked her now, sitting to her left and right respectively, while Rem sat at the other side of the table. Her stomach was still writhing with nerves even after falling weak-kneed into her seat. The men that shared this table with her, they were her family. She lifted the glass and took a long, slow sip.

And still, no words would come. She had opened her mouth a few times but had just closed it again wordlessly. For a long moment, a distant banging had resounded in Lark's ears; her emotional walls trying repeatedly to slam shut against the truth before her. Fear began to claw into her guts as she realized those walls were failing.

The older man had wept as he told the story of how his wife had insisted on taking their daughter with the troupe to Cuttah alone. How the troupe had been raided by thieves. How neither of them had ever come home.

He dropped his head into his hands and spoke into the table, pushing through what Lark hoped was the end of this painful story. "We searched the city high and low, we found nothing. So..." He swallowed hard. "We started looking everywhere else. For ten years I dragged these two around the galaxy looking for my wife and daughter. Took bounties for money but in time... I had to let go."

"Hunting bounties is all we've ever known," Jaimy interjected. "It was hard for us to come back here and stay when Dad was done, so Liem and I went back to it. We met you a couple of months after that."

Lark stirred, sensing that it was her turn to talk. She took a deep breath, downed the rest of the liquor and then chewed on her lip. She looked at Liem who was still barely there, and she envied his distance from the conversation. She splayed her fingers out on the dusty table and stared at her red fingertips. It was the only logical place she could thing to start.

"Grew up on the rust streets... Until Raxx picked me up. Taught me how to be a plugger." She swallowed, watching as Liem refilled her glass. "When I met you, I was just starting out on my own. My first independent mark was the one I stole from you two," a smile forced its way onto her face—either from the sudden fondness of the memory or the sudden shot of booze hitting her system. Elbowing Liem, she turned that smile up to show all her teeth, "You remember that, don't ya?"

Liem looked at her out of the corner of his eye then finally came to life with a dark chuckle, "How could I forget?" Looking at his father, he jabbed a thumb in Lark's direction. "Trying to bring the guy in alive and she bounds in, stabs him in the neck, snags his DNAsig, and has enough time to kiss starry-eyes over there on the cheek before we can even register what happened."

Jaimy let out the breath of a chuckle, but the mirth didn't have the strength to survive in the dark silence that followed.

Rem smiled ruefully, his hands winding around his glass. "Twenty years of your life, we missed. And this... Raxx. He raised you?"

Lark held up a hand, stopping that train of thought before it left the station. "Raxx never raised a damn thing that didn't raise his bank account in return. Pulled me off the street when I didn't want to go, forced me into killing in his name whether I liked it or not. And when I tried to get out on my own..."

Her throat closed on the rest of her words, and Lark dropped her eyes to her empty glass. Had she taken that second shot? Chewing her lip, she pushed the glass away when Liem offered to refill it again. She was afraid she had opened her heart too easily, revealed to them things she had said to no one but Mags. These men were her blood, but she hardly knew them.

Jaimy leaned toward her. The few shots he'd had weren't even close to getting him tipsy. "You can tell us. We've been looking for you all our lives. You were right in front of us and we never even asked you where you grew up."

Lark never thought she would be ungrateful for Jaimy's personal skills. His smile, his warm and gentle nature made it too easy to feel comfortable, to want to love them all at once. To give them what they wanted—which was her— even if they didn't have an inkling of what they were signing up for; every little lie and painful secret. Liem, she could have gone on and on with and never told him a damn thing. She would be safely distant. And so, would he.

As a personal rule Lark did not dwell on the past. In fact, she had neatly sheathed the darkness and pain behind a thick black curtain years ago. Drawing back that curtain now, the memories got darker the farther she peered into the long-forgotten past. She did not wish to make them feel any guilt for her upbringing. It hadn't been their choice she was alone. The people she held responsible for the things that had happened to her got theirs in the end. Mostly...

"The rust streets?" Liem prompted when she didn't offer any details right away. Lark glanced at him, and she saw it growing already, the blame he was so ready to carry. Rem shot him a censuring glare.

"No, it's alright," Lark spoke up. "Rust streets really weren't that bad..." She realized she was now viewing her earliest memories through the lens of everything that had come after them. The rust streets had been terrible. Nights full of fear and danger; days empty with hunger and hiding. She decided to spare them those gritty details; it was bad enough they knew what they did. "Got by," she added. "Bet the only reason I survived is... whatever you taught me before I got there."

Jaimy leaned forward. "You don't remember anything before that?"

Lark shook her head, "Just the rust streets... then Raxx." She paused and collected herself, finding the strength to push forward. "I wasn't the only one. He collected a bunch of little girls from the rust streets, thought we made the best pluggers because we were quick and quiet. Trained us and..."

Lark tried to swallow but found her throat had suddenly gone dry. It had been so long since she had given Raxx the luxury of her memory, she thought she would be distanced enough not to be affected by it.

Talking about it now, actively walking back behind that curtain, it was like he'd been right behind her the whole time. She could feel his grip on her arm, yanking her back into a nightmare she thought was long over. "Well," she croaked. "If there was any fear or weakness left in any of us... he got rid of it."

Maybe it was the hollowness in her voice, but they seemed to see right through her words to the truth beneath them. Raxx had successfully beaten what would become a trademark fearlessness into her.

However, try as he might, he could never seem to destroy her self-worth. She tipped her chin up and looked directly at her new father and brothers. Lark was not ashamed of how she had gotten away from Raxx.

"I was the best of those girls. Tougher and smarter. Brought in more money than anyone else, but I gave Raxx back as good as I got so he kept me on a short leash. Wanted out, so I started taking independent jobs and got my own accounts set up. When Raxx found out he..." Lark's tongue sought the false tooth at the side of her mouth. "Sold me to a place called Izlatana."

"Sold you?" Rem repeated.

Lark gave a slow nod. "Resort up at the edge of the Brink by Tavis Minor. Wasn't the worst place. Guess picking peaches and serving rich people ain't as bad as plugging, but I still wasn't free. And Izla didn't turn out much better than Raxx."

It was a toss-up, in truth. Izla lacked the power of Raxx's fists, but she made up for it with patent cruelty and an electrified whip. The ruthless business woman that owned Izlatana—and Lark, for a short time—had left her mark on the skin of Lark's back. She tugged her jacket tighter.

So, here's where the rub came in. Izalatana had been an awful place, but Lark knew the next part of the story was the first and one of the brightest moments in her life. She had met a lone darkspawn as she'd been running through the orchard in the early morning. How beautiful his smile had been in the golden sunlight, and how her life had been tremendously altered from that moment forward.

And she couldn't tell them any of it.

Knowing things about Kyro, knowing any of Mags' secrets, that would be more dangerous than the bounty on Jaimy's head. It was painful knowing that she could share with them the shit-strewn blackness she had hidden behind that curtain but not the glorious happiness of the life she had built despite all of it.

"How did you get out?" Jaimy asked.

"I..." Lark stuttered, took a breath, and thought through the truth for a moment.

"After Izla and I got into it for the last time," a meticulous glossing over of the actual occurrence. "I—" and by 'I' she very much meant 'we' "—staged a riot and broke myself out."

Along with the handful of darkspawn Izla had collected over the years.

"I went back to plugging, independent this time." With the help of Crotis' manipulative disdain and a healthy dose of heartbreak.

"Not much story after that." That lie left the sour taste of guilt in her mouth; it wasn't even half the story.

Maybe they could tell she was lying; maybe her eyes revealed more experiences and victories than she had been able to tell them. Lark found herself uncomfortably close to tears. Her brain and her heart were just too full.

The drink was making her foggy and unfamiliarity with all this emotion was becoming hard to deal with. Determined not to crack now, she yanked the curtain closed and turned away.

That was the last time she would give those memories any light.

24

THE GOVERNOR'S compound on Kar'ju was expansive. Built to Crotis' specifications and initially constructed to give the governor a place to call home far from the hellish world of the d'javu he'd been sent by the Consul to oversee, this was where Magnimus had spent his childhood. Over the years, as Mags had grown, Crotis had acquired a staff of darkspawn that served his every need. Mags could vaguely remember being hopeful for their companionship and had found himself disappointed when there was none to be found.

It became remarkably clear to him, even when he was still young, that these d'javu had been provided by Nyhman. They had been broken and trained for the purpose of remaining obedient and loyal. To Crotis' darkling staff, the governor's word was gospel.

Since the rebellion, Crotis had recruited for his compound d'javu that had never been touched by Nyhman. Free thinking, free acting darklings that were just as fanatically loyal to the governor as the augmented ones had been. The only difference had been that they'd had the choice. Mags trusted them about the same. Crotis had, after all, instilled in him a healthy distrust of those beneath him.

"No one, Magnimus," the old man had told him. "No one is above usurping you. Be especially mindful of those who serve your closest allies, for you will always have something they desire but cannot attain."

It was a battle in and of itself to find common ground with the d'javu on Kyro that he was attempting to lead, but at least he understood their incivility. The Kar'ju darkspawn were another breed altogether. Like Crotis, their motives were not entirely obvious to him.

The halls of the governor's palace were well lit, unlike Katarak Keep, and Mags saw every detail of the architecture, designed with intents that he could never fathom. He approached the door to Crotis' personal living quarters and was lifting his hand to knock when the door opened. A young d'javu he did not recognize, thin and plum-skinned and apparently mute, was in the process of slipping out the door with a furtive expression on his face. He was in such a hurry, he nearly ran straight into Magnimus and pulled up short to avoid the collision. The d'javu's gaze rose to the face of his leader, and fear colored his eyes, shame tightening his expression.

Mags raised his brow, but the darkling executed a deep and cursory bow before scurrying away as quickly as he could. Another thing that bothered him about these Kar'ju darkspawn. Those from Kyro bent their backs to no one, but Crotis insisted upon it.

Mags grimaced as he stood in front of the open doorway, reticent to enter his mentor's chambers with the knowledge of what had gone on in there. Before he could flee, the door swung open the rest of the way, and Crotis stood before him tying a silk robe. He greeted the darkling leader with a welcoming smile.

"Oh, don't give me that look," the old man said, though he could not stop the smile from crossing his lips. "We stopped hiding things from each other years ago, old friend."

"I wish you would hide this one thing from me," Magnimus answered, the withering look did not fade from his features. For a long time, he had simply pretended the rumors were not true. Mags had particularly chosen to ignore those more specific and recent murmurings regarding why this man would take a darkling child and raise him in secret.

The truth, of course, was unavoidable. Magnimus tried his hardest to erase from his memory the night when Crotis had slid into his bed. When it came back to him, unbidden, he was overcome with the sensation of the frigid, skeletal hands that woke him. He could feel them snaking across his midsection even now.

It was the only time he had ever attacked his mentor. It was the night they had become equals. Crotis had been forced to realize that Magnimus, though still young, was no longer a boy and certainly not prey for his manipulations. Mags had learned that Crotis needed him.

Mags shared this memory with no one. He shuddered to think that Lark might view him differently if she knew; what she would have to say of his working relationship with Crotis. The girl was as possessive and wildly protective of Mags as he was of her. It was a volatile situation that Magnimus felt easier to avoid entirely. Even if it meant keeping something from his wife.

Not two months after that fateful night, Mags had been on his way to Izlatana. He had thought then that it was punishment for rebuffing Crotis' advances. Now, he wondered if Crotis regretted sending him there, considering he had brought Lark home from that adventure.

Crotis, his good humor faded now, left the door open and waved him in, "And I wish that you would leave that girl in some corner of the galaxy where she can do no more harm."

"That *girl* is my wife," Magnimus countered, stepping over the threshold and closing the door behind him. The tension had been settled slightly by the familiarity of this candor, this argument they'd had a dozen times. "And she has been of great use to you."

Crotis' apartments were lush and comfortable. The furniture was of a vintage design from an era of civspace history apparently long past—dark woods and curving metals. The walls and floors were a polished burgundy marble while the rugs and fabrics were soft and white. The lights had been dimmed, but Crotis brightened them now. He took an additional glass from a shelf and filled it with a dark red wine, handing it to Magnimus before refreshing his own. Mags ignored the third glass, sitting on the low table with only the dregs of wine left behind. It should not have bothered him, but it did.

Speaking of Lark had worry gnawing at the back of his mind. She had been gone far too long this time. Even the boys, accustomed to having their mother leave for long periods, were beginning to ask about her frequently. Sometimes Mags found himself suspicious that Crotis sent her away on purpose. It certainly would not be below him to organize things that way.

"My people hardly believe me when I tell them you are on their side," Mags said, gesturing toward the door and indicating the darkspawn in general. "How do you think it looks when you—"

"Magnimus, I was not taking advantage of a weak creature," Crotis turned and cast him a glance of reprehension. "I invited him here. I offered him wine and food and company. He gave me nothing unwillingly."

Mags scowled and waved his hand, closing his eyes to keep out the images of Crotis' evening with the young darkling. He could only assume his revulsion was natural to anyone with a parent who was dating. Mags didn't want to talk about this. Ever again, if possible. He shouldn't even have said anything, knowing that Crotis would not censor himself.

Crotis chuckled and settled into one of the over-sized chairs. "How are the boys?" he asked conversationally, crossing a leg and easing back into the upholstery with his wine steadied against his knee. "Growing as always?"

"Sever is more like his mother each day," Magnimus sat, but he was much less at ease. This was in no way a criticism of Crotis' hospitality, Mags found himself most often ill at ease these days.

"And Gunner?"

Magnimus eyed him cautiously. He had been honest with Crotis regarding his feelings toward Lark's first son, hoping to gain some paternal advice on how to overcome his disdain and be what it was Lark wanted him to be.

Crotis had been unhelpful, merely taking pleasure in the fact that Lark had come with more baggage than Mags had anticipated. The more trouble in paradise, the happier Crotis seemed to be. Magnimus hesitated to betray information about his marriage these days, giving Crotis ammunition when it came to Lark always seemed to come back to bite him.

He forced himself to think of the boy and make some assessment of his growth. "He has energy and determination," he responded placidly.

"You were much the same at his age."

He couldn't help the glower that formed on his face and, to his dismay, Crotis was greatly cheered by it. Lark said that often, how much Gunner was taking after him.

Despite his promise that Gunner's existence changed nothing, Mags could not stand to have the child compared to him. The boy was not his blood, he belonged to some other man that had hurt Lark. The more Gunner's temperament resembled his own, the more Mags was reminded that it was his own failures that had done Lark true harm. With all his power, he could have stopped it; he should have been there to stop it. The manifestation of his guilt into his inability to feel anything for Gunner did nothing but further her pain.

Mags closed his eyes for a moment to clear his mind, pressing a hand over them. Without opening his eyes, he took a heavy breath. "The prisoners…"

"Yes," Crotis lifted a glass to his lips and settled forward in the armchair, his tone immediately changing from subtle mockery to conspiratorial business. Magnimus did not move, but he dropped his hand away and opened his eyes. "They arrived safely on Lystor but no attempt at communication has been made. Perhaps they think we are satisfied and content with being left alone. They will not expect invasion."

"They will not be prepared," an unexpected grin found its way onto Mags' face. The shadow of the former conversation dissipated when his hunger for battle, and for revenge, returned. "The galaxy will be ours."

"Yours, my friend," Crotis raised his glass and smiled in a way that reminded Mags of himself. "The galaxy will be yours."

Lark realized she had been lying awake for some time. Liem had let her borrow a shirt, which was about three times too large for her, and his bed that was beginning to smell familiar. Beside the bed, her clothes had appeared clean in a neat pile, her gauntlet and her pistols sat on top gleaming in the dull light. Her jacket hung on a hook beside the door.

Liem's bedroom on the *Udancea* lay in stark contrast to the bunk on their ship. Here, in place of piles of research were remnants of a childhood abandoned. Tokens from around the Fringe took up spaces on shelves, damaged posters from obscure musical acts Lark had almost forgotten about still clung to the walls. The space was clean, underused even. Whenever Liem and Jaimy had decided to go off on their own, Liem had left his past here. Lark found herself humming one of those old catchy tunes as she stood up to dress.

Her knives were hidden under her clothes. Instead of carrying the pistols—a more obvious display of her paranoia—she placed each of her knives in their hidden places of her jacket and slid it over her shoulders. It was doubtful she would need to use them, but she was alive right now because she was always armed.

Everyone was still asleep from what she could tell by the tender silence of the apartment. She found Liem lying on a bench in the living room, his long legs draped over the end of the bench but sleeping soundly. Their glasses and extinguished cigarillos still sat unattended on the table.

Lark gathered the glasses together in the middle of the table and lifted that locket from where it lay in front of the chair she'd occupied the night before. She tucked it into her pocket for safe keeping and later reflection, making a mental note not to forget to give it back to Rem before they left.

Something stirred in her, a feeling as if she'd forgotten something. Then she cursed aloud before she remembered she was trying not to wake Liem. He sat up and stared at her, bleary-eyed. "What happened?" he called without opening his eyes.

"Hey, Liem," she answered softly. "Want to go back in your bed?"

He shook his head and lay back down, rolling over to face the wall. Lark pulled the undersized blanket up over his shoulders then headed out into the corridor. After making note of the markings on the door so she could find her way back, Lark retraced their steps from the night before, heading for the docking bay where she was hoping she could find some privacy.

Luckily at this hour, there was no one here. Lark could not believe she'd forgotten to call Mali to let her know she wasn't dead or sold to the Protectors. Mali had been the last person she'd spoken to, the only person that knew beyond a shadow of a doubt that she'd been taken by the Coin Brothers. Poor girl was probably losing her head.

At least Mali couldn't call Mags either. Otherwise, the war was about to come to the Fringe. Mags knew how much money the Protectors were offering for her alive. He also didn't have an even head when it came to things like this.

Mali sounded as if she'd just woken up when she accepted the call, her voice made thin by distance. Lark switched on the recorder to send her initial message. "Hey Mal, it's Lark. Listen, wanted to let you know I'm safe. Coin Brothers did pick me up but then we figured out that... well, sounds like I'm the long-lost Coin Sister."

After confirming she wished to send the recording, Lark was forced to sit and wait while it transmitted. Sending live voice communications between planets could be tricky the further apart you went. This connection was dodgy but surprisingly well established.

She waited several minutes in which she scanned the docking bay and examined details that she didn't commit to memory. When her comm chimed at the incoming response, she indicated it should play.

[What?]

Lark's lips pressed together into a line. Well, what response did she expect?

"Just as surprised as I was. Did a quick DNA compare and it's true." She paused, shaking her head. "Don't really know what else to say about it, never thought I'd ever find out where I came from."

Another several minutes passed, more than it would take if she had immediately responded. Lark found herself staring at the comm light and chewing her lip. She had been hoping for some advice from Mali on how she should feel. Even if Mali's emotional compass always seemed to point to the negative it at least allowed Lark to gauge where she should be.

Her finger hovered over the record button, just about to send another message prompting Mali to reply when the chime came back, and Lark played Mali's response.

[When you disappeared, and I couldn't track you, I sent a message to Kyro on a drone telling Mags you'd been picked up by the Coin Brothers. That was almost a week ago, Lark.]

The message ended there, even if the tone in Mali's voice made it sound like she wanted to say more. Lark was already running back toward the apartment. She sent some sort of message back to Mali, but she was only half paying attention and would not be able to recall exactly what she had said.

If she didn't make it to Kyro, and soon, then the *Udancea* was going to have a lot more to worry about than pirates.

Lark pressed her hands to the outside of the coffee cup. The warmth of the cup was as steadying as the liquid within—which was much better than what they'd served her back on Cuttah. She watched the three men around her, their faces blank at first, then thoughtful.

The name sounded familiar to them and they were trying to figure out from where. The darkling rebellion had rocked the galaxy, but the Fringe had hardly winced at the tumult they had caused. The darkspawn were shadows among shadows as far as the Fringers were concerned. Just another threat to be accepted as the dangers of living in anarchy.

Liem pulled it together first, which didn't surprise Lark. He worked so hard, kept himself well informed as to the comings and goings of bounties and events in the Fringe and civspace. That stack of papers on the desk in his bunk room was evidence to that, but Lark knew now that he had been looking for her.

"Let me get this straight," he began, holding up a hand as if to slow her down even though she hadn't been speaking. "You're married…" He paused, digesting that for a moment. Lark guessed it was sort of a shock, considering he'd never heard mention of this in all the time they'd spent together. "To the guy that blew up Salva?"

Lark nodded, a smile coming to her lips unbidden, "Sure am."

She wasn't sure what type of reaction to expect. Not many humans had ever even interacted with a darkling, let alone befriended, married, and built a life with one of them. For the moment, they only seemed surprised and maybe a little confused. She could only hope they wouldn't judge her for such a strange affiliation—or Mags for what he was going to do when he found out she'd been taken by bounty hunters.

Rem had a smile on his face, tempered with a bit of surprise. "I am glad to hear that you have a good man, Lark… even if I never expected to hear that he is, well, not a man."

Lark looked at him and did everything she could to form an unpatronizing smile. "He is just like anyone else. All the d'javu are. May look different and their culture may be strange, but they've been outcast from everyone else for so long you can hardly blame them."

"Some people say that about us," Jaimy chimed in.

Lark waved a hand toward him, "Exactly. In fact, Liem reminds me so damn much of Mags sometimes, you'd think they were the twins."

Liem scowled and that only made Lark laugh. Jaimy gave a chuckle, "Bet they don't look as much alike as we do."

"No," Lark allowed. "But they have the same sunny disposition."

"I resent that," Liem growled.

"You should," Lark gave the breath of a laugh, but then reality returned. "Problem is that Mags... can be a little over protective."

Liem settled his arms across his chest, raising his chin in approval of this description. "Don't see how that's a problem."

Lark cut him a glance across the table. She didn't want to blow their cover with their father, but none of them were aware of the urgency of this matter. "That's because you don't realize that you tipped Mali Hardstrom off when you were looking for me. Called me right before we met up because she thought the Coin Brothers were turning me in for my Alliance bounty. Didn't think to call her until just now to tell her that everything was fine, and she already sent a message through the Devil's Tongue to Mags."

Jaimy's brow pulled together, and then his eyes went hard to his brother. Liem gave an aggravated shrug. "Didn't know she had those connections at the time."

Lark watched the way he glowered and wondered what they'd done to Mali. It was a dark question with, more than likely, a dark answer. Mali was alive, at least, and fully capable of handling it on her own. Later.

"What do we need to do?" Jaimy asked after shaking his head at Liem.

"Need to get to Kyro before he can leave. Before he gets that fucking message, if possible. Then explain to him what happened. If we don't, can't imagine what he'll do…" she turned her worried gaze on Rem and saw the disappointment there. Leaving, so soon. Lark reached out to take his hand. "I'm sorry…"

Rem looked up at her. "Don't apologize. You had a full life before we came tromping through it. Boys, take your sister home."

Both twins started to rise, but Lark didn't move. She didn't want to let go of her father's hand. "Can I tell you one more thing?"

Rem sat forward, covering both of their hands with his other one. "Anything, little one."

Liem and Jaimy had paused just after standing and they towered over the table now. Lark looked into her father's eyes, knowing this would give him joy made her happy. "We have two sons, Gunner and Sever. And when all this blows over, first chance I get, I'll bring them out here to meet you. Gun will love it here."

Rem pulled her hand toward him and pressed a kiss onto her knuckles. "Child, you have made me a very, very happy old man in the last few hours."

Lark smiled solemnly, "Wish I didn't have to go…"

"We got you into this mess, Emmy, it should be us who gets you out. I'll be here when you are ready."

"Emmy?" Lark froze, suddenly reminded of the fact that he was still a stranger.

After allowing a sigh, Rem shook his head. "Emelia. That's the name we gave you." Lark swallowed, unsure how to respond. He squeezed her hands, "Lark fits you better."

Rem released her and walked them to the docking bay where Liem and Jaimy disappeared into their craft. Lark paused to hug her father once more. She almost forgot, but she turned back to pull the locket out of her jacket and hold it out to him.

"Keep it," Rem told her. "I have my memories and now I have all my children back. Not a slave to the past anymore."

Lark clutched the locket in her hand and kissed his cheek. She cast him one last smile before heading up the ramp, where the boys were arguing over who got to pilot.

"Will you two knock it off!" she shouted as she waved at Rem and brought the boarding ramp up.

25

"Ain't a good sign, is it?" Liem commented, nudging the brutalized, charred wreckage of what had once been a drone with the toe of his boot. The shattered robot lay on the tightly woven blue carpet just inside the large security door of an apartment within Katarak Keep. The apartment was warm and welcoming, the lights dimmed due to the lateness of the hour, but it was bright in comparison to the inky darkness of the keep behind them.

The thing let out a reverberating electronic noise then Mali's cool voice filled the small foyer, bouncing off the walls of the two corridors that branched off before them. [Mags, it's Mali. I've got some bad news. Lark was picked up by the Coin Brothers, some of the best bounty hunters in the Fringe.]

"Hey, that's nice," Liem crossed his arms and beamed. Lark cast him a frown then looked back down as Mali's monolog continued.

[They're going to turn her into the ACP for the bounty. I'm tracking them, but I lost the trail on Cuttah. Let me know when you're in the Fringe.]

The message went dead, and Lark chewed her lip in silence. She could only hope that the warmth radiating from the damaged robot meant they'd gotten here before

Mags had left. He wouldn't call Mali when he got to the Fringe. When he failed to locate her on Cuttah, Lark didn't want to think about what he would do.

"Ya know what, I'm actually impressed," Jaimy said, just as Lark was getting ready to head down the hallway toward the bedrooms. "She put up a fight and kept on swinging... not bad." She looked up at him and found that he was grinning.

Lark gave the breath of a scoff. "Ain't your type, Jaimy."

Jaimy looked at her, his elegant brow drawing together over his eyes. Lark thought she might have hurt his feelings. When he asked her rigidly, "What's her type then?" She didn't really know what to say. She gazed at him tentatively while she thought about it. Coming from her, she was sure it sounded plainly as if she was saying her friend was too good for her brother.

Liem saved them by snapping gruffly, "C'mon, bro, we both know what her type ain't."

Jaimy's eyes hardened when they turned to his brother. "Shut up, Liem." That was awful defensive. Lark felt a stab of guilt for embarrassing him. "You're the one who beat her friend senseless then shot him."

"Yeh and you pistol whipped her then left her lying on the fucking sidewalk," Liem countered with a mirthless chuckle. "That's your new pick up line, I say it's gonna be a dud."

"*Alright!*" Lark hissed over them. "Could you two quit fucking arguing for half a fucking second? And keep your fucking voices down, I have—"

"Mama?"

Lark whirled at the sound of the child's voice. Gunner stood in the middle of the corridor clutching a worn stuffed brado cub to his chest. His eyes were alight with

207

uncertainty in the dimness of the hall, shifting between his mother and the two strangers.

"Gun, baby, what are you doing up?" Her hand extended toward the panel next to the door to raise the lights. Just before her fingers brushed the panel she smelled it, brimstone and sulfur. As the lights rose a shadow remained.

"Gunner, get back," Mags growled as he dissolved from the darkness, pressing a hand briefly against the child's shoulder and giving him a gentle push backward.

"Mags, no!" Lark cried out, but it was as if he hadn't even heard. He swept passed her and blasted the Coin Brothers backward with a wave of dark power.

Liem flew into the stairs and grunted. The pistol, which had been halfway out of its holster, clattered down the steps and misfired, a catalyst pulse fizzled into the wall above Gunner's head. Lark dove for her son but all she had to protect him from was a spray of plaster.

Mags followed Jaimy and slammed his back up against the wall with enough force to knock the wind out of him and buckle his knees. A dark clawed hand slid around Jaimy's throat and squeezed. The strange gleaming light of Mag's ember eyes illuminated the features of Jaimy's face, etching deep caverns of shadow in his brow as he grimaced in discomfort and fear.

"Mags, stop it!" Lark started toward him, but Gunner held fast to her hand. She turned to reassure her son as Liem rolled and slid down a few steps, grabbing his pistol from where it had fallen and swinging it up to aim at the back of the darkling.

"Let 'im go, you bastard!"

"*Liem*," Lark hissed.

Ignoring her with the skill of a man who'd had a sister much longer than he had, Liem repeated himself with a gravelly shout. "Let 'im go or I swear I'll shoot—" He paused and glanced at Lark, "*At* you!"

Mags turned and curled his lip, flashing sharp fangs and holding on to Jaimy's throat. Liem answered in kind, though his teeth were far less intimidating, and raised his pistol.

Lark let out a frustrated growl. "For fuck's sake, Mags—" she was interrupted by a howling noise from the end of the hallway. Liem glanced at her, confused, and Lark gestured toward him. "Will ya just fucking show him?"

Liem lowered his gun with some hesitation before he pulled his shirt and jacket aside to show the Lecorza tattoo on his shoulder. "They're my brothers," Lark explained. Mags' eyes shot to the tattoo and then to Lark, his brow furrowing over eyes bright with bloodlust. Her voice was calm when she gave the final plea, "Let him go, Mags."

Clearly, he'd forgotten he still had Jaimy's throat crunched between his fingers. He released his grasp and watched indifferently as the man crumpled. Liem shoved him out of the way to get to his twin.

Lark moved toward her brothers, casting Mags a withering look before placing a hand on Liem's shoulder. "You guys alright?"

Jaimy nodded, "Yeh. Easy mistake to make…"

"He always this fucking happy to see you?" Liem grumped, heedless of the fact that Mags was only steps away.

Lark didn't take the bait. Gunner pressed himself into her leg and she touched his hair, watching Jaimy rise and reassure her that he was uninjured. The howling had quieted and a quick look over her shoulder confirmed Mags had responded to the call of their son. Jaimy said softly, "I'm sorry we woke up your kids…"

"That's alright," Lark turned to the young boy at her side and slid a hand under his chin. "Gunner, these are your uncles."

"Uncles?" he repeated, his green-blue eyes studying the older men with suspicion.

"Yeh, they're my brothers. That makes you their nephew." She crouched beside him and pointed, "Jaimy. Liem."

"Nice to meet you, Gunner," Jaimy reached out to shake the small hand.

Lark looked up to find Liem glaring down the hallway and sighed. "It's late, Gun. Gotta go back to bed."

Gunner's eyes were curious as he peered at the two older men. Lark realized that the only other human male he'd been exposed to was Crotis. She repressed a shudder. "Uncle Liem and Uncle Jaimy will be here when you wake up."

"Really?" she could not remember a time when he'd had a reason for such disbelief.

"Promise. But we all need rest. Had a big day."

"Okay," Gunner gave in and said good night, trying to cover a yawn as he padded back down the hallway.

"The living room is that way," Lark pointed up the stairs that Liem had been sprawled upon a few moments before. She dimmed the hallway lights again, "I'll be right there."

Jaimy gave her a nod and Liem a shove up the stairs. After tucking Gunner back into his bed and dodging a dozen questions before he let her leave, she entered the room across the hall. Mags stood over the crib with Sever clinging to his arm. When the toddler saw his mother, he began squealing until she pulled him into her arms. While she rocked him, her eyes rose to Mags. "Sorry…"

He shook his head, eyes glowing with indignation. His voice was a rumble of stones in this throat. "I cannot believe you brought them here. What were you thinking?"

Taken off guard by the reproach, she didn't reply for a moment. She half expected him to break into a smile and admit he was joking, but Mags didn't work that way. "I-I was thinking I'd bring my brothers to meet my husband and my sons. Thought you'd be happy for me…"

"They were going to take you to the Alliance for your bounty. I was prepared to invade Lystor." He heaved out a hot breath of fury and left the bedroom.

Lark settled Sever into his bed and followed, closing the door behind her. Mags stood seething outside their bedroom door. His eyes were orange pools of bright hostility in the shadows, "Do you have any idea what I would have done…"

Lark did have some idea. Back on Izlatana, during the riot he had started to get her and the other darklings out of that place, he had taken out his frustrations by murdering guards with some of the most uncalled-for brutality she had ever seen. It was all she could do back then to keep him from tearing the place apart and destroying every last one of them. For her.

It could have been touching. If it wasn't so damn dangerous.

"I know," she soothed him. "It was a mistake; the whole thing was a fucking mess…"

"You should have come alone."

Lark pressed her lips together. "Little fucking late for this, Mags. It's done." She tried to change the subject, to eek some sort of gratification out of him. "I met my father, Mags. Look…" she tugged the locket up out of her jacket to show him. It had a cool blue glow to it, competing with Mags' eyes.

The look on his face was painful. His brows drew together, and he looked away from the picture. He said nothing.

Lark closed the locket and shoved it inside her jacket. "Are you *jealous*?"

"Of course, I am," his eyes were hot.

Well, at least he was honest. Lark reached out to touch his arm. "Mags…"

"It won't be safe for your friends here much longer. They should go."

"Brothers," Lark corrected, letting his arm go when he pulled away. "And just because you send them away from Kyro doesn't mean they're gone for good." She moved closer, lowering her voice. Her throat burned tightly with a dozen emotions, all of them caustic. "I have shared you with Crotis since we left Izlatana. Think about that for a bit and get back to me."

She turned away and headed down the hall, taking a deep breath when she heard the bedroom door close. She felt suddenly tired but not sleepy. She pressed her palms into her eyes as she turned the corner where she ran into Liem, leaning against the wall and eavesdropping. She glowered up at him, "Hear anything interesting?"

"Nice guy," Liem dropped blankly.

Lark narrowed her eyes at him. "Can we do this later?"

"Tomorrow?"

"Wha— sure…" Lark shook her head to clear away the frustration. "Whatever. Just… not now." She stepped around him and climbed the stairs. "You sure you're okay?" she asked Jaimy who sat on the couch.

"I'm fine," he gestured at her with his flask. "Can't tell you how many times I've been assaulted for showing up to a party with someone else's wife."

Lark couldn't help but laugh at that. She lifted one of the cushions to pull out some blankets and pillows. A dark cloud settled onto the opposite couch, and Lark threw a blanket over Liem's head. She handed Jaimy the controls for the electronics then headed back to her bedroom.

"You can't stay for breakfast?" Lark asked Mags as she joined him in the foyer. He was fully geared in his darklite jerkin and hide duster, but she pushed his hood back to get a good look at his face.

He had held her all night, relishing in every inch of skin against his. The thought of losing her to the Alliance had been one of the greatest fears he had experienced. Eclipsed only by the fear he'd felt on the day of Sever's birth when he had come very near to losing them both at once.

Then, he had been absorbed by the urgency of the task and had cut Lark open himself to relieve her body of the child that was going to kill her. Sever had survived his violent birth, though Mags would not have been so lucky had Lark had the strength to take out her anger on him. He would have sacrificed their child to save her life.

Sever sat on her hip now and Mags rubbed the small gray dome of his head, felt the formation of horns on his skull. A well of pride grew in his chest when he looked at his son. He knew there was no other woman who could have given this child to him.

"No," he answered Lark's question quietly. He could have stayed. Hurshek would wait for him. Lark knew the truth of it and, although he could see the sadness in her face she must have understood because she didn't push it. His hand rose to cup her cheek, ignoring the fading purple-green mesh bruise on her cheek bone and looking into her eyes. "When I come back, there's something we need to discuss."

"Why can't you tell me now?"

He glanced up the stairs toward the silent living room. It wasn't the only reason, but it was a good one. Stroking the soft skin of her face with his thumb, he pressed his forehead to hers and wrapped his other arm around the pair of them. Lark sighed, "Just come back to me, okay? I love you."

He kissed her, gave Sever's head one last gentle touch before he slipped out the door and secured it behind him.

Lark climbed the stairs and cocked her head at the scene in the living room. Jaimy was still sleeping but Liem sat up with Gunner next to him, the pair of them eating out of oversized bowls. Projected against the window was a children's program, the volume turned low. "Morning," she announced herself.

"Mornin'," Liem's eyes were wide when he turned. He pointed at the bowl and the brightly colored cereal within then to Gunner. "This okay? He said it was okay." Gunner passed him an indignant glance for telling on him.

"It's fine," Lark chuckled, letting Sever down on the couch beside Gunner.

Liem looked down at the toddler and his expression faltered with surprise. He looked from one child to the other before he could recover, then he said too loudly, "Who's this guy?" Jaimy stirred at his brother's voice and sat up, bleary eyed.

"Sever," Lark answered, grinning as the ash gray toddler crawled over his brother to investigate his uncle. "Say 'hi', Sev."

"Hi," he mimed to no one in particular.

"Coffee?" Lark was moving into the kitchen.

"Sweet god, yes," Jaimy smoothed his hair and yawned, watching Sever climb up onto Liem's shoulder and perch there.

They drank coffee and ate breakfast in the living room and for a moment Lark was able to forget about Mags and his cryptic promise. "More coffee?" she asked Jaimy as she lifted his cup from the table.

"I'm alright, thanks."

Liem stood and picked up some dishes, following her into the kitchen while Jaimy leaned forward to engage with the boys. "So," Liem began as he placed the dishes in the sink and hopped up on the counter. "Who's the kid's father?"

Lark looked at him, false puzzlement written across her face. "You kidding? Mags."

"Not Sever. Gun."

When she went still and didn't answer, Liem raised his voice, "Should I ask Mags? Hey—"

"Shut up," Lark moved closer. "Mags ain't here."

"I know."

Lark spread her hands. "So... why?"

"Because he left this morning and didn't say goodbye to your son," Liem pointed at her. "And Gun didn't even seem surprised."

Her lips tightened, and she looked away, determinedly not at the living room where they boys were playing. "What are you tryin' to say?"

"That I see what's goin' on here and I don't like it."

Lark wished Mags was still here. Then she could bang his and Liem's heads together. "It ain't what it looks like."

"Then tell me," Liem slid off the counter and moved close to her, dropping his voice so the others couldn't hear. "Make me understand the asshole that nearly killed my brother last night. That treated you like a traitor for bringing your family home without his permission. That acts like *your* kid," he pointed toward the living room. "Doesn't even exist. What else am I supposed to think?"

His eyes were hard but not cold. He cared. Probably more than Liem Lecorza had cared about anything in a long time. Lark so badly wanted to be a part of their life; she couldn't blame him for nosing into hers. "It's a long fucking story."

"Ain't going anywhere." He crossed his arms and raised his eyebrows, prompting her to go on.

She closed her eyes and let out a breath through her nose. She hadn't ever planned on telling this story. Leave it to Liem to stubbornly force her hand right off the bat. "Izlatana."

"What about it?" He responded immediately. If she'd been trying to dodge, he was prepared.

"Where I met Mags. They—we weren't supposed to be together. We got caught and Izla whipped me for it. She made Mags watch." She ran her right hand over her left arm, feeling the slick edges of the scars that traced across her back. "Mags broke it off the next day; he didn't want me to get hurt again. But that wasn't enough for Izla."

Her eyes opened and rose to Liem's. His face hadn't changed. No remorse for making her relive this, no dread as to where the story was going. Liem wanted all the facts, and he was prepared for whatever they may be.

"It's a whole underground business at the resort. They have these special invite parties. They drug servants, mostly girls and a few of the younger boys, and auction them to guests. Don't remember much of it. Woke up in bed with a man I didn't know."

Liem's jaw tightened. Lark recognized the expression of a man who wanted blood. It was the expression on Mags' face when she had shown up in his room in a torn party dress with her face a dripping bloody mess. Then, as now, it didn't change what had happened.

"Mags got me out of there," she went on, eyes trained on him. "Brought me back here, but Crotis wouldn't have it. Like a coward, I ran instead of being rejected." Lark leaned against the counter. "When I found out about Gun, I thought—I hoped he was Mags'. But…" Looking up at him, Lark spread her hands. "Here we are."

As if he'd sorted out all the answers, Liem proclaimed, "Mags blames Gunner for that."

"No, he doesn't," Lark responded with the same certainty. "You don't fucking know him. There's only one person Mags blames for that night, himself." She glanced over toward the living room.

Liem had more to say, but a loud pounding on the front door interrupted whatever accusations he'd conjured during her story. Lark stared at the door and only seconds ticked by before another pounding resounded through the quiet apartment. She left Liem in the kitchen and pulled her utility belt from where it hung on the wall beside the door, strapping it around her hips before she opened it.

Two large, armored darkling guards stood outside the door. Lark recognized them as belonging to Crotis though she did not know their names. The taller was green skinned and especially ugly, his snaggle-toothed incisor was broken at the level of his chin. The other was shorter but broader, a dark red with mangled horns, one of which appeared to dig into his skull.

"Morning, friends," she said to them with a decidedly unfriendly tone. "What can I do to make you go the fuck away?"

"Crotis requests your presence," Red growled at her.

Lark pressed her lips together in a thin line. That wasn't good. Crotis rarely spoke to her directly and even less frequently when Mags wasn't around. She'd either done something to tick him off, or he needed something from her. Neither situation was favorable.

Turning, she found that Jaimy had joined Liem in the kitchen. "Can you…?" she began, her words dying when

Liem started toward them. She shook her head at him, and Jaimy grabbed his arm.

Liem would never understand a situation in which his boldness wouldn't win him the fight. Lark, frankly, liked that about him. On Kyro it would get him killed. "Watch the boys," she said more forcefully, and Jaimy nodded slowly.

Even in her own home, Lark remained armed. Things just got hairy so quickly, and she had never felt safe. This time, her paranoia paid off. She hooked her thumb into her utility belt above her white enamel CCP and turned back to the waiting darkspawn.

"*Yat*," she said to them and waved them forward. They never seemed to like it when she used their language, which was more reason for her to do so at every appropriate juncture.

Her two new friends exchanged glances of hatred before turning to lead her silently through the halls. "You know I can get there on my own, right?" she muttered to them after the heavy door had closed behind her.

Green leaned over to say something in d'javu to his companion, and Lark grinned to herself as she realized his teeth gave him a mild speech impediment. It took the edge off the harsh language. They had to know she spoke fluent d'javu. Then again, they had not been given this duty for their brain power.

She ignored them, as they only seemed clever enough to repeat the same things she had heard a hundred times before. Things neither of them would have had the stones to say if Mags had been here.

Both guards stopped outside the door to Crotis' Katarak office. Red opened the door and announced her. When Lark was allowed in, the darklings closed the door behind her and she faced Crotis, who was smiling.

◻   ◻   ◻

Lark stormed back into the apartment, no guards escorting her this time. Not surprisingly, her discussion with Crotis had not gone well. What he had asked her to do went against her basest instincts as a mother, and she had told him point blank she would not do it. He had not appreciated being turned down. Nor the detail in which she had told him where he could put his request.

Then she had turned and left, instructing him to take it up with Mags as he seemed to be the only one the old man would listen to.

Up the stairs, she let the door slide closed before she secured it and then pounded up to the living level where Gun was helping his uncles get the dishes put away. Sever was sitting on the floor clapping his hands at her. "Ma!" he cried when she reached the top of the stairs.

"Ma!" Gun echoed. "We cleaned up!"

Jaimy must have seen it in her face, in the urgency with which she entered the room, heading for her son like a woman possessed. "What's wrong?" he asked, moving toward her tentatively.

"Nothing," was Lark's knee-jerk response, though she made no attempt to hide the distress on her face as she lifted Sever into her arms.

"Liar," Liem snapped the accusation out without thinking. She was holding Sever like she would never see him again. Like someone was going to march in here and take him from her.

Liem and Jaimy looked at each other, "Lark..." Jaimy began gently. "You need to tell us what's going on. We can help you..."

She looked at him, her cheek pressed against Sever's forehead while he toyed with the locket around her neck, "Crotis—"

The searing sound of cutting metal filled the apartment. Gun dropped the plate he had been carrying to cover his ears. The crash of shattering stoneware and Sever's protesting cries were nearly inaudible over the shriek coming from the doorway. Lark whipped around and stepped back away from the top of the stairs.

Jaimy moved in front of her but she reached out and fisted the back of his shirt, shaking her head when he looked over his shoulder at her. This was beyond any of them. In the kitchen, Liem had pulled Gun back behind the counter and stood over him.

The metal sound ceased abruptly, and silence reigned for a short moment before a deafening slam punctuated it.

"Dearest Lark," Crotis' voice preceded him up the entry stairs. When he appeared, flanked by four elite darkspawn guards, Lark pulled Jaimy back. These were not the errand-running type of guards she had snarked with earlier. These were the type that enforced their leader's will. Huge, hulking brutes in spiked metal armor. They carried heavy weapons and, unlike Red and Green from before, possessed two brain cells to rub together. They would have the strength and endurance that their size denoted, a match even for Magnimus if they so chose.

Crotis smiled, content in the knowledge that he held all the cards today. "I am offended you would attempt to lock me out of the home that I so graciously provided for you and your family." He paused at the top of the stairs and his eyes played off each face, withholding the surprise he had to feel about seeing the two unknown humans here.

Lark's eyes boiled as she held tight to Jaimy and gripped her son to her chest, "Mags provides this home, *not* you."

Again, Jaimy and Liem exchanged looks. As proud as it made them to see Lark's famous fearlessness had not dwindled, even the Coin Brothers knew when they were outmatched. It was probably not smart to piss off this man when her husband wasn't here.

Crotis waved a hand in dismissal, "I gave you an order, my dear, and I am here to see that it is done."

"Ah yeh," Lark growled. "You want me the Protector's baby so bad, you fucking get her. I ain't taking a child from her mother's arms! I won't fucking do it! I told you to take it up with Mags."

"Magnimus knows the consequences of disobedience. I am disappointed to discover he has not shared them with you."

With a raise of his hand, the d'javu moved. Two came at Lark and the others toward the kitchen. Jaimy tore from his sister's grasp and stood solidly in front of her. These d'javu did not laugh in disdain, for all their size and brute strength they lacked a sense of humor. So, they simply sneered down at him.

Gun screamed, growling and grunting as he fought the hold of the large darkspawn that hauled him from the kitchen. Aside from a brief shout, Liem was nowhere to be seen or heard. In the same moment that Lark turned to demand they release her son, the d'javu directly in front of Jaimy brought his fist across the man's face. Jaimy hit the floor, blood pouring from his nose and soaking into his long silken hair as he went limp before her.

"Stop!" Lark shrieked, but there wasn't time to protest. The two darklings closed in, and one of their large, spiked hands reached toward her. It closed around her neck, holding her still while another wrapped fully around Sever and tore him out of her arms. "NO!"

Between Gun fighting, Sever crying, and Lark screaming, it appeared this entire thing was giving Crotis a headache. He rubbed at his temple as the four darkling enforcers walked down the steps on either side of him with Sever squalling and Gun spitting like a tethered wildcat.

Lark had fallen to her knees and her hands sought her CCP.

"Please, don't make this harder than it has to be," Crotis said to her from the stairs. "If you shoot me, there is nothing stopping the darkspawn from destroying your misbegotten children."

"Just fucking give them back," she snarled, aiming the pistol at him even if she had no intention of using it. She hadn't even activated it. Her hands shook on the grip, a tremor of withheld murder, "Give my sons back to me, Crotis."

"I will," he assured her calmly. "When you bring me the Consuls' daughter. Not a moment before. Work quickly, my patience grows shorter as I age."

He disappeared from view, climbing down the stairs and leaving her in silence. Lark fell forward, dropping her pistol onto the metal floor and trembling for a moment. Then she scrambled to her feet, jumping quickly to Jaimy's side and checking for a pulse. He was alive, just unconscious.

"Liem?" she didn't know what had happened to the other brother, he was just gone once they took Gun. Turning the corner around the bar, she found Liem crawling forward. A smear of red across a counter door was the only evidence of where he'd struck it.

Dropping to her knees, Lark inspected the head wound. "Jaimy?" he forced out, his voice breaking over the name, pain revealing concern he would have rather kept to himself.

"He's okay, just out like a light." He'd already stopped bleeding, so Lark leaned back and stood.

"They took the boys..." he grunted when she pulled him to his feet.

"I know," Lark answered. "And trust me, he's gonna fucking pay for that."

◻   ◻   ◻

Lark waited until Jaimy had piloted the *Stalker* out of the red cloud of the Devil's Tongue. She was sitting on the floor at the base of the ladder to the cockpit watching the display on her gauntlet for the indication that it could make a connection. Once the icon lit up, she pressed the send key and waited some more

With her hood back, the speakers played the message Mags sent back loud enough for her brothers to hear in the cockpit above her head. [Lark, your last message was in three different languages, two of which I do not speak. Repeat in universal.]

She recorded her response quickly, loudly, and without thinking. "They took our fucking kids!"

Jaimy was about to point out to Lark that she may want to be more specific when the response chime came in. Liem was shaking his head anyway, cautioning Jaimy not to involve himself. Mags voice was calm but edged with impatience when Lark played the message. [Who did? And why?]

It was a reasonable request for clarification. By Lark's response, he might have been inquiring about the weather. "Will you fucking *listen*?! Crotis took them! He tried to order me to kidnap the fucking Protectors' new baby, and I told him I wouldn't. So, he had his enforcers *break* into our fucking apartment and take Sever and Gun hostage!"

The pause afterward stretched. It might not have been any longer than necessary to send the message to wherever Mags was, but every millisecond that ticked by made Lark more agitated. When the chime finally came, she grunted when she indicated the message should play. [And you're going to do it now?]

Lark made a sound that made both of her brothers flinch despite the fact that she was nowhere near them. Her fingers curled as if she could crush her husband's face from across the galaxy. After spitting a curse, she answered in a frigid tone, "Yes, Mags. We are on our way to Lystor right now. And *you* better be getting your ass back to Kyro and tell that sick fuck to keep his hands off my kids."

[They are safe with him. Do you understand that?]

"They broke down our fucking door, attacked my brothers, and *tore Sever out of my arms, Mags*!"

[I'm going, Lark.]

"If he touches my sons, I will *castrate* him."

[Don't forget that Sever is my son as well.]

He'd barely finished the statement before Lark was holding down the record button and screaming into the pickup. "*They. are both. your fucking* sons!"

Liem and Jaimy tensed when Lark's boots rattled up the ladder. Her communicator chimed two or three more times, but she ignored it, placing her hands on the headrests of their chairs. She sighed, and Liem chanced a look back to find her grinning in a sardonic way.

"So," she began, moving a hand down to Jaimy's shoulder and gently smoothing his hair. "How would you two like to collect on my bounty?"

26

IT WAS raining on Lystor when the *Stalker* set down. The type of rain that had people peering out their windows in fear, as if the clouds were to cease their harmless tantrum and get to serious business at any moment.

Cracking, roiling thunder shook the starship. Lightning briefly flashed in the darkness, shedding daylight on the slick platform. A set of guards, outfitted in the light blue regalia of the Alliance Legion, stood under an outcropping that hung over the palace entrance. They seemed unwilling to step out of their shelter, even when the strange ship landed, and they stood squinting into the downpour as the trio approached.

The Fringers hurried across the landing platform, shoulders hunched up to their ears against the driving rain. Once they were under the outcropping, the guards stepped forward to block their path. Jaimy raised a hand and spoke patiently, "We are here to see the Consuls."

"Who are you?" the first guard asked, surveying them.

Liem gave a mirthless chuckle, "They don't recognize us, Jaim."

Jaimy grinned, "We're not in the Fringe, Liem."

The second guard caught on and his mouth opened in awe, "The Coin Brothers..."

Grin widening into a smile, Jaimy started forward. The guards pressed back defensively, raising unlit catalyst pikes. Jaimy held his hands up, "We're here to claim the bounty on this one," he pointed a thumb back at the prisoner onto which Liem was holding tightly. "Willing to bet you recognize her."

"Burn in hell you low life sons of bitches!" Lark shouted. She growled and whipped her head back and forth while Liem tried to hold on.

With a nervous laugh, Jaimy showed the guards a forced smile. "The quicker we get this over with the better..."

"No, no, *no!*" Devi slapped Ryk's hand away and stabbed a finger directly into the projected map that floated just above the tabletop ringed with the best military advisors the Alliance had to offer. "Ilia is the beginning of the Sya trade route. If we block it off, half the galaxy loses access to—"

"And if we do not," Colonel Hampted spoke over her. He was one of the few men who had the gumption to do so. "Nyhusa will be invaded by the Ilian prince within a year and we will have lost two systems before we could even hope to resolve the conflict."

"Consuls?" Devi dropped her hand and looked toward the door where Zak, one of the Salvan guards who'd been stationed outside the door to the meeting room, had stuck his head in. "I'm sorry to bother you... something has come up."

Devi gave frustrated sigh, "I was in the middle of telling off the Colonel, Zak, can't it wait?"

"I don't think so, Consul..." he swallowed hard and glanced at the Colonel before going on. "The Coin Brothers are here. They want to see you right away."

Ryk gave him a puzzled look. "The Coin Brothers?" he glanced at Devi to see that she was just as perplexed as he was. "The bounty hunters? What do they want?"

Zak turned to Ryk and spoke assertively, "They are here to claim the bounty on the assassin from the Fringe..."

"Give us a minute, gentleman," Zak had hardly finished his sentence when Devi rose and switched off the projection table. "Something has come up." The assembled company muttered quietly to themselves as they sat back in their seats. Ryk gestured for Zak to let their visitors in.

In they came, the long-haired one first. He was followed by his twin brother, the only difference being the length of their hair and that the second was dragging a spitting, snarling blond woman with him. "You'll fucking pay for this!" she was growling before her captor gave her a sharp tug, and she came to a stop in front of him.

They were dressed in clothing so nondescript it must have been intentional. Against the polished walls of the palace and the crisp sky-blue uniforms of its guards, the trio appeared to be viewed through a dingy filter.

"So, you are the Coin Brothers?" Ryk asked.

"We are," the long-haired twin replied.

Devi spoke up, her arms crossed. "Which one of you is Jaimus and which one is Liem?"

"Jaim," he said, bowing his head respectfully, with just a hint of bravado. "This is Liem," he indicated his brother who gave a curt nod. "Brought you the war criminal, and we'd like to collect that bounty now."

Devi and Ryk both moved forward to peer at the girl. She had been relieved of anything even slightly resembling a weapon, and her arms were exposed, cluttered with a mass scars. Devi would never forget that face from Kyro; pink lips curled in a sneer and bright turquoise eyes dancing with a bloodlust that was almost animal.

"Nice to see you again, Lark," Devi said with a sour grin that might have led one to believe it wasn't so nice to see her.

"Fuck you!" the young assassin spat. "You think just 'cause you got me here means you fucking won. But you ain't! And you!" she gave Liem a particularly hard tug then, and he had to struggle to keep hold of her. "Turnin' in another fucking Fringer! You're as good as fucked when you get home!" She gave him a shove with her shoulder. "Weaklings! *Fusalia*! Fucking Cowards!" Liem took a hold of her hair and yanked her back toward him until she was subdued with a yelp.

"Liem!" Jaimy scolded.

His brother pointed at him and responded in the same tone. "You do your fucking job, I do mine." Then his attention returned to Lark. "Stay still, dammit!"

"Anyway..." Jaimy turned back to the Consuls, his face carrying a very forced looking smile as he tried to remain calm in the face of dealing with this woman—a punishment that did not suit even their crimes. "You put the bounty out there, here she is. You don't get her till we get paid. And we want eighty thousand."

"The bounty was fifty," a steep price, for sure, and Ryk had been forced to beg, borrow, and steal to get the money allocated. It would take a lot of temptation to get the Fringe to turn on one of their own, but it had, apparently, paid off.

"Yeh, and this is pretty much the end of our career," Jaimy responded, spreading his hands in an easy and open gesture. "Turning her over to you isn't going to make us any friends back home. Me and my brother want to retire. An extra thirty thousand and we can live peacefully where no one will ever find us."

"That's why the bounty was fifty-thousand."

"Listen, you don't want her?" Jaimy countered with mock impatience. "We can take her back where we found her. I don't think anyone else will be catching her any time soon, it took us almost two years. Think you can wait another two years for this opportunity to knock again? Fine. C'mon, Liem, give the pretty girl her gun back."

As if a wild animal were about to be set free, the room tensed all at once and fear swelled from the table. A large man who had been seated in the corner stood and moved toward the table. Zak took a step forward as well, moving toward the Consuls with his hand on his belt.

"Alright!" Devi's hand cut through the air before Liem could release the prisoner. "Stop haggling, we'll pay it." Moving over to the wall unit computer, she plugged in a money chip and loaded it up then tossed it to Jaimy.

He caught it and grinned at his brother. "Told you this would be fine."

"Says you," Liem muttered. "You didn't have to deal with th—OW!" Lark stomped on his foot with the heel of her boot. Then she brought her knee up toward his crotch but missed when he grabbed her and pushed her to arm's length. Growling out a curse, he stood to his full height and took a breath, a grin plastering itself across his face. "Think we want to stay here tonight, too."

"What?" Ryk leaned slightly toward him as if he truly did not hear what Liem had said.

"Yeh, we'd like to celebrate. Have some food, maybe some drinks, sleep in the most comfortable beds we've ever seen." His grin split open into a toothy smile. "Brought you a war criminal. Pretty much makes us heroes, right?"

27

ONCE SEPARATED from her brothers, it was time for Lark to play the waiting game. It wasn't her favorite past time, and she wasn't particularly good at it, but it was her part in this script for the moment.

Four big burly guards were assigned to bring her down to the empty holding cells. Lark thought this might have been overkill. She was also certain she could get away from them if she really wanted to.

Meant to house political prisoners, the cells were spotlessly clean and climate controlled. The benches were padded, coupled with shiny tables and moody reading lights, the beds were far better than anything Lark had ever slept in.

Shuffled in through the door and uncuffed, Lark rubbed her wrists and took in her surroundings. "Fancy 'ccommodations," she commented, looking around at the gleaming marble walls. "Could stay here awhile, ya know?" She passed them a salty grin as they stepped around her to exit the cell. "Any o' you want to join me?"

The guards gave her little more than scoffs in response. Lark kept smiling until that metal door slid smoothly, silently closed on its oiled hinges and they were gone. She wasn't entirely sure what she would have done had any of them taken her up on that offer. The Protectors needed to think she was the ingrate they billed her as—a traitor to her kind, an unscrupulous murderer who fed off chaos and war.

Pretty close to the mark even if it was only half the truth.

The baby girl was probably better guarded than Lark, who could see only one soldier at the end of the hall through the small barred window in her cell door. No one else around. She had faith in the Coin Brothers, and in herself, but this was still the worst idea she'd ever had.

Lark ran her hands over her arms, feeling the scars under her fingertips. She had protested with vehement pouting when Liem had asked her to shed her jacket. Jaimy had been close to giving in, too. Especially when he saw the way she had rubbed at the exposed scars, clearly wanting to hide them. Liem was right, though, no one would have believed they would let her keep it. The thing was chock full of hidey-holes and nefarious items. The Brothers certainly hadn't been dumb enough to let her keep it the first time they had her in captivity.

There was little else to do, so Lark dropped herself onto the cushy bed without bothering to take her boots off. She had to squirm for a while to get comfortable. This bed was too soft, she decided. Lark didn't like to sleep deeply when she was alone. The last thought she had before falling asleep was that she should probably not fall asleep.

She woke an indeterminate amount of time later. Feeling sluggish and disoriented from her deep sleep, she rolled slowly with her eyes closed, her hands seeking weapons that were not there.

Finally, whatever woke her repeated, and she realized it was a voice. Lark turned to see Devi, tall and bold with her hair tightly pinned to her head. Her arms were crossed, her face hard and angry. Lark smiled in greeting, but Devi shook her head. "I'd ask how you sleep at night but clearly the answer is loudly."

Lark yawned and wiped the corner of her mouth on her arm, then swung her feet onto the floor and sat up, regarding Devi coolly. "Could ask you the same damn thing, ya know. 'Cept as you're clearly giving me the self-righteous routine, I'd say the answer's gonna be 'Like a baby.'" Lark gave a slow sigh and pushed her hair away from her face as Devi's scowl deepened. "Girl, you need t'smile more. All that frownin'll give you the worst fuckin' wrinkles."

"Do you think this is funny?" Devi snapped, tightening her arms. "All the things you've done, to your own people. How could you do it? How could you betray your own kind? For... *them*?"

Lark didn't think this was funny. She'd have very much preferred it if Devi hadn't chosen to go this route. That was a nerve, a tender nerve that the Protector had just struck. Her hands balled into fists, but she did her best to contain the brewing storm inside her.

It had been a long, long time since she'd felt like this without Mags around to keep her from doing something stupid. They had a plan here but if Devi kept talking about the darkspawn like a bunch of animals that plan was going to be thrown into the dirt.

"What I did is nothing compared to what you fucking did," she answered with acid, her throat tight as she tried to force the words out in a way that sounded controlled.

Devi took a step back as if Lark had struck her—which she really did want to do. When she recovered, Devi reclaimed that step and another, coming toward Lark aggressively. "You destroyed an entire planet. You killed women and children, families. Our entire race wiped out!"

Lark stood. "How many darklings did you fucking kill so the children on Salva could sleep without nightmares?

Were just as innocent as your families! Didn't do a fucking thing to provoke you except to be born on Kyro."

"They aren't human!" Devi's voice rose, barreling over the last of Lark's words.

"Doesn't mean they deserved to fucking *die*!" Lark shouted at her. Devi was taller than Lark and armed, but Lark was not about to back down from this. If the Protector wanted to come to blows then they'd settle this Fringe-style. "We hadn't fucking stopped you, how many more darklings would be dragged from their beds and tortured? How many more darkling babies would be pulled from their mother's arms and killed in front of them? All because you were *fucking* scared of them!"

Devi hesitated. She would have expected a heartless, ignorant butcher—not a woman with passion and conviction. Nothing new; Lark had surprised a lot of people by having a brain in her head.

It didn't slow Devi down for long. She was a woman with passion, too—and a chip on her shoulder for every person lost on Salva.

Good for fucking her. Lark felt no shame.

Devi's voice having fallen several octaves with repugnance, "They are monsters,"

Lark was ready for that one, too. "Known more fucking monsters in this life than you ever have or ever will, sister," she snarled, showing Devi her teeth. "Every last one of them been more fucking human than anything on Kyro."

"You chose to live on the Fringe—"

"About as much as you chose to be a Protector. Or any of those fucking babies that choked on stardust when the bubble popped on Salva."

A smile threatened Lark's composure when she realized she'd paid Devi back in kind. The woman's stony face was turning a particularly horrid shade of magenta, she let out a sound like a wounded cat and took a step.

"Devi, stop!"

Lark hadn't even realized he was there—or had he stepped in through the barely open door?—but there was Rykstar Os, that thin figure she'd only seen briefly in person. He grabbed Devi by the arm and pulled her to a stop. The woman froze almost immediately, but her anger hadn't cooled. "Did you hear what she said?" she hissed at him, her eyes still burning at Lark.

"I heard her," Ryk responded, he glanced at Lark. She didn't want them to, but his eyes sent a deep ache shooting through Lark's spine. Sadness, the kind that time can't wash away. He'd lost things more precious than most. Lark would be lying if she said she felt nothing when she saw him, but she had long ago come to terms with what she'd done. All that she had said to Devi held true.

Would they feel anything if they looked into Mags eyes and saw the parents he'd never known? Or any darkling who had lost loved ones because of them?

No, they would't.

Ryk didn't look at Lark long; he soothed Devi with a low voice. "Justice is what we can do now, Devi. Not revenge."

"*Wraakitak fan tagif batikar.*" Lark spat, her lips pulling away from her teeth as she watched them feeling sorry for themselves, making her feel things she didn't want to.

Devi stared at her in disbelief, her mouth twisting like she had just tasted something sour. Ryk blinked those sad eyes at her then turned back toward the door, speaking calmly, "What did she say, Bae?"

The door swung open further and Lark cocked her head at the man on the other side. She knew his face, but it had been a long time since she'd seen it. A bushy beard had been trimmed up, covering long healed scars. He crossed his arms over his big chest and watched her carefully as he spoke. "She said 'revenge is greater than justice'."

Lark's eyes narrowed. The Protectors didn't make a habit of learning d'javu, as they preferred to go on misunderstanding their enemies. It was then that it clicked in her head. The last time she'd seen him was in the war room when Mags smashed the darkstone table after they'd returned from Salva.

When had Crotis released the prisoners? Did Mags know? This man looked well fed and healthy; he'd had weeks to recover. Why hadn't anyone told her? Especially considering she was running directly into Protector territory!

Anger raged in her chest, but she kept it under wraps, letting a smile creep across her face. "Good to see you, too, friend."

"Better to be on this side of the cage."

Lark gave a noncommittal shrug and rocked her head back and forth. "Each his own."

"That's enough," Ryk finally spoke up, his voice harder than it had been. He pushed Devi into Bae then regarded Lark with thinly veiled disdain. "You will be treated fairly and humanely. Unlike the way our people were treated. Your justice will be swift."

She lifted an eyebrow at him. "I meant what I said," she told him. "Every word. You think you're right and that's all fucking great. But I helped to free a people that were being brutalized. Gotta die for that, I go clean. What it's worth, I hope that spoils your fucking justice."

Ryk's jaw was tight, but he apparently didn't have Devi's verbose anger issues. He gave a nod and left her alone, closing and locking the door behind him.

Lark listened to their footsteps and hushed voices until they were gone, glad that exercise in futility was over. What she and Mags had accomplished was a long way from upstanding, but it was simple penance for generations of torture and death because of fear and ignorance.

235

Of course, it helped to know she wasn't going anywhere near their 'justice' system. If her brothers ever got their pretty little behinds in here to get her the hell out.

28

LIEM REACHED out and grabbed a fistful of Jaimy's shirt. Already off-balance from too much to drink, Jaimy pitched backward and hit the wall with a grunt. Liem slapped a hand over his brother's mouth and pressed them both against the wall, holding his breath.

Ryk, Devi, and the big guy strode passed, unaware of the two miscreants hiding in the shadows. The moment they passed the brothers, lightning flashed outside the opposite window. For a split second, Liem's face was lit, contorted as it was in horror as he watched the figures pass. If they had but glanced to the side, all would have been lost.

"You should get some rest," Ryk said, barely loud enough for Liem to hear.

"No," Devi responded immediately. "We're going to finish our meeting."

There was a pause. Liem leaned out to see if they were gone. As they turned the corner, he heard the big guy yawn, "I'm tired. I'll take Dia to bed..." The rest of what he said was lost in distance. Liem released his brother when he felt Jaimy's tongue on the palm of his hand.

"Gross, man, c'mon! How old are you?"

"Couldn't breathe."

"Use your fucking nose, stupid," Liem wiped his hand on his jacket and cast his brother a resentful glare before stepping out of their hiding spot and heading toward the holding cells. Jaimy followed closely, his path considerably more winding than his twin's.

"Look like you're sneaking," Jaimy commented at full volume as he watched his brother crouch and creep through the halls. "Act natural." He smiled at Liem when he turned. "Gotta chill out, Liem."

"Knew I should have stopped you from ordering that last round," Liem shook his head but he relaxed slightly. Ahead, a guard was talking at length to a steward holding a glass tray loaded with food. Liem glanced at Jaimy, and they exchanged a brief hand signal.

"I know, I know... Why she gets the good stuff is beyond me," the steward was saying as they approached.

"Evening, gents," Liem said by way of greeting, and both the guard and steward turned to look at the approaching duo. He nodded and forced a smile.

"You're the Coin Brothers," the guard said, pointing at them.

"That's us," Jaimy said with undue pride, smiling widely and sincerely. Both the steward and the guard seemed instantly at ease. Liem tried not to smirk. Jaimy had a talent with people that he just couldn't ever figure out. Even at his worst, Jaimy could make a friend where his twin made a rival. "That for our friend?" he pointed at the tray.

The steward looked down at the tray and nodded. "Lark, the war criminal. She's the only prisoner we have right now."

"Course," Liem tried to use his brother's smooth laugh and smile. He spread his hands. "This is a peaceful place, don't get a lot of us hardened criminals around here."

All three of them stared at him. Liem looked to his brother, who somehow managed to remain subtle despite his state of intoxication and waved at Liem to shut the hell up. "We have some choice words for the little thing," Jaimy went on to say to the guards. "Why don't you let us take that off your hands? Kind of a bitch," he laughed like they were talking about a girl they'd all dated. "You know what I mean? Why don't you guys head out for a smoke? We won't tell."

The steward looked up at the guard who shrugged and then handed the tray to Jaimy. During the exchange, in that moment just before the steward had let go of the tray, that was when Liem attacked. He slammed his fist into the guard's throat, jammed his thumb down on the plunger of the syringe hidden in his palm and pumped him full of some nice hard sleepy medicine that would blank out the last half hour or so of his memory for a couple days.

As the guard slid to the ground and Liem pocketed his small syringe, he turned to find Jaimy standing over the steward who was in a similar state of unconsciousness. His long-haired twin was holding the tray in one hand and downing the wine with the other.

"Really? Had to save the wine?" Liem asked in disbelief, bending to grab the guard and sling him into an empty cell.

Jaimy licked his lips and nodded. "Not gonna waste it." He put the wine glass down and started picking through the food.

"Whatever, just put the grub down and help me with this. We don't got a lot of time before alarm bells start ringing."

A few minutes later, Jaimy was finishing the last of the food and supposedly standing watch as Liem climbed into the ceiling and set a round device that was smaller than his palm on the cables that ran from the security cams. When

Liem hopped down he looked at the empty tray, "Save any for Lark?"

Jaimy stared at him as if he'd spoken another language. "I..." he began, mouth full of food. "Didn't even think about it."

Liem nodded in acceptance. "Well, I'm not the one you're gonna have to hear it from. It's her."

Jaimy quickly finished the last bite and threw the tray an empty cell. "Doesn't know won't hurt her."

"Nice," Liem shook his head. "Real fucking gentleman when you're drunk, you know that?"

With a snort, Jaimy followed him. "At least I am a gentleman at some point..."

Liem ignored that. The differences between himself and his brother were minor annoyances, but they were honestly the only things that made them able to stand each other.

They took out two more guards and locked them into cells before they heard Lark's voice coming from another at the end of the hall. "The hell took you two so long?" She was gripping the bars in the window of the cell's door, clearly holding herself up so she could peer through as she was not tall enough to reach that window. A crash of thunder punctuated her statement, the rumble dying as the brothers approached.

Liem smirked at her. "Good crowd in there. Thought Jaimy was fascinating." He rolled his eyes and started examining the door controls.

"Ah yeh, don't we all—" Lark shifted her grip but her eyes remained visible, peering out through the bars at her other brother. "Are you drunk?"

Jaimy grinned stupidly at her. She turned her eyes to Liem, silently inquiring if this behavior was normal. He shrugged, "Somebody had to make friends and it wasn't gonna be me."

"Just about drank the big guy under the table, too," Jaimy told her proudly, beginning to wander and peer into the other cells.

Liem caught Lark's eye and shook his head insistently. She smiled and dropped out of view for a moment. When she returned, Liem had relieved the control panel of its cover plate and turned toward his brother. "Jaimy," he whistled to try and gather his twin's attention. "Jaimy. *Jaimy!*" He held his hands out when the distracted man finally turned.

With a dimwitted 'oh,' Jaimy reached into the pocket of his jacket and tossed Liem a small device. Liem went about attaching it to the wires that ran from the control panel to the door lock.

"That the new interrupter from Catalyst Corp?" Lark was pressing her face against the bars, trying to peer at what Liem was doing.

"Nah," he didn't look up from his work as he manipulated the console. "It's a knockoff. Dad reworks them and sells them for twice the price."

"That so?" There was a sharp electronic noise and the door swung open with her still clinging to it. "Guess it works." She hopped down and Liem stood, detaching it from the wires.

"Best in the Fringe."

"Can I have one?" Lark gave him a wide, girlish grin.

Liem chuckled and threw the thing in the air as he passed her to collect Jaimy. "All yours, little sis. Plenty more where that came from."

Lark caught the device and turned it over in her hand before tucking it into the pocket of her pants. "Goin' back to the ship," she said to her brothers, turning toward a rain-battered window at the end of the hall. "I'll see you shortly."

"You know where you're going?" Liem asked.

"What're you, my grandma?" Lark retorted, throwing a smile over her shoulder. "Been finding marks since before you were fucking born, Liem, I can find this one."

Liem smirked and called after her, "That doesn't make any sense!"

"Yeh," Jaimy chimed in, louder than was necessary. "He's older than you."

"You and me are the same age," Liem said to him. "You realize that, right?"

"Yeh…" from the tone of Jaimy's answer, it was clear he hadn't considered that when he chose to speak. Liem rolled his eyes and started out of the cell block.

It was getting late. As a result, Jaimy and Liem were seen by almost no one until they came upon the Consuls' living quarters on the western side of the building. There, two Salvan guards stood watch on a corridor of rooms. Jaimy could easily persuade a common worker like a food steward. These guards, trained Protectors, had Liem unsure of this brother's skills. The only thing that eased his paranoia was that one of them was a young woman.

Liem slowed, allowing Jaimy to take the lead. "Evenin'," he said cheerily, approaching the tense guards. "Name's Jaimy. Might've heard that we're here celebrating the fact that we brought in the war criminal from the Fringe." He gave them a slight, flourished bow and then gestured swiftly at Liem. "This is my brother." Liem scowled as Jaimy asked for their names.

"Eiley," the young girl answered, smiling and blushing.

"That is a pretty name," Jaimy grinned at her. He shook the hand of the male guard, Zak, who was relaxed. Liem tried not to harrumph. "The party downstairs played itself out, but the big guy invited us up here to play some cards. Said he was ordering up some grub, mind if we go in?"

Eiley looked at Zak, and his face became grave. Liem had experienced this before when Jaimy asked people to do things they shouldn't do. As if afraid to disappoint him, but hesitant to forget their duties. Liem closed his hand around the small CCP in his pocket while Jaimy smiled some more.

"Tell you what," Jaimy began when they didn't give an answer. He began moving toward the door, somehow making it seem like the guards were escorting them. "Why don't you guys join us?"

"Oh..." Eiley responded, her shoulders dropping. "Our shift doesn't end until later..."

"That's alright," Jaimy reached out to run his fingers down her cheek as Liem opened the door and stepped inside. "I'll save you a seat." He turned to follow Liem then snapped his fingers, "I forgot I told Bae I'd bring up an Invokin whiskey I've got in the ship. I'll be right back."

Liem met the eyes of the guards. Jaimy always told him not to smile; his smile always seemed to provoke mistrust or violence. Liem wondered how they could have the same face but completely different expressions. He pressed the panel to close the door before he gave into the urge to smile maliciously at the two dumbfounded guards.

The door whooshed closed behind him. He brought his elbow back onto the panel, hearing it crack as it shattered. Then he strode across the room silently and opened the window, reaching down to pull a sodden Lark in through the opening just as a crash of thunder rattled the glass.

"Jaimy went back to the ship?" Lark asked in a whisper, shaking out her soaked hair and pushing it away from her face. The downpour had made that climb more treacherous than she had anticipated. It was more annoying than frightening to her. Which was pretty much a summary of how she felt about this entire ordeal.

"Yeh," Liem confirmed quietly, securing a cable that disappeared out the window through which Lark had entered.

"Right," she nodded with less enthusiasm than she was accustomed to experiencing during a job. "Let's get this over with."

Liem raised his pistol, thumbed the mechanism that activated his tranq darts.

Thunder rumbled in the distance, rolling closer and breaking right above them with a shuddering crack. The flash of light cut sharp shadows behind Liem as he clung to the adjacent wall, moving with slow intent.

One of these rooms had baby Nadia in it, any other one might have big boy Bae snoozing. Whatever it was Jaimy had slipped in his drink, she hoped he'd given him a heavy enough dose. The guy hadn't seemed off when Lark had spoken to him, but she wouldn't put a delayed release past the Coin Brothers. With any luck, they'd find the baby before they found him.

A gentle hiss of air behind her and Liem entered another room. Lark waited until he came back out and gave her a shrug. Taking a few steps, Lark palmed open the door closest to her and then motioned for Liem. This was not what they had expected.

The child's crib was nestled against a wall, a mobile with gently flickering stars rotated slowly above it, casting soft lights onto the ceiling. Opposite the crib was a large bed, which to Lark's great surprise and dismay was occupied with a large body. Liem stuck his head in the doorway and identified the problem. He gestured that the guy was sleeping soundly and pushed her toward the crib.

On eggshells, Lark tiptoed across the dark room toward the crib. She reached it without incident and peered in at the tightly swaddled little girl. Lark was reaching, sliding her hands under the little girl's neck and behind when she heard someone moving behind her.

"Dev?"

Lark snapped around and pulled the child quickly to her chest, waking her and causing her to begin whining. Bae stood, half naked and woozy. "What the hell are *you* doing here?!" he slurred, slumping against the wall. "Put her down!" he was trying to yell at her but could hardly get his voice above a mumble.

Lark was slow to react, her normal quick reflexes and violent impulses hampered by the wriggling child in her arms. Liem was just as stunned by the bumbling giant and stood stupidly in the doorway without an inkling of fraternal instinct.

Bae pressed one large hand against the wall and grunted as he pushed himself upright. The other hand gripped and lifted a catalyst ax, thumbing it on and swinging it wildly at Lark.

"Lost your fucking *teeth*?!" she yelped as she ducked to the side and wrapped her arms tightly around the squalling baby. The weight of the ax nearly toppled him, but Bae recovered just in time to see Lark slide behind Liem. The tall bounty hunter stood solidly in front of her and raised his pistol at Bae.

"Why don't you just go back to fucking bed, big guy?" Liem suggested, firing several dosed darts that struck Bae in the chest and neck. The big man lunged at them but hardly made it two steps before he plummeted and met the floor with a resounding crash. Liem smirked at the prone giant, "Won't draw any attention to us..."

"Nah," Lark responded offhandedly, but she was heading toward the window and shushing the baby. She kicked the glass pane outward, wind and rain pounding in through the opening to whoosh around her. The platform was several stories below. Liem secured the grapple to his belt and tucked Lark tightly against his chest. Then they jumped.

Nothing—no amount of experience or recklessness made the feeling of a free fall comfortable. Least of all with a screaming infant crushed between you and your brother's large chest. Rain swirled around them, made into sharp pinpricks by the upward rush of air and blinding them as they plummeted. Lark was keenly aware of the building behind her with a thousand imagined outcroppings as well as the quickly shortening drop to the platform below.

"Pull it, Liem!" Lark ordered, squeezing the child probably more than was comfortable. Her stomach was in her throat and she felt about as secure against Liem as she would in the arms of a stranger. "LIEM!"

"WAIT!" he grumbled at her. "There!" The blast of thrusters roared below them, and Liem pulled the grappler. Their descent was abbreviated with jarring suddenness. Dia's crying had abruptly stopped, and Lark could only guess she'd lost her breath for a moment.

The ground disappeared. The *Stalker*, slick with rain, swept up to meet them.

Liem sealed the hatch while Lark slammed herself into a seat, awkwardly strapping in and clinging to the child during a hurried takeoff.

Their feint was successful, and they were rocketing out of Lystor's atmosphere while the Alliance were still scratching their heads at the speed of their departure. When they were in free space, cloaked, and heading toward Kyro,

Lark unbuckled and took the baby back to one of the bunks to dry her off and try to get her to sleep.

Lark felt for Dia. A starship was no place for a baby and, more than likely, this little girl was already yearning for her mother. Whining and gurgling, Dia made it clear she was not entirely happy or comfortable. Lark thought about how Devi would feel when she found her child gone and a fist of guilt gathered in her stomach. Despite their less than cordial conversation, Lark's disenchantment with this mission had diminished none. It wasn't right, taking a woman's child.

Killing, genocide... These things Lark could swallow easily. But kidnapping? Lark's morals might have been skewed, but she had discovered that at least she had them.

"You alright?"

Could have been either one of them, Lark had to turn to see which one. She hadn't spent enough time around her brothers to tell their voices apart. That was just salt in her already wounded emotional state. Lark was glad to see that it was Jaimy in the doorway as she wasn't in the mood for Liem's gruffness.

Nodding slowly, Lark ran her hand over the baby's silky soft hair and tightened the swaddle around her. She rubbed Dia's middle until the baby started to drift off to sleep. Lark looked up to find Jaimy standing next to her.

"Not too bad for two hunters and a hit man," he said quietly. "We make a good brother-sister team."

"Yeh..." Lark let herself grin, even if it was rueful. Jaimy was coming down from his binge and had become melancholy. It matched Lark's mood all too well. "Doin' our best anyway..."

Jaimy touched her shoulder and pulled her away from the bunk in which she'd secured the baby. The door hissed closed behind them. He bent to look her in the eye when they were alone in the corridor. "Did what you had to do.

Think your boys are in far greater danger than that little girl."

"Maybe," Lark allowed, looking into his eyes but feeling herself pull back. She found it difficult to express her feelings to Jaimy, and she couldn't quite pin point the reason for it. She sighed in resignation, too tired for her own misgivings. Then she realized Jaimy was smiling at her somberly, "What?"

"I know this is going to take some time... This," he gestured between them. "Someday we will feel like a family again, but until then it's just going to be difficult. Liem doesn't get that, he feels like we should pick up where we left off when we were kids."

"Wish we could," Lark admitted quietly. She reached up and touched the end of his long brown hair, feeling a thrill of nerves at the new affection. The sensation was at the same time exciting as it was depressing. "Wish I could remember any of it. All the shit things I remember, and I lost the stuff that matters."

Jaimy's larger hand wrapped around hers, pressing it over his heart. He could easily make any woman swoon by doing so, but Lark could see sincerity in his eyes that she knew he never showed to anyone. He ached, just like she did, and that honest moment brought Lark home for the first time she could remember. "We'll just make new memories."

Lark was going to hug him—because she needed a damn hug—but his face suddenly contorted, and his body lurched forward. The hand that had been holding hers so gently was now gripping it for dear life. He curled, his other hand cradling his stomach. Lark whispered his name, unsure of what was going on, and steadied him, trying to lift his face back to hers.

When he finally turned to look at her, blood was trickling from the corners of his mouth, and he crumpled against her.

"Jaimy?!" she cried out, struggling to catch him. "What is it?" He gathered enough strength to roll onto the floor then lay there on his back, trying to catch his breath. Lark fell to her knees and pressed her hand to his forehead; the skin was cold and clammy to the touch. Her voice sounded desperate and terrified when she spoke his name again.

Jaimy didn't respond, his body jerked and curled in pain, his mouth gaping wide and blood spilling to the floor. Lark felt herself shaking, panicking.

"*Liem*!!" she screeched it, trying to keep Jaimy's arms down as they kept flailing. Lark yanked her gloves from where she'd stowed them on her belt and stuffed one in his mouth as he began to seize. "Liem!" she called again, just as he was turning the corner at a pace that could have broken the sound barrier.

"What happened?!" he demanded, falling to his knees on Jaimy's other side and doing a much better job at holding him still. "Jaimy? Can you hear me, brother?!"

Liem bent over him, calling into his face, but if Jaimy could hear him he couldn't respond. When Liem looked up at Lark, she saw the same soul-twisting fear in his face that she felt in her chest. "What happened?" he asked her again, with much more dread in his voice this time.

"I don't fucking know." Her throat caught on the words tears threatening as the depth of her helplessness settled in. "We were talking..." she tried to catch her breath. This was no time to fall apart. "And he just..."

Jaimy stopped seizing. Lark pulled the glove out of his mouth. He began to cough and heave, but for the moment he was breathing. Lark shushed him and smoothed his sweat drenched hair back from his brow. Jaimy groaned, his face growing paler. "Hang on..." Liem ordered, jumping to his feet and disappearing down the hall.

"Lark..." Jaimy muttered weakly, his eyes searching blindly.

"I'm right here," she leaned over him. His hand found her arm and gripped it.

It took him a long moment, but he found the words and the breath to whisper to her, "Glad I ate your food."

"What are you talking about?" she asked him, but he was suddenly and terrifyingly unconscious. "Jaimy?"

"Here," Liem reappeared with a syringe full of black liquid.

"What the fuck is that?" Lark asked him, wide eyed.

"Black gnesium," he replied rapidly, tearing Jaimy's shirt sleeve up his arm.

"What the fuck—"

"Gypsy Blood," Liem snapped and Lark's mouth clamped shut around the question. Gypsy Blood was a rare thing indeed. The gypsies sold it in their on-planet troupes at exorbitant prices to paranoid business men and cheating lovers, anyone desperate enough to believe there was a magical substance that could dispel almost any poison. It wasn't available anywhere else, even on the blackest of markets.

Lark had heard stories that others had tried selling it and had wound up dead under mysterious circumstances. Fringers weren't normally a superstitious bunch, but for some reason, the gypsies were regarded with an unprecedented amount of fear and misunderstanding. Lark was beginning to sense that the gypsies did everything in their power to keep it that way.

Lark had never had the pleasure of seeing Gypsy Blood work. If whatever had done this to Jaimy was a poison, and if it was one that could be jumped by this stuff, they'd know soon enough. If it wasn't, what would they do then?

Jaimy's whole body went tense when Liem injected the stuff into him. A pained howl escaped him and his back arched. "Hang in there, buddy," Liem urged his brother, throwing the syringe down and grabbing his brother's shirt to keep him from writhing. "You hear me in there? Keep it together, Jaimy, it's gonna be over soon!"

Remotely, Dia's cries could be heard echoing Jaimy's. Lark chewed her lip and hung on to him, watching Liem as he stared with rapidly depleting hope at his twin. The moments dragged on as if pulling through mud, and Lark felt her tenuous hold on her emotions weakening. Her knuckles were white as she held onto Jaimy's arm. She couldn't bring herself to raise her eyes to Liem again. If she saw him give up, she wasn't sure she could keep holding on herself.

Finally, Jaimy stopped fighting and went limp. Lark's breath escaped her in a soft sound like a sob. "Is he okay?" she asked quickly, searching his neck for a pulse and blissfully finding it. "Liem...?"

But the other twin had fallen backward, the adrenaline having taken everything out of him. He sat against the wall, heaving breaths and staring at them. He nodded after a moment, "He should be okay. If he's not dead yet, he ain't gonna die. Not from this anyway."

Lark allowed herself to breathe. Propping herself up against the wall, she pulled Jaimy's head onto her lap and watched the color slowly return to his face. They sat in silence like that for a long time, until Dia had stopped crying and had gone back to sleep.

Finally, Lark looked across the hall at Liem who was watching his brother just as closely. "He said..." Lark began, pausing when Liem's intense gaze rose to her. She'd never seen him look like that, and her chest went rigid at the sight. "Said he was glad he ate my food. The hell was he talking about?"

Liem winced and brought his hand up to rub at the tension in his brow. After taking a deep breath, he pointed at Jaimy. "We stopped the steward who was going to bring you your dinner. Drunky over there ate what was meant for you. If he hadn't..." Liem pursed his lips and a strange expression overtook his face. Something of a somber relief. "That would have hit you a lot harder than it hit him...It was probably in the wine, giant lush." Petulantly, he kicked Jaimy's boot.

Shocked, Lark looked down at the man sleeping against her. She'd feared for his life, in a way she'd only feared for Mags, and to find out that what had nearly killed him was intended for her came as a tough blow. Her shaking hands smoothed his hair back, and she suppressed a sob.

"Fuck them," she whispered morosely into his hair. "Almost makes me glad I took their damn baby..."

Liem gave a mirthless chuckle, "All's fair in war, baby sis. Makes you even in my book."

"Yeh," Lark frowned and traced the subtle lines on Jaimy's brow. "Almost."

29

DEVI HADN'T moved in hours. Bae had been relocated to the medical wing for treatment of the injuries he'd apparently given himself and to monitor how his body was processing the plethora of sedatives they'd pumped into him. Ryk stood just outside the doorway to the bedroom, watching Devi sit on the edge of the bed and stare at the empty crib.

"All the holding cell cams were scrambled," one of the security officers was telling him, though Ryk was only half listening. "But we have them on another—the Coin Brothers and the assassin together."

Ryk's eyes closed slowly, his mind barely able to comprehend how severely they'd failed. Allowing the Coin Brothers into this place had turned out to be a grave mistake. Underestimating Lark had proven to be much more devastating.

"Thank you," Ryk said quietly and waved the security team away. It made little difference how or why at this point. They knew that their child had been taken, and they knew where she was headed.

It was not a place Ryk ever thought he would go again. Imagining his beautiful baby daughter among all those devlish faces... He wasn't entirely sure how he was still standing here.

He opened his eyes and found Devi sitting there, still as death, utterly broken. Ryk would not move until she did. It worried him that they were not already on their way. Devi never hesitated. Devi never stopped. Seeing her like this disturbed him. If she never moved, how could he possibly go on?

"Consul, the attack squadron is preparing." Words he was not at all prepared to hear from Colonel Hampted, a man who should have long ago retired.

Battle, again. An act of war from the darkspawn, even as personal as this, was a serious matter to all of the Alliance. "Shall we deploy as soon as they are ready?"

"No," Devi's voice answered. Ryk looked up to find her standing. "They are not going anywhere without us."

"Yes, Consul," Hampted bowed sharply then retreated.

Ryk held a hand out to Devi that she didn't take. "Dia will be alright," he assured her emptily. "They wouldn't dare hurt her."

"That is a stupid assumption, Ryk," Devi responded unkindly, eyes that rose to his were dark and hard as the satinite stone of Kyro. "They have murdered thousands like her. They wouldn't hesitate to hurt her."

Ryk nodded slowly. She was right, of course, but she'd killed the lie he was telling himself. With that, a weight seemed to fall heavily on his shoulders. "If you're ready..."

30

LARK HELD the infant against her chest as she strode stoically down the dark hallway accompanied by her two large brothers. One of the d'javu enforcers posted in the docking bay had informed her that Mags and Crotis were on the observation deck. A long lift ride and several flights of stairs later, the corridor widened to reveal a large but mostly empty room.

Segmented windows framed in black metal dominated the eastern wall, letting in cutouts of crimson light. Outside sprawled the broken, black landscape of Kyro enveloped in the red twisting light of the Tongue.

Crotis, old and bent, stood in sweeping purple robes that hid his diminishing body. Beside him stood Mags and it appeared they had been conversing closely. The latter stood with his hands behind his back, leaning toward his mentor and listening to the old man's whispers. Mags straightened when he heard them approach and turned to regard them.

"Lark," Crotis greeted smugly. "Welcome home."

"Save it," spat Lark, coming to a stop before them with her brothers pulling closer on either side. Mags gave them a brief glare, but his eyes snapped back to his wife when she spoke sharply to him. "Where are my sons?" she demanded.

Crotis was not one to be ignored, "I see you did as you were told." He patronized her, "It wasn't all that hard, now was it?"

"I got the girl," Lark snapped. "Ain't fucking giving her to you. Who knows what you'll do to her—"

Mags stirred suddenly to take a protective step between them, darkness peeling off him as he stared his wife down. "That is enough."

Lark felt Liem at her elbow, closer than was safe for him. He didn't know any better, but Lark could see that his vigilance was only putting Mags on edge. However, to be completely honest, she didn't really give a crap about Mags' feelings at this point. If he decided to snap on her brother, he had a surprise coming. She made no move away from Liem.

"Keep the girl, Lark," Crotis interjected. "I only instructed you to take her and bring her here. She has served her purpose."

Lark frowned, vexed, and rocked Dia slowly when the girl began to fuss. She looked up at Mags. "You just wanted them to attack Kyro..."

"Yes, my dear," Crotis said with a condescending chortle. "They will attack here while we invade civspace. Their forces scattered, attention divided. They will be nearly defenseless. And we will take what we deserve."

Magnimus was watching her closely, but Lark couldn't meet his eyes. Why hadn't he told her any of this? Weren't they supposed to be partners? Hadn't she proven her capability when she helped him with his first victory? But no, he went to Crotis. He always fucking went to Crotis. Lark would never be the confidant that old man was to him...

Grinding her teeth, swallowing monumental anger and hurt, Lark turned hot turquoise eyes on her darkling husband. "Where are my sons?" she asked him, her voice little higher than a growl. "Ain't gonna fucking ask again, Mags."

"I'm surprised at you, child," Crotis took a step toward them. "Can you not see your own progeny before your eyes?" He pulled his robes to the side to reveal where Sever was clinging to them. When he saw her, a bright smile lit his face and he reached out to her. "Yes, my boy, your mother has returned at last." Crotis bent and lifted Sever into his arms.

Mags nearly flinched when Lark's eyes shot to his. She had never been so angry—at least, not at him. Her jaw was tight and her eyes on fire. Lark fumed silently, watching her husband try to look like there was no reason to be upset. She shifted the infant in her arms, wanting nothing more than to have her hands free so she could tear Sever from the arms of that man.

Her eyes slid over to Crotis holding her son and narrowed as he pressed a crooked hand against the child's back and hugged him close, smiling wryly.

Lark considered her position quickly. Dia was in real danger here among the darkspawn. She was safest with Lark, as Mags would never let anything happen to his wife. Or Sever, so she had to risk showing her hand. "Jaimy," she said suddenly, and he leaned toward her, his eyes never leaving Sever. "Get my kid."

Jaimy stepped forward without hesitating. He approached Crotis, arms out for the child. The old man hissed and squeezed Sever tightly, pointing a finger at Jaimy. "Come any closer to me, Coin, and you will find your life in very real danger."

"Quit fucking around, old man," Liem growled, his catalyst pistol appearing in his hand. "Don't threaten my brother. Just hand the kid over."

Crotis stared at the other twin, incredulity in his eyes. "If you pull that trigger, Magnimus will kill you both. You are risking your own and your brother's life for a darkling child," he told Liem. "You will not shoot me."

"Ah yeh, but you ain't my fucking blood," Liem replied, activating the pistol. "The kid is. I'm willin' to risk it. Now give him up."

A sharp intake of breath from Lark and a grin slowly spread across the face of Magnimus. It was an unkind grin, full of malice and dark satisfaction. Liem caught a sidelong glance from his sister before Crotis started speaking again.

"Blood?" the old man croaked. He looked at Lark, who was glaring hotly, and a laugh escaped him full of nothing even resembling joviality. Cruelty, that's all she heard in that laugh. "Did our little orphan find out something about herself?"

"Ain't your fucking business, Crotis," Lark ground out. "Give my kid up." She threw a disparaging look at Liem, "Big mouth." Then turned her eyes back to Mags. "Where's Gun?"

"At home," Mags replied flatly.

Crotis was chuckling to himself, making no move to give Sever to Jaimy. He ran his hand over the back of the child's head and smiled darkly. "This is the heir to the throne of Kyro—"

"And my nephew," Jaimy cut him off. "Give Sever to me. You really want to cause a fight?" He nodded toward Lark and Mags.

"Marital discord is not my concern, young man, so much as the future of this people."

Lark growled, shifting the baby in her arms. Her eyes were acidic and reproachful as they passed to Mags, "Ain't gonna say a fucking thing, huh?"

She shoved Dia into Jaimy's arms and held her hands out to Sever. There was nothing Crotis could do, Sever dove for his mother's arms, and Lark pulled him away from the man. "Touch my fucking child again and you're gonna have to switch spots with the next darkling you get in bed."

Magnimus made a threatening noise, but Crotis waved him away. "Don't worry about it, old friend. As I have told you time and time again, your wife's priorities do not reflect my own. Which, of course, always align with yours." With that, he slithered off.

Lark rounded on Mags, "How long were you going to let him keep fucking with me, Mags?! And—"

Mags took her by the arm, sneering down at her, "That is enough. I don't want to hear any of this. What you said to Crotis—"

"Was true. And if he touches your son again I'll do it. Let me go."

Mags didn't release her arm. "I want you to go back to our room and gear up. I need you here, Lark." There was slightest softening at the end of the statement, pitched to be heard by her only. Lark looked up into his eyes and saw the emotion deep within their molten glow, calling out to her to understand what no one else could.

"Why don't you just let the girl go," Liem cut in, stepping right into deadly range of the darkling. Lark's eyes widened but, to Mags' credit, he simply glared at the man. Liem went on, his hand wrapping around his sister's wrist. "I don't care how you treated her before, I ain't gonna let you lay a hand on my sister."

Lark let out a long breath. In her anger, she'd almost forgotten the Coin Brothers were here. *Her* brothers. Her stupid, giant brothers.

"Liem, don't," she said gently, forcing reason into her voice. "Mags, let me go and I'll get ready." He released her arm slowly and Lark passed him a pleading look before heading for the corridor that led to their apartments. "C'mon, boys," she called to Liem and Jaimy who were hanging back. Over her shoulder, Sever was waving happily and babbling to his father.

Jaimy gave Mags a slight nod of deference before following Lark. Liem, however, continued to glare for a long moment. Then he smiled; a wide toothy grin that was reminiscent of his sister. When he was gone, Mags shook his head and returned to the window.

"You think Gun is alright?" Jaimy asked. She could hear him quietly shushing the girl in his arms who was probably getting a nosebleed from being held at that height.

Lark's answer came in a muttered growl, "He better be."

"Better be!" Sever chimed in happily, grinning at Liem over her shoulder.

Jaimy watched his sister's back. "Mags wouldn't have let anything happen to him, right?"

She didn't answer right away, and Liem only grew darker. "Right," Lark responded, so belatedly Jaimy seemed to have forgotten what he had asked her.

They remained silent the rest of the walk back to the apartment. Sever rubbed his head against his mother's jaw. At the top of the dark stairway, she called for Gunner as she opened the door. The boy came out from around the corner, "Ma?" he breathed in disbelief.

"Gunnn!" cried Sever, wrapping his arms around his brother. Lark pushed her son's hair away from his face. He seemed to be unharmed, just scared. Lucky day for Crotis—and Mags, too.

"Did they hurt you?" she asked him, looking down into his face as Sever clung to him.

Gun shook his head. "They put us in a dark room until daddy came and got us out." He looked down at Sever. "Grandfather Crotis came here, and they got in a big fight. Never seen daddy so mad. Said lots of mean things." Lark swallowed a victorious smile, smoothing Gun's hair. "Grandfather took Sever," the little boy looked up at his mother. "Dad told me I need to stay here and protect Sal. I wasn't supposed to let anyone in unless it was him. He said if anybody broke in like they did last time, I needed to run and find him."

"That's my brave boy," Lark said softly, glancing toward the kitchen where the darkling nanny's low singing could be heard. Then she kissed his head and stood to relieve her brother of the baby girl.

When Dia was settled into Sever's crib, she quieted quickly. Poor thing was as worn out as the rest of them. Lark took a moment to run her hand over her silky hair and warm cheeks. Devi was a lucky mother, she thought, to have such a beautiful and content baby.

Pushing her regrets aside, Lark returned to the living room. Only to be confronted by Liem, who lashed out at her the moment she came into view, "Why do you let him treat you like that?"

"Like what?" Lark demanded in return, her brow furrowing at the sudden outburst.

He crossed his arms and looked down at her. "Lark—"

"Liem," Lark interrupted him flatly. She had recognized the look on his face, had seen this coming from miles away. In his defense, he'd held off a lot longer than she thought he could. "I get that you want to protect me, I do. But Mags is the last person in this universe you need to protect me *from*. That?" she pointed toward the door, indicating the show that had set him off. "You think I can't handle that then I should take you down to the rust streets where I grew up."

His jaw had clamped shut, but the look in his eye told her that he wanted to say more. Not yet, she was going to make her damn point before he piled on Mags. "You can trust me when I tell you that I am not the type of girl that would let a man push her around. Mags respects me—not just as his wife but as a warrior. So, don't you start trying to tell me what you think he is because I know what he is. And I love him. For all that messed up, ragged shit inside him and for everything you won't ever get to see."

Liem watched her for a moment, his anger cauterized in the face of her defense. Then he gathered his determination and pushed on. "Ain't sayin' I know anything about the two of you. But he just can't fucking treat you like that in front of me, alright? Don't care how tough you are—I'm your brother and I won't sit back." He let out an aggravated breath and added, "Just don't fucking like it, alright?"

"That's fair," Lark answered swiftly, apparently as much to her surprise as to Liem's from the way the words fell out of her mouth. "When all this is over, I'll talk to Mags. He's gonna just... he needs to learn to respect your wishes."

He gave a slow nod and looked at her out of the corner of his eye, unsure who had won the argument. "Right."

Jaimy chimed in as his brother ran out of steam, "What about Gun?"

She frowned and thought for the moment before giving a shrug. "It's complicated."

Liem scoffed, "It isn't *that* fucking complicated, Lark."

"He knows that," her defensiveness returned as quickly as it had lapsed. "And he tries."

Liem regained some of his resolve, "That ain't what Gun needs." She turned her glare on him. "Trying isn't enough."

"Gun is safe and he's with me. There are worse places."

Jaimy pressed a hand to her shoulder, squeezing it gently. "There are better places, too."

She shook him off, tired of listening to them vilify Mags and annoyed at being cornered when there was so much she already had to deal with. "What're you tryin' to get at?"

Jaimy's voice remained level and his words were measure, aware of how inflammatory they were going to be, "I'm trying to say that Gun could be a lot happier with a family that accepts him."

Lark stared at him, telling herself he wasn't saying what she thought he was saying. The only defense she had left was to mutter, "This is home…"

"This is *your* home," Jaimy agreed. "And Sever's." Lark pressed her lips together, studying the face of a brother she hardly knew, but Jaimy pushed on. "I know that you want to be with your kids. But you also want the best for them, don't you? This is no place for Gun."

Liem chimed in. "Being cooped up in a place like this will fucking kill him."

The harshness of her face drained away, and her eyes dropped to the floor. It didn't matter how many times she'd entertained these same thoughts in her own head, hearing them out loud turned them into knives of truth that cut into her and stayed there.

Lark ran a hand over her eyes and turned to look across the apartment at Gun. He was playing on the other side of the living area with his brother, a toy ship in his hand that Sever continually tried to grab from him. Right now, as he so often wanted to be, he was lightyears away from here. Lark pinched her eyes closed. "I'm his mother," she said lowly. Her last argument, given with resignation. "I'm all he has."

Jaimy stepped close to her and spoke softly, gently grasping her shoulder. "You *are* his mother. Time and distance aren't going to change that." He wrapped his arm around her shoulders. "But you are far from all he has."

She didn't open her eyes for a long time. Distantly, she could hear her son pretending to swoop through space and shoot lasers. When Lark finally spoke, her voice was little more than a whisper. It was a statement, not a question, "You want to take him with you."

"We just want him to be happy," Jaimy assured her, the warmth of his hand soothing her with his enduring calm. "And he isn't ever going to be happy here. Sever has his dad and all these other darkspawn. Gunner needs…"

Lark held up her hand to silence him, her eyes finally opening. She had exhausted all arguments and now had no choice but to admit that they were right. It would be the most painful thing she ever did, but she owed it to Gun to do everything she could for him. Even if that meant letting him go.

"You should get out of here, it won't be safe here for humans much longer," she turned turquoise eyes bright with restrained tears on her brothers. "Give me a minute to say good bye to my son."

Across the living area, next to one of the glastine windows, Sever and Gun were still playing quietly as if their world was not about to change. As she approached them, she tried unsuccessfully to veil her pain. She did not wish to frighten them or to preemptively steal Gun's joy. Somehow, he saw through it, as he always did, and immediately put down his toy to move toward her, sympathy on his face without even knowing why.

Lark moved to her knees, "Sev, go say good bye to your uncles." The ash colored boy looked up at her, confused at first and oblivious to the tension in his home. Lark pointed toward her brothers, and Jaimy crouched down, opening his arms. Sever ran happily toward them.

Meanwhile, Gunner moved into her arms, and when she turned back to him he was peering up at her, precocious and concerned. "Gun," Lark forced herself to begin, her voice throttled and quiet as she ran her fingers through his hair, "Remember how I always said things would change one day?"

Tentatively, Gunner nodded. "Yeh…"

"Well, things are gettin' ready to change." He blinked up at her. Pasting a thin paper smile over her heartbreak, Lark forced herself to keep going. "You're gonna go with Uncle Jaimy and Uncle Liem. They'll take you to meet your grandpa."

The small boy stared up at her, mouth slightly agape. Then, an expression of delight like none she'd ever seen on his features spread across his face.

"Really?" he asked, more in excitement than disbelief. She nodded. Just as suddenly as the glee had filled him, he became uncertain. He glanced around him at Sever and toward the doorway to the rest of the keep. "But…"

Lark shook her head, cutting off his questions. "This is just for you, Gun. Sever and me are staying here but we'll see you soon."

"Ma…" Gun leaned into her, burying his face in her shoulder, "I wanna be with you…"

"I wanna be with you too but…" she lay a hand against his smooth, warm cheek. "You wanna see the rest of the galaxy and fly a starship, don't you? You want to be away from here…?" After a moment of consideration, Gunner abandoned his indecision.

He hugged her tightly, but the excitement was making him restless. Lark could feel in his embrace an eagerness to go. "Go pack your things," she said to him, willing her arms to release him. "Just take what you can; I'll bring the rest when I come see you."

Like a catalyst pulse from a pistol, Gunner took off toward his bedroom. Lark stood slowly, moving back toward Liem and Jaimy as if her body was weighted to the floor. Sever, upon seeing his brother's excitement, bolted to follow. "He's packing," Lark said to her own brothers.

"Are you going to be alright?" asked Jaimy, almost apologetically.

She shrugged in response and forced herself to smile. "I always knew I had to let him go. Their freedom is important to me, I wasn't going to hold on forever." Giving a sigh, for a moment Lark revealed that this was much sooner than she had ever expected. "I'm just glad you two showed up when you did. The stars know how badly I needed you..."

Liem touched her arm. "He's gonna be fine, you know that. Kid's tough."

Lark gave a breath of a laugh, "Ain't him I'm worried about, fellas, that's my kid you're taking. I'm much more worried about the two of you."

When her brothers and her elder son were gone, Lark asked Salmalaina to return. The dumpy darkspawn woman had taken her leave shortly after Lark had shown up with her brothers as she had not wanted to intrude.

"Where is Gunner?" Sal had skin the color of red wine, with a round face and bright, red eyes. The female d'javu all had black hair on their heads, and a lot of it as if to make up for the fact that their males had none. Sal's flowed down to her shoulders, thick and wavy over dark horns that reached toward the sky. She spoke in d'javu exclusively and had been instrumental in ensuring both the boys were fluent.

"He's going to the Fringe," Lark answered her, letting Sever down so the child could greet Sal.

"Oh," Sal looked down at Sever and pinched his cheek. "We will miss his wisdom, no?"

"There's a human baby girl in Sever's room," Lark told the nanny tiredly. "I want to keep her safe, think she's in a lot of danger."

"Sever and I will protect her together," Sal said, gesturing toward Sever's room. "Come, little warrior." She patted Lark's shoulder as she passed, aware of the young mother's emotional exhaustion as only another woman could be. Lark moved to her own bedroom and got in the shower.

In the comfort and privacy of the shower, Lark leaned her weight against the cool metal wall and allowed the hot water to mingle with her tears. The sound of her grief echoed freely in the steamy room.

Regret is a cruel thing; offering clarity without resolution. Lark waited so long to put Gunner's needs first, squandered the years he'd been all hers. She had given him up now, and there was no going back. From now on, she would see his growth in spurts, catches of his face over comm waves and abbreviated visits.

Lark longed to say goodbye to him again, to hold him tightly until she knew she would never forget the feel of his slight form in her arms.

No one could have judged her pain, not even Mags, but she wanted to own these private tears. She lingered in the shower and allowed herself to feel the full width and breadth of her sorrow. Lark and Gun had spent less than two years alone together. He had given her purpose when she had lost all hope. She had the best reason to rise above

267

and push forward. He had been a good natured, obedient child. She hadn't deserved that, and she hoped he grew out of it. Liem and Jaimy were up to that task.

Assembled and geared, tears dried and pain subdued, Lark twisted her hair up and bid her younger son goodbye. "Lock up behind me, Sal," she said to the d'javu nanny. "Don't know who's comin' to get that girl."

Mags was alone inside the observation room. When she entered he was standing in front of the great round window silhouetted in red, his legs and arms were spread loosely as he stared up into the Devil's Tongue. He was deep in thought, so Lark approached slowly, quietly.

"He could have told me," she said lowly when she decided he'd had enough time to notice her. "I'm capable of being part of a feint..."

"I know," he replied, turning. "He didn't tell me either."

"Jaimy and Liem are gone," she said to him flatly, revealing none of the pain it had caused her to let them go. "Took Gun with them, bringing him to my father."

"That is good." In his sincerity lay the proof of his own regret, "It will be better for him than Kyro."

"You tried," she told him, wanting so badly for someone to believe her.

"Not hard enough," his answer was a blow of honesty Lark had not been prepared for. She closed her eyes and let out a sigh. The pad of his thumb brushed her cheek where she had scrubbed away the evidence of her weeping, "Are you alright?"

His concern leveraged her, and Lark steadied, opening her eyes. "We all did what was best."

Mags shook his head and said her name softly. His arm slid around her waist to pull her close, and she rested her head against his shoulder. "I am sorry it came to this," he whispered in her ear.

"I know," Lark breathed, fresh tears threatened in her throat and began to fill her vision.

"I cannot do what they can."

Lark let out a low chuckle and looked up at him, a teasing smile tugging at the corner of her lips as she sniffled and blinked the tears away. "Takes only two humans to do what the great and powerful darkling warrior can't?"

He pressed a gloved finger to her lips to silence her, the shadow of a grin visiting his face. "You know that I love you, don't you?"

The words were seldom spoken but that in no way diminished their truth. He'd never given her cause to doubt that he was steadfast in his affection. Still, hearing him say it, his comfort and support as she let go of a child that had caused so much tension between them, touched her deeply. "I do," she said around his finger. His other hand rose to cup her cheek, and he kissed her.

Lark leaned into his embrace. Pressed close to him, she could smell the darkness of his skin against the hard leather of his armor and it reminded her that their love had been forged in battle. So close to it now, their bonds heated to strengthen despite all that sought to pull them apart.

A low fizzle and the smell of brimstone that came from him intensified. Lark opened her eyes when he released her, finding they were no longer in Katarak Keep. She looked around as Mags' hold on her loosened, and she was surprised to see through the view port just in front of her that they were now in the expanse of space. The red glow of the Devil's Tongue was nowhere to be seen.

Confused and disoriented, she hardly noticed when Mags collapsed in her arms.

31

"MAGS!" LARK shouted as she tightened her grip around his waist and strained to keep him from crumpling to the ground. In the end, she was only able to slow his descent. She helped him as safely as possible to the floor and, after propping him up against the wall, Lark found with distress that the orange glow of his eyes was barely a flicker. She knelt beside him and looked over his defeated body, "What the fuck did you do?"

"He teleported the both of you across the galaxy using the ancient powers of our people," a familiar voice broke. Lark looked up at the figure standing over them. "Something I cautioned him against attempting. He has always had a problem with patience."

"Hurshek. They finally get you off that fucking rock?" a relieved smile broke across Lark's face. He looked down at her with the same old seriousness that, at this moment, reminded her of his reliability. To her prone husband, Lark cocked her head. "I didn't know you could do that," she said to him.

Without opening his eyes, Mags gave a weary, cockeyed grin. "Neither did I..."

Lark smirked at him and then turned back to Hurshek. "Well?" she prompted.

"Well?" he mimicked, staring down at her intently. A wealth of wisdom and knowledge, he still had not managed to develop an understanding of human idioms. He also lacked anything even remotely resembling a sense of humor.

"Is he gonna be alright or are we fucking doing this without him? Wait, are we..." At first, she had been too focused on Mags' sudden debilitation, but now she recognized her surroundings.

They were on the bridge of a warship; the larger half of the room was outfitted from floor to ceiling with a permaglass starshield marred by a crack that had been filled and sealed but carefully preserved. The computers and navigation equipment had all been retrofitted to accommodate the darkspawn physiology; the monitors scrolled readouts and updates in the severe d'javu typeset.

There was still no mistaking it. The construction of this vessel was a human design. "Is this the *Salvation*?"

"It was," Hurshek amended, turning and gesturing to another darkling in the corner. "You will remember that it has been renamed as the *Wraakitak*."

Vengeance. Sense of humor or no, she was sure the irony wasn't lost on Hurshek or anyone else. The juggernaut had been the glory of the Protectors, the largest ship they had ever constructed. Lark hadn't seen it since they had used it to destroy the Protectors' home planet. She had never considered where Mags had sent it.

Hurshek was handing her a metal cup and gesturing toward Mags. She took the cup in one hand and immediately the sharp, sweet smell hit her nostrils. "This is rakku juice," she told Hurshek insistently, shaking her head. "He hates it." She started to hand it back to him, but Hurshek held up a hand.

"The rakku flower has healing properties to the d'javu. With that and a short rest, he will recover quickly."

Lark felt Mags' fingers find their way into her hand, and she turned to find him chuckling quietly. Was it embarrassing for him to have her pander to his private preferences in the presence of others? Lark helped him drink and then with a large darkling's help brought him to the ready bunk not far from the bridge.

"It alright if I leave you here?" she asked quietly when they were alone. She tugged his boots off and pulled a blanket up over him.

"Not if you're going to make me drink any more of that rancid juice," he answered her, his eyes closing. His breathing deepened as he dozed off almost immediately until she slapped his chest. The sound of her hand striking the tough leather was loud enough to wake the dead. Through the shadow of the cramped bunk she saw slits of orange light appear on his dark face, the glow was already returning to them. "Why did you do that?" he asked. Mags had become very skilled at hiding a teasing tone, but Lark knew better.

"I tried to talk them out of giving you the damn juice— you fucking hate it. Made it out like I was being overbearing..." She sat down on the edge of the bed and rested her chin on his arm. "I know I'm a just a human woman here among all your people. But I feel like... somehow I got left out of something big..."

Mags' tired eyes blinked once, the glow disappearing for a moment. "If you don't wish me to treat you as a woman—" Playfully, she slapped him again before he could finish that statement. Mags laughed in his throat, catching her hand in his and pressing her fingers to his lips. "You have never been *just* anything to me. What is going on out here... it wasn't complete until you arrived. I would never fight a war without you by my side."

Lark gave a short sigh and shook her head, digging her chin mercilessly into his arm. "Don't be sweet, it's confusing." He muttered something slurred about distractions, his eyes beginning to close again. "Get some rest, I'll talk to Hurshek and see if there are any other foods you hate that have healing properties. I may need to start keeping kayat stew around." She hardly heard his groan of revulsion as she rose to leave the room.

"I know I should know this," Lark began as she approached Hurshek on the bridge. He was watching the d'javu work the navigation controls and scanning space as it slowly passed by the starshield. "Mags hasn't gotten a chance to fill me in... any chance you'll tell me what the hell we're doing out here?"

"Of course, my queen," he answered glancing at her briefly. "We are on the outskirts of the Philanthian cluster. We will commence our attack on Vargo once Magnimus awakens."

"Why are we attacking Vargo when the Protectors are attacking Ky—Did you just call me queen?" Lark was starting to become less and less enthused by Hurshek's little surprises.

"I did," he answered, giving her that same un-readable expression. "If Magnimus is to become the d'javu-khan, then you will be the d'javu-kheen." He turned back to the stars as if this were something that should have been common knowledge.

"D'javu-khan...?" she prompted when he failed to elaborate.

"The d'javu-khan is the darkling king. Magnimus freed us from the bonds of the oppressive Alliance. Now, he will unite us and take his rightful place not only as our leader but as our ruler. And you will be at his side."

"But... I'm human. Don't you think some of you are going to have a little bit of a problem with that?"

Hurshek gave a nearly undetectable shake of his head. "When he is d'javu-khan, his word will be law. If he says you are the queen, there is no darkspawn alive who would dare combat him. You will be his equal in all our eyes, and your son will be his heir."

"Even though he's..."

"Even though he is a half-breed," Hurshek nodded. He didn't seem to notice the way she tensed at the word.

Lark fell silent for a beat, peering down at the floor of the bridge and then at the stars punched out of the velvet blackness before them. "I didn't know any of this..."

"Nor should you have," Hurshek turned to look at her. "When the galaxy exiled our people, much of our history and tradition was lost. That is why Magnimus brought me here from Sulok, to help him restore the d'javu to what we once were." A rare smile tugged at the corner of his blue lips. "You didn't think he brought me here for my military prowess, did you?"

Rarer still, was something of a self-deprecating joke. Lark chuckled, feeling the weight of ignorance begin to slide from her shoulders. That explained why all of the sudden she was getting blindsided by new information constantly.

"We are attacking Vargo," Hurshek went on. "Because the Protectors are attacking Kyro. With their forces divided, our numbers will appear swollen while they scramble to defend on several fronts." His dark red eyes studied her. "Crotis brought this upon us prematurely. Magnimus did not want to share his plan with the governor until after he had discussed it with you. One of the young darklings in Crotis'... service may have temporarily misplaced his loyalty. The attack on your children was meant as much to send a message to Magnimus as it was to you."

Lark chewed on that for a long moment. Then she offered Hurshek a grateful smile. "Thanks for bringing me in on this."

With customary distance, Hurshek gave a nod. "Magnimus views you as his equal, so I will treat you as such."

Lark said little else, but she got the feeling as she stood there next to Hurshek that how the Kabalak viewed her had less to do with what Mags said and more to do with their own history. Perhaps, back on Sulok when she'd refused to back down, she'd gained an inkling of the priest's respect. She decided to put that one away to needle him with later.

32

Mags awoke in the bunk on the *Wraakitak* and found Lark sleeping next to him. Or, rather, sprawled out on top of him. Her legs were thrown over his, her elbows tucked in awkwardly in the tight space. She hadn't bothered to remove her holster belt, and her right-hand catalyst pistol was digging painfully into his leg. The low sound of carefully sawn wood echoed against the metal wall.

He could smell it: Battle. On her, in the air of the juggernaut. It was coming, and he had never been more prepared.

Mags poked Lark in the ribs until she jerked and giggled, bright eyes opening to glare at him. "Get ready," he told her softly, pulling his legs out from underneath hers and getting to his feet.

"Been ready," she insisted through a yawn, stretching and hopping out of the bunk. She smoothed her clothes then pulled on her jacket and went through the pockets, systematically checking their contents and compartments. Mags re-secured the fastenings of his woven darklite armor, watching her remove and replace items obsessively. She cocked her head at him when she was finished. He offered his arm, and they left the bunk together.

Hurshek was waiting for them on the bridge of the juggernaut. Outside, the civspace world called Vargo dominated the starscape. On this side of the glass, war dominated every corner of the bridge. Several star maps were holographically displayed throughout the command center. Each glowing display had a planet at the center, a fleet of ships approaching orbit.

Salvaged from the deserted landscape of the Protector home world, some of the juggernauts had only been half built when the Protectors had been destroyed, and their aft sections had been completed using materials and craftsmanship unique to Kyro. The ships looked something like human vessels that had been half-swallowed by shadow.

The besieged planets formed a line that slashed the galaxy in two. Vargo was closest to the center of civspace, only a few light years away. If they took this planet they would be at the Protectors' doorstep.

Vargo's location was the least of the reasons Mags had chosen it as the planet he attacked himself. "Vargo," he told his wife, "Is where Nyhman is doing his experiments on the darkspawn he has taken from Kyro. He breaks them and then sells them as glorified house pets in the Fringe. Or worse."

The fact that the Protectors allowed this to happen in their so-called Civilized Space meant they had learned nothing since the darkling rebellion. It was time for a supplemental lesson.

And when Magnimus got his hands on Nyhman he'd get what was coming to him as well.

Magnimus gave a growl of anticipation and grinned to himself. The soft leather of Lark's hide jacket yielded when he grabbed her arm, pulling her toward the transport hangar.

"Where are you going?" Hurshek wanted to know, taking only a few steps to follow them.

Pausing and regarding him over his shoulder, Mags gave what seemed to him to be the obvious answer, "To the battle."

"You are their leader, you need to be here. Leading them," said the Kabalak calmly.

Lark laughed at that. "And miss all the fun?"

"Magnimus, you cannot lead the darkspawn from the grave."

Mags scowled at the other darkling, whose wisdom always somehow bordered on the inconvenient. "That's why I'm bringing her with me," he waved a hand in Lark's direction and then started for the door. She followed dutifully but not without flashing Hurshek a grin.

33

THE VALLEY city called d'jaku rose up on either side of the Alliance army. Before them, line after line of darkspawn in dark shades of blue and red and even greens and oranges stood waiting. Each face, regardless of its coloring, was split with a sardonic, hungry smile. Shielded in their barbaric armor, brandishing darksteel weapons, the d'javu stared them down like a long-awaited meal.

Dimly, Ryk wondered if any of these creatures knew what it was that had brought the Alliance legion here. It was doubtful. Even more doubtful would be that they cared. The darklings had long been waiting for the day they could finish what they had started.

The shuttles emptied the Alliance's unimpressive invasion. A few hundred mostly untested troops against what had to be half again as many drooling darkspawn warriors. Not the untrained, repressed rabble they had faced last time, either. This was the true meaning of the ancient darkling horde the people of Salva had sworn to keep exiled beyond the Devil's Tongue.

Devi came to a stop in front of the army and the d'javu let out a deafening battle roar. Ryk glanced behind him to see the younger soldiers shudder and fall back a step. The veteran Protectors held their ground, those who had been in captivity seemed to rise taller.

"Shut up!" Devi's scream brought his attention back to her. She shifted forward to stand beside her. Bae was nowhere to be seen, but Ryk didn't have time to wonder after him. Devi repeated her demand until the battle roar died down. "You know why we are here! You committed an act of war by sending that cretin to steal my daughter from me!"

The darkling heads swiveled back and forth, muttering to each other in confusion. One of the larger, a dark green d'javu wearing spiked pauldrons and shouldering a heavy ax, spoke up. "Who is cretin?" he inquired.

"Lark. Your fearless leader's best friend," Devi spat in disdain.

A rumble went through the closest darklings. Green had a smaller d'javu at his side, whispering in his ear. After a short discussion; he turned back to the Protectors and spoke. "Lark is wife of Magnimus. She is our queen."

For a reason that Ryk was sure he would never understand, this seemed to make Devi even more furious. Maybe it was the way the d'javu continued to flaunt Alliance laws, their insistence on remaining outside the rules of normal society. Everything about them pressed her buttons. "That's not true! It's been forbidden for generations!"

The darklings began to make a noise as if they were revving up to do that battle cry again. The cry itself never came, but the sound became rhythmic. Ryk realized after a moment that they were laughing.

"We do not care for your laws," Green told her when he had composed himself. "Law is Magnimus." They began to chant, then. Something either in d'javu or unintelligible universal. Either way, Devi was having none of it.

"Enough!" she screamed over them. "Where is your leader? He will give me my daughter back, and the darkspawn will stay out of our galaxy!"

"Devi," Ryk warned, gripping her elbow and pulling her a step back. She shot him a caustic look, but he was undeterred. "If you speak to Magnimus that way then we will get nowhere."

Their green compatriot wasn't deterred either. "Magnimus is not here," he said, holding his ax in both hands. "There is nothing to speak about. It will be *you* who will stay out of our galaxy!" He raised his ax and, as if this was the cue they'd been waiting for, the horde began moving toward them, a great dark wave rushing across the face of Kyro.

Devi pulled her catalyst pike from its place on her back and thumbed it on. She raised it and answered the roar of the d'javu with a battle cry of her own. Green came at her and swung his ax, a heavy downward stroke. Devi dodged, spun her pike and then slammed it through his chest.

All around them, darkling met ally in combat, and the battle had begun with an agonizing crunch. Ryk pulled his sword and activated the catalyst core just as the nearest d'javu was on him, a great hammer falling with deadly efficiency toward his head. Ryk swung his sword, and the energized blade bit deep into the darkling's short, stubby forearms, knocking the blow aside. Ryk pushed down, bringing the injured creature to his knees, and brought his foot up against the side of the thing's face.

Yanking his blade free, he barely had the chance to duck beneath the next blow that came. Dark red blood still clung to the glowing metal of his sword as he swung with both hands and buried it between the ribs of the closest darkspawn. He didn't even stop to see if it was the one that was attacking him.

Over the chaos around him and the grunting and roaring of the d'javu, he could hear Devi. She was screaming as she attacked, letting loose all the anger she had been swallowing since they'd found Bae unconscious and Dia's crib empty. Her hot-headed nature had served her well in the past, but this time Ryk was concerned she might have cracked a little.

[Ryk!] He'd almost missed the sound even though it was in his ear. Bae's voice, calling to him through the comm. [Up here!]

Pausing long enough to search over the crowd, he saw Bae standing atop a rampart and waving at him. [I know how to get you inside. Get Devi and meet me at the end of this wall.]

Ryk was going to nod if it had not been for the darksteel laden fist that nearly took his head off. The world spun briefly, and the ground came up to meet him, but Ryk turned his sword up as the darkling came at him. He shoved upward deftly, and the blade sunk deep with the darkspawn's own momentum.

Devi was screaming for him. She stabbed the already dying creature with righteous fury, shoving him over and off Ryk's sword. "Are you alright?!" she asked urgently, reaching down to yank him up, her anger momentarily washed away by worry.

"I'm fine," Ryk responded, leaning on her slightly. When the daze had passed, he nodded toward Bae who was hacking at a d'javu that had followed him up on top of the wall. "Bae can get us inside." Without a word, Devi started through the crowd, clearing the way for Ryk as she went.

By the time they reached the end of the rampart, Bae jumped down and spun his ax before fastening it over his shoulder. Blood dripped from the blade onto his shoulder as he grinned at them. "What took you guys so long?"

34

Lark sucked in breaths, the taste of stagnant water from a stone reservoir sticking to her tongue. While she felt the hot air burning its way in and out of her throat, her lungs seemed convinced she was asphyxiating. Chasing people was her day job; she had no problem with running. But it was the dead of summer and the planet Vargo, apparently, circled about a half meter from its sun these days.

The crowded darkspawn army made a path for Mags. Shouts of his name eagerly filled the air along with war cries Lark didn't bother to translate. Instead, she focused on the pumping rhythm of her legs and the struggling intake of air that was thickening quickly the further into the ranks they travelled. If they said anything to her, she didn't hear it. Her ears had long ago become accustomed to their contempt, and she was not going to waste her energy on them now.

Muscles screaming and sweat pouring over her face, she smothered a cry of relief when Mags began to slow as they arrived at the head of the column. Lark came to a stop behind him, gulping air and taking comfort in the fact that his shoulders heaved as well. Her heart banging around in her chest drowned out any of what Silas said as he greeted

Mags. Instead of attempting to listen in, she moved to the front of their line to get some air and her first look at the city of Hartun.

The ancient walled city stood atop a high cliff at the crest of a craggy bluff. Sprawled out at its base, tight rows of Hartun's warriors stared back at the roiling mass of the darkspawn army that was just waiting for the signal to attack. Lark didn't know much about the city or the planet with the exception that it had been abandoned for a long time before being bequeathed upon Nyhman as a reward for his work on the darkspawn. Work which he continued here, from what Mags had uncovered, in a laboratory beneath the city.

Lark stared through the haze of heat and humidity at the far-off warriors of Hartun City. The late afternoon sun glinted off bronze breast plates and overlarge helmets, tracking the giant orb as it began its descent toward the horizon behind the walled city. The soldiers were uncannily still, as if held there by an outside force. It was an unnatural stillness that forced Lark to stare harder.

A gust of tepid wind off the reservoir brought a moment of relief and tore already loosened hair from the braids across her scalp, catching it in the zipper of her jacket. Grumbling to herself, Lark leaned her rifle against her leg and proceeded to untangle the strand.

At first, she didn't see the movement of the ranks. When she lifted her head to re-secure the honey strands into her braids, she found the Hartun troops had shuddered into movement and began a slow, restrained march toward where the darkling army stood.

Dread began to stir inside Lark as she squinted into the lowering sun. One of the bronze-clad warriors at the front of the column suddenly raised his sword, as if to strike the invaders who were still several meters away. His arm trembled with unseen effort, but he swung and threw the sword to the ground in defiance.

As if released from slow motion once the sword had left his hand, the mutinous warrior fell to his knees, grasping at the collar around his throat. She watched helplessly as he sank lower and lower to the ground. Then the warrior's head abruptly leapt from his shoulders and tumbled to the ground. The decapitated body crumpled, and the army moved on, heedless of their decapitated comrade.

Lark struggled to pull her goggles up over her eyes, fingers trembling in trepidation as she zoomed in on the forgotten helmet. Where it had fallen open, Lark could see the face within. Dusky blue skin and features that would have been ghoulish even without the way the face had distorted in agony.

One after another, bronze laden heads left their bodies and weapons clattered to the ground unused. Lark saw with growing horror that every last one of them was a darkling.

"*Mags!*" she shouted, tearing her goggles down and pushing aside a large darkling that was standing between them. She grabbed a handful of her husband's hide duster and yanked, pointing to the army. From his expression of annoyance at her uncouth interruption, he didn't see it at first either. "Those are d'javu warriors!" she tried not to scream at him, but she could hear the panic in her own voice. "Wearing shrink collars!"

After only a moment, his face contorted in recognition. "*Pull back!*" he ordered in d'javu. Silas repeated the order, and the horde began to march back amidst puzzled growling. Mags pulled Lark with him as he hurried the group into a jog, murmuring into his comm to Hurshek as he did so.

Lark's feet felt leaden as she kept her eyes on the captive army and noted with relief that, after a terrible moment, they came to a halt and regained their unusual motionlessness.

"Magnimus, what do we do?" Silas asked when he called for them to stop, his eyes lingering on the frozen darklings and his grip tightening on the hilt of his sword.

"We will not attack our own people," answered Mags, his voice barely audible. "Hurshek, do you have a layout of the city?"

[I do, Magnimus,] the priest's voice in their ears. [But it is not complete.]

"Send it to Lark," Mags had already begun stalking through the crowd of his army. Lark followed. Her gauntlet trilled, and she shouldered her rifle, bringing the map up on a micro-holo. Mags paused when they reached the edge of the army, turning to address Lark whose eyes had not left her gauntlet as they passed through the ranks, "Can you get us inside?"

Lark's brow furrowed as she scrolled along and filtered through layers. "Yeh," she closed it and looked up at him. "Remember the aqueducts on Izlatana?"

From the look on his face, he certainly did. The caverns of the aqueducts that fed fresh water into the bathing pools at the resort had been the private escape for their illicit love affair. Izla had caught them there together in the end, but it didn't change the warmth of the memories they'd created on wet stones surrounded by the sounds of bubbling water.

Mags seemed unable to fathom what those aqueducts had to do with their current situation. Lark smiled at him and started walking. After a brief pause, Mags followed, volunteering to allow her to surprise him yet again.

Her cryptic words made sense swiftly thereafter when she was leading Mags through the dark, cavernous underground waterway that fed the city from the reservoir.

The rank air was humid, and the water barely moved in the channel to their right, the city having long ago resorted to less archaic methods of water distribution. The stone of the narrow walkway was damp and slippery with all manner of the soggy plant life that grew in this type of environment. Lark's voice echoed down the tunnel ahead of them. "Familiar, ain't it?

"The aqueducts on Izlatana did not smell like this," Mags was steps behind her, and she was silhouetted in the light of the low-lit torch she was using to keep from taking a bath.

Lark gave the breath of a laugh, though her voice sounded distracted. "It was this or the sewers. Besides, how would you remember?" she slowed as she took a corner. Mags saw the blue-green illumination of the holo-map on her gauntlet appear and disappear at irregular intervals. "Unless you were paying more attention to the scenery than you were to me."

With a chuckle, Mags scanned the ceiling and found nothing of interest. There could have been surveillance equipment or some type of trap but so far, he'd seen little evidence anyone had been down here since the Alliance had formed. "You know very well that you are apt with your methods of distracting me."

The butt of her rifle slung over her back dug unpleasantly into his thigh when he ran into her. His eyes on the ceiling, he had not realized (and, he would recall to her afterward, she had not notified him) that she had stopped. Boots slipping in the scum, Lark's feet swept out from under her, and she plunged face first toward the dark water.

His hand seized her waist, the other shot out to grasp a ladder that ran up the wall to his left. With a jolt, she came to a stop, suspended over the water only by his arm. When she turned to look over her shoulder at him, her braid fell from her shoulder and the tip brushed the water. Or it would have, if she had not been so quick to swipe it away.

When Mags set her on her feet, she cocked her head at him and drew her hand across her forehead to wipe away the sheen of sweat that had gathered. "Ya sure I'm the only thing distracting you?"

He offered no explanation, and Lark shook off the adrenaline that had soared through her veins as she'd fallen for what felt like forever toward a dirty dip. "This ladder," she indicated the one he'd grabbed to steady himself when he caught her. Mags wiped scummy algae from his hand. "Leads up into the basement—"

A sound deep in the darkness quieted them both and Lark turned to look behind her. Mags touched her shoulder, peering around her, but he saw nothing. He shook his head and she turned back, bringing up her holo-map. "We'll come up near the outside wall. We can follow it around to the western wall, hope we don't catch any guards and turn in two streets from the lab."

Mags fisted the padlock that secured a metal plate over several rungs of the ladder. Lark's head swiveled in paranoia while he gave a tug, and the lock fell apart in his hand. It clattered across the path and dropped into the water with an echoing plop. Lark's hand fell on the railing of the ladder, but Mags grabbed her wrist. "I'll go first."

"Be my guest. I'll enjoy the view." He could see her grin clearly despite the gloom. He brushed her cheek with the back of his knuckles before gripping the ladder and hoisting himself up.

They came up in the basement of an occupied home. A half empty wine rack and several containers of unused items blocked a staircase that led to the main level. A haze of light came in from just below ceiling height. Lark kicked a wooden box over underneath the window and climbed up up, pushed open the dirty glass, and crawled out onto the street.

There was still far too much daylight for Mags to shadowwalk his way through the city, so they were forced to hug walls and move slowly. The space between the line of stone houses and the thick outer wall created a narrow alley which turned off toward guard houses and other infrastructure areas.

Lark approached a corner and came to a stop, pressing her back against the crumbling foundation of a home and listening intently. Under her breath, she let out a low curse. Voices. Guards approaching. Mags' hand caught her arm painfully and tugged her back, unsure if she had heard them as well.

The sound of a baton striking across Mags' shoulders was made no less sickening by his armor. He fell to his knees, momentarily void of breath, but rose just as quickly to combat his opponent. The man was tall and lithe, armored from head to toe in brown leather with shiny brass plates over his more vital or precious organs. He went for Mags again with the thick, studded baton, but he did not have the element of surprise this time. Mags lunged, and they clashed with deadly force.

Lark's hand plunged inside her jacket for her CCP, but even as her hand closed around the grip, she was yanked backward. Someone had grabbed her rifle where it had been slung across her back. They shoved her forward into the unforgiving stone house. A hand on the back of her head restrained her movement, the sharp edges of the crumbling rocks gnashed against her face. She could feel every one of her hidden weapons when the man pressed his weight against her.

A shout of pain and frustration escaped her, blood trickling into her eyes. She felt his hot breath on her neck; his body confining hers against the stone foundation. He hadn't been fast enough; Lark still had her CCP in her hand even if she hadn't been able to free it from its holster strapped against her ribcage. She wrenched it from where it was wedged between her and the wall, tearing her holster and jacket as she did so. She aimed downward and between them, firing repeatedly into the man's foot.

Howling, he fell backward. Lark spun just as he recovered and slammed into her, plastering her back against the wall again. As she fought him, Lark saw Mags turn. Having dispensed with his opponent he started toward hers. What he didn't see was the crowd of them behind him, blackened teeth glinting from sour grins.

"*Aketi!*" she shouted at him in d'javu. "*There's no time! Get the shrink collars, I'll catch up!*"

He paused momentarily, puzzled at the order. Lark was sure he felt he could easily save her, and they could move on together. Then he passed a look over his shoulder to find that they were upon him. When he turned back, Lark saw agony on his face.

She swore at him foully, her voice guttural with the effort of fighting to keep her hands free from the repressive guard. "*GO!*"

35

BAE PAUSED. After running swiftly across the expanse of the main hall, ill lit and full of dusty air, he came to a stop at an intersection that led in four different directions. Ahead of them, the hall turned several meters off and followed a wall broken by windows. To the left a set of stairs that disappeared into darkness, to the right a shadowed hall. Behind them were only the main hall and the sounds of the battle from which they'd come.

When he stopped, Devi slowed with Ryk beside her.

"That way goes down to the dungeons," Bae indicated the left. His eyes lingered on the endless stairs, alight with fearful memory before he moved on. "This way…" he squinted toward the windows then pointed to the right. "I haven't been that way; I won't be of any help to you anyway."

Devi stared down the empty hallway. "What do you mean?"

"Go," he ordered them and began walking forward without missing a beat.

"Bae!" Devi dove to grasp his armor, hauling him to a stop. "You aren't going anywhere alone."

Bae disconnected her hand from his clothing and clasped his own at the back of her neck. The aggressive gesture caught her off guard. Devi went silent, staring into the eyes of a stranger. "You have a daughter here, Dev, and her father is with you. I know where I'm going if I go this way, and we'll cover more ground if we split up. I *will*," he spoke the word with certainty that shook his hand where it held her, "see you after."

Releasing her abruptly, Bae strode away. Devi stood stunned, rubbing her neck where he had grabbed her. She let out a breath then turned to look at Ryk. The sympathy on his face only seemed to enrage her again. "Let's go," she snapped petulantly, storming down the righthand corridor like a teenager being sent to her room.

With each passing intersection that offered no resistance, Ryk slowed. They had been interfered with by no one. When they had come here following what they considered an act of war or terrorism by the darkspawn, they had expected the army waiting at the gates. They had also expected Magnimus to meet them here, most likely with his jagged hands around the throat of their beloved daughter. Instead, they found Katarak Keep all but abandoned.

The map Ryk had pulled up on his tablet dated back to just after the death of Jiktar Avrok. Since then, the Protectors didn't bother much with the Keep. Ryk himself, even as High Commander, had never set foot in the place. Crotis had assumed maintenance of the place and, as far as they'd known at the time, it had been forbidden to the d'javu. After Magnimus claimed it as his home, several additions and alterations had been made that the map didn't account for. Twice now, they'd had to double back without making any progress.

"This is pointless," Devi huffed from ahead of him, defeated. "We haven't seen one guard. We can't be going the right way."

"All their warriors must have been sent outside," Ryk answered absent mindedly, his eyes trained steadily on the map searching for something they'd missed. "Or at least they want us to think they have nothing in here worth guarding."

Devi squinted up a broad staircase that smelled faintly of decay, wrinkled her nose and turned back toward the main corridor. She muttered in disdain, "They would do something like that, wouldn't they?"

She wasn't wrong. If they had learned nothing else from the rebellion, it was that the darkspawn were far more apt than they had realized at reading their enemies, manipulating even the most insignificant advantage, and exploiting weaknesses. The Protectors had failed to give the darkspawn credit for this in the past, and it had been their undoing. Ryk did not think it best to repeat such a mistake.

"They would..." he mused, raising his eyes from the tablet slowly to allow them time to adjust from the bright light to the darkness. Blinking, he realized suddenly that this particular area of the corridor was much darker than it had been previously. "Which could mean..."

He pulled a flash-torch from his belt and pointed it into the gloom. The beam of light disappeared into shadow straight ahead of him then swung around and tracked up the silky black carvings of the wall.

What he saw when the light struck the ceiling was nothing less than a nightmare.

Ryk made no noise to alert Devi to the scene on the ceiling. The darkspawn, clinging to the outcroppings and sculptures high above, grinned at him with wide mouths, teeth glinting in the light of the torch and dripping with drool.

Devi snapped around and then looked up in the direction of the light. She gave no reaction before she pulled a small controlled catalyst pistol from her belt and began to fire. The pulses of chemical energy glowed brightly as they sored into the ceiling and splashed against the darkspawn.

The darklings screamed and fell. Some were dead by the time they hit the ground, others were merely injured and lay there squirming and screaming through the din. A few of them managed to dodge the chemical pulses and land on their feet with black weapons in their hands.

Ryk dropped the tablet and drew his sword from his back. While Devi continued to fire at the ceiling and bodies rained around them, he charged the upright darkspawn before they could do the same to him.

They were in the right place. The subversive attack was nothing if not evidence that their daughter was here. Ryk did not care if he had to kill every darkspawn on Kyro to get her back.

Bae entered the vaulted war room through the southernmost door at the top of the tiered steps that led down to that great table. He clutched his ax, dripping with fresh blood, in both hands and started down the stairs toward where Crotis stood with his palms pressed against the surface of the darkstone table.

The old man's face rose without surprise, and his eyes leveled on the intruder. "Baelfor," he croaked, lifting his hands from the table and steepling them before him. "After all the time you spent here, I would have thought Kyro would be the last place I'd meet you again."

Bae's eyes narrowed as he stepped down a tier. It felt like it hadn't been that long ago that he and his fellow Protectors had stood in this very room surrounded by the darkspawn, watching them celebrate the destruction of Salva and the genocide of her people. Magnimus, that great ax falling into the table and cracking the stone carving of the Protector home world. The cheers of the rest of the darklings at the despair of an entire race.

Years of captivity had dulled Bae's wits, but they had not dulled his memory of that day nor the anger that had darkened his dreams since then. "I came back for you," said Bae darkly, stepping down another tier. "You were put here to govern the d'javu, to keep them under control. You betrayed us. The galaxy, its people, Salva. All of us. For what?"

Crotis did not hesitate a moment, he gave his answer with calm self-assurance. "For a people that had been ostracized from the rest of the galaxy. Slaughtered and exiled simply because they were different from the rest of us. I was put here to control them, yes. But I came to see another side of the d'javu that the Protectors and the rest of the Alliance had refused to see. The darkspawn have been misunderstood and mistreated, as I had been, and they simply deserve more."

Bae shook his head in disgust. "You're a liar. You wanted power. You knew the easiest way to get it was through those weaker than yourself. That is why you took Magnimus when he was young. You used him and all the darkspawn. You used Kyro."

Crotis spread his hands in a gesture of pacification, watching Bae closely as he descended the tiers. "Did you come here to tell me all that, Baelfor? Your people are going to lose this battle, as they lost the last one. Except this time, we will have more than just shallow victory. We will have it all. It will not matter how far you go, you will never escape us."

Bae let out an ironic laugh as he took yet another step closer to Crotis, his ax held high. "Us?"

36

HE KNEW she could take care of herself, he knew that she was more than capable of slipping away from those men. She had lived in this galaxy on her own most of her life. She had fought battle after battle alone. She had lived through hell and come out of it a warrior as a benefit of her own strength and perseverance.

All of that had made it no easier to walk away when she was in the midst of a battle—his battle, nonetheless. If she was killed he would never forgive himself.

Still, he ran on. At least he had managed to pull some of them away from Lark. He could hear them following, loud and slow. Every breath that heaved in and out of their lungs gave Mags an indication of how far they were falling behind.

He must have been charging forever, listening for them as his mind clung to Lark, anger swelling inside him. The things he was going to do to that man when he came back for her. He could already taste his blood; feel the inside of his head as he filled it with a darkness that would have him tearing his eyes out. That man who had put his hands on Lark would not die quickly. He would suffer.

Mags was lost in thought when the wall rose up in front of him. The alley that followed the outer wall had come to a swift and final dead end. Mags slid to a stop before it, aghast at the unexpected terminus. He had missed a turn. Distracted by thoughts of avenging his wife, he had possibly undone everything she had sacrificed herself for.

The fury that had been focused on those humans suddenly turned inward, morphing into a black self-hatred. He may as well have ended this war and taken his wife's precious life himself. Belatedly, he remembered the guards that were pursuing him. They were closer now.

Mags gathered himself for the impending confrontation. There were only three of them, though the tight quarters would make working them over more difficult than it needed to be. It was time wasted on top of too many other foul-ups, but he had little choice in the matter. Die here and Lark suffered for nothing.

Heavy footsteps faltered, and Mags listened more intently. Rapidly, those footsteps became tangled and with a rolling thump, one of the guards fell. Another second and the other guards tumbled as well. Mags peered back around a corner and saw them lying dead several yards behind him. A flash of movement at the top of the rampart caught his eye and he turned to peer up into the setting sun.

She was lowering her rifle and giving him a savage grin that was as mirthless as he'd ever seen it. The right side of her face glittered in the sunlight like a half-mask made of bloody fire.

The rifle rose to her eyes again and she fired. Mags barely dodged, the blast came within a breath of striking his left arm, and he snapped around quickly, assuming this meant there was someone close behind him. A dark, smoking burn mark in the stone wall was the only evidence of a target. When Mags turned back to Lark, she was already moving swiftly along the rampart. Mags chuckled to himself.

He could almost hear her voice. *"I didn't get my ass kicked so you could stand there and stare at me, lover, now hustle."*

So, hustle he did, back-tracking to the turn he had missed and keeping an eye on her as she followed him above. She was a silhouette now, backlit by the twilight sun. He could tell by the focus of her movements that her customary playful viciousness had been replaced with furious determination.

In words more closely derived from her own vocabulary, Lark was through fucking around.

37

"Is this... someone's home?" Devi asked when Ryk had forced the door open, and they stood in what appeared to be an apartment. A wide stairwell faced them, leading up to a sparsely furnished living area and open kitchen. From the entry way, the ceiling was visible, domed in glass and lit by the red glow of the Devil's Tongue. A narrow hallway with three doors, opened and closed, stretched to their right.

Ryk peered through the dimly lit corridor. "Someone who is not here..." he gestured up toward what they could see of the living area. "This was built after the rebellion."

"Crotis?" Devi assumed, following him as he started down the hallway. He stopped and bent suddenly, lifting something small into his hand. "What is it?"

Ryk turned, holding up a half-broken toy. "Children... I know there are rumors about Crotis but..."

Devi shook her head, taking the toy from him. "That was teenage boys, not babies..." Her forehead creased. "Lark... Lark lives here. She must have brought her children here..." Devi frowned deeply. She didn't believe what the darkspawn outside had said about Magnimus and Lark, but if the woman had children of her own... "How could she take our child? She is more heartless than I thought..."

Ryk gave a noncommittal shrug. "This is the only place in the galaxy she can be safe after what she did, it doesn't surprise me she would hide her children here." He turned back. "To people like her, money trumps common decency. Even if she is a mother herself."

Giving a nod of understanding, Devi dropped the toy on the floor. Her head snapped up when a cry came from down the hall. "Dia!" she exclaimed, slipping passed Ryk and heading toward the room from which the cry had come.

38

SALMALAINA KIRINSTAN knew the Protectors were coming. After all these years, she hadn't forgotten the sense of them—the percussion of their words. They weren't human. Humanity had nothing to do with it. The Salvans were beasts of some vile nature.

She had not always known. She had been young once and foolish enough to believe her happiness could not be taken. The Protectors had come and proved her wrong. It was a lesson Sal would never be free of.

Her hands twisted around the grip of her dagger. These were hands that were not meant to hold a weapon. They were hands that had been empty for far too long, since the Salvans had pulled her Zalik from them and murdered him when he failed their test. He had been only months old and would remain so for all eternity. Her only comfort was that his father had followed him. While Sal was left alone, at least they were together.

"Hide," she whispered sharply to Sever. The young boy obeyed almost instantly, perhaps sensing the danger himself. Sal pressed herself behind the door and held the dagger to her chest. Not for the first time, she wondered why they had not killed her that day as well. Such cruelty, to ask a woman to live on after killing her husband and son before her eyes.

Crotis had saved her during the chaos. He had absconded with her to Kar'ju in the wake of Jiktar Avrok's final days and placed the gray skinned child in her arms. The Protectors thought they had washed the galaxy clean of the black blood d'javu they feared so much. Magnimus would never know his parents, but their sacrifice was in his blood. Sal never let him forget that.

Her childless hands put to work, Sal had raised Magnimus as much as Crotis would allow. The old man had expressly forbidden anything he considered coddling, admonishing comfort for something as small as a skinned knee. The very moment the boy had shown even an ounce of autonomy—shortly after his fourth birthday—Sal had been removed from his presence. She would watch him grow into a powerful man from afar.

Sever was nearly four now, and she would be leaving him as well. At least she knew Sever would be in good hands with his mother. She swore silently she would bring a message with her to the place beyond life, to tell Jiktar and Hosta their son had made them proud. Twice over. Now it was time for her to repeat their sacrifice to ensure their grandson would have the same chance.

The Protectors were in the apartment now, Sal could hear them through the closed door speaking low to each other and coming closer. Their voices and the fear in her throat took her back to those horrible moments when her child and husband were ripped from her.

Sal would die before she allowed Lark to feel that same pain. She longed to hold her sweet boy once more, to tell him to be good to his mother. And to say goodbye. There was no time. The Protectors were at the door.

The door opened, and Sal pressed herself more firmly against the wall, hoping the slamming of her heart against her ribs would not give her away.

"Dia!" Sal jumped when the woman cried out, heading quickly toward the bed with the man at her back.

Once they had passed the threshold, Sal pulled in a deep breath and steadied her courage. "*Filthy Kotumcyst!*" she screamed in d'javu, the blade held above her head as she threw herself at the man's back.

The woman shouted something, and the end of a pike cracked against Sal's wrist. Her hand blossomed in pain, and her fingers released the blade. "*I will not let you hurt him!*" Sal cried though she knew they did not understand. She attacked again with the nails of her good hand slashing at the human woman.

The white-hot blade of the catalyst pike bit deep into her belly. Sal froze. She was not a warrior. She was merely a mother to children that replaced the one they'd taken from her. She stared at the human woman on the other end of the pike, her sharp features screwed up in anger. Sal recognized the look on this woman's face—another mother protecting her child.

It was wholly unfair that this Protector got to save her child when it was the Protectors themselves who had rendered Sal incapable, twice, of saving the children she loved.

"*I hate you*," Sal spat in d'javu before her knees gave out. "*Murderers. Child-killers.*" They both stared at her as she slumped to the floor, her final curses falling uselessly on ears that could not decipher them.

Sal fell onto her back and stared at the ceiling, listening to the Protectors speak words she could not understand. Helpless, she wept as darkness filled her vision.

39

TWILIGHT WAS turning to dusk and Lark was beginning to lose Mags among the infinite shadows inside the city walls. She scouted around each corner from her bird's eye view and, if a soldier was lurking ahead of Mags, she paused to shoot them before they even knew he was coming. He hardly had to slow down as he made his way through the city.

The tops of the ramparts were void of a walkway, slightly crenelated and heavily decayed in places. Lark was only just able to navigate them with her dignity intact. None of the guards thought to look up here for her so she remained un-accosted throughout the entire ordeal. When she wasn't trying to keep up with Mags, she kept herself low and out of the light of the sun.

Mags had nearly disappeared into shadow by the time he entered one of the buildings. As nondescript as any of the other structures in the city, Lark didn't know how he could tell that was where he needed to be without the map that was stored in her gauntlet.

Dread rose like bile in her throat, and Lark choked on the internal hope that Nyhman was not in that building. Selfishly, she prayed to any god or spirit that her husband would never find him. Even if it meant Mags would spend the rest of his life searching.

Shaking her head against these insidious thoughts, Lark chewed her lip. Her eyes never left the door through which Mags had disappeared, as if staring at it long enough would reveal what was going on beyond it.

Crouched down, she watched the last tongue of red sunlight lick at the top of the tallest buildings before it fell below the horizon. What the *hell* was going on in there? She had no way of knowing what he was up against, no way of knowing if he had found Nyhman or the collar controls or if he had ended up at the nasty end of some lucky fuck's catalyst pistol. Tapping ruddy fingernails on the barrel of her rifle, she squinted through the fading light at the door.

A pattering and lazy summertime rain began to fall. Lark turned her face to the sky and closed her eyes, letting a few of the large warm drops loosen the sheen of sticky blood that had layered over her skin. She ran the back of her glove over her face, streaking the dark leather with brownish-red stains.

When she'd finally had enough of waiting, she threw her rifle across her back and began searching for a way down. That was when she felt it. Anxiety rose in her so suddenly her knees quaked, and she was forced to grip the ramparts to save herself from tumbling over the edge.

Fear; abrupt and inexplicable fear. Lark turned to look into the city and found that people were beginning to stream from the buildings, eyes wide with panic as they ran full tilt out into the darkening streets. Unable to face such terror, some had chosen to fling themselves from windows or balconies. Their unfortunate landings did nothing but heighten the frenzy of those already on the ground.

Years upon years of standing at Mags' side while he pulled this trick, one would think Lark would have gotten used to it by now. Unfortunately for Lark, even her body could never get used to this type of fear. She had, however, learned how to work around it. At least this meant Mags was alive.

Pulling herself up, Lark swallowed the terror in the back of her throat and started back the way she'd come, watching the ebb and flow of the crowd as it flooded Hartun's streets. Rich men, whores, soldiers, and servants—fear made them all equal.

Once on the ground, Lark bolted through the chaotic streets, shooting anyone that came at her. She was unsure if the fear she felt for Mags was real or manufactured, and she wasn't terribly inclined to care. Mags had gone into that place and he hadn't come out, that was as much reason to be frightened as what he did to cause this riot.

Disoriented by the blinding terror and forced off course due to the idiotic panicking of the occupants of the city, it took Lark longer than she'd expected to get to the door where she'd last seen Mags. Once there, she found it locked and wasted no time kicking it in.

She had meant to charge in guns blazing, find her husband and plug whoever had forestalled him. Her rifle already raised, she glared down the sight and right into another door at the bottom of a steep staircase.

This one was more healthily secured, and it took almost a full minute of slamming catalyst pulse after catalyst pulse against the lock to get it open. Again, she prepared herself for an assault on whoever happened to be unlucky enough to be keeping Mags from his work.

What she saw when she kicked open the door froze her in her tracks. The room was windowless and dark, lit only by dim bluish light coming from large water tanks that lined the far wall. It was what was inside those tanks that had her feet rooted to the floor.

Darkspawn—dead or unconscious—floated in the murky water, tangles of tubes and wires sprouting from their skin. A lump of revulsion gathered in Lark's mouth, and she had to force herself to breath around it, her knees growing weak as she studied the darkspawn laid out on tables in similar states of consciousness. The floor was dark and wet with blood, Lark's eyes tentatively followed the trail of it to the opposite side of the room where a camera had been set up over a d'javu laying on a table.

It was all she could do not to wretch. The darkling's scalp had been cut open, his skull sawed away. Raw, bleeding brain exposed and half-dissected.

Nyhman. Sick bastard. Sicker than even Lark had guessed.

Light-headed and hyperventilating, Lark was close to collapsing when sounds of pain and anger from a corridor to her left brought her back to the moment. Terror seized her anew as she realized her husband could very well be on his way to one of those tables. Gripping her rifle, which had nearly fallen from her hands during her panic attack, Lark pushed herself out of the room and into the dark hallway, following the sounds of the scuffle.

Human bodies were slumped against the walls and lay mangled in the middle of the corridor, a sign that Mags had been through here searching for Nyhman. A distant sound of screaming made her press her back against the wall, holding her rifle against her chest. When the shouting didn't come any closer, she slowly peered around the corner to find the next corridor empty with the exception of a dead man that lay sprawled only a few yards from her.

Eyes trained on the opposite end of the hall, she crouched and approached the dead man. His earpiece had fallen from his ear and lay across his cheek, buzzing with the small sound of his comrade's voices. Lark lifted it and held it a few inches from her own ear, listening to the breathless but controlled shouts.

[He knocked the lights out on two,] the first voice reported. That meant Mags was alive and, for the moment, had the upper hand.

[Lifts are out, and stairwells are secured,] another answered. Alive, but trapped.

Lark tugged on the thin wire running from the earpiece until the box sprang free of the dead guard's uniform. She gave the earpiece a cursory wipe across the sleeve of her jacket and then plugged it into her ear, making sure to mute her end of the connection before shoving the box into her pocket.

They updated infrequently while she made her way to the stairwell. It sounded as if they had lost him. She found the stairwell and slipped up to the second-floor landing, watching the stairs above her for signs of fellow travelers.

One of the guards was breathing endlessly in her ear either from exertion or trepidation. [I think we cornered it.]

It?! Lark had to restrain herself from opening up the comm and giving that man a piece of her mind. He went on a moment later, whispering noisily, [At the end of the west corridor, near stair A.]

Curiously, Lark leaned forward to check the sign on the landing above her. A large block letter 'A' winked at her next to a door with a dark window. She appeared to be alone in the stairwell, but she climbed cautiously anyway, her finger settled gently on the trigger of her rifle. Other than the man's breathing, the stairwell and the building beyond had gone still and silent. Her boots scuffed quietly on each stair as she made steady progress toward the door.

[WEGOTHIMWEGOTHIMWEGOTHIM!]

Lark jumped when the crack of a catalyst bolt echoed simultaneously through the door and the earpiece, the guard's exhilarated call drowned out by the repeated firing.

Catalyst pulses flashed on the other side of the window, coming from both directions.

Caution forgotten, Lark lunged for the door and shoved with all her might, but they had indeed secured it. She kicked it once, out of frustration rather than any misconception that it might help, and then she began the process of emptying her rifle into the hinges. A high-pitched whine, growing in strength, told her that the catalyst chamber was beginning to get low. She paused to check it and heard the fitful, angry noises of a caged animal and repeated orders to hold him. There was no time to work on the hinges, she needed out of this stairwell now.

Slinging her rifle over her shoulder, she pulled a palm-sized charge from her belt and slapped it over the lock. On the lower landing, she pressed the detonator and didn't wait for the explosion to complete before she scrambled back up the stairs.

The catalyst pulses had ended. The stairwell was full of smoke, but the door didn't even resist her weight when she threw herself against it. Momentum brought her into the opposite wall, pulling her dual CCPs from their holsters.

"Hey!" she shouted at no one in particular. Not far from where she stumbled out of the thinning dust cloud and into the darkness of the hallway, she could see the glow of flood lights and the gathering of guards on high alert.

Mags was in the center, on his stomach. His hands were bound by a rough black tether that wound around his neck. In the harsh light of the handheld floodlights, everything about him was in stark detail. The darkness of his skin, the hatred on his face, and the raw, bloody skin where the cable bit into his throat.

One of those flood lights shifted in Lark's direction, temporarily blinding her.

She fired anyway. Twice.

By the way the mouth-breathing in her ear suddenly ended, at least one of her pulses hit home. Those guards not directly involved in detaining Mags scattered, many of them directly into Lark's line of fire. Her teeth clenched until they hurt, every free catalyst pulse she had went toward the light carriers that held her husband in place. One of them dropped, screaming as the light clattered to the floor. Another fell a moment later.

A pulse splashed on her shoulder, and Lark fell back a step. Her jacket absorbed most of the heat, but it ate its way to her skin quickly. Turning back, she squeezed both triggers and didn't let up, screaming as she did so and sending one last pulse to the final light carrier.

The flood light dropped, and Mags disappeared.

It didn't matter which one had said it, Lark shoved her pistols into their holsters and turned to the closest dying guard. Bringing her boot into his midsection, she cursed at him, "My husband is not a fucking *it*, you civspace bastard!"

A deadly shadow took care of the surviving force in the hallway. Lark followed the sound of the invisible struggle until she found him at the end of the corridor. The cable was still around his neck, and he'd utilized the other end in kind, strangling one of the guards while he pressed his hand to the side of the man's face. "Tell me where the controls are." His voice sounded calm, almost suggesting instead of demanding.

Lark fell back against the wall and drew in heavy breaths, adrenaline pounding through her veins until she heard her heartbeat banging around inside her head. She stared at Mags, his glowing eyes mirrored in the terrified gaze of the dying man. His forehead was bleeding from the butt of a rifle or some other blunt instrument they'd used to try to knock him out, repeatedly.

When he let the body drop, satisfied by whatever information he'd found, Lark lifted the rope over his head and squinted at the bloody ring around his neck. It was too dark to see it well and he was already on to the next task, anyway.

"Mags…" Lark said, without meaning too.

He turned, and his eyes pierced through the darkness, causing her to swallow her misery and fear. "Nyhman isn't here," he bit out.

Good. That's what Lark wanted to say. Instead, she said nothing. She just tried not to think about what her husband's insides would look like if that psychopath ever got close enough to take them out of him. Again, Lark felt as if she might throw up.

"The controls are this way." Mags was already walking down the hallway.

Lark hurried to catch up and slipped her hand into the crook of his elbow. He looked down at her and she arranged her face into what she thought was her customary Cheshire grin. The corner of Mags' lips curled slightly, and he turned his gaze into the dark hallway before them. "You were afraid."

"Was not," the retort came out of her mouth unbidden, but even she didn't believe it. Her eyes fell to where her fingers clutched his arm, and she squeezed the leather and hard muscle beneath. "After what I saw in that lab…" her own voice sounded weak and she knew that she had been afraid for him; terrified, in fact. "If he ever got his hands on you…" He pried her locked fingers from his arm when he came to a stop before a doorway and pressed them to his lips.

"When I saw that wild woman shooting her way into that hallway, I thought to myself. 'That is *my* wife.' And I cannot fathom for everything in the Fringe why she keeps following me into these messes."

"Why I keep saving your ass, you mean?"

The breath of a chuckle, and he swept her braid back over her shoulder. "As long as you love me, I have nothing to fear."

Lark felt her cheeks warm and a stupid, girlish smile spread across her face. She gave him a gentle shove and turned toward the door, shaking off the mortifying puppy love he'd evoked from her. She couldn't wipe the smile from her face, even as she forced open the door and they stormed the control room together.

40

THE OLD d'javu woman spat her ugly words before she collapsed to the floor and died. Devi removed her pike from the darkspawn's stomach. Did this old woman think she would stop them from taking their daughter back? She was wrong—nothing would stop Devi.

A small cry pulled their attention from the dying woman and Devi saw a small, light-gray d'javu toddler running toward the bed where Dia slept. He looked at them, eyes wide with fear, and Devi gasped.

Those eyes were... they were human! She had never seen eyes like those on a darkling before. Darkspawn all had eyes in orange, strange inhuman orbs that glowed soullessly. This child's eyes were turquoise and could have been—

Ryk spoke the words before Devi's mind could even fathom them. "This is Lark's child."

"Impossible," Devi replied immediately.

"I don't think that darkling was lying..."

Devi looked at him, "That's disgusting, Ryk."

Before he could respond the child began to climb into the bed, trying to reach Dia. Devi didn't think, she swung her pike at the toddler and knocked the child down. He tumbled with a cry and impacted the wall, falling to the floor unconscious. Devi slid her pike into its holster on her back and lifted her child from the bed.

Dia cooed happily as her mother tightened her blankets and kissed her face. "Let's get out of here," Devi said to Ryk, who was still staring at the child on the floor. "What's the matter with you?" she snapped at him.

"If she had a child with Magnimus... if they were able to conceive. That means—"

"It means nothing. They are monsters, Ryk. All this proves is that she's a monster, too. Now let's get our daughter out of here." Devi strode from the room hastily, holding tightly to Dia. She wanted to find Bae and get off this terrible planet, never to return to it. Or destroy it the way they'd done to Salva.

If only they'd had the power—if the d'javu hadn't stolen it all from them—Devi would have done it in a heartbeat.

41

THE MAIN square that led to the front gate of the city was clogged with frightened humans, jostling and trampling each other to escape an unknown terror. The rain, however light, had already stopped, and the sun had fully set. Pools of light hovered at the bases of tall street lamps. Lark paused as she came to the end of the alley that led into the courtyard from Nyhman's lab, studying the crowd and the ramparts.

A panicking human male came out of nowhere and ran straight into her. She gripped his sleeve to keep from falling, but the man tore free, pushing her to the ground where her holdout pistol fell from its torn holster. He snatched it from the ground and held it in both hands, leveling it shakily at Lark.

Panicking people were unpredictable. She'd been shot more than once by an idiot who found his courage at the last moment. Given her preference, Lark didn't like being shot. So, she raised her hands, palms toward him, and spoke as calmly as possible, "Listen, friend…"

Mags caught him by the throat and slammed his head into the wall, showering himself and Lark in a spray of blood and brain matter.

Lark squinted up at her husband from the ground and shook a bit of skull from her hand. "Thanks..." she muttered.

"Back the way we came," said Mags as he took her by the hand and yanked her to her feet, turning her to face away from the churning mass. Still pulling bits of her new friend's coconut from her hair, she bent to pick up her pistol while he took the lead and began climbing the outside wall.

"Pain in the ass," Lark whispered to herself, deploying her gauntlet mounted grappling cable and following Mags up the wall. By the time she had reached the top he was already on his way, bounding across the ramparts like the shadow of a cat. Wincing at the pain in her shoulder, Lark was reminded of the fight she had almost lost in the alley and the catalyst pulse that had eaten through her jacket. It seemed like ages ago now, but her body sure hadn't forgotten and that climb back up the wall was a hell of a reminder.

Mags did not wait for her. As long as her legs kept moving he wasn't going to waste worries on her. Lark pushed the pain away, starting after him with far less grace and much more cursing.

He had stopped at the Eastern corner of the rampart, surveying the army outside the walls of Hartun. A sea of barely visible flesh roiled in the darkness, the mass occasionally lit by the passing of flood lights that shown from somewhere on the other side of Hartun's gates—which were opening slowly.

A current rippled through the black ocean and the darkling horde, ranks swollen with the addition of the freed darkspawn captives, flowed into Hartun.

42

OUTSIDE, the sounds of battle were far away. The cries of men and darkling blended together until they were indiscernible from one another. As Bae stepped off the last tier and onto the same level as Crotis, the old man turned to glance at the table and he chuckled darkly. "By now Magnimus has taken Vargo. Your galaxy is falling apart, and all of your veteran warriors are here on Kyro." He waved his hand across the map before him. "He has shattered your so called *civilized* space. As he did your beloved homeworld," Crotis scoffed and his hands rested on the cloven stone carving of Salva. "You came here to begin a war over one child, sacrificing half of your empire to us."

"There's that us again. How long do you think they will continue to honor you?" Bae looked away from the table, unable to continue looking at a galaxy that very well could be falling apart around him. "How long do you think they will give up their boys to you?"

Clucking his tongue, Crotis lifted his hands from the table and regarded Bae patronizingly. "Do I mock who you have in your bedroom? The woman you pass back and forth with the Consul?" He grinned, watching Bae as he moved around the table until the dark rock map was at

Crotis' back. "All I need to do is call them, and you will be returned to the dungeon. And you will not be released again. Is that how you wish for your life to end?"

"I don't care about my life anymore, traitor. It's your life I came here for." Bae swung his ax. Crotis attempted to step back away from the blow, but he had never been the nimblest of men and he stumbled against the side of the black stone table. The heavy, energized blade of the ax fell with full force into Crotis' shoulder, slicing downward and cleaving through bones and organs. Until it met the old man's heart, where it stopped.

Crotis had not even been able to scream. He went limp against the table, mouth agape in surprise while his blood flowed over the carved galaxy at his back, pooling around the mock planets that Magnimus had taken for his own.

Bae tore his ax free and the old man crumpled to the ground. Then the Protector turned. No more words needed to be said. It would not change the victories for the d'javu, it would not win back half the galaxy. But the traitor was dead and if that was the lone victory of this day then so be it.

43

LARK AND Mags watched the invading darkspawn as they tore apart the defending army of Hartun. After the soldiers were all dead, many of the d'javu spread into the city to seek out survivors or those that had tried to escape. If the populous hadn't been smart enough to evacuate, they would all be dead. Lark tried to feel remorse, but the images of Nyhman's lab killed any regret she could have had. Any people who would harbor someone like Nyhman deserved the vengeance of the d'javu.

Until now, adrenaline and pure stubbornness had dulled much of the pain and exhaustion. Lark was leaning into Mags before she even realized it, and she felt his arm grip her carefully, supporting her weight. "Shouldn't you be down there?" she asked him, hearing the weakness in her own voice and clamping her teeth down in frustration.

Mags shook his head, looking down at her. His grip tightened when she tried to take back her own weight. "Hurshek was right. This is my place. I led them here, now it is their victory."

Lark chuckled quietly, pushing onto her tip toes and speaking into Mags' left year. "Did you hear that, Hurshek? Mags said you were right."

[Noted, my queen.] Lark could hardly hear him from the localized earpiece, but she swore there was just a little bit of satisfaction in his voice.

Mags gave a crooked smile and pulled Lark closer, his glowing eyes softened as he gently wiped at the dried blood on her chin. "How are the other battles going, Kabalak?" he asked Hurshek as if inquiring about the weather.

[We have taken the planets of Carbo, Sertisk, and Runtalis. All other battles have yet to yield results.]

"Pull the armies from Yor and Cota. Send them to support the others. We do not require victories there, we will return when the Protectors have abandoned them to pick up the pieces."

[Consider it done,] Hurshek replied.

"Regroup and begin spreading our declaration. We will take every planet from here to Kyro. Kill anyone who opposes us."

[Yes, Magnimus.] With that, the comm when silent.

When the darkspawn had finished ripping the meat from the bones of Hartun City, they returned to the gates. They gathered below the platform where Mags and Lark stood and raised their bloodied weapons over their heads. "*D'javu-khan!*" Someone yelled at the back. Another echoed and slowly, the chant took hold. "*D'javu-khan! D'javu-khan!*"

Mags squeezed Lark and raised his hand. The chanting quieted. "D'javu!" he called to them and they let out a roar in kind. "I gave you back Kyro, but it was hardly enough to quench our thirst for revenge.

"Now, I give you half of this broken galaxy. Let our darkness consume each world from here to our home. Today, my darkspawn empire is born!" They all cheered, and Magnimus gestured toward the darkspawn transports that were breaking the cloud cover, scooping toward their masses. "Go!"

Over the howling and chanting, the darkling Laus stepped forward. "Are you not coming with us, d'javu-khan?"

"No," Mags replied without looking away from Lark. "I am taking my queen back to Kyro."

He wrapped his arms fully around her. It took Lark a moment to realize what he was going to do. "Mags, no—"

But with a fizzle, they were gone.

44

DEVI HELD tightly to Dia, her arms like chains around the baby girl. Her eyes were not focused on her daughter. With Ryk beside her, soldiers and Protectors saluting them as they passed, her eyes were trained upon the shuttle crafts that belched the battle-worn onto the rain slicked landing platform on Lystor.

The wounded were carried swiftly to the medical wing, while the dead were shifted solemnly onto an open portion of the platform where the ever-present drizzle soaked into the shrouds that covered them. Most were draped with the ACP's flag to remind their families they had died for the Alliance. A few, too many to Ryk's eyes but far fewer than the Alliance soldiers, were draped with the old flag of Salva. Protectors felled by the darkspawn with no one left to mourn them but friends.

A sound escaped Devi that startled Ryk, pulling his eyes from the dead. He'd never heard Devi make a sound like that before, was that joy?

"Bae!" she cried out, squeezing the child to her but nearly leaping. Ryk relieved her of their daughter. To her credit, she only hesitated a moment before she allowed him to. Then she threw herself into Bae's arms, gasping at the blood stains.

"It's not mine," he told her. His voice was not his own, it was grave and low without a hint of his normal cheerfulness. "It's the old man's."

Devi stared up at him, her hand cupped his face. "Did you...?"

"He's dead," Bae confirmed. Devi wrapped her arms around him and let out a sob. Bae cast his eyes at Dia and then he, too, began to weep.

Hours later, Devi had refused to leave her daughter's side. Ryk didn't push her, but he needed to review developments of the ACP.

Bae accompanied him to the war room. They had both had the opportunity to shower and several hours of fitful sleep. Bae seemed more like himself now, grinning as they strode into the darkened room.

At the center, a hologram of the galaxy spread before them, illuminating the faces of a handful of sour looking men and women. Globes that represented each of the planets rotated slowly around their suns.

"Consul," Ambassador Hiku Trang from Ilya stood straight from leaning over the table. "Congratulations on returning from Kyro with your daughter."

"Thank you, Ambassador."

Runia Yuoy, a tactician from Rimbosi, inclined her head at Bae, "And I believe we have you to thank for the execution of the traitor Crotis."

Bae had never been humble; he smiled broadly and gave a comical bow, "That's me."

With a soft chuckle, Ryk nodded to them both. "What is the state of the Alliance?" he asked them.

"Half the Alliance," Trang amended. "Is well, though shaken and mourning their dead."

"Half?" Ryk questioned, moving toward the hologram.

"While the Consuls battled the darkspawn on Kyro," Youy activated a switch on her side of the console.

"Magnimus Avrok led an offensive against a dozen planets across Allied space." The globes began to turn red. A dozen of them formed a line that cut the galaxy in two. Youy continued. "Avrok took Vargo himself," she indicated the most central of the planets.

Ryk remembered that this was the planet Nyhman had been given as a gift after he'd discovered the genetic anomaly in the darkspawn. It had been largely uninhabited then, but several colonies had begun and flourished under Nyhman's less than attentive rule. "They took every other planet they assaulted with the exception Yor and Cota." Those two planets returned to green, but they were on either end of the line and mattered little when it came to reclaiming those that were lost.

Hiy Bultak spoke up from the other side of the table. "Avrok released a statement this morning. He claimed all planets between here and Kyro as a part of the darkspawn empire. Any humans that did not wish to stay were welcome to leave, those that stay will be treated fairly so long as they obey his laws."

Ryk eyed the planets, "Did he give any indication as to what those laws might be?"

"Only that slavery of any kind is illegal." Hiy gave a whisper of an ironic smile. "That all authority comes definitively from him. And…"

"And what?"

Youy answered him, "He has decreed that darkspawn and humans are equal citizens of his empire and intermarriage between them shall be considered legal and binding."

Ryk pursed his lips and thought for a moment. They could not afford to fight this war. "Send cruisers to pick up refugees at the border."

"What border?" Trang blustered. "Don't tell me that you are going to accept his proclamation!"

"Do you wish to fight them, Trang?" Ryk asked bluntly. "There are about to be plenty of empty uniforms to fill. Unless you have forgotten that the ACP's largest military organization was destroyed nearly six years ago, you would know that we do not have the forces to take back twelve planets let alone the other thirty that now lie in enemy space."

Trang frowned. Deeper than Ryk had ever seen him frown, which was saying something because Trang had a lot of practice at the expression. "We are weak."

"We have been weak since the d'javu destroyed Salva," Ryk snapped caustically. "Thinking that we have ever been anything else was foolishness. We will take those planets back, some day. But for now, we must give our people new homes and then things will need to change in the Alliance."

Youy's eyes narrowed. "Change how?"

Ryk's hands curled into fists. "No Alliance citizen is safe. We need to start acting like it."

Ryk and Bae were silent as they left the war room. Ryk's eyes saw far away and into the future. He saw now that the ACP had never been a safe organization, that they had never been prepared or capable of war. The Alliance had always leaned upon the Protectors to fight their battles for them. Salva was gone, and with it the only military strength in the galaxy. Until now.

How had he not seen this coming? How had he never thought to be more forceful with preparations? Ryk had not wanted to be Consul. They had begged him, forced him in the end. It was far past time that he was to do something with the power that had been thrust upon him.

Bae had opened his mouth to say something, but Ryk spoke over him, stopping in the hall. "I want you to take Devi and Dia and leave here."

"What?" Bae turned to stare at him. With his brows pulled together in consternation, he looked much meaner than he ever was.

"Take them and hide. I will have to make some changes to the Alliance, and I know they will not go over well. It will take time before we are able to defend ourselves against the d'javu. Until then, I will not allow Devi or Dia to remain in a situation where they can be used to exploit our weaknesses."

Bae remained silent for a long moment. "She won't go."

"Make her." Ryk stepped closer to him. "You and Devi can raise Dia well, in a place away from all... this." He gestured back toward the war room. "Sacrifices will need to be made if we are ever going to combat this. It starts with me."

For a moment, the big man looked like he was going to continue to argue but, finally, he clapped Ryk on the shoulder. "For you, my friend."

"Thank you, Bae."

45

IN THE blink of an eye, a fizzle and a burn, Lark and Mags stood in their living room on Kyro. His knees wobbled, but Lark had been ready for it this time and pulled his weight onto her despite her own dwindling energy. Pushing Mags into a chair, she stumbled into the kitchen and poured a glass of rakku juice that she kept around for the boys. "You okay?" she asked, squatting down to look up into his face.

"I'm fine..." said Mags as he stared down the juice as if it were a long-forgotten enemy. "Check on Sever," he muttered to her, tipping the glass up and forcing himself to drink.

Lark rose slowly, feeling her knees pop in protest, and she headed toward the staircase that led to the bedroom hallway. At first, she found it odd that Sever's door was open but thought nothing of it as she stepped through it. "Sever?"

The first thing she saw was the small, contorted puddle of him on the floor. She rushed in and slammed to her knees. Her heart went still in her chest as she gathered his limp body into her arms. Time slowed for a dragging, heartbreaking moment as she clung to the tiny form and sought any sign of life. She may have said his name, she may have even screamed, but she could hear nothing when she cupped his cheek and lifted his face to hers.

With a cry, Sever stiffened and then howled in pain. Lark gasped in a breath, relief flooding through her as she wrapped her arms around him despite his protesting cries. Rocking him back and forth, as much for her own comfort as for his, her eyes caught the glint of a discarded knife on the floor. Not far from where it lay, a pool of blood.

Ice shot into her veins as she followed the trail of it to the source. In her haste to retrieve Sever, she hadn't even seen her. Hand outstretched toward where Sever had been, trails of tears down her burgundy cheeks, Sal's body lay cold in the middle of the floor.

Lark fell backward from her knees, clutching Sever and letting out a howl of her own. Moments dragged on, and all she could do was stare at the body and hope that Sal, too, would suddenly regain consciousness. She never would.

A shadow filled the doorway, but Lark's eyes were too full of tears to see Mags' expression as he looked down upon the dead woman. She pressed her face into Sever's shoulder and closed her eyes, racked with pain.

"Is he alright?" Mags asked her after a moment, his voice sounded far away.

Lark lifted her head and looked up at him as he ran a hand over Sever's head. "I..." she couldn't hear herself in her words. "I don't know... he was out when I got here... I thought he was..."

Mags ran his hands over her hair, "He's alive, Lark. Salmalaina gave her life for him."

A sob escaped her, and Lark nodded, "I know..."

Mags pulled her to her feet and gave Sever one more inspection to ensure he was unhurt. The child whined and curled into his mother.

"We must go to Crotis," Mags said, barely above a whisper. She nodded and wiped her eyes. Mags looked down at Sal, and Lark wanted to reach for him. He turned before she could, stalking from the room with his hands in fists. Lark followed her husband tentatively, already dreading the moment when he could no longer dam up the emotion and it was unleashed upon them like a flood.

If he was still dragging from the use of his powers, he was covering that well, too. As they approached the doors to the war room, Mags instructed one of the lingering warriors to gather the darkspawn clans around the table, so they could celebrate the new empire together as they had after the destruction of Salva.

Silence greeted them as they entered the war room, and Lark paused at the doorway. Something wasn't right. Her nose itched, and she pressed the back of her hand against it. "Do you smell that?" she asked. "It smells like..."

"Death..." Mags was already moving, loping down the tiered steps toward the table. Lark followed, slowly as she was carrying Sever who had grown quiet. She stopped when she saw the puddle of dark blood.

Mags came to a stop on the opposite side of the table. "Tell them not to come," he ordered her hastily. "Lock the doors," he stepped into the syrupy puddle and knelt behind the table.

"Stay here," Lark set Sever down on one of the middle tiers before she ran up to the doors. When she swung the heavy stone door open, it slammed against the opposite wall, the sound echoing in the corridor. A large group of d'javu was approaching, glowing eyes turning to her in surprise. Lark called out to them, "Stop the others from coming, lock these doors. Mag—"

She was going to justify the order by stating it came from her husband, but the closest of the group cut her off by moving toward the door and beginning to close it. "Yes, d'javu-kheen."

Lark blinked. Hurshek had been right, of course, he always was. Lark just hadn't expected word to travel so fast or for the change to take effect so effortlessly. She had expected at least some disdainful tone or maybe an eye roll, but the guardian had almost sounded respectful when he spoke to her.

She didn't have a lot of time to think about it. "Thanks," she said to him uneasily. The door closed along with several others that led into the war room. Lark swallowed painfully as she watched Mags from across the room, dread slowing her footsteps as she started toward him, not sure she was ready to see what was on the other side of that table.

46

Magnimus knelt in a sea of drying blood.

The man who had raised him leaned against the darkstone table. His body had been nearly cloven in two, his eyes open and staring blankly into eternity.

Mags felt adrift in a sea of a different kind. Pain and loss swept away his composure as he stared at the crumpled governor. Crotis' last few acts had undermined the authority he had vested in Magnimus, endangered Mags' children, and bred derision between himself and his wife. Those last few acts, as insidious as they had seemed at the time, had won Magnimus half a galaxy and the admiration of his people.

And they had cost Crotis his life.

Lark came to a stop behind him, and Mags heard her breath catch in her throat. He didn't turn. He couldn't turn away from this man. Crotis had groomed him for this victory, made him who he was. Mags had known nothing but Crotis for half his life, had followed him and it had led him here against all odds. If the man had ill intentions, they had never come to fruition and he had paid for them regardless.

"Mags..." Lark said softly. He didn't reply. He reached out his hand and closed Crotis' dead eyes.

Finally, he stood up and looked at his wife. "This does nothing to change our victory," he said, his voice low. "The d'javu are free, my empire is born. That is what he wanted."

He saw her lips pull tight across her teeth, the taste of the sour words sticking to her tongue. She withheld comment. Mags felt a grin slide across his face. That was the most respect she could gather for Crotis. Despite the fact that it came on the heels of his death, and mostly for Mags' benefit, he knew how difficult it was for her.

Stepping through the blood, he joined her at the other end of the table. His hand slid down her arm to grasp her fingers, then he turned to gesture toward the carved galaxy in the center of the room, over the dead body of his mentor.

"Half of this galaxy is ours," he told her, grinning wickedly. "My d'javu-kheen."

Her dagger slid easily from its sheath, still slick with blood from the battle, and he leaned over the table. Stabbing the knife into its surface, he dragged it across the middle, carving a jagged line to separate Vargo and the other planets they'd taken today from what remained of civspace.

Drawing a line to claim what was his.

What was theirs.

DARKSPAWN

Acknowledgements

This book could not have reached its final form without the help of Kathleen Van Pelt, who edited this thing from cover to cover and found some of the most ridiculous word transpositions known to man.

I would also like to thank those that read the early scenes and not-so-gently gave me the very warranted criticisms I needed to mold a chunk of my brain into a story that could be released into the world. David and Cande—your harshness will always be welcome (even if I whine about it). And Nikki, who has believed in me since I was sitting on a school bus scribbling in a notebook—and maybe re-wrote a school paper or two.

Finally, I am eternally grateful to my mother who, aside from teaching me important life skills such as breathing, swimming, and remembering to get my car inspected, fostered in me an insatiable love of books and words. It is an invaluable gift that you gave me, and I cherish it.

DARKSPAWN